Praise for

MW00770040

"Author Diana Dempsey's admiration and affection for her subject shines throughout *The Unstoppable Eliza Haycraft*, a beautifully written, compulsively readable tale that gives voice to this fascinating, larger-than-life figure from a neglected corner of history."

— Indie Reader

(*The Unstoppable Eliza Haycraft*) "I loved it. The characters, history, and the emotions it brought out made for an excellent read. And (it) shows that if you put your mind to it, you can do anything."

— Sandra Vandelicht, Chief Deputy, Callaway County Recorder of Deeds

(*The Unstoppable Eliza Haycraft*) "WHAT A WOMAN! Diana Dempsey creates a fascinating tale, based upon an unforgettable real life character. Faced with ignorance, poverty, and betrayal, a brave young woman struggles at a time when women had little say in their lives. Using determination, shrewdness, empathy, and friendship, she is led through struggles, historical events, romance, loss, and triumph. Dempsey had me from the get-go to the very end."

— Sheila Guthrie, Kingdom of Callaway Historical Society

"Perfect Ten! ... Debut author Diana Dempsey soars with *Falling Star*, a powerful, moving, riveting tale of greed and betrayal, love and self-discovery ... Excellent characterization, great dialogue, and non-stop action make the book almost impossible to put down ..."

— Susan Lantz, *Romance Reviews Today*

(*To Catch the Moon*) "Skillfully plotted and filled with realistic detail, this fast-paced story deftly interweaves romance, murder, and ambition with issues of social status and trust."

— Kristin Ramsdell, *Library Journal*

(*Too Close to the Sun*) "Spicy, sexy, and sultry: popular Dempsey has another hit on her hands."

— *Booklist*

"*Ms America and the Offing on Oahu* is excellent summer reading material ... The writing is first class."

— *The Mystery Site*

(Beauty Queen Mysteries) "The characters remain lovable because they have family values (in the truest sense of the word) and none of them are superhuman. They fumble. They fall. They temporarily fail. Just as we would in the same position ... The Beauty Queen Mysteries are on my must read list, and I can't wait for the next installment."

— Jacqueline Vick, A *Writer's Jumble*

THE
UNSTOPPABLE
ELIZA
HAYCRAFT

A Novel

DIANA DEMPSEY

BRAMERTON
PRESS

The Unstoppable Eliza Haycraft

Copyright © 2023 by Diana Dempsey

All rights reserved. No part of this book may be reproduced, stored in a retrieval system, or transmitted in any form or by any means whatsoever—electronic, mechanical, photocopy, recording, scanning, or other—except for brief quotations in critical reviews or articles, without the prior written permission of the author.

This book is a work of fiction. References to real people, events, establishments, organizations, or locales are intended only to provide a sense of authenticity, and are used fictitiously. All other characters, and all incidents and dialogue, are drawn from the author's imagination and are not to be construed as real.

FIRST EDITION July 2023

Cover Design by Tim Barber, Dissect Designs

Author Bio Photo by Silverlux Photography

ISBN 978-0-9906964-6-9 (Ebook)

ISBN 978-0-9906964-7-6 (PB)

ISBN 978-0-9906964-8-3 (HC)

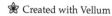 Created with Vellum

To the dear friends we lost far too soon

Bill Aiello

Nahid Aram

Leo Levin

"Eliza Haycraft was born in Callaway County, Mo., on the 14th of February, 1820, of humble and honest parents. Possessed of unusual personal attractions and a warm and confiding nature, she early fell a prey to the arts of the seducer, and became an outcast from home and country. She had never received any education, and to the day of her death was totally innocent of letters. When a young woman of about twenty years she fled from her home, and, embarking all alone in a frail canoe on the turbulent bosom of the Missouri, started for St. Louis… "

— "Remarkable Career of a Remarkable Woman"

— *Missouri Democrat*, December 8, 1871

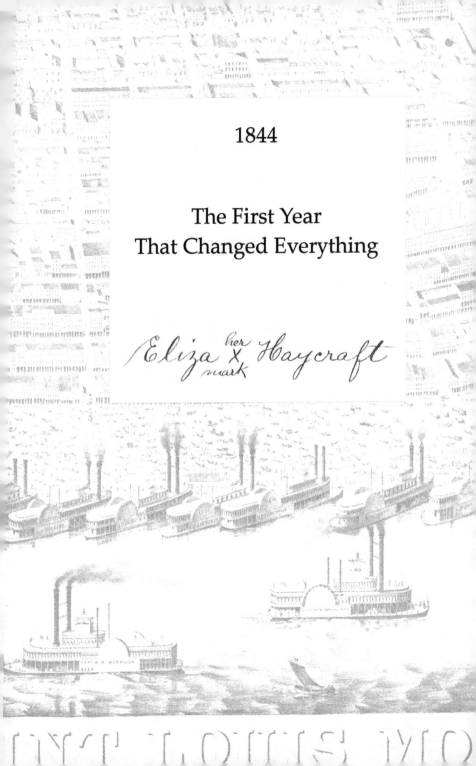

1844

The First Year
That Changed Everything

Eliza her X *Haycraft*
mark

Chapter One

I'M NOT ONE TO PASS MUCH TIME THINKING ABOUT THINGS BEFORE I DO THEM. My father shakes his head and says that's how his beauty Eliza got into this trouble. My mother smirks and wonders out loud how I can think I'm so special when all I know how to do is get into trouble.

Alone in the midnight blackness, for once I do stop and think. I stand on the riverbank thick with cottonwood and willow trees and stare at the water as it rushes past, brown like the mud that nearly brought me skidding to the hard ground as I stumbled to get here. I shiver even in all I'm wearing, both my skirts over my drawers and corset, two blouses, little jacket, two moth-bitten shawls, stockings and best boots, the only ones with no hole in them. I dare not leave anything behind. I'll need it all, the coins, too, tucked inside the string bag stuffed in the pocket of my inner skirt. Even under all that, the chilly air squeezes in on me like a too strong boy who wants what he wants and sees no reason why he shouldn't have it.

I push my dark hair back from my forehead. Tonight of all nights I dare not start thinking. I should just lay hands on John's canoe and *go*.

He'll hate me for it when he comes to. But that's the least of what he'll hate me for. And what do I care anyway? For every speck of hate he'll have for me, I'll have twice as much for him.

The liar. The cheat. The brute I married. Though now I half wonder if I really did.

I shake my head hard, as if that will clear it, and tell myself again that tonight is no night to dwell on the past. I can't spare the time. Or lose my courage. If I linger too long, the drink will wear off and John will rouse. He'll come looking for me even before he sees my clothes are gone; I know it. Then what?

I shudder. Almost better that a wolf or bear find me first. And either would be better than a ghost to rise before me, unearthly white from the plague that got him. Who knows how many souls are buried along this river? If you make the mistake of dying on a steamboat, that's your fate: eternity under the riverbank or your corpse swept away with the water when it changes course.

It's the fear of creatures both alive and dead that sends me edging again down the grassy slope, closer to the river. It's so dark I can't even make out the bank on the other side, but I know this clutch of trees and believe it's close by here that John lays his canoe. The water is moving fast—faster than it looks when I see it in the day. When I see it but have no scheme to climb inside that old boat and let it free on the river to carry me far, far away. Now that I can truly imagine myself on that treacherous journey, I shudder again and my foot slips in my stupid shoe. I give a little shriek and grab at the shrubs around me to stop from sliding into the current.

When finally I settle again, I try not to pant but to keep silent. What if someone heard me cry? Yet I pick up no shuffling among the trees. I can hope it's too cold for anyone to be afoot. And hard as my ears strain, all I can hear is the river. No, I hear something else, too, that familiar screech. A panther. Distant, thank God. And upriver, not the way I'm going.

I'm going to Hermann, I remind myself, where the Missouri meets the Gasconade. I hear tell there's a post office there, and somebody once said there's an inn, not that he'd seen it. I could find work, and not the kind I do here, that leaves my hands blistered and crusted with dirt and my back bent as if I were already old.

I'm not old yet. Yes, I'm four and twenty, but if I hold my tongue and keep my eyes downcast I can pass for younger. I still have my looks, near fresh as ever. When my courage is up I don't doubt I could marry again, though I wonder why I'd want to. I know now all that does is make a man free to do what he wants with you and in near one year I've had enough of that for two lifetimes. But if ever I changed my mind, what's to stop me? For if John Haycraft could amble into this town and forget everything that went before, why couldn't I go to Hermann and do the same?

That thought makes me feel like a girl again, strong and bold. I remember when I would lie in the grass and stare up at the blue, blue sky, dreaming of being far away from here, away from these rutted fields, away from these people who don't care if they never see past this stretch of river. Even if they came from somewhere I can't conjure, from Kentucky or even Virginia, they don't think about that anymore. It's as gone from their minds as if they woke from a fever. Even for my father it's that way. When I was a girl I thought all the time about what lay beyond the curve in the river and for a time I was fool enough to think John Haycraft would take me there. Lately I've started wondering about it again, knowing if I only dared, this coursing water could lead me to a different life than the one I'm stuck with now, these pitiful days that stretch out one after the next all the very same. If I stay put here, the days won't change until the day I'm dead.

I've walked further downriver—due to the fact that's closer to our place and John is more likely to be lazy than not—when I startle at a soft laugh behind me.

"Well, well. What're you out looking for this time of night?"

A woman's voice and I know it in an instant. My head spins around and I see my sister Sarah.

"You're not looking for John's canoe!" She says it in a triumphant kind of way, eyes gleaming, like she's sure that's what

I'm after. "Why do you need that? You're not going anywhere. You wouldn't go in the day," she tells me, "let alone in the dark."

If somebody had to find me I wish it were our sister Visa Ann, but she would never be out at this hour. Even our brother Asa would be better to find me than Sarah. But it's Sarah who can pick up a change on the wind.

She eyes me. She's dark-haired like I am but older and harder of feature. People shouldn't tell her that, but they do. Even our father does. "You're not going anywhere," she repeats. She's sure she's on top of me in this. "And even if you do, he'll come after you."

I don't want to tell her much because every word will make it back to our mother's ears, and maybe John's, too. "This has nothing to do with you," I mutter. That Sarah keeps telling me I won't go puts even more fire in me. I spin back around and lose my footing, which only makes her cackle louder. I know she won't think for a moment of helping me. Sarah's our mother's daughter through and through.

"You're wearing both your shawls, too," she mocks me. "You must think you're really going. Why this time?" and in that question I hear a curiosity she can't hide. We all in our family live so close, one on top of the other, which means she knows my shame, and like our mother she enjoys it. *Look at our beautiful Eliza! So special but still getting* that *from the man she begged to marry.*

"Because this time was one too many," I tell her. I wonder if John will admit the true story once I'm gone. I doubt it. It casts no good light on him. I doubt he'll stay, come to think of it. There's nothing for him here. Like us Harpers, John Haycraft owns no land. Couldn't he hunt anywhere, and trap? He'd be better off trying his game somewhere new. He's the sort of man you don't mind seeing the back of once the shine's worn off and you have to look straight on at what little is really there.

But despite everything, the thought of John gone, forever gone, does pain me. I feel a sting behind my eyes and look away to hide my face. See? It did me no good to start thinking again.

"He woke up, you know," Sarah says, in that same triumphant tone. *I know something you don't.* "I heard him calling for you and not in his nice voice, either. I came out to warn you."

That's a lie. Sarah doesn't want me to get away from John. She wants him to find me then see what he does after. I put my back to my sister and keep moving, my eyes madly searching.

"So where you think you're headed?" My sister's voice taunts as she matches me step for step. "Hermann," she guesses, and I hate that my plan is so obvious it rises to even her mind. "That's not far enough," she tells me. "Haycraft will sure enough find you there."

Then I spy the canoe, my salvation, in front of me to the left, its paddle lying in the middle like it's aiming to split the boat in half. It's always John who puts the canoe in the current, laughing that I'm not strong enough, but tonight I will find the strength to do it.

Sarah must see the canoe, too, because she rushes forward to set herself between it and me. She pushes her hands into my chest, hard, so that I stumble backward. "You're not leaving me to mind Mama's brats on my own," she tells me. Now her voice is rough as her hands. Then she puts her fingers in her mouth and lets loose a whistle so sharp and loud it could wake all those ghosts under the riverbank.

I scramble past her for the canoe. And though she yanks on my skirts and my hair and bangs on my back, somehow I push it closer to the river. I feel as if a kind of mad force has gripped me, as if I can do things I never could before. Sarah whistles again, even more of a shriek this time, and after that I hear a commotion behind us and figure it has to be John coming this way, just my luck, scrambling fast through the trees and the shrubs. So he was out already, roaming and looking, just like Sarah was. They were a pair, the two of them. My sister just found me first. And if she was going to warn anybody tonight, it was going to be him and not me.

She's on his side and no wonder. This wouldn't be the first time she wants what I have, but this time I'm ready to give it up.

Maybe she's drunk the potion I must've drunk when I first met John Haycraft, which full wore off tonight.

I've got the canoe only a few feet from the river when he finds me. I spin around to face him. My clothes are torn from Sarah's pulling and my hair is crazy wild, but I'm calm inside now I can't undo what I started. Sarah backs off a pace as I watch John's eyes move to the paddle I've taken in my hands.

"Put that down, woman."

I will not, but I don't spare the breath to tell him that. I just raise the paddle higher in the air.

He stares at me, panting, hands on hips and eyes narrowing. People didn't trust him when he showed up here out of nowhere, since they didn't know him and they didn't know his family. It wasn't much more than a year ago, but I must've been young and stupid then because he won me over with his sweet talk and his stories. Then his kisses started and that sent me over the edge. Even now, when there's dirt on his trousers and I can smell the drink from here, any woman would tell you he's a fine-looking man. I must've thought that was good for something when I married him.

"What I said before doesn't matter," he tells me.

It does matter, but I won't give him the satisfaction of another go-round on the topic. "Just let me go," I say, though now I doubt I need his permission.

"I don't think so." He cocks his chin at the canoe behind me. "Don't start thinking that belongs to you."

"If I'm your wife"—I keep my voice low—"I've as much right to it as you."

I hear a little whoop from Sarah. She knows John'll take those as fighting words and that she wants to see.

He steps closer. I can tell it's one of those times he doesn't know how to handle me. "I say what you've a right to. And woman, you should know by now that I'm the one who'll do the leaving."

Truth to tell, by this sorry point I'm not sure he'd mind my going. I think he's had enough of me like I've had enough of him. I just think he doesn't want me to best him, especially not with Sarah watching.

"She means to go to Hermann," my sister offers. Then: "She's got coins in her skirts."

John lurches forward faster than I can do anything about it and grabs the paddle from my hands. He throws that aside and knocks me backward, pushing fierce on my shoulders. I fall hard, half on the canoe and half on the ground. Pain grinds through me and I taste blood in my mouth.

He's on top of me then and I worry he's going to want to do what he always wants to do, never mind Sarah's watching. That brings me to. I push at his hands, beneath my skirts now, but for once it's not my drawers he's after.

"Her pockets!" Sarah shrieks.

He's ripping at me, he's tearing at me, I can smell the drink strong in my nostrils, and when I know he's going to find my string bag with the coins, I stop fighting. That really makes him mad—it always makes him mad when I pretend I don't care what he's doing—and I can tell I'm right because he doesn't just rip the bag out of my pocket. He rips the whole pocket off then raises himself halfway up to hold it high above me in the air. Still astraddle, he stares down at me for a moment then whips the bag down and across my face.

I close my eyes tight and don't let loose the tiniest whimper. I know what he wants and I won't give it to him.

So he does it again.

Behind John, Sarah makes a sound. This might be too much even for her.

"You gonna cry, woman?" John grunts.

I will not. I don't care how many times he does it. I don't care how much blood I have in my mouth. I didn't cry when he threw those words at me tonight and I won't cry when he throws his fists at me now. He hates when I go cold like this, when I don't react at all, because he knows he can't get to me then, whatever he does. I surprise him with the strength I have. Really, I surprise myself.

He relaxes and I find that crazy strength again. I kick my legs out at him and hit him somewhere, I don't know where, or care, but this time it's him toppling backwards. I scramble to my feet and whirl around and push the canoe closer to the river, it's so very close now, and then it's edged out over the water and I fling myself inside and the force of my body pushes the canoe all the way into the river.

The rushing water takes me fast, so fast. I turn around on my hands and knees in the rocking canoe and see John and Sarah on the bank staring after me. I don't think I'll ever forget their faces, splotches of paleness in the black night, looking like they're seeing something they'll never forget, either.

I feel a stab, then, quick and sharp, for the life I've lived here, for my father, for my younger sisters... I may never see little Minerva again, or Lucinda, or Visa Ann.

The canoe takes no heed. It's moving and I'm in it. I have no paddle, I have no coins, I'm spitting my own blood out of my mouth, but I'm in it.

Chapter Two

"Of all the variable things in creation the most uncertain are—the action of a jury, the state of a woman's mind, and the condition of the Missouri River."

— *Sioux City Register*, March 28, 1868

I T'S NOT MY FIRST TIME ON THE RIVER, BUT IT'S MY FIRST LIKE THIS—at night, alone, shivering from a chill wind, and with no plan ever to go back. I see no other craft and don't expect to until the sun comes up. No one fusses with this river in the dark if they don't have to and Indians avoid it even in the day.

With all the rain we've been having, all manner of things are floating along with me in the current: splintered trees, parts of houses, even some poor bison drowned and bloated. Everything snags on the bottom from time to time, that shifting bottom John gripes about. Without a paddle, the current sends me whichever way it wants. I've seen no sign of Hermann yet, but maybe I floated right past. I can't guess how long I've been out or how far I've come. It's still dark as ever. And now I wonder how I'll get myself to the bank if I *do* see Hermann, for the canoe stops when I don't want it to but I can't think how to make it stop when I do.

There's little moon to speak of so no steamboat will come upon me; they won't risk running in this blackness. I've watched the passengers on the upper deck, whiling away the hours, so mysterious to me they might have traveled from the moon herself. Even from a distance I can tell how fine their clothes are. And they've nothing to do but steam from place to place and watch the world with bored eyes?

In time, I don't know how much, the sky ahead gives off some light. The morning will come soon and no way to stop it. When I imagined setting off on the river, I never let myself imagine too far ahead, for fear I wouldn't do it. Now I don't have to imagine. I just have to look around me. The scene is much the same as the one I left: river, trees, and sky. Somehow, though I couldn't say how, I'm different. Hard to think why, since it's far from the first time my teeth chatter or my stomach rumbles. It's not the first time, either, I've felt myself alone in this world.

I'm hoping the canoe snags near the riverbank so I can pull off. It's not for thinking, for I've as little interest in that as ever, but to sleep. And some time later the canoe does snag and I do pull off. It feels strange to be aground again, and in a place I don't know. I pull the canoe off the water and set it under a giant willow with drooping branches to hide me away. When I climb back inside, I curl into a ball under the only shawl I have left—the other got lost fighting John—and try to get warm. I'm careful not to touch my face. It hurts now from all the work John did to it. I shut my eyes and hope sleep will take me. I'm not sure I'd half mind if I never wake up.

It's a commotion that brings me to, a racket on the river. *Boom. Boom.* Louder that second time. I crawl out of the canoe, now under the light of the sun, limbs stiff and heart jigging, and edge toward the water, keeping low to the ground, gentling aside the branches of the willow. Then I see it, floating toward me on this narrow stretch of river, and it takes my breath away, same as always.

A steamboat, mighty and proud, white as you like it, coughing smoke from two stacks high as can be and firing its cannon just because it has a mind to. Those were the booming sounds that woke me. This steamboat is a real beauty, three decks in all. It has two side wheels with sunbursts painted all around them, a red stripe above the waterline, and flags of many colors whipping in the wind.

I've heard tell the Indians call the steamboats fire canoes. They say they walk upon the water. I swear they do, palaces made for the river but rising tall above it, grander and more powerful than anything I've ever seen.

Those fine people are up on the top deck like they always are. I hear them laugh and carouse as they float by. I get a fright when one man hoists a shotgun in my direction, but he keeps raising it higher and higher still then fires it into the sky far above my head. Everybody around him makes an *ooh* sound and I hear a crashing through the thicket behind me and realize he's shot something out of the sky. A duck or goose most likely and of course no one will bother to fetch it. Poor beast died for no good reason.

I could go find it, but what then? I've no knife to clean it. I might've been smart to take one last night, but that's what happens when you're scheming to leave a man. You forget a thing or two you might find handy. Though if I'd had a knife, I wager John would've found it and then what?

That thought gets me full awake. And reminds me it's past time to be thinking of the man I put behind me or the goose I can't eat. I must get somewhere I can put something in my belly. That means back in the canoe and back on the river.

I never imagined I'd see that steamboat again but not longer after I do. It's stopped a ways ahead on the left riverbank, to wood.

I watch as I float nearer. People, not the fancy ones, are carrying sawed-off pieces of timber onto the boat. It's Negro roustabouts mostly doing the work but also white men and women, too, and children I'd guess are Betsy's age, boys and girls both. Arms full they go from the wood yard then along the sagging plank to the boat. From time to time somebody shouts to move faster. Some of the fine-dressed people are ashore, too, but only watching. Most of those are men sitting on a log or leaning on a tree to have a smoke.

When I'm nearer still, a dark-haired young man carrying a load happens to look my way. He stops and frowns until the man behind urges him on. But then that man looks my way, too, then the woman behind him. All three stop, wood in their arms, and stare.

I'm a sight, I know. For one thing, I'm a woman alone in a canoe. And I've been on the river all night, my hair askew, my clothes ragged. Oh, and around my mouth my skin is probably black and blue, and who knows? There may be dried blood. Everyone ashore will be quick to figure none of that happened on the river.

Somebody curses loud at the three to get them moving. Then a barrel of a man with a beard so dark and thick a bird could make a home in it shouts out to me. "You aiming to come aboard? Make it fast if you are."

Some fancy people are staring at me now, too. A few men have moved closer to the bank for a better look. I've no mind to be a freak in a show. I raise my chin that way my mother always mocks and that gets another man to call out to me.

"Where's your paddle?" he wants to know.

"I'll give her a paddle," another man mutters, loud enough for all to hear. I catch the titters, too.

The current with the mind of its own has decided to carry me closer to the bank. And as it does, I get an idea. There's sawed-up wood here. Maybe I can get a piece to use as a paddle. So this time it's me calling out, asking for help to get ashore.

The barrel-bodied man orders men to drag in my canoe. They glance at my face and look away fast when I meet their eyes. I know why and it shames me. A few of the children come to stand on the bank, but they don't drop their gaze. They give me that wide-eyed curious stare children are prone to.

I smile at them. I never could resist a child though thank God I didn't get one by John. There'd be no leaving for me then.

When we get to the bank I step out of the canoe and thank the men who pulled me in, making sure the canoe is far enough off the water there's no chance it'll get swept up by the current. A woman with a frizz of reddish hair hands off her wood and nears me, worry on her face. She looks about my mother's age, but I understand fast she's another sort of person entirely. "You'll be needing cleaning up," she says, her words different than I've ever heard before. She pours me water from a stone crock and more when I finish that, without me even asking. Then she holds out a piece of bread she pulls from a pocket.

"Thank you, but I can't take your food," I make myself say. It may be small, it may be dry, but still I want it.

She gestures to the steamboat. "We've more on board."

I need no more invitation. I turn away as I bite into the bread. I don't like the fancy people watching me eat, as if I'm a creature born to entertain them. Some of the women have edged closer now, too, wearing their straw hats and tasseled shoes with buttons. I feel their eyes roam me, from my moth-eaten shawl to the rip in my top skirt. Maybe it's my shame but I most feel their eyes on my face, that part that's too bruised to touch. They might think I deserved that. I'd set them right if I had a mind to.

The barrel-bodied man brushes past the red-haired woman. I get the idea he's running things, or least means to. "You aiming to board?" he asks me again.

If I had coins, I might. "What I'd really like is wood I could use for a paddle."

"You think they hand that out?"

My experience, nobody hands anything out. "I only need one piece."

"It's ash," he tells me. "Seasoned."

"I only need one piece," I repeat, then: "Please."

The red-haired woman has been watching. "Look at the mite of a thing," she says to the barrel-bodied man. "Shame on you if you don't give it to her."

That prods him to show pity, though he's not happy about it. He calls to a skinny lad about Asa's age. "Get her a piece for a paddle. Not too big."

"I'm going to clean her up," the red-haired woman declares.

"Make it fast," the barrel-bodied man says. "We don't wait for you deckers." He spits on the ground then stomps away.

The red-haired woman tugs me away. "Don't they do just that," she mutters, "leave us to lighten the load, no matter we've paid our fare." She pulls fabric from her pocket and wets it with water from the stone crock. She does what she can with my face and hands, her touch quick and gentle. If she asked me how I got to the state I'm in, I might tell her, but I fancy she's already guessed and that shames me even more.

Finally I think to ask her a good question. "You're riding on the steamboat, then?"

"Deck passage."

"Have you gone past Hermann?"

"Couldn't tell you. Can't see much from down where we are."

Not like the fine people on the top deck. By now the wooding is finished. The barrel-bodied man is telling the quality to step back on board.

The red-haired woman hurries me back toward the steamboat. The skinny lad runs up with a piece of timber I can make do with, but now I've got another scheme in mind. I push my way through the "deckers" to the barrel-bodied man. He cocks his chin at the timber in my hand. "Not good enough for you?"

"I'll sell you my canoe," I tell him. "For deck passage."

He throws back his huge dark head and lets fly a laugh so

loud some of the fancy people peer down from their deck high above. "Why would I want your pitiful boat?"

"It's a fine canoe. Sturdy. You never know when it could come in handy."

"I need your canoe like I need the pox!" he shouts up at the fine people.

They laugh like he hoped they would, at my expense, but he can't mock me like my mother can and that I learned long ago how to suffer. "I'm only going as far as Hermann," I say.

"She wants to go to Hermann!" he shouts skyward.

"To live among the Dutch!" one of the fine-dressed men shouts. "She must like sauerkraut and sausage!"

Another man mutters something about sausage and even the tasseled-shoe women titter behind their gloves.

"You want to sell your canoe?" A man's voice without a speck of laughter in it booms down from the top deck. "I'll give you fifty cents for it."

Everyone goes silent as dawn. I look up to see a man, not young, not old, not at all fine-looking like John and certainly not tall like him, with side-whiskers the color of mud. Dressed fancy but somehow not as smooth as the others. He was one of the men watching me before, standing ashore smoking. Sort of a gnome-like man, but that bellowing voice makes him seem bigger. Something about the way he's waiting to hear how I'll reply, eyes keen under the brim of his hat, makes me think it's a game he wants to play. He's not the first man to have that thought where I'm concerned. "I'll take no less than a dollar," I call up to him.

That gets whoops and cries.

"Seventy-five cents, then," the gnome man says, as if he's struck the deal.

"Seems to me that's still less than a dollar," I call back.

More whoops. The gnome man bites back a smile. Then the barrel-bodied man raises his voice so all the crowd can hear. He wants some of this laughter for himself. "How much less than a dollar, you reckon?"

He's thinking the best I'll manage is to say twenty-five cents. "Twenty-five percent," I state clearly, a strange thrill pushing me on. "But I'll make you an offer," I call to the gnome man over the ruckus. "I'll cut my price by ten percent, which makes ninety cents, and add a thank you kindly."

The gnome man spreads his hands wide as his smile. "Now I ask you," he says to the crowd, "what man could say no to such an offer?"

I can tell the barrel-bodied man doesn't like it when the gnome man, come down from the top deck, makes sure I pay no more than the rightful fare for deck passage. He's shorter than I imagined, not even tall as me, but wearing a fine watch chain on his vest that sparkles gold in the sun. "Thirty cents will get me to Hermann?" I ask him.

Again he gives me that sharp eye. "It'll get you there."

So I will get to Hermann and have sixty cents besides. "Thank you kindly," I say, and smile.

I watch the skinny lad stash the canoe belowdecks as the gnome man disappears upstairs. I almost miss the canoe when it's toted out of sight. It's half of what got me this far.

Chapter Three

"We used to separate the men from the boys at the mouth of the Missouri River. The boys went up the Mississippi and the men up the Big Muddy."

— Captain William Louis "Steamboat Bill"
Heckmann

IF THEY COULD SQUEEZE ANOTHER HUMAN BEING BELOWDECKS, I'd be surprised as a babe at a cockfight. There's all manner of barrels and crates stacked so high there's barely room for the pigs and cows. And so many deckers from young to old—I suppose I'm one now, too—not to mention the roustabouts, all crowded so close I'm not sure I see a spare bit of floor to squat on.

They aren't my kind, either, most of them. The ones who aren't Negro, or don't talk funny like the red-haired woman, speak a language I can't even name. Any other day the smell of their cooking would turn my stomach. Today I feel it rumble.

But for a few canvas curtains, almost all around us the steamboat is open to the outside, which is a mercy because I don't know how I'd bear the stench otherwise. And the boilers, now I see them close, they frighten me. Big and black and belching, hot as hell itself and eating the wood fast as they're fed it, they put up a roar so loud God can hear, not that he gives much mind to the likes of us.

I can't fathom how the boilers make the paddlewheels move, but they do. And so our white palace runs down the river, with me on it, every minute taking me further away from John. And my father and sisters and everything I've ever known. What must they be thinking now they know I'm gone? Wondering if I'll be back, most likely. Wishing for it in some cases. But not all, if I know my mother.

I force my mind from those thoughts and search for the red-haired woman instead. Finally I see her. The mother of six, it looks like, with a wee one in her arms. She gives me a cool look as I push toward her. "I'm thinking I've no need to worry about you," she says, and I wonder again why her words are so strange-sounding.

"I must do what I must." I say it just loud enough so she can hear me over the boilers' racket. "I have only myself now."

She bounces the babe and makes her voice low. "You know what he'll be expecting."

She's speaking of the gnome man. "That makes him no different from any other man. Least he bought my canoe."

Her lips curl at that.

"And more at my price than his," I add.

Her lips curl further. "How'd you learn calculating?"

"My father taught me." He taught Asa, too, but I took to it faster. A memory rises, that sometimes I would add up numbers fast to make my father laugh. The recollection of that laughter stings me sharp as a needle. "I'm going to Hermann," I say. "The man who bought my canoe is likely bound for St. Louis." I know already that's where the fancy people go.

"You mind if he quits the boat at Hermann, too." Her eyes drop to my bruised mouth. "You've had your share of troubles," and her voice softens. She lets loose with her own story then, that her name is Ina and the eight of them came from Ireland, which must be why her words sound funny. They crossed the whole wide ocean to join her brother in Iowa only to wonder why they came so far just to farm again when they could go to St. Louis and do better. "In four years it's grown twice as big," she tells me. Her light eyes are huge at the wonder of it. "There's a factory on every block, and the port, too. Only New Orleans is busier." She cocks her head behind her at a spindly man I take to be her husband. "Better than farming. And we're not too old to learn a new way."

I keep inside that her husband looks too frail to manage farm work or factory work. Instead I reach into my pocket for my new coins and pull out the dearest. "You've been very kind to me. Please take this."

Ina looks down at the coin and back up at me. She wants it; I see that plainly. Oh, there were days I'd sell my soul for a coin. How old was I when Sarah and I walked to the general store only to get shooed away because our feet were bare and our dresses were all patches? I can still hear the titters. I don't recall if I hated those more than the looks of pity.

"I'll keep you fed till Hermann," Ina says, and the coin disappears in her palm. "We've some to spare." She glares at a man who's set his eyes on me in a way she doesn't like. "Stay put by us," she tells me, "there by Bridget, my eldest."

I'm grateful to squeeze next to the girl, red-haired like her mother but thin as a tree branch and biting her nails until they bleed. I feed myself with Ina's stringy meat and hard bread. I don't even know that I sleep until I wake as the steamboat shudders to a stop. Outside the light is faded. The wind is chill and I wager it will bring rain.

"We're to wood again," Bridget tells me, and off we march,

leaving on board only the oldest and tiniest. Now I'm in the throng crossing back and forth over the plank and again I notice the gnome man ashore with his eyes upon me.

When finally the barrel-bodied man shouts that our work is done and we're stopped for the night, the gnome man finds me. By now the rain has found all of us. "Obadiah Darby," he says and gives me an expectant look.

I hesitate before I repeat what I told Ina. "Eliza." Haycraft or Harper: I don't know which to say.

His brows rise. "Only Eliza?"

When I say nothing, he speaks again. "Well, Eliza, I'm from Massachusetts. What about you?"

I don't know that Obadiah Darby would find a way to send me back where I came from, but still I don't want to say. "Upriver."

He chuckles, watching me with those keen eyes. Again I get the idea I interest him, maybe even more than the way Ina is fretting about. "When's the last time you ate?" he asks me.

"Belowdecks after I boarded." I don't want him thinking I'd starve without his help.

"So you're good at making friends." He glances at Ina, who's scowling at us from a distance. "That can get you far in life."

"I'm going only as far as Hermann."

"So you keep saying." He narrows his eyes. "You know it's full of Dutch? *Sprechen Sie Deutsch?* You speak German?"

"I can learn," I say, though I'm not sure I want to.

Now Obadiah Darby is scowling. "Better stick to your own kind."

"There aren't my own kind in Hermann?"

"I already told you. There are Dutch in Hermann. It's their town, made for them." Of a sudden he seems impatient, his voice rough, and disappointed in me somehow. "We stop at Hermann tomorrow," and he backs off, "less we hit a snag or have an explosion," then he disappears among the fancy people climbing back aboard, faster now as it's raining harder. The barrel-bodied man, who's made sure to catch every word, sniggers at me and doesn't hide it.

Like Ina I'm restless all night and rise before dawn. As we huddle in the dark and she brings the little one to her breast, I ask in a low voice if they're Dutch, the people around us with the stinking food and the rough language.

"Be sure of it," and I think she'd spit if she didn't have a babe in arms.

No snag, no explosion, keeps us from landing in Hermann. I go ashore to stare at it. Under ornery clouds it looks as if it's sitting in a bowl, with thick-wooded hills all around and buildings made of red stone in a neat row, as if a child has set up blocks he'll soon tumble. I learned long ago not to trust my sister Sarah, but her words come back to mind. *That's not far enough. Haycraft will surely find you there.*

In the end, just like something flung me into John's canoe, something prods me back onto the steamboat. "Too many Dutch," I tell Ina when I reappear and she needs no more explanation.

It's later that day, after I have a go-round with the barrel-bodied man paying him more fare, that we deckers are once again called to wood. Again I see the gnome man. Those bright eyes of his light up as he sees me, arms laden with timber. When we're allowed to stop he comes near, Ina's gaze narrowing as he corners me.

"You didn't stay in Hermann," he says. "So you *do* have a head on your shoulders."

I like the praise, but all the same I bristle. "I have my own reasons for doing what I do."

"I wouldn't mind hearing what those reasons are."

"Those ninety cents bought you a canoe." I step around him. "Nothing more."

I hear him chuckle behind me. This is something I know about men: they like their games. If a man expects me to say one thing, sometimes I say another, just for the surprise of it. Like as not, he enjoys it.

But it costs me belowdecks that Obadiah Darby talks to me. Ina and her family don't shun me, not quite, but tonight there's no piece of meat put in my hand, never mind I gave Ina another coin this morning. The other deckers stare at me, too, with chilly eyes, and keep their distance.

The next day is warm and bright, as if the sun has a mind to go back to work. I welcome the wooding just because it gets me out into the clean air. I never really knew before how much humans could stink and wish I didn't have to learn. When we're all back crammed belowdecks, I bend my head down so the stench I smell is mostly my own. Maybe the sun gets to the pilot, too, or the captain or whoever is running this steamboat, because of a sudden we're going faster than ever. This stretch of river must be deep and straight, because with all those snags and sandbars, most times we'd get beat by a funeral march.

As usual when something's amiss, the men and boys crowd to look outside and the women stay put. I'd go look, too, if I didn't have to cram myself among the menfolk. Given half a chance no man on this deck would keep his hands to himself.

It's hard to believe, but a second later we're going even faster.

"Maybe it's Indians," Bridget whimpers, "shooting arrows at us."

"If that's so, we'd fire our guns back at them," I tell her.

"I hear sometimes they get aboard." Her eyes are huge and light as her mother's.

I tell her not to worry, but Ina grips the baby tighter and makes a sign of the cross. I cast an eye on the boilers, raging so loud I half expect them to raise the devil right in our midst. The barrel-bodied man—I can't see him but I know his voice—is yowling at the roustabouts to feed the boilers faster, faster. Their skin, black as the boiler beasts they're feeding, is running with sweat.

"There's a steamboat behind us!" a man looking off the side of the boat cries.

"We'll beat it!" another hollers.

Ina's baby doesn't understand a word, but she sets up a wail and she's not alone. Now even the pigs and cows are putting up a ruckus.

"What nonsense is this?" Ina hisses. "We're racing?"

Most of the men and boys are shrieking with the thrill of it, getting drenched from spray as we churn through the river. But some move to the front of the boat to try to push up the ladder to the upper deck. Somebody, I don't know who, throws each man back.

"A boiler goes," one man yells, "and we're done for!"

Ina's children are jumbled around her and all but the oldest boy are crying. "Those fools think this is comical?" Ina shouts at me, but I can't answer. I haven't made it my business to understand why men do what they do, but I am more than sick of putting up with it. And I didn't give up my canoe to get blown to smithereens on a steamboat.

I rise and pull Bridget up beside me. "Let's go stand by the side," I call out to Ina, and add what's likely a lie. "We can jump in the river if we've a need to."

"Get back down," Ina orders her girl and scowls at me. "Don't you go scaring my babies. There'll be no jumping in the river for any of us."

They're not moving; that's plain. So I make my way alone to the side of the boat and push through the cluster of men. Now I'm one of those leaning out and it's a mercy. The air is fresh and the river spray hitting my cheeks bracing. Here you can almost forget the boilers are one mad belch from killing us all.

The other steamboat, too, is a beauty, but now I know for sure that if I threw myself off this boat, I'd lose my life, not save it. Not going so fast and with that other white palace bearing down like a thunderhead. Above us the fancy people are putting up a clamor, too, and there's only one thing I think about that. Now more than ever I'd be up there, too, if I could.

I move to the front of the boat and the crowd of men at the bottom of the ladder. One man's halfway up and another's right behind. I guess they both make it all the way up because whoops rise to the sky. Men are behind me now and pushing hard against me but it's no time to take offense, not if I want to make it to that ladder. So I push fierce, too, against the man in front of me. I make it a little closer when the boat hits something, I couldn't begin to guess what, and we're all shaken loose and thrown to the floor like dice.

My leg screams—somebody's stepping on me—when I feel hands grabbing. I flail at them like a beast gone wild until I hear a man's voice shout my name. Above me a face looms into view. It's Obadiah Darby.

He's a small man but a strong one, as he pulls me to my feet with one yank. "Keep behind me," he bellows, then grabs my hand and pushes forward—it's easier now because most of the men who wanted to get to the upper deck toppled—and before I know it, Obadiah Darby lets me loose to climb onto the ladder himself. I clamber up behind him, my skirts wrenched from behind by another desperate soul I never see. For when I alight on the upper deck all I can do is suck in the air and marvel at the sight: the river so wide in front of me and so far below, churning brown; the trees on both sides tall as green kings; the crows above my head cawing so close I believe I could grab one if I tried.

But I don't get to gawk. Obadiah Darby grabs my hand and pulls me along, away from the barrel-bodied man cuffing another decker. The fancy people are mostly in the back—though we're not racing anymore, so there might not be so much to look at—but some are up here in front and they see me all right and even with all the commotion we've just been through, I can tell they don't like it.

I don't know what I'm seeing as Obadiah Darby runs me fast as a jackrabbit, but it's all very grand, like the pictures I saw once in a magazine in the general store. I was a thief that day because I tore those out the better to remember and carried them home stuffed in my pocket. I'm glad I did because they come back to me now. Here's a kind of saloon near as long as the steamboat, with fancy glass for a ceiling so the sun shines through and makes the colors in the carpet sparkle like marbles. I can't begin to take in the furniture because I've never seen any like it, but it makes me imagine that even a queen could sit here and find no cause to complain. And this dreamland is only one ladder's climb from belowdecks. It was up here all the time and I just never knew how to picture it.

Obadiah Darby pulls me into the saloon and my shoes sink into a carpet soft as rabbit fur. Only one soul sits here, a snoozing old man so close to dead he could sleep through the racing. We stop at a door with fancy glass that makes a window and Obadiah Darby opens that door and pushes me inside.

Right away I know what this is. This is a room with a bed. Small but grander than any I've ever seen except for those pictures. I spin to face Obadiah Darby and my face must be saying something even if my mouth isn't because he raises both hands, palms facing me. "I mean you no harm," he tells me.

"Why'd you come belowdecks?"

"Captain gets paid better than God, but he's a damn fool." He brushes past me and pushes his dark mop of hair back from his forehead with a rough hand. "Didn't want you to die down there if the boilers went."

"What's it to you?"

He turns around and frowns. "Nobody ever give you a hand up?" I'm trying to think of somebody who did when he speaks again. "Come to think of it, my canoe's belowdecks and boilers going wouldn't have been any good for it, either." That gets us both to smiling.

But Obadiah Darby doesn't have it in him to stand still and grin. He strides around the room again, staring down at the carpet as if it'll tell him what he wants to know. Then: "You truly called Eliza?" he asks, and I nod. "Why not speak your family name, then?"

"I don't know what it is, Haycraft or Harper." Obadiah Darby must be wearing me down because that slips out before I think about it. "One is my married name and I don't know if I'm really married."

His brows rise. I've surprised him again. "Your husband could be dead?"

Not John. John will squirm out of being dead longer than any of us. Maybe only Sarah will have him beat. "He has no reason to be."

We both jerk our heads toward the door. I can tell from the ruckus that people have come into the saloon now the racing is done. Obadiah Darby signals me to stay quiet though I don't need to be told. I know what'll happen if I'm found in here and it doesn't involve me staying put in all this comfort. He motions to a desk by the wall. Resting there is a plate with painted flowers and gold trim. What really catches my attention, though, are the two slabs of crusty bread on it, good and buttered. "Sit and eat," Obadiah Darby orders in a low voice, "and fast, before somebody finds you."

I'm too hungry to mind him watching. I sit and do as I'm told.

"Should've thought to bring back more," he says. "Last night's dinner was turtle soup and oyster pie with a side of fried plantains." He talks quickly as if he wants to get it all in before somebody throws me back belowdecks. "I'm guessing you've no plan for when we land in St. Louis."

That's so obvious I don't stop chewing to answer.

"So I have a proposition for you."

You know what he'll be expecting, Ina told me.

"I could help you," he goes on. "It'll be hard for you to set up on your own."

I set down the bread. "Why would you do that?"

"It's like I said before. I've been given a hand up. Today wasn't my first time belowdecks, you know."

He's saying he used to be like me and maybe in a fashion he was. Except that he's a man and that makes him different.

"I'm sure there are ways you could help me, too," he goes on, and since I've known John Haycraft I have no trouble imagining what those ways might be.

Still, he's right that I need help. He's also one of the fancy people, with plenty of help to give if he has a mind to. "I still don't understand why you'd want to take the trouble."

He stares at me. "There's something about you." Those keen eyes of his don't shift. "Something I can't put a name to."

It's quiet in the room when Obadiah Darby says that. We have that moment that comes sometimes when a man and a woman are alone together. They could be under a blue sky wide as heaven, but it's just the two of them in the world right then and they both feel it. Still, the commotion in the saloon is getting louder. I hear shouting and get the idea some of it has to do with me. I go back to the bread and finally shove the last bit in my mouth.

Obadiah Darby eyes the bruises there and doesn't hide it. "I won't ask how you got those. But I'm not that kind of man, so you know."

I don't think he is another John Haycraft. What he is, though, I couldn't say.

Somebody pounds on the door.

"All right," I say, and rise from the chair. I have no plan, like Obadiah Darby says, so this time, too, I'll follow what my insides tell me. "I'll take your help when we land in St. Louis."

There's the pounding again, then a man hollering. "Obadiah Darby! I know you have a female decker in there! Open this door!"

"Good," Obadiah says to me. "But it's not St. Louis I'm speaking of." He heads toward the door, no rush in his step. "You and I are bound for New Orleans."

Chapter Four

"She remained in St. Louis but a short time, and went to New Orleans in company with a male companion… "

— "Will of Madam Haycraft"

— *Daily Democrat*, December 9, 1871

TODAY ISN'T SUNDAY, BUT MAYBE PRAISE IS DUE THE LORD ALL THE SAME, because Obadiah Darby is standing right where he told me he'd be when our steamboat docked in New Orleans: ashore on the lookout for me to walk down the plank. I can tell he's waiting for me from how his eyes under his hat's brim light up when he spies me. This makes two times he's stood waiting for me: St. Louis and here.

I step off the plank onto dry land. Another thing is the same here: I can barely breathe.

Almost, almost, I'd step back on that steamboat if I could.

Because if I was scared when I pitched into John's canoe near two weeks ago, it's nothing compared to what I feel this hot afternoon. I know that river; I've known it all my life. I know the trees and the sky. But *this*, this madness of people, fancy people, plain people, Negroes, boats big and small, carts and wagons rolling pell-mell, dogs barking, horses whinnying, machine arms swinging overhead from most all the ships, aiming to knock you cold if you're not watchful; smoke belching from ships and shore where buildings are packed so tight they can scarce breathe any better than me; peddlers shouting to buy their wares; men thick as giants throwing crates and casks around like toys, and if a cask gets loose you best be careful because it might take your legs out from under you or send you smack into the river. Where you'd drown and no soul would notice unless they had a mind to pick your corpse clean.

I make my way through the hubbub to Obadiah. He told me to call him that and said it meant servant of God. I don't know him well, but I understood from the laugh he let fly that he'd be no slave of God or anybody else.

He pulls me sharp aside when I reach him. "Take a good look around, Eliza." He throws one arm wide so I'll take in the whole scene. "Commerce. You smell it?"

"I hear it." That's the other thing I can't fathom. The noise so loud I fear my ears might break from the work of it.

"No city in this country is richer," he tells me. "Or growing faster. It's the wonder of our modern times."

"Aren't we forgetting something?" I point back at the steamboat I just left. "The canoe?"

He just laughs. "We don't need that any more," and off he strides in that jumpy way of his, carrying what I now know to call his portmanteau. That's French, he told me: expect to hear it in New Orleans. I heard it where I grew up, too. But it didn't sound the same as here. I'll wager nothing there is the same as here.

I scurry behind, catching only part of what Obadiah says, about the boats that line the riverbank far as the eye can see, sometimes three and four deep. The steamboats I understand already, but not the brigs or the arks or the barges.

Obadiah points to one especially grand "sailing vessel." "Look at that three-master. Flying the Tricolor, so you know it's from France." I think I know what he's talking about: a red, white and blue flag. "You're in little Paris now," he tells me, and I hear pride in his voice as if he's responsible for that name himself.

He is responsible for me being here, no disputing that. It's Obadiah who paid my passage belowdecks from St. Louis. It's Obadiah who paid for me to pass the nights in a boardinghouse there, with rich meals to boot, and he's the one who saw that I had thread to mend my clothes, and soap to wash them, and food and bedding for the steamboat ride to New Orleans.

When we docked in St. Louis, Ina and her clan walked ahead of me leaving belowdecks and I could tell from the showy way she harrumphed and picked up her pace that she saw Obadiah waiting for me even before I did. After the steamboat race she had no time for me. The story of how I was found in Obadiah's so-called stateroom made the rounds and I know what everybody thought even though no part of it was true. Getting off the steam-boat Ina hurried her children along that plank as if she believed Obadiah Darby and I would get to fornicating right there on the levee and she didn't want her brood's innocent souls corrupted on a bright and shiny Thursday morning.

I have no doubt Obadiah is "expecting something." Well, why wouldn't he be? I may be a rube from the country, but I know well as anybody there's nothing free in this world. And Obadiah hasn't demanded anything yet. That shows he's got well more patience than John Haycraft did and I don't recall getting much more from him than bruises.

All the same, now we've got to New Orleans the reckoning with Obadiah can't be long off.

Right now I have to move fast not to lose him. With sweat trickling down my back I wonder how far we're aiming to walk when we get to a wide road loaded with drays and carriages.

Shops and I don't know what else crowd both sides. Obadiah tells me not to slow him down even though that's the last thing I'm doing.

I shudder what would become of me if I did lose him. I don't know what to make of these people. They're even less my kind than the Dutch in Hermann. Half the bodies here are Negro. Many speak French, too, least I think so. Of course we had Negroes where I come from, all of them belonging to somebody— though not our family: we couldn't afford that. One Negro girl I ran with one summer, till my mother caught me and told me to stop, and we never mixed after.

Ahead Obadiah jerks his arm upright and looses a loud whistle. Up rolls a small carriage drawn by a horse nearly the color of Ina's hair and inside holding the reins is a skinny-as-a-rail Negro man, whiskers pure white, who clambers out to grab hold of Obadiah's portmanteau. "Welcome back, sir," he says then hands Obadiah a flask and swings the portmanteau into the carriage. If he's surprised to see a wild-haired woman of four-and-twenty years standing behind Obadiah, he doesn't show it.

For the first time since I met Obadiah Darby, who's thrown back his head to guzzle whatever is in that flask, I think to myself that maybe I am the fool my mother always said. Because only this second do I have the idea that I might not be the first female he offered to "help" here in New Orleans.

Obadiah pulls down the flask and licks his lips as if he tasted something he's missed. "Good to be back, Matthew. This is Miss Eliza. You'll be riding in the back now," but he didn't have to say that because Matthew's already headed that way. Obadiah slaps the horse friendly on the rump and waves me into the carriage. I try not to show it's my first time. Off we go with a jerk and my hands fly, grabbing at something to latch on to. That makes Obadiah laugh, and maybe the horse, too, because it's tossing its head and prancing like it's happy to have Obadiah home.

What would John Haycraft think of this, or Sarah, or my

mother or father, me in this conveyance in so-called Little Paris, headed to who knows where with one of the fancy people?

I know what *I* think. I better be careful.

I better have no pretty pictures in my mind where Obadiah Darby is concerned. He told me straight out he has a wife, two sons, and a daughter in someplace called Lowell, Massachusetts. He told me he lives there sometimes and he lives here sometimes and he likes both but in different ways. Not that I'm aiming to marry again, even if I could, but with Obadiah I can't unless his wife passes and that I won't wish for. It's not in my nature, but maybe I should've done more thinking before I threw myself in John's canoe because the time beforehand all I thought about was how to get away and the time since I've been preoccupied with getting away far—first to Hermann, then to St. Louis, and now here. Now I'm farther away than I ever thought I'd be. Now what?

Since I can't breathe right and I can't think right, all I know is that New Orleans is a sight to see, even more than St. Louis. Everything is big and bright and fast. My eyes are so full I can't follow what Obadiah is saying. That's the Cathedral St. Louis he's pointing to now. If you're fancy enough to pray in there, I'd say God has to listen. And there are so many fancy people here. I can't fathom the clothes I'm seeing, or the bonnets, or what Obadiah calls the parasols. The buildings show so much color, too, from pink to yellow to blue, as if they were flowers sprung from the ground. There are real flowers, too, everywhere, and you don't just see them, you smell them, sweet and fruity. And the glass! The windows are all glass, if you can believe that. Obadiah points at the balconies and something called wrought iron and tells me how fine it's made, even to look like vines and flowers. It's like nowhere else in the world, he says. I try to look everywhere so I don't miss a thing, but I think I could stare for whole days and there'd be a hundred things I'd miss.

Well, I used to wonder what was beyond the bend in the river. I guess now I'm finding out.

Obadiah passes me the flask. Maybe he's thinking things'll go easier if I'm liquored up, but I'd rather keep a clear mind to the extent I'm able. He stashes the flask in his pocket. "You'd be smart to learn what New Orleans has to teach you, Eliza. Enjoy life while you can. You don't know what tomorrow will bring."

Not long after that, when the sun's about to quit for the day, the horse stops without being told. Matthew jumps off the back and I figure we must be where Obadiah lives. Fine houses line up one after the next, pushed back from the road, every last one with a garden. Obadiah raises his hand to a Negro woman stepping out from one of them. She's twice the size of Matthew, with a kerchief on her head and an apron round her middle. The house behind her isn't wide but has one story in front, two in back, and four windows near as tall as me.

"That's Esther," Obadiah tells me. "Matthew's wife."

So much for her smile, because that fades fast as a snowflake when she catches sight of me. And once Obadiah is past and can't see, she makes me step around her to walk the path to the front door. Funny how she speaks no more than her husband does but says what she feels just the same.

Going up those stairs into Obadiah's house, it's possible I'm even more breathless than in the carriage. Up to now it's been only a log cabin for me, the chinks daubed over with mud and greased paper. This is a home built of brick, cool and hushed, like you're leaving the whole world behind. With the sun so low I can't see clearly, but I make out a parlor with chairs and couches that take me back to the steamboat saloon—there's the same kind of rug, just as fat—and real paintings on the walls. I smell cigar smoke and catch a whiff of something so delicious I might faint from hunger.

Obadiah speaks up. "Esther, show Miss Eliza her bedchamber. And get her a basin so she can wash up before supper."

So I'm staying here. And I'm eating here. No boardinghouse for me.

Esther more grunts than answers, but Obadiah gets something

like a smile out of her when he asks if that's her shrimp wrapped in bacon he smells cooking. "Same as I make it every time you come home," she tells him then turns to me. "Miz Eliza," she says, making plain she thinks I've no more right to that Miz than she has.

I follow her to a rear bedchamber with a narrow bed and wooden stand with drawers and chamber pot and window with curtains white as daisies. While I wait for her to come back with a basin—and I thank her when she does—I stand at the window and wonder how I got here. I wonder what other females have been in this room and what happened to them. Far away I hear New Orleans' noise but hereabouts it's almost quiet, save for a dog upset about something and a few carriages rolling past. I'm too hungry and tired to ponder what my future holds and don't need much imagination to figure it out anyway. So I use Obadiah's fine-smelling soap to wash best I can and go back out to find him.

He's sitting in a room set up for eating, lit soft by candles. I can tell he's washed up, too. He sets his eyes on me, but it takes him time to speak. Then: "Eliza, I don't know that I've ever seen a woman prettier than you."

I don't know that I believe him, especially as I'm wearing clothes so old and tatty, but he motions me to sit across from him at the heavy dark table, just us two, with Esther in and out to make sure it all goes right. It's not just shrimp with bacon she's cooked but soup with beans and okra, and biscuits so buttery they melt on your tongue. And she had enough flour and sugar left over for a peach cobbler.

Obadiah does most of the talking. That's a mercy because I can't stop my fork from moving or my teeth from chewing. He tells me all manner of things I doubt I'll have straight in the morning, about New Orleans and how big and rich it is, mostly because of its port. New Orleans is like places I've heard of—New York and London—and places I haven't. Liverpool? Obadiah has something to do with the cotton business, big in these parts due to the plantations. I guess that's how he went from belowdecks to fancy.

I try to understand. "So you help the plantations sell their cotton to people in the other state you live in, Massachusetts, and you get a share?" I pass again on the whiskey and try not to worry about Obadiah drinking. I know what whiskey did to John Haycraft more times than not.

"I help the plantations sell to the mills in Lowell, yes." He sits back in his chair. "So if I sell a hundred dollars' worth and I get" —he stops, I suspect to make the calculating harder—"fifteen percent, what does that make for the plantation?"

I think hard to make sure I get it right. "That means it gets eighty-five."

Obadiah smiles. It's that same smile as when he talked about Little Paris, like he had something to do with New Orleans being called that. He knows he's got nothing to do with my calculating, but for some reason he seems proud of it just the same. "You like Esther's cooking?" he wants to know.

"It's God's honest truth I have never eaten food this fine." I stop for a moment, then: "Thank you, Obadiah."

I didn't plan to thank him now, but there it is. He goes quiet and we have another of those moments when it's like nobody else is alive in the world. Maybe I got him to thinking about the other ways I could thank him. I don't know where Esther and Matthew have got to, that's for sure. He gets up from the table and comes back with two fancy glasses, very small, filled with something pretty and orange. "This is French liqueur," he tells me. "Try it."

I sniff it—"it smells like oranges"—then I taste it. That makes him smile again. It burns on the way down in a way I like. I sip it again.

I know where we're headed—I think I've known ever since I was in Obadiah's stateroom and told him I'd take his help. I don't know how to think about it except I do need help and far as I can figure I've got only one thing to give in return and that's as clear to Obadiah as it is to me.

He sits back down at the table but closer this time. "So how can it be you don't know if you're married?"

I feel like a fool not to know. "Well, I can tell you I got married right and proper. It was June twenty-ninth last year and it was in front of a judge with my father as witness."

It came after a lot of screaming and crying on my part. My father wanted no part of John Haycraft for me. Now I think back, I believe he saw what I didn't want to see, what I kept telling myself I didn't see. Every worry, I pushed to the side. I believe my mother also saw trouble, but she was just as happy not to have my mouth to feed. Even better, she could lord it over me when it all went bad.

Obadiah frowns. "And your husband's still alive?"

"He was alive the night I left him." I'm admitting it, then. I left him. But I had good reason, least in my own mind. "He told me" —I stop, because it's the first time I've said it out loud and it's hard to make the words come—"the night I left him, he told me he had a wife before. In Kentucky, where he came from."

I don't know why he picked that night to tell me. I'd been short with him all day, but that was nothing new. I'd had near enough of John Haycraft by that point and I believe he could sense it. Some time after I married him, I couldn't say when, the dreams I used to dream when I stared up at the blue sky were gone as if they'd never been there. I'd had enough of him coming after me with his fists when he'd had too much from the bottle. I'd had enough of him pulling down my drawers whenever he had a mind to. I'd had enough of him being lazy as a dog when I thought he was a man who would make something of himself. And I'd had enough of being so wrong about him, which meant my mother was right about him, which meant I was a fool after all, just like she said.

"The wife in Kentucky," Obadiah is saying, "so she's dead?"

"She wasn't dead when John left her. He said she was sickly, though."

"Sickly's not dead," Obadiah says.

That's what I'd told John, even though he didn't want to hear it. That wife could still be in Kentucky breathing, for all he knew. Didn't help that the winter had been so long and cold, snow piling in drifts so high you could lose a body in them. He was on very friendly terms with the bottle, too, so I can add that to the things I didn't cotton to. I felt caged up and ready to bust out. I guess all I needed was an excuse and he gave me a good one when he said he had a wife before and just never saw fit to mention it before that occasion.

"If you're married to one woman," I say, "can you rightly be married to another?"

Obadiah shakes his head. "Not a Christian man."

"Not even if one wife is in Kentucky and the other in Missouri?" John tried to make me believe that. I wanted no part of that if I could help it.

Obadiah obliges me by shaking his head again. "Just one living wife, that's all a Christian man can have. So, I guess we'll call him your husband, his name is John?"

"John Haycraft. John Neville Haycraft."

"Haycraft or Harper. Those are the names you spoke to me before."

"Depends whether or not I'm really married." I think about what Obadiah just told me, Obadiah who knows the ways of the world. "I'd say I'm not."

There's a good chance John Haycraft knew that all along. He knew I wouldn't let him into my drawers unless he married me and I guess now I understand why he didn't object overmuch. In the end, though, he was spitting mad. When he threw those words at me about his wife in Kentucky, I knew what he wanted back. He wanted tears, tears and agony. I gave him anger, least at the start, but even that didn't last long. I knew the best way to get back at him was to go cold. By then I was just as happy to be rid of him. I don't think John Haycraft bargained on that.

I watched him yell and drink and yell and drink and I stayed cool and quiet and out of reach. I knew a heavy sleep would take him and I had a plan hatched for when it did. I didn't know that I'd do it, but it was there. So finally when he was snoring good and loud, I didn't let myself think. I just put on all my clothes and the coins we'd stored up inside my string bag and crept outside silent as a ghost.

Later that night John Haycraft told me he's the one who'd do the leaving. Well, I don't think so.

Obadiah pushes my glass closer. I realize all this time he's been watching me and I've been thinking my own thoughts with no mind to him. I take another sip of that orangey liqueur like I know he wants me to then I set down my glass. It's almost like he made me invitation and I took it. Obadiah looks at my mouth where the bruises are near gone by now then he leans forward and kisses me.

I've had other boys kiss me, and men, not just John Haycraft, but of course it's the first man who's not John Haycraft since I got married, or leastwise thought I did. I'm not feeling all fluttery and alive when Obadiah kisses me, like my heart's about to take off on golden wings, but his lips are gentle and his moustache tickles and I can tell he likes it when I giggle. He smells nice, too, since he washed up, and I taste that orange liqueur on him. That's nice and I'm happy to kiss him back. That gets him going stronger and I get a little shocked at myself thinking what I'm about to do.

But I am about to do it because it's what I owe Obadiah. And, I think I can say this even though I might be a fool for it: Obadiah Darby is a friend of mine.

He takes my hand to lead me up the staircase, the light of his lantern a full moon rising on the wall. Matthew and Esther, I don't know where they are, but I don't hear them and they don't seem to hear the stairs creaking so I throw them from my mind. Obadiah takes me into a bedchamber and this one has no narrow bed. This one has a wide bed so high you need a step to climb onto it.

When I think about it later, I think how strange it is that Obadiah didn't say a word and I didn't, either. I guess we both knew what was about to happen and there was no point talking about it. I stepped out of my shoes and let him take off my dress and drawers and shift and just stood there for him to look at in the lamplight.

I didn't crave Obadiah's hands on me like I craved John's at the start, on my breasts and my private parts, all wet and deep and aching. Not even a young Obadiah Darby would set a woman's heart to racing, but he's wiry and hard and I liked the way he looked at me. Maybe he hadn't had a woman of four-and-twenty years in a while, maybe that was it, but he looked at me like he couldn't quite believe his luck. He touched me that way, too.

I don't ever remember anything like that from John Haycraft.

Chapter Five

Frenchmen, Spaniards, West Indians, Creoles, Mustees,
Yankees, Kentuckians, Tennesseans, lawyers and trustees,
Clergymen, priests, friars, nuns, women of all stains;
Negroes in purple and fine linen, and
slaves in rags and chains.
Ships, arks, steamboats, robbers, pirates, alligators,
Assassins, gamblers, drunkards, and cotton speculators;
Sailors, soldiers, pretty girls, and ugly fortune-tellers;
Pimps, imps, shrimps, and all sorts of dirty fellows;
White men with black wives, et vice versa too.
A progeny of all colors—an infernal motley crew!
Yellow fever in February—muddy streets all the year;
Many things to hope for, and a dev'lish sight to fear!

— Colonel James R. Creecy

— *Scenes in the South*, 1860

THERE ARE PEOPLE LIKE CHANTAL ROSSIGNOL IN NEW ORLEANS. I've known her for near two weeks now but still find it a wonder. I sit next to her in Obadiah's parlor, drapes putting up a fight against the afternoon sun, and watch her bend over her needlework. I shake my head at that skin of hers that looks like coffee loaded with rich cream. Where I come from, there's nobody like Chantal. Negro but not Negro, nobody's slave, fancier than most white folk, and speaking French, too. John Haycraft doesn't know any like her, I wager, but if he did he'd think they were uppity and want them put back in their place.

"Tell me that word again," I say, "that says what you are?"

She shakes her pretty head with her hair piled high and laughs her soft laugh, never looking up from her needle. "*Mulâtresse.*"

"*Mulâtresse.*"

She giggles because I can't say it like she does, with the growl deep in the throat. She's taught me other words I can say, like *jambon* and *café au lait.* I try them out on Obadiah, but every time I do it ends the same way and so I pick and choose my times. Otherwise I'd be on my back more than the morning and night I am already.

"Here's a new word for you," she says. "*Aiguille.*"

It's so hard I don't even try it. I just laugh. These weeks I've been at Obadiah's house, with more ease and comfort than I've ever known, it's easy to laugh. I know it won't stay that way for long.

"*Aiguille,*" she repeats. She holds up her needle and tries not to giggle. "*Aiguille.*"

"*Aiguille.*"

"*Aiguille.*" The way she says it, it sounds like three words.

I try again—"*aiguille*"—but really all I can do is laugh.

Esther stomps past the parlor with a harrumph. Esther is very busy the days Chantal is here because she has to scowl at Chantal least as often as she has to scowl at me. Chantal doesn't seem to care. She's uppity with both Esther and Matthew; I see that plainly.

Some of Chantal's sewing tools hang from a silver brooch she clasps to her bodice—a *chatelaine*, she calls it; that's another new word for me—but some she spreads on a length of rich red fabric on the low table. With the sun that's sneaking in—the drapes can't be full closed or Chantal couldn't see her stitches; that's another thing Esther grumbles about—dust dances in the air like tiny fireflies. I reach for a needle but Chantal stops me with a mild shake of the head. "Not that one. Try the one with the double eye."

"That one's harder to thread."

"The needle with the single eye gives you the problem of a strand of thread stuck on the wrong side of the fabric. Then you must separate the two and pull the stopped one through. All that takes time."

Chantal keeps saying she has no time to waste. That's one way it's not easy to sit and watch her. It makes me think I should worry about wasting time, too, though that's hard to do when the days pass in such a nice way that I'm not aiming to change them.

Chantal is sewing dresses for me that Obadiah is paying for. The first day she came to Obadiah's house she buzzed about me with lengths of fabric, measuring every which way and smiling in that way she has, as if she's tending a happy secret. It makes a body want to know what that secret is.

I could tell from the easy way she spoke to Obadiah that they are not strangers. It shames me that she must know what I do here. How many times has she been in this house sewing dresses for women he plucked off steamboats? Maybe when I screw up my courage I can ask her what happened to them. It's not as if I think their bones are stuffed beneath the floorboards, but still I'd like to know.

I'm wearing the blue-colored dress she made me—it's the finest thing I've ever owned, the color of bluebells—and now she's making another in yellow. Obadiah has also given me high-button shoes, a far sight different from my clodhoppers, both of those good for the left foot and the right. I have a new corset, and drawers and petticoats made with lace and something called broderie, though why anybody has suchlike on their drawers is beyond me. Not even Obadiah, who paid for them, can be bothered to spend more than a few seconds admiring them before off they go.

Chantal lays aside her needlework and stretches her fingers and neck and shoulders. It's coming on late afternoon and she began sewing before I was finished with breakfast, not that I rise early these days. I'd like to know how old she is but can't bring myself to ask. She looks young but frets like someone old, not just about wasting time but about losing her eyesight and her fingers growing numb. More than anything she frets about her daughter. I'd like to know how Chantal got her, too, but that's even harder to ask about than her age.

That night after Obadiah and I are done eating a stew made with beans and sausage—I can't believe I eat like this every night, and in a dining room, too—I ask Obadiah how can it be that Chantal isn't a slave. I know enough to wait until Esther has carried away her scowl and the empty bowls.

"Chantal is a free Negro woman," he tells me. "Her mother bought her own freedom and so Chantal is also free."

"Didn't her mother need money to buy her freedom? How did she get that?"

"She was a seamstress, like Chantal." Obadiah rises to pour us the orange-flavored liqueur. Esther returns with cherries soaked in syrup. She keeps her harrumph at Chantal's name low and quiet since Obadiah's in hearing. "Her owner gave her a price and allowed her to do needlework on the side to earn the money."

"Why would he do that?"

Obadiah winks at me. "Maybe he liked her."

It doesn't take me long to add one and one. That white owner is Chantal's father; that's how she got her *café au lait* skin. "How did Chantal get her daughter? And is she also free?"

But Obadiah has had enough of talking about Chantal. I know

already that mostly he wants to talk and have me listen, which might be the only way Obadiah Darby is like John Haycraft.

It is not until the next morning that I point out how seamstresses must make a great deal of money if Chantal's mother could get enough to buy her freedom. Obadiah laughs at me over our beignets in a way that makes me think I would be on my back again if he didn't have to go early to one of the plantations.

"Will you take me with you?" I ask. After all, now I have the blue dress to wear, and the high-button shoes.

Obadiah's smile becomes a frown. "Aren't you happy here?"

"How could I not be happy?" I have gone from a shack to a palace. My belly is so full that it sticks out. I need do nothing all day but sit and watch Chantal. "But I'd like to see what's outside, too."

He wipes his mouth with his napkin and throws it on the table. "How long have you been here? Not yet a month?" He leaves without kissing my forehead. Esther makes sure to look down her nose at me when she comes in to collect the dishes piled with crumbs and sugar.

Usually I understand what Obadiah likes to hear and what he doesn't, but this time I don't.

It's noontime when the weather turns. Soon it matches Obadiah's mood. The air grows heavy and gray clouds square off like pent-up boys fixing to fight. For the first time I get restless watching Chantal sew and pick up a needle myself. She allows me to work on a small part inside the dress that no one will see. But that doesn't go right, either, since I can't stitch as fine as her and I can see she worries she'll have to rip out my stitches and do them over. "Don't worry, Chantal," I say. "I don't mind that the stitches are big."

"If I must pull them out, the fabric could be harmed and then I would have to buy more."

"Don't worry," I repeat. "Obadiah will never see my stitches."

"Mr. Darby. That is what you must call him when you talk

about him to other people." Her hands full of needlework fall to her lap. "I'm sorry. I should not have said that."

"I don't mind."

"It's just that I'm putting in the sleeves and that's tricky and takes so long."

"Why must I call him Mr. Darby?"

She looks at me surprised I don't understand but doesn't answer as if I were a fool, as my mother would. "Even if he were your husband, you would call him that to people who aren't in your family."

Fancy people and their strange customs! "Have you seen his wife?"

"One time. Years ago."

"He told me she doesn't like it here. It's too foreign." Unchristian, he said she called it, that the gin shops and gambling halls are open on Sunday as if that day isn't devoted to God. Once she even saw a cock fight on a Sunday, across from the exchange building. Then there are the French people, the Creoles they call them, and the Spaniards and the free Negro people, too. All of them are a problem for one reason or another, though I wonder why because aren't they all God's children she's supposed to love?

"Don't worry," Chantal assures me. "She won't be back."

"He didn't want to take me today to the plantation."

Her eyes fly wide open. "You asked to go with him?"

"I want to see more of what's outside. I haven't been out even once since we came here from the steamboat."

Chantal says nothing. Her eyes drift back to the tricky sleeve as if she'd rather sew that than talk to me.

"Do you know why he, why Mr. Darby didn't want to take me with him?"

She glances around to make sure we're alone—Esther is probably snooping; she always does if she's not catching a wink—and leans across the table that holds her sewing things. "It's because you're not his wife." I must look as if I don't understand because

Chantal keeps talking. "Many people know Mr. Darby. If he is out and about with a strange young woman... " Her voice trails off.

I know what they would think. And they would be right, too. "But does that mean I never leave this house again?"

"You and I could go for a walk," she offers, "on a day when it's not raining. I will take you to the market," and then she takes up her needlework again, and I'm touched because going to the market would take Chantal's time and she seems to have so little of it to spare.

I decide to do two things then: to be more careful with my needlework so Chantal doesn't have to do it over, and to ask what I want to know, because it seems she can tell me and sew at the same time. "Are you married, Chantal?"

That question stops her needle from moving. She looks across the parlor in a dreamy way, as if she's seeing something there. Or someone. "I was not allowed to marry the man I loved. Nor he me."

"Why not?" Maybe he had a wife already that he was truthful about.

But she surprises me. "Because I am a *mulâtresse.*"

I think back to what Obadiah told me about Chantal's mother and father and take a guess. "Is he a white man? Like Mr. Darby?"

She nods, dreamy as ever. Maybe he is the secret she's tending.

This next part is tricky, though, as Chantal would say. "You have a daughter?"

Her eyes light up. "She is called Honorine. She has six years. She is the love of my life, Honorine." Chantal sighs, and it stings me because my mother would never say that of me and sometimes I worry I may never have a child of my own I could speak that way about.

Now I know why Chantal worries so much about her daughter. Honorine is a bastard child. Maybe people don't care so much if you're a *mulâtresse*: they don't expect you to have everything right and proper. I'm surprised Chantal says Honorine is the love of her life and not the man she loved. Maybe later he went off and married a white woman and pretends Chantal and Honorine don't exist. That is what John Haycraft would do. But then why would Chantal still be lovesick? "You still love him?" I am being bold and asking what I like. "Honorine's father?"

No more dreaminess. She looks straight at me. "I will love him all my days. But he is dead. He died of the yellow jack."

I know that fever. "I have heard it is horrible."

"First you have chills, then fever. Then you spit up black vomit. Then your skin turns yellow. Then you die." Up goes the needlework. Chantal is back to her sewing. "It was three years ago. That was a bad year for it. It comes in summer."

"That's now." I look down in my lap at the fabric we're sewing. Yellow like the yellow jack turns your skin before you die.

"Most of the good families leave in summertime. They go to Lake Pontchartrain or stay at their plantations. It's not so much a problem for Mr. Darby as he is mostly at the plantations."

I must look worried—I haven't gone back to my needlework because I'm still busy imagining yellow skin and black vomit—because Chantal tries to reassure me.

"I don't think it's bad this year." She frowns. "Though you don't always know if it is. They try to keep the news down because it's bad for trade and the men of business want the port open. And can you guess what some people say? That if people like me had white owners, we wouldn't get sick." It's the first time I've seen Chantal look disgusted. I didn't know her pretty face could form such an expression. "The white owners themselves get sick and die. How do those idiots explain that?"

I can see why she's angry. The white man she loved died. Now the only way she can be with him is at the graveyard and, no matter what people say, that's not much good to anyone.

In honor of Chantal's sadness, I thread a different needle, a short double-eye whose stitches will be finer. I pull the thread tight by looping through the knot after the first stitch, like she does, and when I've done the whole seam I return the other way to fill in the empty spaces in the stitch line. This gives my needlework strength, but it will be harder for Chantal to tear out if she wants to. At the end of the day, I'm proud because Chantal wants to tear out only the stitches I did first thing in the morning when I was sloppy and working with the long needle. Those come out easily and don't hurt the fabric.

"Please don't ask Mr. Darby again if you can go to the planta-tions with him," she says when she's done fixing my work. "He's a good man. He'll want to say yes but know he shouldn't."

I say nothing. I don't want to be a problem for Obadiah, but all the same I don't want him to hide me in this house as if I'm mad as a loon.

"He's a good man." Chantal says it again as she gathers her sewing things on her red fabric. "Some of these people"—she waves her arm across Obadiah's parlor—"they make me work all day and all night to finish the dresses fast but don't want to pay what they owe. Sometimes the people with the biggest houses don't want to pay. By then they have the garments in their hands and what am I supposed to do? Mr. Darby never does that."

"You can't ask them to pay before you start?"

"I can ask. But that does not mean they will do it."

And even here in rich New Orleans, I suppose there are only so many people who can pay to have Chantal come to their house to make dresses.

She makes me promise not to step out on my own. "There is much danger and you could get turned around this way and that and not find your way back."

I protest but don't want to be another worry for Chantal, who has enough already. After she leaves, I sit in the parlor while Esther clatters about in the kitchen. For some time now I have thought of Obadiah as my friend and now I start to think of Chantal that way, too, even though she is a *mulâtresse*. Obadiah doesn't seem to care and I am thinking I don't, either. It is not how my mother would think and that makes me even more fierce in the feeling.

I'm especially nice to Obadiah that night and not just because of what Chantal said about him. I don't like to think about it—and it's not like it was with John Haycraft—but it frightens me to make him angry. He could turn me out quick as he brought me in. I inquire about his day at the plantations, well past the point that I really listen to the answers, and when he gets to asking me to do calculations I do them fast to make him laugh, just like I did with my father. I even sip whiskey and watch his eyes grow brighter. He's thinking that when we get upstairs I might allow more wickedness than is typical. And indeed I do. At the end of all that, I wager I'm back in his good graces.

It's a funny life I have now, though. I lie in the soft bed beside Obadiah, who's sleeping placid as a babe, and I feel the black night all around me and wonder again how I got here. I suppose one thing just flows into the next and you find yourself where you are. But this life I have now has a strange feeling to it, as if someday I will wake up and that will be the end of it. Gone—like a dream you can't pull to mind in the morning.

Chantal doesn't want to go to the market the next day as the roads are so muddy from the rain and our skirts would be much the worse for it. It's the first time I've ever had to worry about a thing like that. But it might be just as well, as I've got Obadiah again in a good mood and don't want to put him out of it so soon. I've already decided I will ask him permission to go to the market, though it chafes me to do it, as if I were a child, and what if he says no? Then I can't go? If it were just me I would sneak out, but I know Chantal won't cotton to that—she does want my dresses paid for, after all—and Esther would tell Obadiah before he even took off his hat. I see the road all of that would take me down and I don't care for it.

Chantal will risk our skirts two days later and sure enough I get Obadiah's permission the way I know best. Like Chantal he also talks of danger—it seems everyone here carries a dagger or a pistol and isn't afraid to use them—and demands that Matthew follow us even though that means Obadiah must drive his own gig that day. Chantal does not mind as Matthew will carry what we purchase, but I don't like it as I am sure Esther will demand he report every detail. And what use will skinny old Matthew be in case of real danger? I cannot complain, though, especially after Obadiah gives me coins for the outing.

My eyes are big as I walk with Chantal. She walks me on Canal Street, which has very grand shops but may be as crowded with people and carriages and dogs and horses as the port, and near as much belching smoke from the ships. Many items for sale are from real Paris. Some of the women are dressed in the sort of things I see in the windows and I am amazed to think that this fine garment that I am wearing is simple beside theirs. The fancy men don't look only at their fancy women, though. It reminds me of floating up to the steamboat in John's canoe. Even though I looked crazy and beat up and wild, many men's eyes turned toward me. Now it is the same, so it doesn't seem to matter whether I am dirty or wearing a fine dress with my hair piled prettily on my head like Chantal's.

Chantal pushes me past women calling out to sell things, women who look like her but have bright fabrics twisted about their heads and baskets of wares on their arms. Flowers, eggs, meats, and something called pâté, which Chantal buys and which I think would make me sick if I ate it. Very soon I spend my coins on earbobs and a white bow for my hair that has a ruffled edge, too. And I see it's not unusual that Obadiah enjoys whiskey in the evenings. The men here in New Orleans must drink all the day long because even now in the morning they stand in the hot sun outside a beautiful building with glasses in hand. They're served from bottles all the colors of a rainbow.

"That is a hotel for pleasure seekers," Chantal whispers to me. "Many come from as far away as Europe. Much money can be made from a bar. The hotel serves a buffet table twice a day, too. From one to two and from eight to eleven."

I am becoming less ignorant as I listen to Chantal and Obadiah both. It is amazing what your eyes can see if you just look. And what your ears can hear if you just listen.

The market, when we get there, is a sight I will never forget. Such people, from black to brown to white and in between, their clothes bright as the fruit and vegetables on offer, speaking every language anyone ever thought of, all pushing and laughing and staring and yelling and buying and selling. We even see Indians who look very savage, half naked with long black hair dangling from their scalps and knives in full view.

"Choctaws," Chantal tells me in a low tone. "It is said they are the most honest people of all. And their women the most chaste."

That may well be. But still they frighten me.

With no time to waste, Chantal marches through quick as you like—it's a wonder Matthew keeps up; she doesn't try at all to keep him behind us—but from time to time she stops to point at something and tell me what it is. I learn about the green fruit called plantains that can be fried for dinner; cocoa and pecan nuts; and the names of different types of silver fish, dead but nicely laid out on what Chantal calls palmetto leaves.

We're halted at the seed sellers, their neat packets spread on woven mats, when a carriage clatters to a stop behind us. It's the racket that first brings me round, but the carriage is so large and grand that once I see it all I want to do is stare. Long and shiny and black as a crow it is, with the top raised to block the sun. It's pulled not by one horse but by two and the Negro driver sitting up top is wearing a fancy red jacket with gold buttons down the front and gold braids at the shoulders.

Two women sit inside—it fits four at least—and once my eyes light on them I cannot look away. On the old side they are, with plenty of wrinkles, and dressed rich like the ladies wearing the Paris clothes but with more color. They both have bright hair the color of a robin's breast and faces powdered white and red paint on their lips and cheeks. They're looking at me, too, as one gets out of the carriage with the help of the driver. She squints at me and doesn't look away and even says something to the other lady as she points in my direction.

"Come." Chantal tugs at me. She has looked up from a packet of seeds. "Don't look at them."

"Why not?"

Chantal pulls harder and calls to Matthew to come fast even though he couldn't do that to escape the gates of hell. "They're bad women," she tells me.

"Why are they bad?" The one who got out first is waving her old hand at me and calling out and pointing at me to her driver.

"They run bawdy houses. Come," and Chantal pulls me around a corner into a crowd even though I don't think Matthew can see us to follow.

They are very rich whatever they do because I am amazed at the size of their carriage. And the jewels hanging round their necks are the biggest I've seen.

Chantal keeps pulling me as she walks, fast as ever, but I glance back once and see the bawdy ladies' carriage driver far behind us in the crowd, back where we turned the corner, standing in the sun looking this way and that. I don't know why I believe it, but I'd lay down good money he's searching for me.

Chapter Six

"To all men whose desire is only to be rich, and to live a short life but a merry one, I have no hesitation in recommending New Orleans."

— Henry Bradshaw Fearon

— *Sketches of America,* 1818

CHANTAL DIDN'T LOOK BEHIND US TO SEE THE BAWDY LADIES' CARRIAGE DRIVER, but she speaks as if she knows he was there. "If you should ever see those women again," she says, "or women like them, you must not speak to them."

It is the afternoon and we are back at our needlework in Obadiah's parlor when she says this. I'm threading a double-eye needle the way she taught me, through the bottom hole first then through the top hole the opposite way.

"And," she goes on, "if a man tells you he works for the city and will help you find a situation, or a proper boardinghouse, you must walk quickly away from him."

"I think you don't want me to talk to anyone." I say it mildly though I do not like all these Musts and Must Nots from Chantal.

"A man like that is not working for the city. He is looking for young women to work in the bawdy houses."

"He couldn't make me if he tried."

"He would tell you stories to make you follow him. Then, when you are settled in the boardinghouse, which wouldn't be proper at all, you would be charged high rents you couldn't pay unless you worked at the bawdy house."

Chantal sounds very familiar with the situation. "Has this happened to you?"

Her eyes fly open. "No! This happens to young women who come to New Orleans from the country. Or from Ireland," she adds quickly, probably because she remembers too late that I'm a rube from the countryside and might be insulted.

"From the looks of them, those women would have no trouble paying high rents." I say this knowing it will annoy Chantal, but I am annoyed that my one chance to be outside and see interesting things ended so soon. Now I am back in the house, which I thank God for, but when will I get out again?

"Those women could pay because they own the bawdy houses. But the young women who work for them have no money at all. Especially"—and I know she adds this because she is annoyed at me, too—"because they spend what little they earn on earbobs and hair bows."

Maybe because it surprises me to have Chantal be sharp with me I get careless and prick my finger with the needle. Before I know it Chantal has pulled the yellow fabric from my lap. "If you bleed on it, it will be ruined." Her face is very stern. "And then I shall have to buy more."

"I'm sorry, Chantal." I suck on my finger to catch the blood. "I don't want to make you worry. And I really believe Obadiah, I mean Mr. Darby, would pay for it."

"Maybe yes, maybe no. But I cannot afford the chance."

It quiets me to see Chantal worry so much about money. How did her mother ever earn enough to buy her freedom? Chantal won't let me sew because of my bleeding, and because now I am vexed with one thing and another I leave Chantal by herself in the parlor and go sit in the small bedchamber at the back.

Of course that night Obadiah hears all about the market trip from Esther, because Matthew could not keep up with us, as I knew he couldn't, and so he returned home alone, and so did we, and with all of that Esther could not keep her mouth shut.

"I didn't die," I remind Obadiah later. We are doing something new and drinking the orange liqueur in bed, which like our antics won't be good for the bed linens and so Esther will have another reason to holler at me when we're alone in the house. She doesn't like that I make more work for her and I can't say I blame her. I am naked but for my earbobs and hair bow, which makes Obadiah smile as I knew it would. He is smiling now, running his fingers over my nipple in a lazy way that makes it stand straight up and will make me spill my liqueur for sure. "Are bawdy houses legal?" I ask him.

"Of course. They cater to a natural need."

"Have you ever been to one?"

"I don't need to go now," he says, and his hand drifts away from my nipple to other parts and so much for my liqueur. I know he thinks he's flattering me when he says that, as if I can be sure I am all the woman he will ever need, but when I think about it later I'm not sure I am flattered. Does he mean that if it weren't me it would be a bawdy lady and so there?

I get a shock the next morning when Chantal tells me she's almost finished with my yellow dress. She will want me to put it on in the afternoon so she can hem it to the proper length. "Then you will stop coming here?" I ask.

"You won't miss me." She double knots a length of thread and neatly trims the end, her eyes on her work. "You have Mr. Darby."

I don't think Chantal really believes that, though I don't know her to be someone who speaks untruths. "Truly, I will miss you, Chantal."

Her voice is soft when she speaks again. "I will miss you, too." She raises her eyes to mine. "I just want to make sure you understand things because there might come a day when you don't have Mr. Darby."

Like she doesn't have her lover. I take my usual place across from her and think what to say. I have thought of ways in which I might not have Obadiah. He could find another woman. Or his wife could decide she doesn't really mind that New Orleans is unchristian and want to come here, maybe to reform it. But I say the way Chantal would understand best in her heart. "He could die of the yellow jack."

"And then you would be turned out, as I was. From a beautiful house to furnished rooms."

"Worse than that if you can't pay for furnished rooms." I think for a moment. "I hope the rents aren't too high."

We both smile at that. But Chantal grows somber fast. "Yes, I must pay the rents, every month without fail. And feed myself and Honorine."

That is why Chantal has no time. Because what time she does have, she must spend it earning money.

"What would you do if that happened to you?" she demands of me.

I tell her honestly that I don't know and she sighs and goes back to her needlework. You can count on Chantal not to have idle hands for long.

That afternoon I put on the yellow dress and like it even more than the blue one, which I did not think was possible on God's earth. I spin till I'm dizzy and my giggles get Esther to slamming pots in the kitchen. "I have an idea," I say to Chantal. "We can tell Mr. Darby I need a green dress, too."

"You would be very pretty in green, Eliza." It is the first Chantal has said my name and I couldn't say why but it near makes me tearful. "But you're very pretty in yellow and blue, too."

I know a body shouldn't even think that, but I believe it to be true. Not that it's done me much good. Until now, I suppose, with Obadiah Darby.

"Mr. Darby has never had another young woman here before," Chantal says. "Not that I have seen."

Maybe I won't lose him then. But I can't stop the yellow jack if it comes.

I wish I could slow her down, but Chantal finishes the hemming that very afternoon. "I will come visit you," she says as she gathers her things.

"You won't have time, Chantal." I hear myself and realize I sound like my little sister Visa Ann, pouting when the last sweet is gone. When I think of her, small as can be and with hair the color of wheat, I must stop all talk to keep from crying. I turn away from Chantal. Oh, I do remember the delicious feel of Visa Ann's tiny fingers in my hair when she begged to plait my locks, so dark and different from her own. I would sit on the stoop and she would stand behind me, taut with concentration, her fairy breath light on my neck. Silent she was but for little coos, like a dove.

"Eliza?" It is Chantal, speaking softly to bring me back from where I've gone.

"Maybe in a week you can come back." I spin around and force a bright voice. "Maybe I will tear my skirt and you will have to come back to fix it."

"And maybe between now and then," she whispers, "you will think what you would do if you should ever lose Mr. Darby."

I tell her honestly that I have been thinking about it and earn a smile and a squeeze of the hand.

Esther is only too happy to shut the door behind Chantal. Then she goes to the parlor and pulls all the drapes full closed.

That afternoon I can't sit still—I know it's because of the thoughts I've been having—so I step out to walk. Of course Esther sends Matthew after me and he might as well be an old woman, he is so nervous that I am outside, that he will lose sight of me again, that maybe this time it will be for good, that in the end I give up and go back with him to the house.

That day is full of unease and shocks because that night I get another. Obadiah does not return at the usual hour. When even the time for dining has come and gone and still there is no dinner and no Obadiah, I go to find Esther. She is in the kitchen shucking peas in the lantern light. "If you'll be wanting a meal," she says, not sparing me a glance, "you'll be making it yourself."

It took me some time, but finally I came to realize that Esther must know Obadiah's wife and so is not happy to have me in this house, a young woman who sleeps with the master and causes more work to be done, too. I hate to bother her or ask her anything about anything, but I am so desperate that I do it. I remember to ask after Obadiah in the way Chantal taught me. "Do you know where Mr. Darby is?"

She takes her sweet time answering. Then: "Not mine to know."

"He went by himself in the fancy carriage today."

Esther's fingers may be fat, but they fly as she pushes peas from pods into a bowl. "No need to tell me my husband's been in this house all the day long."

"I'm worried about Mr. Darby," I confess.

"He's his wife's to worry about." Esther gives me a sly smile. "Not yours."

No denying it. I go to bed with an empty stomach and not in the big bed, either, because it doesn't seem right without Obadiah. The next morning he's in the dining room drinking coffee with cream as if it's the same as every other morning and both of us slept the night through like kittens. He's smiling, which relieves me, though it makes me fret that I can be happy only when he is, too. I busy myself pouring coffee.

"You weren't in bed when I came home," he says behind me in a low voice. "I almost came to find you."

This is a game I know how to play. I turn around and keep my voice quiet, too. "I know what would have happened if you did."

Esther didn't bother to cook last night, but she does this morning, bacon and eggs and fresh-made buns, too. After my empty belly gets its share, Obadiah and I go upstairs and he gets his share of me, no matter that it's bright sun outside and Esther is clattering around downstairs and there must be a plantation waiting. When we're lying about after, which never lasts long in the morning because Obadiah is one to get jumpy, I feel bold enough to ask why he got home so late.

"Passed some time at a gambling hall. Playing billiards, mostly."

I don't think his wife would like that, but I don't mind. Of course Esther would remind me it's not mine to mind. "Did you win or lose?"

"I only wager what I can lose." He puffs up. "And often I win."

"You are very smart, Obadiah, so I am not surprised by that." He puffs up a little more. I don't know why I ask it, but I do. "Will you take me with you one time? So I can see you win."

He calls me a minx but laughs when he says it, and after he's washed and dressed he stops to look at me, still on the bed feeling lazy, and letting him see what he likes to see, full sun or not. "It's not a natural thing for you to be in this house all the day long," he says. "But if you're going with me to a gambling hall, you'll need a new dress."

I smile—"please, one in green"—and he kisses me, and my eyes promise him another thank you in the nighttime.

I picked a good time to ask for what I wanted. But I don't understand why Obadiah said yes about going to the gambling hall, because I'm no more his wife now than I was Tuesday. But I will get my green dress, and Chantal again, too.

That takes weeks because Chantal has other customers to keep her busy. I pass some of the days without a care in the world—it's funny how when you're looking forward to a happy thing, you can push your worries to the side—but on others I do think what I would do without Obadiah. When finally Chantal does come, I tell her why I need a new dress. "I don't know why Mr. Darby will take me to a gambling hall and not to the plantations, but he barely put up any fight at all."

Chantal can see I take pride in that, but she purses her lips in that way she has. "That is not a place a man would take his wife."

"Because it's not proper? Still, people will see us there."

"Men will see you there. But they won't talk about it." Chantal busies herself laying out her sewing tools, and since she does it murmuring all the while I get the idea she doesn't care to answer questions about men and gambling halls.

I sit in my usual stuffed chair and watch her buzz about. I think I understand why Obadiah will not take me to the plantations but will take me to a gambling hall. I believe it is because the men who see us will keep Obadiah's secret.

I am Obadiah's secret.

This is not a new idea to me. I see Obadiah writing letters and I am guessing they are to his wife. I don't say a thing about them. He doesn't say a thing, either. But both of us know he doesn't write one word about me.

I am still thinking about all this when Chantal shows me the green fabric she has chosen for my dress, in a color she calls jade. I tell her I thought it would be a brighter shade, though she's not one to choose those, but she says this color is better and look how lovely it is against my skin and once the dress is done it will be my favorite and I will look more beautiful than ever wearing it. We're talking about my dress, but I know that really Chantal is trying to make me feel better because she understands that I am vexed. She understands about being a secret because she was one, too, for her white lover.

"This is a dress for evening." Chantal glances around to make sure there is no Esther in hearing. "You will be very beautiful in this, Eliza." Even lower goes her voice. "Beautiful enough to find a husband."

Chantal doesn't know I found one already, or least thought I did, and in the end that's what set me loose on the Missouri River.

"Mr. Darby is kind to you," she goes on. "But marriage is one thing he cannot give you."

It would be a wonder to get marriage and kindness wrapped up in the same man, and what if he were a fancy man, too? I would not hesitate to take that if it were on offer. And who's to say I could not get such an offer? Where I grew up there were no fancy men except the ones floating past on steamboats. Now here they are standing still and for the first time they can see me in return and they are looking closely, almost to a one of them. That must mean something.

That night in the big bed, Obadiah spent and snoring, I think how Chantal doesn't know about John Haycraft. Obadiah wouldn't know, either, if I hadn't told him. I could keep that entire sorry episode to myself if I had a mind to, just like John kept to himself that he had a wife in Kentucky. If I don't tell people what a fool I was, they would never know it.

As the days pass, I watch Chantal sew my jade dress in a way I didn't watch her make my blue or even my yellow one. Every time I ask a question about how she does this or that, she gives me an answer. And fine as those dresses are, this is finer, with the bertha, the tucks, the pleats, and the special trimming. The jade fabric is so delicate, as Chantal calls it, that she'll let me work only on the underskirt and overskirt, cut of cotton, most of which a body will never see. "I don't know how you keep all these steps in your mind," I tell her.

"I learned from my mother, starting from a child." She's sewing her fast way, laying in two stitches before pulling the thread through. "She was a seamstress, but I was able to learn under a dressmaker, too. Thank God for that, for I tremble to think what else I would do to earn my keep."

"There must be something else." I wonder about this more and more.

"If I were a man, there would be. I could make shoes or cigars or barrels or things out of iron. Or be a carpenter. Some men do lithography, which has to do with prints. I would enjoy that, I think. There are harder things, too, out in the sun, like stone-laying or brick-laying." In, out, her needle goes. "I could be a *domestique*. But that is hard work, worse than needlework, bad for the back, with low wages, and most often you must live with the family you work for, usually at the very top of the house, where it's always the coldest and the hottest, and what would become of Honorine? Do you know your letters?" she asks me suddenly.

"My brother does. But not my sisters or me." There were too many of us and my father didn't have time and my mother said why should he bother anyway because all we would do was marry and have babies. My father taught me my numbers, at least.

"I do not know my letters, either." Chantal jabs at her fabric as if it were the reason. "Some people like me do, but nowadays the men of business don't want that." Often Chantal has complaints about the men of business and I can see her reasons even though I think she is bold to have such ideas. "It is a shame you cannot read because you could be a teacher if you did."

"I have had an idea." Something has come out of all that think-ing. "I know it would be very hard, but maybe I could learn to be a seamstress. Like you."

Her eyes fly open. "You do have skill for it." She lowers her needlework and moves down into a whisper. "And meanwhile you could keep your eyes open for that husband."

I am amazed we are sitting in Obadiah's parlor speaking this way. "That is what I am thinking, too." It excites me to whisper it aloud. It almost gives me the feeling I had as a girl, looking up at the blue sky. "But what about Mr. Darby? He is giving me so much."

"Don't you give him something in return?" Chantal fixes me

with a steady look. She knows exactly what I give in return. "You must think about yourself. He is a good man, but he is thinking about himself."

Yes. But I have still another worry. "I cannot look for a husband while I am under Mr. Darby's roof. That would not be right."

Chantal sews for a time in silence. Then: "I don't know what he means for you to do in this house when he returns to Massachusetts."

"He's returning to Massachusetts?"

Chantal gives me the same look as when I didn't understand why I must call Obadiah Mr. Darby. "He will not spend winter away from his wife and children. Think about Christmas. He will travel back to be with them before the weather turns cold."

"That is a long ways away," I remind her.

"But that day will come."

Maybe this is why life here in New Orleans feels like a dream. It has been very pleasant to be asleep, but now I am waking and fear that too soon all the dreaminess will leave me.

I pick and choose my time to ask Obadiah about Massachusetts. I let a full night and morning go by because he is upset about some matter of business, but the next evening he is smiling again soon as he's taken off his hat. As we eat dinner he tells me about the conversations he had at the plantation. I am always glad when things go the way Obadiah wants but especially tonight because that means I can ask my questions.

We're lying in bed after, my head on his chest, when I tell him I'm worried when he'll go back to Massachusetts.

He sighs. "Ah, Eliza. I knew you would think of that before long."

He is telling me again that I have a head on my shoulders. These days I am trying to use it and be planful. "Are you going soon?"

"Not for months, no. But in the autumn, yes." Chantal was

right as usual. "You're worried what will happen to you. You may stay in this house. I'll come back in the spring."

I'm not a crier like my sister Lucinda—she will cry every time she hears an owl snatch a bird—but that brings tears to my eyes. What would Obadiah get for his kindness over the long winter, with him in Massachusetts and me here? I would have a roof over my head and be fed and, yes, I would have to listen to Esther holler, but that would be a small price to pay. Not a high rent at all. I kiss his chest and a tear runs off my cheek and he must feel it because he kisses my forehead in a tender way he hasn't before. "You told me on the steamboat you would give me a hand up," I say. "And you have."

"Sometimes people do what they say, Eliza."

I have lived long enough to see it. But I don't think it's commonplace.

"I often think," he says, "what luck it was that I met you. If I hadn't paid a visit to my brother in Kansas City and been on that steamboat—"

"I don't even want to think about it."

Obadiah moves on top of me again, though we've just finished, and we are together but different this time, with some sadness in it. It's not just Obadiah sad; it's me, too. Later I stay awake thinking about it.

The next morning I show him the seams Chantal let me sew in the yellow dress. "I'm not doing Chantal's work for her," I tell him, for I do not wish him to be angry with her. "I ask her to show me. She's slower when she shows me and she hates being slower."

He nods but says nothing. Knowing Obadiah, he has an idea what I'm about. We're quiet over our beignets and this morning, too, he kisses my forehead before he leaves.

Chantal is making fast work of my jade dress and that means I will be able to go soon to the gambling hall. But one fine day when the sun is out and the air is not too heavy, needlework is not the only thing on her mind. "I don't want to insult you," she tells me.

It is after midday and she is leading me into the rear garden, to the corner furthest from the privy, where sometimes she goes to eat food she brought from home. I imagine Esther peering from a rear window trying to figure what we are about, out here together.

Chantal spreads white fabric on the grass and pulls from a basket plates, knives, forks, cold meat, bread, cheese, and grapes. "I want to show you something that will help catch you a fine husband." She holds up a knife and a fork. "A knife is not a fork and a fork is not a knife."

"You're not insulting me by telling me that."

I am smiling but Chantal remains stern-faced. "You are beautiful to look at and have a warm way about you, Eliza, but you must not give a man reason to object. If you do, he will simply move his eyes to the next woman."

I nod. I know that.

"The man you want to marry must have proper breeding." If I had known that, I would not have gone before the judge with John Haycraft. "You must show him you have proper breeding, too." Again she raises the knife and fork. "You must never carry food to your mouth with a knife. And you must get used to using the fork with your left hand only."

Here are more Musts from Chantal, but I will listen. I learn that the knife rule is easy, but the fork rule is not. "Mr. Darby does not mind if I send the fork back and forth between my hands," I tell Chantal.

"He is not marrying you, is he?" She gives me that fierce look of hers. "He is not expecting you to raise his children?"

Then follow more rules—use the fork to remove small bones from your mouth; cross your knife and fork on your plate when you are done, tines down; squeeze grape pulp into your mouth then return the skin to the side of the plate—and one more that has nothing to do with eating, which I know already. "When you don't know what to say, say nothing at all."

I nod. "Simply smile."

"With your mouth and your eyes, too."

Yes, I know that one already. Men never object to that.

Chapter Seven

"Certainly New Orleans seldom does things by halves."

— Sam Clemens (Mark Twain)

— Letter to Pamela A. Moffett, March 1859

I T IS ONLY A FEW DAYS LATER THAT CHANTAL FINISHES THE JADE-COLORED DRESS. The night before, I warned Obadiah that she was close to done and he laughed and asked if I always got what I wanted and I teased him by saying, well, yes, Mr. Darby, I do.

I did a lot of spinning in the dress when Chantal helped me put it on for the hemming. She sat back on her heels and watched. "I'm not sure you'll stay long at the gambling hall," she told me, and I knew what she was really saying.

She helped me dress and arrange my hair for that night and made me swear to remember everything because she would return the next day to hear the whole story even though Mr. Darby would have no work for her. Once dressed, I realized that being indoors all the day long was good for something. Usually this time of year I am brown as a nut, but now the skin beneath the jade-colored fabric is pale as the cream Obadiah and I pour into our coffee.

"All eyes will be on you, Eliza," Obadiah says when he sees me. He's smiling, but there's sadness again, too. Maybe he is thinking how someday he will return to Massachusetts, away from me. Tonight I don't want to think about that, though.

It is near midnight when Obadiah's carriage, the fancier one I have never ridden in before, rolls to a stop outside the gambling hall. I have the same feeling as when I first saw the port here in New Orleans, and Canal Street, and the market. It is such a madness of noise and light that I can scarce think straight for the wonder of it. The grand building I am walking into has more windows than I can count, on each and every floor, and light pours from all of them as if the sun itself were lighting the place from inside. And God will be kept awake like it or not because the noise bursting through the flung-open doors must reach all the way to heaven. Gamblers are winning and gamblers are losing and you hear both their cries and their groans; the men who run the place never stop shouting at the gamblers to do this or do that; one man spins a giant wheel that sends a white ball jumping from red slot to black slot to red again until the ball decides it has had enough and picks a place to settle and then another roar begins its way heavenward.

Obadiah has me take his arm and pulls me further inside. Among all the gambling tables I see richness I've never seen before: if I may say so, it almost makes the steamboat saloon look like a tavern. There are paintings tall as me, many of naked people not bothering to hide it; sofas and such-like with so many cushions and pillows I don't know how a body could find room to sit; silk fabrics hanging on the walls; and more figures of people in the form of statues, but not dressed high and mighty like they are on the city squares; no, these are naked, too, and most of them women.

Then there are the gamblers, all men, but women are watching, and now I understand why Obadiah said I needed a new dress for the occasion. I can hold my head high in my jade-colored dress, but that is not to say it couldn't do with more trimming. Chantal insists it's the woman who wear the dress and not vice versa—that's how she explains her light hand—but the dresses around me make mine look almost simple. The other colors, too, they're very bright compared to my jade. And, probably I shouldn't be surprised in a gambling hall, which isn't really proper, but many women's faces are powdered and painted like the bawdy ladies, though these women are much younger.

Still…

"You are the most beautiful woman here," Obadiah tells me.

It is happening again, even as he says that: men turn to look at me and not just to look but to stare. Women look at me, too, and I at them, but it's each other's dresses we examine, and jewels. The other women can find none of those on me, but I don't feel the lack of them, not with this dress and with my hair half piled high and half left loose the way Chantal arranged it.

My heart beats a jig as Obadiah leads me to what he calls the roulette table. We take two places and I am served something pretty in a beautiful glass, not that I will touch it. I will drink not a drop tonight; I don't think I will speak a word. The other men nod at Obadiah and stare at me with bold eyes.

What am I doing in a place like this, only two months' gone from when I threw myself in John's canoe? I can scarce believe I am the same woman. John Haycraft, my father, my mother, Sarah: would they even recognize me? To think they are living and breathing on the river as if nothing has changed, while I am sitting in this place and everything is new for me.

Obadiah has chips now, in piles like the others, and the gamblers begin calling out their bets using words Chantal told me I would hear, like *rouge* and *noir*, and the chips are moved onto a green mat covered with numbers. The *croupier*—she taught me that, too—makes a show of spinning the wheel. Obadiah has placed only a small bet to start and the ball does not land on a spot where he will win. It does for a younger man sitting across the wheel, dressed very fine, with dark hair, surrounded by women laughing and patting his arm. I will say he is handsome, especially when he collects his chips and gives me a wink.

Obadiah looses a snort that only I can hear; I don't know if it is because of the win or the wink. As minutes pass Obadiah places more bets, bigger now, and sometimes wins, though his pile of chips does not go so much higher. It is the same for the handsome man across the wheel. Finally Obadiah turns to me. "How about I put some on twenty-four?"

That is the number of my years; I finally confessed it. Obadiah did not think it was so very many and now he is saying that number will bring him luck. I nod and smile and feel the younger man's eyes upon me.

Obadiah places chips on this bet and the wheel is sent spinning and this time the ball does land where Obadiah wants it to. I cry out despite myself and so does Obadiah, laughing, and so does everyone who saw him look to me before placing his bet. "Now you have seen me win," Obadiah says to me as a large pile of chips is pushed his way, "and I say it's thanks to you." The younger man raises his glass in our direction and calls out something to Obadiah that I think is in French. Obadiah tips his glass in return.

It is as Obadiah said it would be: he decides he is done and leaves the table with more silver than when he started. He and the young man nod at each other and I feel the young man's eyes burn into my back as Obadiah and I walk across the hall to rest on a sofa. "New Orleans royalty is out tonight," Obadiah tells me.

"What do you mean?"

"That was Charles Pierre Chouteau across the roulette wheel."

That name means not a thing to me. "Who is he?"

"He is from one of the richest families in Missouri, though

they started here in New Orleans. They make their money from fur, mostly. The family helped found St. Louis."

I don't really understand how to "found" St. Louis. But I do understand "one of the richest families." I also understand that the Chouteau who seems to have about as many years as me could be staring at any woman here, but he is staring at me across the whole of the gambling hall.

Obadiah speaks again. "They are the kind who think the most of themselves. They even named the street in St. Louis on which they built their mansion the *Rue Royale*. Creoles," Obadiah adds in a way that makes me remember his snort at the roulette table.

"You don't like them?" I say. "Aren't there many in New Orleans?"

"Too many. They don't like us, either, us Americans."

"Aren't they Americans, too?"

"They're French"—Obadiah drains his whiskey—"so they are indolent. Lazy," he says when he sees I don't understand.

I've learned another new word, though I don't see how the Chouteaus could make so much money in fur, or help found St. Louis, if they're *indolent*. "What do they think of us?"

"That we don't belong here. That Louisiana is theirs and not ours."

I don't remind Obadiah that New Orleans is called Little Paris.

This is one way I am very ignorant: about who people are. This was important even where I come from. Who were the families who owned land, and how much? Who were the families who owned slaves, and how many? Which families didn't like each other, and why not? I know none of those things about these New Orleans people.

"I'll be damned," Obadiah says, "Chouteau is walking over here," and I see him make his way in our direction. Not alone: the women who were with him before walk behind him now.

My heart picks up its jig. I can tell Obadiah is surprised, and other people, too, as all around the gambling hall eyes watch Chouteau move toward us. Obadiah stands and so do I. Even if it were to stop myself from being thrown into hell, I don't think I could speak a word.

"*Bonsoir*, Darby." Chouteau turns his eyes to me. He is taller than me and much taller than Obadiah. I have never seen clothes so fine.

"Good evening, Chouteau. Allow me to introduce Miss Eliza" —Obadiah stops; then—"Haycraft."

Chouteau takes my hand and lifts it to his lips. He is very bold as he does it, staring in my eyes all the while. It is almost as if Obadiah isn't standing right there.

Obadiah speaks up. "Did I hear you've been in London lately?"

My hand is let go. Chouteau turns to look at Obadiah but keeps glancing back at me. There is business talk I try to follow but don't catch the whole of. I think it's the same with the other women, who eye me closely as I eye them. None of them could be Chouteau's wife; I know that from what Chantal explained.

After a while Chouteau again turns his eyes to me. "It is my very great pleasure to be back from London for a time. My very great pleasure." He bows to me then to Obadiah and then walks away. The women follow. I think it is their very great pleasure to turn their backs on me.

Again Obadiah holds out his arm for me to take and turns us toward the doors still flung open to the night air. He leans close and chuckles. "It didn't take you long to make quite a conquest, Eliza."

Even though I never heard that word before, I understand what Obadiah is saying. It is the first thing I will tell Chantal.

We walk back out into the night. We're leaving the gambling hall early, as Chantal said we would, but I don't mind as my head is so full already. "Why did you tell Chouteau that I'm called Eliza Haycraft and not Eliza Harper?"

"Because Haycraft is an unusual name." He hands me up into the carriage. "It is rare, like you. You remember what I told you the day I bought your canoe? That you're good at making friends."

I do remember. I had helped with the steamboat wooding for the first time. And Obadiah had come to watch, I believe so he could talk to me again. "You said that could get me far in life. That day I wanted only to go as far as Hermann."

"And look where you are now."

We are inside the carriage now and I lay my hand upon his arm. "I am here because of you, Obadiah."

If it were my mother, she would rub my face in that. But that is not Obadiah's way. "You did well tonight, Eliza. I saw something in you when you floated up to the steamboat in that canoe and I was right. Something I couldn't put a name to." He chuckles. "You have that rare quality that has no name."

I don't know what to think of that, but Obadiah is happy and proud and so I feel the same. When we are back at his house and upstairs, it's the orange liqueur for us, and much time spent undressing me, with stops in between when I am wearing only some of my garments. I've learned a few things about what a man and a woman might do since I've known Obadiah Darby.

As I lie on his soft bed after, it makes me feel very far above John Haycraft. I imagine him now on our pallet of straw. I know what he would call me for doing the things I do with Obadiah, as if we were man and wife. Well, didn't he do those things with me even though he wasn't my husband and knew it all the while?

If I know John Haycraft, he's thinking I'll go back to him; I'll get frightened and run out of that fierce feeling that got me into his canoe; I'll crawl back to him like a she-dog to its master, no matter I've been whipped.

That is very far from the way I am thinking.

The next morning Esther fries eggs and Obadiah notices the new way I hold my knife and fork. I must eat slowly because otherwise the egg slips off and drops back onto the plate, but Chantal tells me men like to see women pick at their food like birds. She must be right because Obadiah smiles as he watches me.

Chantal knows the word *conquest*—it is almost the same in French: *conquête*—but she does not know much about the Chouteau family. I was sure the most exciting thing of the day would be telling her the details of the evening, but it turns out I am wrong. Very wrong.

In the late afternoon we are in the parlor and hear a carriage clatter to a stop on the street. Esther draws back the drapery to peep out the window. It takes her a long time to turn around and when she does she is frowning. "Gentleman in a barouche carriage is out there."

Chantal lowers the needlework she brought with her. "A barouche?"

I don't know what that is. I peep out, too, and see Chouteau standing beside a very grand carriage like the bawdy ladies have. "It's Chouteau." I drop the drapery as if it's on fire and step backward. "It's him."

Chantal's eyes grow wide as plums. "The same as last night?"

"It's Chouteau." What are his given names? I need think only a moment. Charles and Pierre. Like the bawdy ladies, his carriage also has two shiny horses and a Negro driver dressed in a coat with many gold buttons. "Maybe he has business with Mr. Darby," I say. "They spoke of business."

"Mr. Darby isn't here." Chantal rises.

"Driver's stepping up to all the houses." Esther is peeping out again. "He'll be stepping up here soon." She walks toward the front door.

"I will talk to him," I say. If I can: I couldn't manage even one word last night. I'm glad I'm wearing my yellow dress, for even though it has less trim it's prettier on a sunny day.

"No," Chantal says, "it should be Mr. Darby talking to him."

"Mr. Darby isn't here." I have an idea I can't really believe. *Maybe it's not Mr. Darby Chouteau has come to talk to.*

"Driver's stepping up," Esther says.

I'm standing behind Esther, and Chantal behind me, when Esther pulls open the front door. The driver gives me a little bow and one to Chantal, too. On the street Chouteau sees me and makes a big bow. "He has come all this way," I tell Chantal, "we must talk to him," and without turning around—she'll try to stop me if I do—I move past Esther to step down onto the stoop. I walk past his driver toward Chouteau. Chantal follows. I hear my heartbeat pounding in my ears.

Chouteau's eyes never leave me. It is the same as at the gambling hall. I stop a short way away and must lick my lips before I can speak. I say the only thing I can think of. "Hello."

"*Bonjour,* Mademoiselle Haycraft." Another smile. Another bow. He raises his eyebrows at Chantal. Behind me she says something in French that ends with her name. "Chantal Rossignol," Chouteau repeats, "*bonjour.*" Then he turns his eyes back to me. "I hope the day finds you in good health."

"I am healthy." Chouteau's eyes twinkle as if he might laugh. "Thank you." I struggle to think what else to say.

"That is a beautiful dress you are wearing," he says.

"Thank you." I don't know if this is the right thing to say, but it is all I have. "Chantal, Miss Rossignol, made it for me."

"Ah." Again he glances at her behind me. "You are a very talented dressmaker, I see." But his dark eyes cannot stay off me for long. They return to fasten on mine.

I manage another sentence. "Mr. Darby is not at home."

"That is a shame," Chouteau says, but he does not sound disappointed. "I was hoping to speak with him further about the Blackfeet. My father's business has dealings with them, but the arrangements are not always satisfactory."

I don't remember hearing those words last night, but there was much I didn't catch.

Chouteau speaks again. "I do not believe I had the pleasure of seeing you before last night here in New Orleans, Mademoiselle Haycraft."

"I am from Missouri."

"Ah!" Chouteau sounds very enthusiastic and says many things about Missouri and St. Louis. He talks so much I don't have to say a thing. I smile with my mouth and my eyes both, but mostly I get distracted wondering why he is here and why he is talking to me for so long. And I watch his eyes roam my face and my hair and my throat and my bosom and my waist. Once he even steps back and looks down as if he wishes to see my shoes beneath my skirts.

Suddenly all talk of Missouri stops. *"Je suis désolé,"* Chouteau says, "but I must return to town." He steps forward, takes my hand, and moves it to his lips. Like last night, he stares into my eyes as he kisses my fingers. But this time the kiss is bolder: it lasts longer and leaves my hand moist and even after all that he does not let my hand go. "I very much hope to see you again, Mademoiselle Haycraft," he says and finally my hand is again my own.

He nods at Chantal behind me and then is gone into his carriage. If it were not for Chantal I might have stood watching it roll away down the street, but she hisses at me to follow her inside.

When we are again in the parlor, Esther frowns at me and sets her hands on her hips. "What that gentleman want?"

"You heard every word we did," Chantal snaps. She is agitated, like I am.

Esther stomps off.

"He wanted to talk to Mr. Darby about black feet," I say.

"The Blackfeet," Chantal corrects me. "Indians."

"That is why he came here," I say.

"He came here because he wants to take you as his mistress." Chantal turns to stare at me full in the face. "He wants to take you from Mr. Darby."

"Can he do that?"

"He is a very rich man. He can do anything."

He is from one of the richest families in Missouri. I drop onto a stuffed chair. *It didn't take you long to make quite a conquest, Eliza.*

"This is the problem with going to gambling halls," Chantal goes on.

I am not so sure. *You have that rare quality that has no name.* I keep my voice low as Esther is near. "Chantal, if that is true, is it really a problem?"

She looks at me, still breathing fast, and cannot answer.

I must wonder if this is my chance, better than I could have imagined. I do think there is something special about me, though it shows conceit to think so. My mother mocked me for it, but my father would say there was something, and John Haycraft said so in his way, and so did Obadiah. Maybe now Chouteau is saying the same thing.

I'm surprised that evening that Esther leaves it to me to tell Obadiah the story. I must because if I don't she soon will.

"Chouteau came to this house?" Obadiah says.

I explained that already, but he doesn't seem to believe it. "He said he wanted to talk to you more about the Blackfeet, like last night."

"What do I know about the Blackfeet?" Obadiah pours himself whiskey—"he knows we didn't speak a word about the damn Blackfeet"—then he throws it down his throat. "What else did he say?"

I try to remember. "Things about Missouri, St. Louis... " I'm able to repeat some of it, but most of it I cannot bring to mind.

Obadiah rubs his forehead. "It is very odd that Chouteau would come to this house."

"Why? You are both"—I remember Chantal's words—"men of business."

"Chouteau and I are not the same. He is from one of the richest families in Missouri."

I know what Obadiah is saying: he is not rich like Chouteau. Chouteau is from a family that has been rich for many years. I'm sure he has never been belowdecks. It frightens me to say what is in my mind, but I am not one to stop for that reason. "Chantal says Chouteau wants to take me for his mistress."

"No." Obadiah shakes his head with vigor. "He came here to see you in the bright light of day. That is all he came to do."

I watch Obadiah turn away and am a little insulted by this. It is as if Obadiah is saying that now Chouteau has seen me in the sunshine, he'll be done with me. No, I was not able to say much, but I'm not sure that counts against a woman. I also know what Obadiah does not: that Chouteau kissed my hand in his bold way and told me he hoped to see me again. He hoped so *very much*.

Near two weeks later, when I'm alone in the house but for Esther and nothing more has happened to liven up our days, I am in low spirits to think Chouteau is done with me after all. For once Chantal was wrong. But that evening I get a surprise: Chantal comes to the house late, at a very strange hour, when Obadiah is already home. She stands in the parlor looking stiff and straight. Without needlework in her hands, she doesn't seem to know what to do with them. "Monsieur Chouteau summoned me to speak with him," she tells Obadiah and me, "and trusted me to make a proposition to you."

I cannot believe I am hearing it, but this is what Chantal says: Chouteau wants me to go to St. Louis, where he is traveling himself, where he will put me in a little house of my own and where I can learn to be a seamstress with the help of the dress-makers who work for the Chouteau family.

"He said you would learn from the very best," Chantal goes on. "You would be again in your home state, which would naturally be more comfortable for you. And of course he would pay your steamboat passage."

"I'll be damned," Obadiah says, and then he says it again.

I am so shocked I have trouble speaking. Finally I can move my lips to ask a question. "Do you believe Chouteau meant all of that, Chantal?"

It is Obadiah who answers. "I don't know Chouteau to be a liar, but if you're rich as he is, few would say it if he were. I'll tell you something else." Obadiah looks at me. "Chouteau does want you for his mistress."

Only a second passes before Chantal nods.

I am breathless. I am hearing things I didn't really think I'd hear. Obadiah is still looking at me as I say out loud what I've been wondering for days. "Does Chouteau have a wife?"

Obadiah frowns. "What does that matter?"

"Because if he does not have a wife, maybe he does not want me only for a mistress."

Obadiah doesn't know what to say to that. He doesn't seem angry with me, but I cannot be sure. And if he is, what have I done to deserve it? I have not been improper with Chouteau.

"That is something you cannot give me, Obadiah." I am repeating what Chantal told me. "You are a good man and you have been very good to me, but you cannot marry me. Do you know: does Chouteau have a wife?"

"Chouteau does not have a wife," Obadiah says. "But you must not think he will take you for his wife, Eliza. No."

"Why not? You told me yourself I have that quality that has no name."

"Because," Obadiah says, "the Chouteaus do not marry"—he cannot seem to find the right word—"anyone who is not a rich Creole like them," he finally says. "They stick to their own kind. Chouteau will marry a Gratiot or a Berthold or a Cabanne or a Pratte."

Not a Harper, Obadiah is telling me. But I am not sure I believe him.

"Eliza," Chantal says, "I do not want to insult you, but you must listen to Mr. Darby. I pressed Monsieur Chouteau very strongly about how you must learn to be a seamstress. I believe that will be a real chance for you, as it has been for me."

"Yes, yes, I will learn to be a seamstress."

"You must not expect to marry Monsieur Chouteau." Chantal is wearing her stern face that I know so well. "You must believe Mr. Darby in this."

I listen and I nod, but even as I do, I know that if I go to live in this little house Chouteau makes for me in St. Louis, most of what

I will be doing will not involve an *aiguille* in my hand. And what is to stop Chouteau from falling in love with me? With all that he is proposing to give me, isn't he saying he's half in love with me already? I am ignorant about many things but not about men. I learned many lessons from marrying John Haycraft, or leastwise thinking I did, and from this time with Obadiah Darby. And one of the things I learned is that fancy men and not-fancy men are not so different after all. In some ways they are just the same.

"I see you think this is your decision to make," Obadiah tells me.

Now he is angry, and who can blame him? This is an insult to Obadiah that Chouteau is proposing to take me away from him. "Is it not—" I begin to say before he interrupts.

"I will not keep you a prisoner if you desire to go," and from the parlor he stomps.

I do not look at Chantal for I know already what her face will tell me and I do not care to see it. Instead I drop my gaze to the tasseled shoes Obadiah bought me, which stand upon his fat Turkey carpet.

I have been trying to be planful. I am trying to think before I jump. Leaving Obadiah would be like flinging myself into John's canoe, only this time I do not leave mostly bad things behind. I leave mostly good: comfort, safety, the dearest of friends. Oh, it is a great deal. I know Obadiah to be a good man. And I would be leaving Chantal, too. I would miss both of them very, very much.

Still.

Obadiah is practical. He would be the first to say I should be, too. And do I really think I would stay in New Orleans forever? I, too, think it is foreign. That might be one way I am like Obadiah's wife.

Of course Chouteau seems foreign. He is a Creole, a Frenchman. For that reason alone Obadiah does not like him. But I do not get a warning feeling about Chouteau as I did about John Haycraft. Though I do not like to admit it, I was a fool, like my mother said, and pushed that feeling to the side. I have suffered for that.

But now with Chouteau, I have no bad feelings to push aside. And he is a young man, much my age, handsome, very rich, with no wife yet, who cannot stop himself from crossing town to come stare at me.

I know it may be, it *may* be, that Obadiah and Chantal are right. Perhaps Chouteau will not marry me. But he wishes me to be his mistress: no one doubts it. I would be mistress of a man from one of the richest families in Missouri. Obadiah cannot give me that. Is it not better to be Chouteau's mistress than Obadiah's? And I might be able to convince Chouteau to marry me. There is a chance of it.

I do not look at Chantal when I raise my head. I spin about for I must find Obadiah. I am ready to say to him almost exactly what he himself said to me when he bought my canoe. *What woman could say no to such an offer?*

Chapter Eight

"She remained a few months in the Crescent City, and then returned to St. Louis... "

— "Will of Madam Haycraft"

— *Daily Democrat*, December 9, 1871

FOR DAYS I HAVE BEEN ON A STEAMBOAT AGAIN, but riding north this time, and not belowdecks, either. I have a stateroom to myself and a trunk inside it, which I keep locked, filled with my clothes. As when I floated up to the steamboat in John's canoe, I am a woman traveling alone, which makes me near as mysterious as the Frenchman who people say is very rich and a famous duelist. Like me, the Frenchman keeps to himself. Not like me, he leaves the boat to hunt and always instructs the pilot not to wait for him if he does not return. *It does not matter if I return*, he says, or so I'm told because he says it in French.

I am not as mysterious as he is. But I am close. And I might think about him more if my mind was not already full with thoughts of another Frenchman, also very rich but much younger and more handsome, waiting for me in St. Louis.

Now, as every day, I sit in the ladies' cabin, where men—I should call them gentlemen—may sit, too, if a lady invites them. I wear my blue or yellow dress, trading off one for the other, and pretend to enjoy the view. I do enjoy it, but really what I do is watch the ladies. I'm trying to learn from them: how they sit, how they eat, how they talk. Mostly how they talk, because I want to be able to talk to Chouteau—Charles Pierre.

I listen to the men, too, and find them more interesting. They have the advantage of more to talk about as they see more of the world. Once on a quiet stretch of river, some of us were invited to the pilot-house way up top of the steamboat. It has windows on all sides and things called speaking tubes and bell ropes that make the engines do what the pilot wants: go forward or back or stop. The pilot told tales meant to scare the ladies: *View the many dents on these walls. They're from bullets fired at us in gun battles from shore!* The ladies cried out but all I did was smile, as I didn't half believe him. Then one man all the way from the state of New York got to talking about something called the Advent. Jesus would come to earth, he said, precisely on October 22nd, and all of us sinners had better be ready. I wasn't too worried, though, when I heard Jesus was supposed to come one day in March and one in April, too, and we haven't seen Him yet.

I say little and believe more than ever that my silence takes me a long way: no one can tell how ignorant I am. Once I made the mistake of telling a lady I was journeying to St. Louis to marry. She had a thousand questions. I finally said I could not speak of it because even thinking of my fiancé made me cry with longing. I brought a tear to my eye and ran from the cabin. No one has spoken of it since.

I may still be ignorant, but not as much as I used to be.

Of course I know who I must thank for that: Obadiah and Chantal. Every night in my stateroom, while the fiddler plays in the saloon and the fancy people dance, I lie in bed and cry for both of them. I tell myself that after I marry Chouteau I will be so rich that I will travel to New Orleans like other pleasure seekers and visit them both. I tell myself that I have not said goodbye —*adieu*—to them forever.

Obadiah believes I said exactly that. He told me so as we lay in his big, soft bed the night before I boarded this steamboat. *You are sure you want to go?* he asked me, and I told him I did, though it hurt me to say so. I could feel in the dark night all around us that he wished to say something more, but he remained silent, a rare thing for him, and so did I.

With all this time on my hands I think of my family, too, and wonder will I ever see them again. I like not to think about it, but on this steamboat I have heard news that makes me doubt it. There has been a great flood since I left Cote Sans Dessein, rain that fell for weeks and made the river rise higher than anyone had ever seen it. Many people moved to higher ground.

Did my family? Will I ever know? And what of our cabin? Surely it flooded. Have they lost what little they had? Did any of them drown? It gave me comfort to imagine them in the cabin, ramshackle though it was, but now I can do that no longer. The news of this great flood makes me think John Haycraft is gone for good—good riddance, I say—but my tears flow hard when I think I might never see my father again, or Asa or Visa Ann or Nancy or Lucinda or Minerva.

I have seen kindness in my life. I don't know if anyone other than my father has shown me more than Obadiah Darby. Even as I was preparing to leave him, he gave me the trunk, the clothes inside it, and money. *You may be needing it,* he told me, which insulted me at first, because why would I need it after Chouteau puts me in a little house of my own? But then I remembered I am being planful and imagined what trouble I could get into with no coins in my reticule.

I am told tomorrow we dock in St. Louis, after a journey of not even six days. It is time again to look forward and not behind. I am ready. I am even settled on my name, an easy choice because it is how Chouteau knows me.

I am Eliza Haycraft.

———

IF I WERE STILL the greenhorn who had never seen New Orleans, I would think St. Louis a great metropolis. But now, under a sky gray with sulking clouds and smoke belching from boats and factories, I step off the steamboat and think only how much smaller and shabbier this city looks. I would say it's not nearly so rich as New Orleans and no one would think to call it Little Paris.

Still. The family of Chouteau helped to found it so I must look at it with bright eyes. Here is one thing: Obadiah told me it was an ancient Chouteau who thought to lay the streets in a grid starting at the riverbank, which must be a fine scheme. I see on the river all kinds of boats, and on the cobble-paved levee deckhands and roustabouts and all manner of laborers bustle about. Men of business stride here and there, men like Obadiah. I will not try to count the drays and pushcarts and mule wagons being loaded or unloaded, nor the bales of hemp and stacks of wood that just came in or will soon go out, covered with tarps and sights to warm Obadiah's heart.

I climb the steep levee. Before me, rising between the river and the city proper, are warehouses built of brick. There are merchant houses, too, as I remember what Obadiah told me. Across the way is the Market Building, also used for City Hall, and next to it the Old Rock House, so-called because it's made of limestone. It's a warehouse for a fur trader, Obadiah said, though I don't believe he spoke the name Chouteau. Not far off the spire of the Cathedral pokes into the dingy sky, perhaps to remind God where it is. I recall that the church was styled in the Renaissance way, whatever that means, and that the chimes for its bells were brought from France.

"Mademoiselle Haycraft?"

This must be Chouteau's driver—a young Negro like the one in New Orleans, this man, too, in a gold-buttoned jacket—come to fetch me, in a carriage not as fancy as the barouche but very fine all the same and with two prancing horses. The porters from the steamboat, who trailed me up the levee, load on my trunk. The driver and I roll off with a slap of the reins. Soon, though I can scarce believe it, I will once again see Chouteau.

A few blocks more on Front Street and then we leave the hurly-burly of the riverfront behind. I wonder where is the ancestral Chouteau mansion Obadiah described, built more than seventy years past? He said the structure is made of stone and boasts a broad porch held up by pillars. With its gardens an entire city block is consumed, protected by a stone wall two feet thick and ten feet high. That would keep out the Indians, and the Yankees, too, Obadiah said, I believe trying to make a point I did not care to hear.

Up Poplar Street we are now, the driver tells me in his Frenchy way, but this is not the view, or the fresh air, I hope for. Everywhere on the dusty street are mounds of manure the driver does not bother to avoid. Mules, dogs, and pigs scatter in front of us. Here is one factory after the next. Ina was right that there is one on every block. Obadiah rattled off what they make in that excited way of his: tin and copper and castings, white lead and red lead, cabinets and chairs, blacksmiths and housesmiths, linseed oil and castor oil. And that is just the start of it.

Near the factories are buildings I must call shanties. The people look hard done by. White they are, mostly. Seeing them takes me back to the first steamboat, and belowdecks. Many are from Ireland, I wager, like Ina, or Dutch who decided for St. Louis over Hermann. A little further we turn onto a still narrower street and here and there I see a vacant lot with the last of the wild white chamomile poking from the dirt.

I guess you can trust horses to know where they're going because these two get it into their heads to turn up an even skinnier lane beside a house of two stories set back from the street. Now the light is starting to fade, all I can see is that it's built of brick with plenty of windows. The horses pull up to a rear coach house, near hidden from the street thanks to a hedge rising high. A body could come and go and no one on the street would be the wiser.

I'm taken in a side door of the house—which doesn't seem right, to be honest—to meet a young Negro woman, thin and with her hair wrapped in a bright fabric, like the *marchandes* in New Orleans. The driver tells me to call her Marie-Christine. She smiles in a way Esther never would and seems happy to show me the parlor and dining room and bedchamber upstairs, cozy in the gaslight. Maybe I am full of conceit now because it is much better than I am used to most of my life, but I'm not sure it's nicer than Obadiah has and I was expecting nicer from Chouteau. When Marie-Christine runs downstairs, I test how soft the mattress is. Soon she returns with a small beer. I realize I am thirsty and give it a sip. "Mr. Chouteau?" I ask her.

She smiles and nods. "Monsieur Chouteau." She speaks in a Frenchy way like the driver.

"He will come tonight?" I point at the floor. "Here?"

She blinks a few times. I think she understands me. But all she says again is *Monsieur Chouteau*. Then she motions behind her as if she must leave and off she runs downstairs again. I hear her laugh with the driver and get the idea the two of them will try to carry my trunk from the carriage into the house.

I hear them step outside. Silence falls. I sip my small beer. The same thoughts I had when I first came to Obadiah's house fill my mind. Have there been other females in this chamber before me?

Where are they now? Marie-Christine is kinder than Esther, but I almost wish for one of Esther's harrumphs. Marie-Christine does not seem displeased to see me, like Esther was, and not surprised, either, as if she is used to having a strange woman in this house.

This bedchamber has a bench built beneath the three front windows, which poke out over a grassy yard, where a body can sit on a cushion and look outside. That is nicer than Obadiah has. I go with my small beer to sit there. It is darkening outside. This street doesn't have near as many houses as Obadiah's; only a few lights wink at me. One raindrop hits the window, then another. The clouds must be tired of holding in the rain. Maybe, like tears, they must just let them go.

I expected Chouteau to be here when I came, but I was wrong to hope for that. He is a rich man of business. I am sure he will come tonight, or at the very latest tomorrow. He will know my steamboat has arrived. And he said he hoped to see me again *very much*.

I sip my small beer and watch the raindrops chase each other down the glass like children after a dog.

THREE DAYS LATER, the sun is leaving the sky and I have yet to set my eyes on Chouteau. I could not have missed him for I never leave the house for fear of missing him. The days are long when you spend them waiting to hear a carriage roll up the lane. Yet every morning my hope is strong. I take much care with how I bathe and arrange my hair and brush my dress so that it is without blemish.

Where is Chouteau? I know he is a man of business and very busy, but I wish he were still acting like a man already half in love.

As for Marie-Christine, she cooks, she cleans, she washes, she mends, and she doesn't spare her smiles; but she hardly speaks. I think she is pretending to be more Frenchy than she is so she doesn't have to. But even if she were that Frenchy, any woman could read the question in my eyes.

As a last thing, there is no seamstress come to teach me.

All of this agitates me, and with so much time and no way to spend it, warning thoughts have started. I remind myself it was a mistake to push those aside when I had them about John Haycraft.

I am pacing the upstairs landing when a carriage rolls up the lane to the coach house. I stop to listen. Whoever it is enters the house through the side door. I am severely disappointed when I hear voices: this is not Chouteau come at last; Marie-Christine speaks to this man too easily. I realize as he and Marie-Christine babble in their quick French that this is the carriage driver who brought me here.

Marie-Christine appears in the foyer below. She runs up the stairs toward me—"*Vite!*" —tugs me into my bedchamber and jerks open the wardrobe to pull out my jade dress. After a quick inspection she says, "Monsieur Chouteau. Planters House."

Finally I am hearing his name. "Planters House? What is that?"

Already Marie-Christine is trying to get me out of my blue dress. "A very beautiful hotel. You go there."

My breath comes faster. What are Chouteau and I to do at this hotel? I need not imagine long to understand.

Perhaps we will dine there, given the hour. I remember what Chantal said about the fine hotels in New Orleans: they lay a buffet table from eight to eleven. If that is so, I will dine in such a place for the first time in my life, in plain view of everyone and especially Chouteau. I hope there are few bones in the meat as I would not like him staring as I try to take them from my mouth with a fork. When I am dressed Marie-Christine steps back and nods at me with satisfaction. I see in the looking glass my flushed skin and bright eyes.

Soon I am in the carriage and the driver and I are leaving the quiet behind. We come to a wide street still a ways uphill from the river—Fourth Street, the driver tells me—and roll to a stop before a very large building. It is made of stone and brick, at least four stories tall, with ornament around the many windows and even a tower of three tiers rising from the center. So St. Louis can boast of something truly grand. "This is wide as the whole block," I tell the driver.

He nods and grins. "Most beautiful place."

So it is. Shops line the lowest floor and a flag flutters from a pole mounted on the highest tower. As at the gambling hall in New Orleans, music and laughter and conversation spill into the night air and light pours from near every window. It is as if heavenly rejoicing goes on in every room.

The driver hands me down from the carriage. Then he steps back and gestures to the hotel. He is telling me I am to enter this place alone.

I turn to face it. I like to tell myself that I am not stopped by fear, but that is easy to say when I am not afraid. I force myself to raise my chin and gaze about me with a confident air I do not feel. I climb the wide marble steps to enter a salon richly furnished with carpets and lounging chairs and paintings and what I now know to call chandeliers. It is noisy with people, men mostly, the fancy type I begin to know. Most have drinks in their hands and cigar smoke hangs thick in the air. I look for Chouteau but do not let my eyes dart about: I don't want to look like a fox on the hunt.

Ahead of me I think I spy the back of him, in a small group by the far wall. I stop so as to be sure, my heart jumping. I believe I recognize the height of him, and the very fine clothes, and the tilt of his dark head. Somehow I draw the attention of the men he is with, all about his age. They turn toward me before he does; their bold stares make him look, too. It is Chouteau and he sees me and smiles; one man says something to him—under his breath, I can tell—but it is loud enough for all four to hear and funny enough for all four to laugh.

I get the idea it is not just Chouteau awaiting me. These men have been, too. It is as if Chouteau wants them to get a look at me.

I have an uneasy feeling. Even where I grew up I sometimes had to walk toward men when I knew they were talking about me and not in the most proper way, either. I wish Chouteau would leave them and walk to me, as if he is on my side and not theirs, but he does not do that so I am forced to walk to him and all I can do is raise my chin one notch higher.

Chouteau makes a show of kissing my hand. The others lay their eyes on every part of me. Chouteau straightens and gestures toward me. "Allow me to present the *très belle* Mademoiselle Eliza Haycraft."

I smile best I can. "How was your steamboat travel from New Orleans?" one asks, but before I can speak another bursts forth with the tale of a steamboat named *Pilot* whose starboard boiler exploded near a woodyard this March past. It sent both the captain and woodyard owner fifty feet in the air. Both were frightfully mangled on landing but survived and all agreed this was a miraculous conclusion to a steamboat calamity.

Chouteau holds out his arm—"Shall we go inside?"—but does not wait an answer before pulling me deeper into the hotel. As we leave them, his friends behind us say things I cannot catch, but from the tone I am not sure I want to.

It is an enormous dining room with a ceiling high as heaven that Chouteau leads me into, crowded with tables filled mostly with men. Many eyes follow us as we pass. Chouteau soon stops at a table along the wall that can be hidden from view by curtains. He sweeps his arm for me to sit and I do, though it is some trouble to arrange my skirts on the cushioned bench that surrounds the table. Then he sits beside me and a man draws the curtains closed around us. This feels not proper and I would rather enjoy the whole of the dining room, but what can I do? Chouteau moves closer. Again he takes my hand and kisses it. Finally he lifts his mouth from my skin. "I am so glad you are come to St. Louis. Will you take wine with me?"

I say of course and he pours and I think as I did with Obadiah that he is hoping to create an abandon in me that I am too nervous to feel.

He holds up his wineglass and I do the same. "Let us toast to" —he pauses—"the deepening of our friendship."

I smile and sip and try not to be surprised. Then I think I should not be. Of course Chouteau and I are to be friends. And then we are to be much more.

He is sitting so close that I feel his breath on my face. "You did not tell me before," he says, "how was your travel?"

I hope he will let me answer this time, as I want to say something that entertains, like the ladies on the steamboat. As I tell Chouteau my stories, the way I practiced them, about the duelist Frenchman and the visit to the pilot-house, I will say that his eyes roam me more than his ears seem to listen to me. Not once does he speak a word and he cannot keep his gaze anywhere but on my bosom, much of which is revealed in this dress. I am thinking I will leave off the coming of Advent in October when he interrupts.

"I have ordered for us," and he snaps his fingers. The curtains fly open and men appear—I half wonder if they've been waiting —to present us with many dishes, from *filet de boeuf* to saddle of antelope to vegetables in French-sounding sauces. After they serve, again they draw the curtains. "*Bon appétit*," Chouteau says, and turns his attention to his meal.

I will eat like a bird so as not to make a mistake. I take a bite or two. No bones yet. I struggle to think what to say as Chouteau seems happy to say nothing. Finally I come up with something. "You must have been busy these past few days."

"Not too much."

Too busy to see me, but I know not to say that. Then I think of something he will want to talk about. "Will you tell me about your work in business?"

Chouteau laughs. "Ladies do not like to hear about such things."

"I do. I am interested."

"Perhaps I should say ladies do not understand such things."

"Well, if men don't talk to us about them, how are we supposed to?"

He looks startled, and laughs.

"Mr. Darby would speak to me about his work in business," I say.

Chouteau gives me a sideways look that says plainly he does not believe it. But all he says is: "Let us not spoil this lovely evening by talk of business."

We go on again for some time in silence, but it is not the easy silence Obadiah and I shared. Of course, I do not know Chouteau nearly so well. "Will you tell me"—I pause but don't really think it's wrong to ask—"about your family?"

It is not a frown he gives me, but it's not a smile, either. "I'm surprised you're so much for talking. You did not seem so in New Orleans."

"Well, I am here now, because of you, and I am grateful, but how else are we to get to know one another?" Before the words even leave my lips, though, I can guess what he will say to that.

Chouteau gives a low laugh. He lets his gaze drop again to my bosom before slowly it rises to my face. "I can think of one way in particular."

"But—"

"No buts." Chouteau smiles, but I hear hardness in his voice. "I know you are very beautiful and that is all I need to know."

I try very hard not to say again the word *but*. "If we are to be friends, and someday more than friends—"

"*Someday* more than friends? My beautiful Eliza"—another low laugh, and a mirthful shake of the head—"we are to be more than friends this very night. And not the type who need to talk."

I try not to feel disappointment, though it flows through me like blood. I knew it might be like this, meeting for the first time in St. Louis at this hotel. But I was hoping with Chouteau it would be as it was with Obadiah, that I would know him, at least a little, as a man first, and enough to judge him a friend. I did not expect him to treat me as a body alone, with no thoughts in my head and no heart beating in my chest. "Still, I was hoping that in time"—I am speaking carefully as I know how, so as not to upset him more —"you would think of me as someone you share your thoughts with. Perhaps even as more than a mistress."

He stares at me wide-eyed. It comes to me he might be struggling not to laugh. "Do you mean"—he shakes his head—"as a *wife*?" He bursts out with a laugh loud as a rifle shot. I picture the men outside the curtains raising their heads from their rich stews. "Do not pretend to be an innocent, Eliza." Chouteau leans even closer. His gaze drops to my bosom then his hand alights there, though we are in this dining room separated from a crowd by only pieces of fabric.

I push his hand down to my stomach and hold it there. "No," I hear myself say. If we were not in this public room, I think Chouteau would try already to have me on my back, with so few words between us spoken.

Now there is hardness in his eyes, too. With a yank he frees his hand. "It is not up to you to say no. I chose you to be my mistress. I brought you here. You say you are grateful, but I believed you also understood the honor I gave you."

I know such a thing is an honor because of who Chouteau is, but would I not be giving him something in return? "I thought I understood. But I was hoping—"

"For what? To learn to sew?" His face twists as if with disgust.

He is angering me now. "A woman alone must provide her own keep."

"Eliza"—he smiles as if to soothe a cranky child—"so long as you are a mistress of mine, you will be well cared for."

Yes, behind the curtains in the dining room and the tall hedge at the house, where no one can see Chouteau's carriage come and go. I do not wish to, but I begin to see a picture. Chouteau has no wife, but still he means for me to be his secret, except for the friends to whom he boasts about bedding me, the beauty on her back in the little house he provides. I hear Chantal in my head speaking of gambling houses. *Men will see you there. But they won't talk about it.* That is because of the secrets they, too, are keeping, all over this city in little houses.

Chouteau is speaking again. "I agreed to have you learn to sew because Mademoiselle Rossignol was so insistent, but it is not attractive to think of one of my mistresses as some sort of tradeswoman."

"*One* of your mistresses?"

"Surely you did not think you would be the *only*?"

Yes, I thought that, of course I did. Who would bring a woman so far, from one state to another, for her to be but one of many mistresses?

But already he is speaking of something else, as if that is put behind us and of no matter. "I hate to think of a mistress of mine being even a governess, though that at least is respectable. It is not attractive to me, though, not at all."

I stifle the words rising in my throat. It is not attractive to have no money, either, but of course Chouteau will never know such a thing. Though I struggle to stop it, anger and shame make a flush rise hot on my skin.

For once Chouteau's eyes stay on my face. His brows arch. "Do not tell me. I am guessing something else." He makes a low laugh. "You could never be a governess, could you? Because you cannot read." Another rifle shot laugh. "You cannot even read, yet you imagine yourself my *wife*?"

I sit still as a statue. It is as if the last breath has been knocked out of me. I could not hide for long what a rube I am and Chouteau blames me for it, even mocks me, though I wonder if it is really my fault.

"As I think about it," he says, "I'm not surprised you're illiterate. I sensed it from your simple speech." He leans back and sips his wine.

I look at Chouteau and hate him in this moment. As I near die of shame, he sits and sips, carefree as a butterfly.

"It is not the sort of thing that would bother a man like Darby." He speaks the name as if Obadiah were a bug to be scraped from his shoe. "I will accept it because of how beautiful you are, Eliza. Only one thing more before we finish these unpleasant topics and return to our lovely evening." He lowers his glass and brings his face close to mine. "Do not presume to speak of my family. Do you not know that Chouteau is the most important name in this city? Never will you meet them, nor they you. Do you understand me?"

I do understand. I force myself to nod. I may be ignorant and illiterate—though tonight, too, I have learned a new word—but I understand everything now.

Chouteau will never take me for a wife. Obadiah and Chantal understood that and told me so, but I did not believe it. Not Eliza with her nose in the air. Nor will he have me as his only mistress, placed high. I am here with a man who wants to bed me so long as he is not troubled to speak to me. Tonight he remembers my name, but how long will he recall it? For this man—and for my own too foolish dreams—I left behind the only friends I ever knew.

Now Chouteau looks at me with a new light in his eyes. "I will say I might enjoy the fire in you. Perhaps I should look at that as a welcome surprise, because in New Orleans you showed no spirit at all. But there is only one way I ever again wish to see it."

I do not know how I do it, as I am trembling fiercely and it is so hard to move from this bench in these skirts, but somehow I manage to rise and stand beside the table. I must hold on to it for some moments before I can speak. Then: "Please, I beg of you, let me return to the house. I will quit it tomorrow, with my things."

Chouteau is staring at me open-mouthed.

I go on. "I made a mistake here, too. It is not just you." I have been such a fool, more than ever before. I hear my mother's laughter in my head, loud and mocking as Chouteau's. *You think you're so special, but you're just like the rest of us.* "Please, let me return to the house. I have no other lodging for tonight."

"Is such drama really necessary? I feel as if I am at the opera." Chouteau shakes his head and sips more wine. "You will feel better if you merely calm down."

I will not tell him that I cannot calm down while I must stare at his face. So I beg him again, much as I hate to do it. "Please, let me return to the house."

At last he relents, or least I think so. With much muttering and shaking of the head, he rises and follows me from the dining hall, but once outside he takes my arm, more roughly than I like, and steers me not the way we came but toward a wide staircase that leads, I am not too stupid to know, to private rooms upstairs. I know what he is about and will not have it.

He tries to pull me up the stairs, but I will not climb them, and we are not alone, either, as we have this tussle, for there are people behind us in the grand salon, watching all, and now a couple passes us, coming down. They keep their eyes away, but they see us all the same, and I know from the way Chouteau's jaw clenches that he does not like it. "Climb these stairs," he orders me between tight lips.

"I will not do it." I remember his friends and thank the angels they are not about, for what if they would help him get me to the private rooms above? Against Chouteau and all of them I would have not a hope.

He gives my arm a yank and I near topple forward, but that is when I think to use the hand I have free to pull out the pin that holds my hair atop my head. I do not let myself think before I do it. I jab the pin into his hand that is clutching my arm.

He looses me with a yelp. I must keep myself from stumbling backward but manage to do it. He stares at me with shock, though it is not that long a hairpin and cannot do so much damage. I see only two thin lines of blood.

Now I am the one spitting words. "It will hurt more if I stick it elsewhere." I let him imagine a place where it might hurt most. "I wish to return to the house. And be alone there."

This time he relents.

It is not as when I entered Planters House. Now I do not care that all in the salon are watching. With my hair tumbled and the bloodied hairpin in my hand, I walk outside with my head high as I can hold it. This is the last time in my life, the last time, I will beg a man for anything.

Chapter Nine

"Would you wish your existence with faith to imbue
Control in the ranks of the sanctified few,
Enjoy a good name and a well-established pew,
You must surely come down with a dollar or two.
The gospel is preached for a dollar or two,
Salvation is reached by a dollar or two,
You may sin at times, but the worst of all crimes
Is to find yourself short of a dollar or two."

— "A Dollar or Two," Arnaud Préot, composer

— Published by Miller and Beacham, 1855

C HOUTEAU TAKES ME BACK TO THE LITTLE HOUSE IN HIS CARRIAGE, least near enough that I can walk there. Soon as I step from the gig, he shouts to the driver to move forward. My skirts near get caught in the wheels, but all the same I thank the angels he has had enough of me for tonight. He leaves me to find my own way in the dark, which is just as well for I do not want his help anymore, if it was help he was ever providing.

Feeling my way by the light of the moon—Marie-Christine is not about; surely she thought she would see no sign of me till morning—I enter by the side door, light a candle, and pour a tumbler of wine. I carry both upstairs to my bedchamber. Mine for one night more.

With those impossible hooks, I cannot free myself of the bodice of the jade dress, but I am able to wrestle off the skirt and petticoats, and so, wrapped in a shawl, I perch on the bench by the front windows. Now it is time to think of what Chouteau was ready to do to me. Now it is time to remember the words he spoke to me, loud enough, I am sure, that all in the dining room heard them through the curtains. Now it is time to remember how those in the salon gaped as I walked out, my hair tumbled as if Chouteau had his way with me there on the wide staircase, before all. My skin burns with shame but with anger, too, and fear down deep. Is Chouteau worse than other men of his station or just like them? How much is the fault mine for not understanding what he was about? Obadiah and Chantal described it plainly, but I would not believe them.

I made the same mistake with Chouteau that I made with John Haycraft. I imagined he would make for me the life I want. I do not know which was more foolish: believing that of a poor man or a rich one.

I will not make that mistake again. As of this night, I must make for myself the life that I want. I am a woman; so be it; I must do it all the same.

This makes me think I must count how much money I have. I leave the window bench to spill it onto the carpet. It is not so much and it will run out, sure as rain; and when it does I have no one to give me more.

I will have to earn my own. Soon.

Not as a seamstress, either, for I have no one to teach me. Even if I did, it would take too long. And even if I could be a seamstress, I would want to be a dressmaker like Chantal. I know from what she told me that a seamstress's lot is not an easy one; harder every year, she said, with wages going down and the number of pieces going up and new immigrants happy to work for less. And the man who pays you, you must watch out for him, too, for often he believes the wages entitle him to more of the seamstress than just her sewing. The same for a *domestique*, she said, and I have seen enough of the world to know she is right.

I must think what choices are left me. I know they are few. Candle in hand, I pad downstairs to pour more wine. After tonight I will be buying my own; under the watching moon I will enjoy what is on offer.

I tuck my legs beneath me in the big stuffed chair in the parlor. Thanks to Obadiah I have enough money to return to New Orleans, of course belowdecks this time. I believe he would take me back. I would be forced to suffer his pity, but it is not in him to mock me. Still, he would not trust me as before and I could not blame him. He would wonder what I might make of every unwed man I meet and I would fret all the day long that he would tire of me, or die, or decide he is done with New Orleans. Then what would become of me? It is the same problem as before.

If not New Orleans: Cote Sans Dessein? No. I could not bear it. I will never go back to John Haycraft. My pride forbids me. I will not give him that satisfaction, or my mother, or Sarah. Nor do I even know if my family is still there after the flood.

The wine is sweet on my tongue, but this night is bitter. I wonder where is that Creole bastard now. I was wrong to think him ever half in love. And I told myself I understood men. Maybe after tonight I finally do. It is not that I think them bad, or worse than women. I have known women whose hearts are empty of kindness; my mother is one such. It is that the price is too dear to depend on men.

I envy the freedom men have. Rich men, men like Chouteau

and Obadiah: for them the world is made for their pleasure. They need only think a thing to do it. Their wives may enjoy ease as well, but I wonder what price they pay. And now, burned again, I cannot count on that life for me.

My mind goes back to the bawdy ladies in New Orleans. They are rich: they have a barouche like Chouteau and in it they ride on a sunny day, sending their driver to do this and that, eyeing the wares at the market. Ever since I saw them, and they sent their driver after me—or least so I believe—my mind has gone back to them. It is not pretty to think how they make their money, but how much of life is pretty? Most of us pay a price for what we have. Many pay a steep price and still have nothing.

Now I have seen richness up close, I will be bold enough to say I wish it for myself. Why should I not have the riches of the bawdy ladies? Why could I not learn what they do? What does it take but work and courage and being planful?

I have also proved I have something special, something Obadiah saw, and Chouteau, and the bawdy ladies, too: even rich, important men turn their eyes to me. What did Obadiah say? *You have that rare quality that has no name.* Should I not be able to use it?

That life is not what I imagined when I lay on the grass and stared up at the blue sky, when I dreamt of what lay beyond the curve in the river. Still, I am where I am. Would I be happier if I had said yes to one of the country boys who wished to wed me, before I set eyes on John Haycraft? I will never know. I am where I am.

I will not let myself imagine what my family would think. I know the shame my father would feel, though I will believe he could never stop loving his Eliza. For my little sisters who look up to me with bright eyes, I will hope for an easier life, though I do not know how such a thing is possible.

I drink the last of the wine in my tumbler. Is what I am thinking so different from my time with Obadiah? I "catered to his natural needs," as he put it. I am not sure Obadiah would fault me for this. Chantal, yes, and I am sorry for that. She would fear for my soul and my heart.

I don't have the time or money—or patience—to fret about those anymore. I am past my youth. In February I will have twenty-five years. With every year that passes I will lose more of my beauty, and when I have lost that I will have nothing.

As I climb the stairs, finally ready to sleep, I think that even then I will have one thing: the head on my shoulders. That is good for something. Obadiah told me so and he has proved right about everything.

"I REMEMBER YOU." The boardinghouse mistress narrows her eyes at me. "You were here in the spring, on the top floor. Paid for by a so-called gentleman."

I stand on her stoop in the hot sun of a late forenoon. If I am past the first blush of youth, she is past the second, with brown hair surrendering to gray and huge eyes that poke out like a toad's.

She smirks at me. "You're not any nicer put together now, are you?"

I don't mind the insult. I donned my old clothes with purpose this morning: the better to bargain. I hold out coins but out of reach for fear she'll snatch them and slam the door. "You see very well I can't afford as much as Mr. Darby."

She shakes her head. "Shame. Lodging rates go up in summer."

That is a lie. "Well"—I return the coins to my bag—"I wish I could offer more." I put my back to her and step off the stoop. "Though"—I turn half around—"if you did have a room for a week, I might be able to add more at the end."

She harrumphs as if she'll believe that when she sees it. "Where might Mr. Darby be, then?"

She's thinking he abandoned me. I won't correct her. "Like all of us, about his business." I step further down toward the street.

"Well, don't we have a deal, then?" she calls.

I turn half around. "If you take what I offered, for a second-floor room for a week, then we do."

She nods and I step back up and hand over the coins. "I'll come this afternoon with my things," I tell her, and take my leave to join the throng mobbing the street, which throws up more dust than I care for. In the fancy parts of town, I've seen, the streets are watered down. Rich and poor alike must suffer the air, though, foul from soot and smoke. I clutch a white handkerchief to my nose and know it will be gray by nightfall.

I'm learning my way about. I'm on Spruce Street now and behind me is Poplar. If I stay this route, I'll see Clark and then Walnut, but if I turn right and go downhill I'll be on the levee. Around me people rush about, plain and fancy, children, too, grimy and getting no education, poor mites. I suppose if they're lucky they might end up peddlers, some with rough carts mounted on two wheels, the peddler himself playing the horse. If a body wanted to buy a remedy, they'd have no trouble finding one, or a canary bird, or an old-time book. Peddlers call out their wares over the din: "Nice new potatoes!" or "Fine fresh bananas!" It's men with dark skin who sell fruits and nuts; Obadiah told me most of them come from Italy.

It's a motley crew in St. Louis. I couldn't say why, but I don't see many like Chantal. Here most all the Negros seem to be slaves. I don't understand how New Orleans can be one way and St. Louis another, both in slave states, but I do know people every-where have strong views on the topic.

I'm not long about examining the city, for the sun is hot and I have an important errand this very night. Though I am a sight to see in my tatty dress and country clodhoppers—I guess some part of me knew I might need them again—I carry my parasol high. I want my skin white, as I want my hands soft. Marie-Christine's eyes went wide this morning when she saw me leave the house, and in these clothes, too: they will go wider still this afternoon when I depart with my trunk in a hired gig.

PLANTERS HOUSE IS SHINING bright as a thousand stars this night, as it was last. I stand a distance away and keep my eyes open for Chouteau's carriage, for if I see it I will hide until it disappears. I wonder if he knows yet that I am no longer in his little house. I will not spare the time to think long of him and my foolishness, though it makes me smile that maybe Chouteau has learned what Haycraft did: it is not so easy to have your way with me.

Because I am being planful, I know what I am about here. I am wearing my blue dress, for it will not help tonight's cause to look a ragamuffin. The boardinghouse mistress's eyes bulged at the sight of my fancy trunk when I went back there this afternoon; they near jumped out of her head when I came down the stairs wearing this dress. *Her royal highness, aren't you,* she said. I smiled and said I would return soon and to enjoy a pleasant evening. The boardinghouse is not so many blocks from here and so I walked swiftly and with a confident air to make it less dangerous to be out alone.

Carriages arrive and fancy men jump out to enter Planters House. Many drivers are Negro. Some remain in the carriage and speak to no one; others stroke the horses; still others seek another body to talk to. I judge my luck will be best with the last type so cross Chestnut Street and approach such a driver, an older man with a ready smile. "I am praying you can help me," I say.

He looks very surprised. "Don't rightly know how."

"I have a dear friend, a beautiful woman about my age, recently come to St. Louis, and I am very sorry to say she might be of a mind to do something desperate."

He frowns.

"I hate even to speak of such a thing." I look away as if I cannot bear to meet his gaze. "She left a husband who was very bad to her. Now her family has foresworn her and she has nowhere to go and might feel she has only one path left." I return my gaze to his. "You and I both know what a woman might feel forced to do. I must find her," I add quickly, "because with the help of God I might spare her that fate. But of course I know not where to look."

He nods slowly, his eyes widening as he grasps my meaning.

"It is just that"—I try to look very embarrassed—"I hate even to speak of it, but it would not be just any place. It would be where important men go, where a woman with remarkable beauty might go, if she became desperate."

Another driver, a younger man, is approaching. I see curiosity in his eyes. The men talk in low tones, glancing at me. I look away as if I could melt into the street for shame, but really I am proud of this story I contrived. These drivers would tell me nothing if they thought I was trying to corral a wayward husband.

"There's one place in town," the older driver tells me, "head and shoulders above the rest."

"Madam Lantos's house," the younger man says.

"Other one is Madam Hunter's," the older man says. "But Madam Lantos's is the top one."

"Gentlemen who come to Planters House"—I look away again —"they might go to Madam Lantos's?"

The older man nods. "Both of them are what you might call institutions. Been around a long time for the gentry." Like churches, I think, or the academies of science Obadiah talked about. "They're the sort your friend might aim for," he adds.

They name the blocks where I will find these "institutions" and describe large respectable-looking stone houses, with wide stairs to the front door and fanlight above and woven rope mat on which to wipe your shoes.

"Right proper on the outside," the older driver says. "Don't let that be a surprise to you."

"And don't go now, mind," the younger man says. Both

chuckle and shake their heads. "They're mighty busy in the evening time."

"Wait till after noontime," the older man advises. "They be done having their coffee then and be ready to greet the day."

They warn me of the dangers of trying to pry a woman from the clutches of such houses. I don't doubt such stories. But I am not seeking to do what these men think I am.

I STAND on the street in my blue dress, umbrella in hand, and look up at a grand stone house, the very picture that the carriage drivers described. It is gone two o'clock on a day made for melancholy: the skies crying, thick gray clouds a blanket thrown over the sun.

It used to be I wasn't one to spend time thinking about things before I did them. Now I must be planful. I'm sure the pious would say that, in this circumstance, that makes me even more a sinner.

I climb the stairs and rap on the door, careful to stand back far enough on the stoop that a body could see me from the front window. It is quiet as a church at midnight. I wonder if the inmates are still abed. I'm thinking I should knock again—though I don't wish to seem impatient—when the door opens far as it can before a chain stops it. A Negro woman much my age peers out. She's thin, with such sharp eyes I imagine she knows already what I am about. "I'm hoping to see Madam Lantos," I tell her. "My name is Eliza Haycraft."

She nods and closes the door again.

I take a deep breath. My heart patters like the rain upon the sash windows. So I have found the right place. When I left Planters House last night, I walked a different street back to the boardinghouse and happened upon a gambling hall. Carriage drivers waited outside and I told one my sorry tale. Madam

Lantos or Madam Hunter: that is what I heard again. One driver named a third, which I will keep in my pocket if I need it.

I hear the chain rattle. The door opens wide and the same woman silently takes my dripping umbrella. I wipe my shoes on the mat.

It is the music I notice first. Someone is playing a piano. It is the opposite of a rousing tavern song: I do not think I have ever heard a tune so mournful. Then the smell strikes me. Cigar smoke and furniture polish I knew at Obadiah's; also the smell of coffee and of something wonderful cooking. Here, add scent, and whiskey. And something else: the smell of women?

I hear female laughter upstairs. Someone is bounding about. Then a door opens and I hear women talking before a door slams.

It is shadowy, near gloomy as outside. I am led past a front parlor—where the furnishings are dark and brooding as in Obadiah's house—then down a hallway past a cheerful yellow kitchen. The carpet is thick beneath my shoes.

It is a rear parlor I am led into. Here is the piano. A woman is playing, her back to me. She wears a gown of lush purple fabric. She is slight of build and her hair, piled in a way Chantal would like, is so light in color that it is near white. But something about her says she is not old; it is the narrow curve of her waist and how she bends over the piano one moment and the next raises her face toward the ceiling, like a prairie flower swaying with the wind.

This must be Madam Lantos. I have not seen her face yet, but I know already she is not like the bawdy ladies I saw in New Orleans.

The young woman leaves. I do not move from behind Madam Lantos. She must know I am here; she must want me to see her play. It feels too bold to walk deeper inside and turn about to peer at her face.

Finally her hands trill all the way across the keys to the high notes, and when I think she is done she plays, very moodily, one last set of low notes that could set a heart to breaking. She is still for a few moments before she turns to face me.

She stands. She is tiny, very pale, her brows nearly white, with large eyes of a startling green, like a cat's. She cannot be young, but her face is unlined. There is no powder or color on her; she looks fresh as if she just stepped from a garden. That is the scent she gives off, too. "Are you an admirer of Beethoven?" she asks me.

I swallow. "I don't know what that is."

"What he is. Ludwig van Beethoven is a composer. That was his Piano Concerto Number Five. People call it the Emperor Concerto."

Her voice is so calming, I feel as if I am lying in a meadow with a soft breeze upon me. I try to think of something to say. "It has a sad feeling to it."

"The slow movement does, yes. Beethoven was lonely, like so many. And, for much of his life, deaf."

I think that means he could not hear.

"That means his ears failed him," she says. Her eyes fix on my face, her gaze keen as Obadiah's. "He was thwarted in love, Beethoven. Is that so for you, too, Eliza Haycraft?"

Here is another question I didn't expect. But I can guess what *thwarted* means. "Love has nothing to do with why I am here."

"I don't believe you. I would rather you speak truthfully and not waste my time." She says this placidly then motions me to sit upon a sofa. She remains standing, though even then she is not much taller than me. She examines my figure and garments with no shame about it. When she is done she speaks again. "Most women care about nothing but love and they do not come to me if they are happy in it. So I will ask you again."

I feel as I did with Obadiah: she will see through me if I fib. "I have been foolish about love. But I won't be anymore."

"Many women say that. What happened to bring you to me?"

She is good at asking questions, this Madam Lantos, but I will not tell her about Haycraft. He is to be my secret now. So I describe Chouteau instead. "I believed a gentleman would marry me. And then he did not."

"You gave yourself to him?"

"No."

She raises her brows. I believe I see hope light her eyes. "Are you a virgin?"

"No."

I watch the light disappear. "So there have been other men. That is part of life; I do not judge. But I want no drama here. Might this man search for you?"

I think about that. "He has no claim if he does."

"That is hardly reassuring." She frowns. "What about your family, then? Will a father or brother try to save you?" Her lips curl at that.

My father would if he knew. But: "My family does not know where I am. And I don't need saving."

"No. I never did, either." She looks away and is silent.

Now I regard her freely. She seems powerful, though she is so tiny. I am not surprised she is running this house where important men come. I wonder if some of these fancy men might be afraid of her, as I realize I am, a little.

Suddenly she speaks again. "You know, I am sure, that you have certain personal attractions. That is all well and good. But for a clientele like mine, you need more than that after a time or two."

"I believe I can hold a man's attention."

"I must make rapid judgments about men and women both and I am concerned you will be trouble. For one thing, there is a man who might come searching for you. For another, I fear you have too high an opinion of yourself."

She thinks of me as my mother does. I bristle. "I am willing to work hard. I am willing to learn what pleases the gentlemen who come to you." Then I remember a word Obadiah would use when he talked of business. "And I believe I would be profitable for you."

"Profitable." I see mockery on her face.

"I must earn my own keep. What you tell me to do, I will do."

"You know a man is king when he comes here," Madam

Lantos tells me. "Whatever he wants, short of drawing blood, you give to him."

"I understand that."

"The men who come here want to remember what it is to be a man, vigorous and strong. I worry you think yourself above them, a woman who would not give herself to the man she loved, who believes she can hold a man's attention, who claims she does not need saving."

"You said the same of yourself."

Madam Lantos allows those words to hang in the air. Then: "Do not mistake yourself for me, Eliza Haycraft. If you are to be of use to me, you must understand that this is my house only."

I am being scolded, but all the same her warning makes me think she may take me after all. I cast down my eyes. "I understand that."

"Then I will allow you to work for me for a fortnight, at which time I will reflect on the matter again. I will pay you twenty-five percent of what you earn."

I screw up my courage and raise my gaze again. "I have spoken with Madam Hunter. And she will pay me forty percent of what I earn."

Madam Lantos juts her chin much the way I do. "You are telling me in your own words that I am correct in my judgment of you."

"I believe I have a special quality and for that reason will be very profitable for whichever house I work for."

"There is that confidence again. I am not happy to see it. By the by, is that your true name, Eliza Haycraft?"

I tell her that it is.

"I will allow you to use it. It is unusual."

I bite back that it is not up to her which name I use, for the simple fact that indeed it is up to her if I want to work at this house.

"If you last beyond a few weeks," she goes on, "I will pay you thirty-three percent of what you earn." I am about to protest when she goes on. "I will not hear more on the matter."

The woman I saw before returns as if by magic, as she was not called for.

"I will expect you in two days," Madam Lantos tells me, "at the same hour. You will have a bedchamber on the top floor."

Madam Lantos is not the same as the boardinghouse mistress. I will have no say in the location of my chamber.

As I walk back onto the street, the sky now pouring rain as if the angels are washing their wings, I wonder if I am again getting myself into trouble. But it may be worth it, because at the knee of Madam Lantos I will learn from a master.

Chapter Ten

"She came to St Louis... an ignorant country girl unable to read or write. Her only recommendations for favor, good or evil, were a pleasing face and a lithe, almost fragile form. Those who knew her at that time describe her as a woman of unusual attractiveness. She came from a county home in Callaway county, and entered at once upon a life of a *femme de joie*... "

— "A Noted Character Gone"

— *St. Louis Times*, December 6, 1871

ALREADY I HAVE LEARNED A THING OR TWO ABOUT A CATHOUSE, though I have been with Madam Lantos only a few hours. As the four o'clock dinner hour nears and I stand in my sun-hot room on the top floor wishing in vain for a breeze to blow, I wonder if I might as well have joined the army, as the number of rules might be just the same.

To start, Madam Lantos told me that every day I must be out of bed by two o'clock in the afternoon and fully bathed and in a clean *negligée* by four. Precisely at that time, we are served dinner. Gentlemen begin to arrive at nine and I am to be dressed and scented for the evening, with my hair arranged. I will be done working by four o'clock in the morning, unless I have an overnight guest—which is not uncommon—or there is a special event in the city after which clients might stop by, or a steamboat has a very late docking and the same might happen. With the help of Joshua, the Negro man about the house, Madam Lantos locks up at five o'clock.

One night a week and one full day, which might be split into two parts, I am free to do as I please. I am told many like Sunday morning to themselves to attend church services. And during my monthly course, I have three days of freedom. That is a mixed blessing as days of freedom are not days I can earn money.

I must pay for my lodging and meals and linens, and since Madam Lantos insists those be changed after every client I am guessing that can add up to quite a sum. Also, she will not permit anything on the walls that might upset a client, such as a crucifix or picture of Jesus Christ. She will allow a portion of watered-down wine so as to be sociable with a client and for that I will not be charged.

She has strong views on health: that I eat heartily at dinner—no picking at food like a bird for her—and take daily walks for the regularity of digestion, strength of muscles, and clearness of skin. She is much in favor of parasols, as I can see given the whiteness of her own complexion. She is glad I do not smoke, for she believes it unwholesome and the smell unpleasant on a woman. She is insistent on bathing: thoroughly after every client without fail. After I arrived and she explained to me the rules, I was served strong coffee in the kitchen and introduced to a few of the others, all in night shifts just rousing from sleep. I watched

Madam Lantos sneak up close to a fair-haired one called Lydia to
sniff her and thought it was because she suspected Lydia had not
bathed with vigor, but later a dark-haired girl named Charity
whispered that no, Madam Lantos was checking for the smell of
alcohol, on which she would frown and which is a concern in that
case.

There are secrets under this roof, I am sure.

But not with the clients: all of them are well known to Madam
Lantos. She says she does not care for surprises in this regard. She
will allow a new client only if a client she already knows recom-
mends him or in the special case of a well-known personage who
has voyaged to St. Louis, such as a senator or actor or judge. Such
a person is of interest to the clientele as they dine or relax with
drinks and cigars. To my amazement, she said that on occasion
clients do not go upstairs at all but simply talk and drink and
smoke and play at cards.

I struggle with my window to open it further. The reward for
this top floor chamber is a view of the riverfront, the water
clogged by craft of all kinds, but this inspection of commerce—
and the smoke it produces, which sits on the city like a brimmed
hat—does not please me as it normally might. I am too nervous
about the coming evening to be so easily distracted.

This bedchamber in which I will both sleep and work is
richly furnished, like the one I shared with Obadiah, but the
carpet is even thicker, with a fancier pattern, and the armoire
has a design painted on it, of vines and flowers. The bed takes
up a large share, which I suppose is fitting, and you don't need
a step to reach it, which would be inconvenient in the circumstance. I have a tall looking glass as well—I can imagine what
use clients will wish to make of that—and a housemaid just
brought me a wash basin of water, soap that smells of lavender,
and thick towels. I have a chamber pot, too, which I am told to
use after dark as it is unsafe to walk outside to the privy on my
own or even with another girl and Joshua will be too busy to
accompany. I don't think the danger is due to the nature of this

place; I believe it is part of city living and so something I must abide.

Since I have my door open for more air, I hear the bustle: female voices and squeals and laughter—I know there will be tears, too: where there are women there are tears—and carpets being swept and liquor bottles being toted to and fro and water sloshing in basins as housemaids set those in the upstairs rooms.

There is a flurry at four o'clock. I take a deep breath—my heart is jiggering like an egg on a hot pan—and follow the rush down to the yellow kitchen, wearing the negligée I was given. A rough-hewn trestle table is set for dinner, benches on both sides. Oxtail soup is first and I see there will be fried catfish, too, bread and butter, roast turkey and potatoes, salad with lettuce and tomatoes, and apple pie.

Lydia, to my right, gives me a glance. She may be fair-haired like Madam Lantos but is the opposite of delicate: she looks as if she could pitch a man from a window. "Don't expect to see Madam Lantos till tonight," she tells me. "She won't mix with the likes of us more than she has to. Where you from, then?"

"Callaway County. And I was in New Orleans, too."

"New Orleans." She repeats it in a mocking way. "One of our best clients who favors me in particular is a steamboat captain. Won't be long before he begs me to go to New Orleans with him."

"I'm sure it won't," I say, but perhaps I don't say it as if I really believe it as Lydia snaps her head in my direction. She inspects me as I spoon soup into my mouth the way Chantal taught me. "Fancy, you are."

"Be nice to her, Lydia." Charity, across from me, has eyes near black as her hair and a sharp widow's peak, which gives her the look of a minx from a faraway land. I can see how she might fascinate a man. To me she says: "Lydia forgets she was new herself once."

"It's excitement for some when there's someone new." Lydia spears a piece of catfish with her fork then turns to stare at me. "But it never lasts."

I know enough to hold my tongue. Around the table are four other girls who haven't seen fit to talk to me and missing is one who's away visiting family as she does each summer around this time. There is also a cook and the housemaid who greeted me the first day and another housemaid who follows her about like a puppy. Above everyone but for Madam Lantos is a stern-looking housekeeper. I get the idea she counts the linens and liquor bottles; today she seems displeased with the totals, but there is a type who likes nothing better than to grumble. Esther at Obadiah's house might be of that type.

After dinner I am again upstairs in my bedchamber until the clock chimes eight. I am called down to the rear parlor to present myself for Madam Lantos's inspection. Earlier she approved my jade dress for tonight. Chantal had such high hopes for me in that dress; it is best I not think about her now.

Madam Lantos is wearing a white gown as if she is playing Queen Victoria as a bride. She looks billowy as a summer cloud. She examines me in the jade then goes so far as to examine the dress's seams. Though she says not a word I know I have impressed her again. Well, really, Chantal has. She allows the fabric to drop from her hands. "Tonight you will not go upstairs with a client. I will call you down from time to time and then send you back upstairs."

Oh, this relieves me. Then I wonder: is it to create a kind of excitement? Perhaps Madam Lantos thinks that she—and then I— will get a higher price from this way of doing things.

She narrows her green eyes at me. "You will meet important men at this house. You will hear them discuss important matters. You are never yourself to speak on the subject at hand or repeat to anyone what you hear."

I look down at the carpet. "I understand."

"You cannot hope to understand what they are discussing. You are to talk about nothing more than whether they desire more whiskey or a cigar."

I repeat that I understand and am sent back upstairs. But really

I don't understand, or believe, what I have just been told. Did Madam Lantos herself never "hope to understand" what the men around her discussed? I wager not. I myself came to understand a great deal of what Obadiah told me, especially after I asked questions, and I believe he enjoyed only one thing more than explaining to me the ways of the world. I plan to do the same under this roof. I wish to learn about the world and who better to teach me than important men who move freely in it?

It is not long before the house grows noisy. A housemaid calls me to the front parlor. As I descend the stairs, my heart jabbing against my ribs as if making to escape, I hear talk and laughter and raucous piano music that I doubt Beethoven composed. I don't expect to find Madam Lantos at the instrument and later find it is a male Negro there. There are men in the dining room and four sit in the front parlor in a haze of cigar smoke, along with Madam Lantos, Charity, Lydia, and one other. As I did the night I walked into Planters House, I keep my chin high and smile with my mouth and my eyes.

Madam Lantos motions me to a chair; Lydia is atop a man's lap, her arms draped around his neck. "Our newest gem," Madam Lantos murmurs, "Eliza Haycraft," and I wonder if I am ever alone with her would I hear such a compliment fall from her lips.

One man is young, another old, and two are in the middle, their years of vigor not yet behind them but preparing to flee. Their gazes are even bolder than I saw in Planters House, but that can be no surprise: these men know that with enough money, they can have me. I have the thought that, yes, my body they can take, in any way they desire, from night till morning and then again the next night, if they pay. But they cannot buy my mind; they cannot buy my soul.

"Eliza is a flower from our own state of Missouri," Madam Lantos says.

"Always have preferred the local talent," one man says with a guffaw, "you never could convince me there was a good reason to voyage far afield," and I see that he is needling the man Lydia is atop, who has ginger hair and an enormous moustache of the same hue. I am soon told that man is a steamboat pilot and wonder if he is the one Lydia says "favors her in particular" because, if so, I am surprised to see in his eyes a particular gleam as he stares fixedly at me.

Lydia must notice, too, as she speaks up. "I think you, sir, like us Kansas girls just fine," and he chucks her under the chin and says that indeed he does and then the oldest man asks if everyone has heard how bad the flooding was in Kansas City.

My ears perk at that—Obadiah has a brother there, I well know—and off the men go about rotting carcasses of buffalo in treetops now the waters have receded and how many folk are dying of the bloody flux, which is accompanied by chills and fever. Is there not a more cheerful topic, Madam Lantos wants to know, and that gets them to the ordinance just passed here in St. Louis ordaining that an obelisk be built to designate the high water mark of eighteen hundred and forty-four.

"What is an obelisk?" I ask before I think to stop myself.

The head of Madam Lantos snaps in my direction. I am watching her decide whether to scold me now or later when the youngest man laughs. "It would be my very great pleasure to show you one tonight if Madam Lantos allows it!"

That sets them all to laughing and I get an idea what an obelisk must be. A flush rises from my bosom to my cheeks, though now I am in this business I should put blushing far behind me. The steamboat captain chimes in. "I expect our delicate Eliza might easily cause a monument to be erected, here on Poplar Street though it's planned for Front," and then the oldest man says he hopes it won't cost the sum of one hundred dollars like the one to be shaped from a single block of limestone.

Madam Lantos laughs, too, and says that one hundred dollars might suit her very well and she would be delighted to discuss it privately. Then she waves me away. As I rise to leave I see daggers in Lydia's eyes. And I am not sure she even noticed the wink her pilot gave me.

I am called downstairs three more times that night—walking past chambers from which come the sounds of giggling, slapping, and more—and on no occasion does Madam Lantos reprimand me. Perhaps since I got everyone to laughing, I have been forgiven. Past two in the morning she waves me away for the final time. Upstairs in my bedchamber, the windows full open to admit a breeze, I douse my candle and wrestle out of the jade dress. I have done nothing tonight but bat my lashes and still I feel I could sleep for a thousand nights.

In my nightdress, I throw myself atop the bed and wonder how am I to do this, when it comes to doing it? I have been with only two men in my life, one I loved—or thought I loved—and one I trusted as a friend. The next man in my bed will be a stranger, and the one after that and the one after that. I will be doing the most private things a woman can do with a line of strangers.

I suppose it will be difficult at first and then become easier. With John, as his shine wore off or when I wanted to anger him, I would go cold. He would work over me and I would ignore him. I cannot do that here—I must pleasure the clients, like it or not—but perhaps I can find a way to close off some part of myself, as if it is some other woman doing what I must and I myself, the true part of me, is watching only. I don't want to be coldhearted and unfeeling—then it is my mother I become—but I must pick and choose my times to feel. I must remember my aim: to have my own money, to have the money to be free.

Have I not long told myself that I could do what I must, when the time came? Well, I proved it when I threw myself in John's canoe. Tomorrow night, and all the nights after, I must prove it again.

A rap on my door wakens me. Sunshine floods my room. A female voice—not Madam Lantos—is quietly calling my name. I prop myself up in bed. "Come in," I call and the door opens a sliver. It is Charity's face in the gap.

"Eliza," she says. "You're up, then."

"I am now."

She pushes the door further open. She's in her night shift, white with tiny yellow flowers. She looks very young in it, and with her hair loose and flowing. I wonder how many years she has. Not so many as me. "It's gone noon," she says. "Will you come with me to the shops? I saw some lace the other day that I took a shine to. There's coffee on."

I sit up straighter and smell it. Heaven.

Charity giggles. "It's strange to call someone by my own name when I can't use it."

I frown. This confuses me. "Your name is Eliza?"

"Eliza Stubblefield. That name wouldn't do for a whore now, would it?" The word slaps me like the back of my mother's hand. "What man wants to think about stubble here?" she says. "So Madam Lantos changed it. Don't call me Eliza: it'll make her mad. Hurry," and she disappears, and I hear her scamper down the stairs.

There is not only coffee in the kitchen but thick bread, too, that we slather with butter. With parasols against the sun, we're soon out on the street. Charity walks near as fast as Chantal and indeed we must be back and newly bathed by four. I don't care to think about that now, or anything that will follow.

I am thinking Charity and I must move out of the way of two respectable-looking ladies walking toward us, but instead they are the ones who cross away. "Why did Madam Lantos want to call you Charity?" I ask her. It seems a strange name to choose in the circumstance, not that I know what a proper name would be.

"To make clients forget I could be a witch." She points to her widow's peak. "I'm from Massachusetts, not so far from Salem. Only think: if I'd been born in olden times, they might've hanged me till I was dead."

Obadiah would say we are indeed fortunate to be born in modern times. "I knew someone from Massachusetts once."

"A man?" Charity turns her dark eyes on me. "A lover?" She looks as if she hopes he was.

"Yes. And very kind to me."

"Then why are you not with him now?"

"He is married."

I think that will anger her on my behalf, but I am wrong. "I will be married some day, probably not so very long from now, and to a man who is kind and rich and handsome."

I cannot say why, but her sureness saddens me. "Have you been long with Madam Lantos?"

"A year and a little more."

I'm about to step aside for a lady and her small daughter to pass, but they do the same as the other two and cross away, the woman steering her child with rough hands. She tut-tuts under her breath and does her best to shield her child's eyes, which only makes the girl turn to stare once we're past. I think of the bawdy ladies in New Orleans and how I turned to look at them. *Don't look at them,* Chantal said. *They're bad women.*

"You're not used to it, are you?" Charity asks.

"How do they even know?" I have done nothing yet. Am I wearing on my face what I will do this night?

"They know me," she says, "and no one would walk with me unless she were the same," then she pushes open the door of a shop and a bell tinkles overhead and she is on to choosing lace. Charity's coins are as good as the other ladies' judging by how fast the clerk palms them. "After tomorrow you'll have some to spend," Charity tells me when we are again on the street, "perhaps more than you're expecting."

This perks my interest. "I was wrong to ask about the obelisk."

"You're one to watch, is what I thought soon as I saw you." She stops to look straight on at me and there's no jealousy in it. She lowers her voice. "I saw Madam Lantos in private conversation with more than one client last night and I think you were the topic."

Who will it be, I wonder? Who will come back a second night just for me?

"Doesn't bother me," Charity goes on, "as there's no shortage of gentlemen. And if you bring in some new, they'll be around to the rest of us soon enough."

"Do you get used to it?" I hear myself murmur.

"Mostly." She looks away and chews her lip. "It won't be forever, after all. Just let them do what they want and let that be the end of it," and she resumes walking and I think how odd it is that she can be so matter of fact and at the same time dream of marrying someone rich and kind.

We are back to Madam Lantos when I see another mother and child, a boy this time, with none of the rich dress of the others and limbs so scrawny and eyes so huge in their heads that it could set a heart to breaking. I don't know why they catch my eye—I see so many like them—but this day I notice they don't look away when I look at them: they stare at me with no flinching about it.

They are not crossing the street away from me and I won't cross the street away from them. Instead I pull a coin from my reticule and walk close and hand it to the woman. She palms it fast and thanks me hard and grabs her boy's hand and then off they go, probably to buy food.

"You've a soft heart, I think," Charity tells me, and I hope I do, because that would make me different from my mother and maybe different from the woman I will become tonight, who must pick and choose when she will let herself feel.

Chapter Eleven

"The old man, especially if he is in society, in the privacy of his thoughts, though he may protest the opposite, never stops believing that, through some singular exception of the universal rule, he can in some unknown and inexplicable way still make an impression on women."

— Giacomo Leopardi

— *Pensieri* (1834-'37)

— Tr. by William Fense Weaver

I DO NOT REGRET PARTING WITH THAT COIN, not even after I climb the stairs to my bedchamber and find that my money from Obadiah is gone, lifted by sticky fingers from the armoire where I had tucked it among my drawers embroidered with broderie. I fancied when I walked inside my chamber that the armoire doors were not full closed and so it must have been.

I stalk about my chamber, angry. Then... frightened. This means I have not a coin to my name. I will work tonight, but when will Madam Lantos pay me for it? I am poor as I was when I flung myself into John's canoe. Well, then I had the canoe to sell. I suppose now I have myself.

I drop onto my bed. I knew such a thing could happen. All my life I've known to hide a precious token—from Sarah, or John; my little sister Betsy might have light fingers, too. One time my brother Asa took a pressed flower a boy gave me, but it was to tease me he did it and once I began crying he gave it right back.

I am glad the thief cannot have been Charity; I am allowing myself to hope she might be a friend. Lydia comes to mind, but it could be any of the girls, or a housemaid, or the frowning house-keeper. Or Madam Lantos, more teaching me a lesson than desiring my pitiful stash.

Save for Joshua, there are only women in this house when the sun shines. I have yet to see Joshua mount the stairs. I am sure it is a woman who took my money. Where there are women, there are tears, and there are secrets, and there are envies. Coming to a bawdy house, I imagined I would need to understand men. Maybe I am learning I must understand women just as much.

Just after eight o'clock in the evening I am called downstairs to stand before Madam Lantos in the rear parlor. Again I am in the jade, though she has told me I must purchase new gowns and garters and hose. I get the idea frocks suffer from this work, as they are rarely removed and so take the brunt of it. Already I feel for Chantal's handiwork on the jade... Tonight, in this heat, with thunder near-abouts and rain coming, Madam Lantos is in rose, pale as an angel, perfect but for the light frizz in her hair. Not even she, with all her powers, can win against a storm. She holds out toward me a white jar and a sort of stick with fabric on one end. My ignorance must show because her brows arch. "Surely you know what this is for?"

I can guess, though I cannot read the words on the jar. Nor is this a matter I have faced before. Obadiah used something he called a French letter, and with John I thought I was rightfully wed so left it up to heaven.

"You must insert it when you bathe." She hands me the items. "Before every client. Religiously." Her tone is mocking. "I suppose you don't have this, either," and from the side table comes a metal contraption I might think was for torture if I didn't know otherwise. Madam Lantos sighs. "I wish I had known I was bringing on a bumpkin. You were out walking with Charity earlier, were you not? She is more levelheaded than some. She will instruct you."

I am hoping Madam Lantos has more to tell me so I stand still and wait.

"You will have Mr. Lewis tonight," she says in a moment, "the steamboat pilot," and my mind calls back his ginger hair and Lydia draped across him and his jesting about *monuments to be erected*. "This is a fortunate turn, as he is not a troublesome client and it is better to start with one such."

"This Mr. Lewis bid the highest?" I hear myself ask.

"You shall earn a fair penny from him." If it is not admiration I hear, it is satisfaction. "In fact, he has requested to stay the entire night with you," and I am sure I hear surprise as she says the word *entire*. "What you must remember, Eliza"—and I perk my ears again, for Madam Lantos has spoken my name for the first time and I believe is about to give me wisdom—"is that men seek a fantasy when they come to us. They have a vision about women they are trying to make reality, and it is your job to give them just so much that they will come again to renew the chase," and she waves me away, and, with both my hands and my mind full I climb the stairs to call for Charity outside her bedchamber.

I find her in a black gown with her hair pulled back severely. There is something of the witch about her like this: it makes her widow's peak bold indeed. She reads the wonder on my face. "It is Thursday"—she pulls me inside and shuts the door—"so I have

Mr. Buehler, who enjoys to be spanked"—she holds up a whip— "and who is a great admirer of my most beauteous feature," and she points to her widow's peak and giggles.

My lesson on the preventative and what I learn to be a vaginal syringe must be quick: Charity has a mask of netting she must fit on her face, which makes her even more fearsome to Mr. Buehler in the half light. But I cannot stop myself from telling her one thing. "It will be Mr. Lewis for me. I have him till the morrow."

Her dark eyes fly open. "If you're found cold dead, I'll know why."

I know it's not Mr. Lewis she frets will kill me. "Have you had him?"

"No one but Lydia's serviced him for an age." Both our heads jerk at a clamor downstairs. Charity pushes me toward her door. "Here they come. Mr. Buehler is always keen to start early as he's old and will tire otherwise," so I am thrust back into the hallway to climb the stairs to the top floor.

Thoughts of Mr. Lewis whirl inside my head. Now that I have seen a steamboat pilot swagger about his white palace, I know these are not men who lack confidence. I wager Mr. Lewis is very much of the type. In the front parlor he sprawls as if he owned the house; he will not trim any story, never mind the pleasure of the company; and his voice booms as if he cannot bear that anyone miss even one syllable. Then there is his moustache. It is huge: one of the biggest on which I have ever laid eyes. For a man to boast such a thing upon his face reveals a great surety about his manliness, in my opinion.

I enter my bedchamber and remember the word he used to describe me. *Delicate. Our delicate Eliza,* he called me. That is not a word any man would use to describe Lydia. I wonder what use I might make of that? If these are my thoughts, I must be a sinner. Yet I walk this path for a reason. Though it is not something a woman should say aloud—or even think—I want the freedom to do as I desire and for that I need money. Men will spend on me only if they get what they come for. They must want to return time and again.

It won't be forever, Charity says, though life has taught me that I cannot dream the same innocent dreams. My desire is to be Madam Lantos one day, maybe even *more* than Madam Lantos. Then I think of Chantal, who would remind me sternly that I haven't even a coin and so Madam Lantos need not tremble yet in her tasseled boots.

I take the last steps to ready myself. By the time I am called downstairs—trembling now—it is a roar of a storm outside. Lightning snaps like Charity's whip. Wind rattles my window as if to tear it from its frame and rain races down the glass in such thick streams I might think the river itself is flowing from the roof.

It does not surprise me that Mr. Lewis wishes to claim his prize in public view. He waits for me in the front parlor with a handful of men. I raise my chin and sense a ripple among them. But I have no eyes for them. It is Mr. Lewis paying for my attentions tonight.

"Eliza." He kisses my hand as if I were a lady, but the gleam in his eyes tells me he hopes otherwise.

I sit beside him, not atop him. I will not mimic Lydia. She is not in this parlor, I'm glad to say; the other girls are two who do not yet speak to me.

"I was just telling these gentlemen a story," Mr. Lewis says to me, "about a night like this, when my steamship was ascending the river and the heavens grew black with a coming storm."

I fix my eyes upon his face. "Will you tell it again so I can hear it?"

He raises his voice as if he were a showman at a fair. "The wind blew from the west with terrific fury. The storm so raged that it drowned even the groans of the engines. On a night like that, upon the river, lightning is more dreadful than the deepest hue of black."

"I would have been petrified," I breathe, "were you not at the helm."

He will not dispute that. "There was no music or dance, of course, and no conversation. Until, at last, two gentlemen came out the east side of the boat—they could not open the doors on the west side, with the forceful wind—and begged me on behalf of the two hundred souls aboard to land the ship. Cool and collected, I was, and told them with assurance that there was no danger. 'I am at the wheel,' said I, 'and no one aboard need fear.' " He pauses for us all to recognize his bravery. Then: "And, as you can see, we did survive it."

"What courage!" I cry, and as the men around us huzzah I lean close to whisper in Mr. Lewis's ear. "Your tale, sir, makes me so very wet for you that I can hardly bear it."

He is still for a moment before he turns toward me. His eyes widen as his mind works then they pop full open. He slams down his whiskey with such vigor that liquor sloshes onto the table, then rises fast as a jack in the box and pulls me to my feet beside him.

"My chamber is on the third floor," I tell Mr. Lewis as we scramble our way up the staircases.

"You are a doxy, aren't you," Mr. Lewis pants when we are inside my chamber, and I assure him that I am, and that is almost the whole of our conversation save for my breathy pleas that he "be gentle with me" as he is "so much man" and I fear he might "rip me asunder." I am, after all, very "delicate."

Later I wonder how Mr. Lewis could possibly believe these words coming from a trollop, but he seems to have no trouble doing so. We make good use of my tall mirror, too, and from what I can tell he admires himself more than me. After midnight is hours gone, I pour him a whiskey and hope he will sleep. But this is Mr. Lewis and telling stories about his prowess will keep him alert. He dozes only after I have complimented him until I run out of words to do so, and I am able to slip out of bed to bathe, more for my sake than for his, as I wish not only to cleanse and use the syringe Madam Lantos pushed upon me but to have time to myself, to be my own self again, to remember who I am when I am not doing what I must for money.

Across the room from the snoring Mr. Lewis I cleanse myself with water now cold. So. I have survived it. What I have done, a whore would do, and so that makes me a whore, I suppose. Have I always been one, I wonder? For I feel the same as ever and I will do the same things again when called upon and there it is.

I do not spend time wondering when God will pitch me into hell—and, things being what they are, I suppose He will pitch me before he does Mr. Lewis—but I do wonder how much I will earn from the night's work. Exactly how much is the "fair penny" of which Madam Lantos spoke? Then, strange as it is to lie down beside a man I barely know, I do exactly that, and sleep well, too.

Mr. Lewis remembers what he paid for when morning comes and so I must submit with a smile to his latest ideas, and in the bright light of day, too, when deliveries are loud outside my window. I earn an extra coin for my troubles and think as it goes into my pocket how it is my first in this business. Much as I am tempted to spend this, I will hide it instead—hide it well so it is never stolen. And some day when I am very rich, I will look upon it, and remember.

The morning's labor is not done, though, not even after I have brought up coffee, as Mr. Lewis desires a soak in the tub—made even longer by certain requests of me—and then we must call in a Negro barber from one of the best emporiums. Finally, Mr. Lewis is ready to depart. I tell him that I dearly hope I have pleased him and that I may see him again so I will have the happy chance to try to please him again. I am only half surprised that not even this is laid on too thick.

When the front door closes behind him, the house is still quiet: well, save for the housemaids scouring the front and rear parlors. There are ashes to be cleared and rings to be wiped from tables and much airing out to be done, and that is counting only the drudgery on the first floor. In the yellow kitchen, wearing my negligée, I drink coffee and slather bread with butter and listen to the housekeeper stomp about the corridors as she bends to her duties. Then I hear the clink of coins. That draws me to the rear parlor, where I find Madam Lantos in a simple frock, her back to the doorway, doling money into small bags.

I so wish to know how much I earned from Mr. Lewis! But I do not care to admit this to Madam Lantos. So I tiptoe back to the kitchen. Not long after, the housekeeper puts her hat on her head and Madam Lantos's small bags into her reticule and clip-clops out the front door. I learn what she was about when I am out walking with Charity.

"It is to keep us all from being arrested," Charity says. "The constables want their take from last night, don't you know, and those at City Hall, too."

It is beautiful a day as a smoke-filled metropolis can produce, the storm having cleared out a portion of the grime. "Why would we be arrested?" Obadiah told me bawdy houses are legal and I say as much to Charity.

"So it may well be, but we need the constables' protection when the raids come. Every so often the so-called reformers get up a head of steam and then we need not just us but the house protected." We step around a pile of horse dung. "Come, let me show you something," and Charity leads me nearer the river, to a part of town I'd avoid if she'd let me.

Very poor it is, with people living one atop the other, so many hungry-eyed urchins, too, and the filth can't be denied. I can imagine the yellow jack here, and the other poxes and maladies, and know without being told what the tarted-up women who look to be lolling about are really up to. It's much the same as us but not made near so pretty.

"I hear they might service twenty men a day," Charity whispers, "and earn near nothing, and then they get fined for 'plying their vocation,' the newspaper likes to say, or for wandering the streets in the night time. 'Vagrancy,' that's a word the constables use, but they don't arrest men for vagrancy, do they?"

It's not a question that wants answering.

"They don't," Charity goes on, "because the men of business want newcomers to keep the city growing faster than Chicago. That's their big rival, you know," and I'm hearing about men of business again. "That's what we're paying Madam Lantos for," Charity says, "to keep our business orderly and behind closed doors." We depart the dismal streets and I'm glad of it. "That's where the muck-a-mucks want it, after all, and their services, too," and she is done with that serious topic.

After all, there is gossip to be traded. I hold some back as I am not sure how much Charity is one to mind her tongue and Madam Lantos did impress "discretion" upon me, another new word and an important one. But I do tell Charity a thing or two about Mr. Lewis.

"You've had your first, then." Charity eyes me. A woman crosses away from us, but Charity is right: already I mind less. "You'll stay for a second?"

"And a third and a fourth." I'm happy to see her smile at that. We're walking past a scrawny lad selling newspapers when I ask Charity if she reads one, as I heard her say.

"My favorite is the social column, to guess who might come by the house."

So she can read. And here she is a harlot, just the same. "You see our customers' names in that column?"

"Even Mr. Buehler!" she chirps.

I wonder if she's ever read about Chouteau. Come to think, I wonder if she's done more than read. I'll want deeper acquaintance before I make mention of him.

"And from time to time," she goes on, "I might see a tidbit about home, though I wonder I still call it that."

"You're a far way from Massachusetts." So was Obadiah, of course, but he's a man, and rich, and so can journey as he pleases.

"I didn't expect to come so far," Charity says. "I thought I'd go only to Boston," and her face takes on a thoughtful expression.

It comes out then, how when Charity was fourteen her mother died of a sudden and her father swiftly married a bride only a few years older than Charity herself. The new bride wanted no part of her husband's daughter and made it plain. "It didn't help I'm the picture of my mother. I had a hankering for the stage, too, to be honest," Charity says more brightly, "and Boston's famous for it, what with the Federal Street Theatre and the Tremont."

Famous or not, of course I haven't heard of either.

"But it turned out I hadn't the talent," she says. "Not like Madam Lantos."

We're back at the house and stop at the bottom stair. "She was on the stage?" I can imagine it. A striking figure she is, despite her tiny size, and musical, too.

"So it's said. And in New York." Charity climbs the first stair. "And even here, we're playacting, aren't we? Madam Lantos stages the production and all of us are the romantic stars," and I step up after Charity with something new to fill my head, and we're inside the house again and I smell dinner cooking and know my hours of freedom will soon be over.

As the days pass, I learn there is a rhythm to life in this house, and I laugh at the tedium of it, which I wouldn't have imagined. There's the endless tidying up and airing out and the mountain of linens—laundered by one who "used to be one of us," Charity tells me, and so "knows our needs"—and gowns to be repaired and new garments to be ordered, those, too, sewn by a former doxy, for who else would come near enough to measure us? Add to that the alcohol, and the food, to be bought and cooked and served and cleaned up from, and seven nights a week, too, no leisurely Sundays in this work.

I doubt Obadiah's wife knows much about bawdy houses, but if she did she would not be pleased that for some there are church services in the morning and ours after nightfall.

One evening as I dress my hair, I think on Madam Lantos's words the day I met her in the rear parlor: *I will allow you to work for me for a fortnight, at which time I will reflect on the matter again.* That fortnight ends this very eve. Tomorrow I might be out the door walking toward Madam Hunter's or I might be snug in my chamber here, earning not just a quarter of what each client pays Madam Lantos for my services, but a third.

As I hoped, I do not want for customers. And though I have been well paid already, money flies from my pockets. New garments are the worst of it, but laundering the linens is a burden, too, and one that will never stop, much as I scowl as they are pulled from the mattress to leave only the waxed canvas beneath.

On this night I share the rear parlor with Madam Lantos, Lydia, and one other girl. Lydia is atop a client, a burly dark-haired man name of O'Connell, who pours a great measure of liquor down his throat but still cannot settle. It comes out he's been gambling at the hall on Fourth Street. And "winning big," he booms. He chooses me and Madam Lantos collects the fee with a smile—she is far better than Chantal at getting paid before the stairs are climbed—and upstairs we go, Lydia watching silent as a cat and not even pouting.

It is not a good feeling I have as my bedchamber door shuts behind me.

"Show me what I paid for," he growls.

I force a smile. "There's no rush we're in, Mr. O'Connell," and I help him off with his waistcoat. It is mostly off when a playing card flutters to the carpet. "Oh, the ace of spades"—I pick it up and hand it to him—"what good luck," though as I speak the words something Obadiah once said half rises in my mind.

He grunts and slips the card in his pocket. "Show me what I paid for," he commands again," and I know I must. With effort I remove the jade dress but keep on my corset and pantalettes.

He pushes down my corset till I am full exposed and paws at me as if he has more than the usual two hands—my skin will turn purple, I'm sure of it—leering as only a drunk can. That doesn't keep him from demanding more whiskey. I pour him a hefty draft and wonder how many drams down his gullet will get him to sleeping? If I strip him naked then, he might believe when he comes to that he got what he came for.

Then: "You remind me of my wife," O'Connell sneers, "that sour expression you've got on you."

"Oh, no talk of wives here. And besides, what you're seeing is amazement at how big you were a winner tonight." I sit on the bed and gesture for him to join me. "Please," I breathe, "tell me all about it."

"It's not talking I'm here for. And I won hundreds! Not that a whore can count that high. Can't get above ten with your shoes on, now can you?"

He chortles as if he can't believe his own wit, though I feel a chill. This is the first I have had a client throw that word at me. I stand and move away from him.

"Get back here, stupid whore," he mutters, and I am forced to near him again, him now unsteady on his feet, his face red and wearing a look of lechery.

Still I keep a little distance away, purring like a cat, hoping I may soothe him still. "Tell me, though, how were you so very clever as to win so much?"

"Shut your filthy whore mouth already," and something about the way his eyes skip from mine snaps me to. I full remember what Obadiah said, about cards appearing out of sleeves at gambling halls and how that leads to pistols coming out of pockets. I don't know what my face is saying, but: "Get on here," O'Connell orders, and even before I can move, "scheming whore," he snarls, and slaps me backhanded across the face.

I crash to the carpet beside the bed but am back on my feet fast. O'Connell may be in his cups, but I am sober as a preacher. He is about to lunge when I send my right foot, still in its high-button shoe, up toward his groin. There's no thinking as I do it, and I manage to hit him somewhere; must be where I was aiming because he bellows then crumples half standing and half keeled over, howling like a bear.

I yank up my corset—this ruckus will draw Joshua, I'm sure—and get close enough to O'Connell that he can hear me hiss. "What you do outside this place is your business, but if you come at me or this house, it's mine. I know a *croupier* at that hall on Fourth"—that will give him something to think on—"and he'd want to know about that ace of spades up your sleeve. So you figure what you're going to say to Madam Lantos," and then my door is flung open and there is Joshua breathing fire, with Madam Lantos close behind.

I watch their eyes take in the bruises rising on my skin. O'Connell, bent over, cannot summon a word to his lips. "That was roughhousing you heard," I lie, "but Mr. O'Connell will have to leave us now as he is feeling poorly."

Madam Lantos holds back both her tongue and Joshua. Not a minute later O'Connell slinks down the stairs and out the door.

I have a frightening thought then: he could kill me so I would never be able to tattle on him. I must carry a dagger and tell Charity who to look for if my corpse is found bloodied on the street. Men like O'Connell stalk this city and it is the fate of all women to meet them from time to time. For once, though, I have something to say about what a man like that does, and he and I both know it.

The morning next, Madam Lantos calls me to the rear parlor. "I knew O'Connell could be a scoundrel," she says, "as there was a time once with Lydia." I must take a deep breath at that: Madam Lantos was testing me even as Lydia was seeking revenge for servicing her steamboat pilot. "I did not know before yesterday," she goes on, "how you would behave with a hotspur like him. What truly happened?"

"That is between O'Connell and me. But if he ever brings trouble to this house, I can do a thing about it."

For the first time I read respect in Madam Lantos's green eyes and know I will be staying, and at the higher rate, too. She hands me a small cloth bag, filled, I can tell, with coins. "Do you wish an accounting? Not all the girls—"

"Yes."

She pours the coins onto a square of black velvet and shows me the ledger page that she says has my name on it, and though I cannot read the words I can read the numbers, thanks to what my father taught me.

It is not as much as I had hoped, given my "starting expenses," but it is more than I have ever seen in one place before, and it is all for me, and it fires in me a desire, a burning desire, to pile up more.

Chapter Twelve

"Though slavery is thought, by some, to be mild in Missouri, when compared with the cotton, sugar and rice growing states, yet no part of our slave-holding country is more noted for the barbarity of its inhabitants than St. Louis."

— William Wells Brown

— *The Narrative of William W. Brown, a Fugitive Slave*, 1847

I DO NOT LIKE TO WALK PAST THE COURTHOUSE OF A MIDDAY, but sometimes my errands force me to do it, and sometimes when I do I see the slave auctions on the steps outside the east door, and I walk fast as my feet can carry me and turn my head away.

I hear the business all the same: the auctioneer who shouts as if it were horses he was hawking. *Look them over carefully before you bid,* he says, *as there is no warranty. Take your time and look them over good.* Over him I hear the sobs of women and children and some-times of a man, too, though he tries to quell it; and I know that after this day many men and women will be separated from each other, and from their children, too, and sisters from brothers, forevermore, and my heart breaks for them.

Sometimes I cannot keep myself from glancing over as I stride past. I see them in pens beforehand, heads sagging as if all spirit is lost, then in a group on the pavement, chained together awaiting their fate. They are chained not just to keep them from fleeing: it is also so that once they are atop the steps, they cannot stop the men who would own them from prying open their mouths to inspect their teeth or squeezing their limbs to judge their muscles.

I think to myself: Chantal's mother suffered like this. If her mother had not been able to earn her freedom, Chantal would have suffered like this. Chantal. It makes me wonder how many of these poor souls are wise as she, strong as she, loving as she. If Chantal were to lose her Honorine, like these mothers will lose their children today, her heart would break into more pieces than she could ever sew back together.

And all this outside the east door of the Courthouse, a grand structure I have learned is built in the Federal style. That has something to do with Greece and Rome, meant to honor the Ancient Past, and even I, ignorant I, see there's something wrong with auctioning slaves on the steps of this building that is tied somehow to everlasting ideas of honor.

The slave trade is a lively topic over whiskey and cigars in the parlors at Madam Lantos, and I listen and keep my mouth shut though sometimes I long to cry out a word or two. Madam Lantos has sternly instructed me that on this topic in particular I must say nothing. I know Missouri was from the first a slave state and Charity has explained that for some years now it is against the law even to speak against slavery.

I will do everything Madam Lantos asks, for after a year with her I have more dollars to my name than I can believe. I saved almost nothing at the start, what with my expenses, but since then I am frugal as a nun. I tell no one about my stash, not even Charity, but I believe Madam Lantos has an idea of it. I have caught her eyeing me and commenting that she has not seen even a new piece of lace on me of late.

That is because Chantal's reprimand after we saw the bawdy ladies never stops ringing in my head. *The young women who work for them have no money at all. Especially because they spend what little they earn on earbobs and hair bows...*

Most of us bawds are scattergoods. Even Charity cannot stop spending. Does a harlot really need combs of ivory or a dozen gowns? I do not think even the steady customers notice if I wear the same gown time and again. They are not here, after all, to admire my garments. I have raised my voice to keep Charity from giving money to some Mack who spins a sob story of gambling debts or of a father who cut off his funds. It seems in the nature of doxies to have a "live for today" attitude. Yet I have remained planful this twelvemonth. What does that make me?

"A delight," says one client I enjoy so much and see so often that I have come to consider him a friend. If he were to go of a night to another girl I would be truly saddened, though I know not to complain. Daniel Godfrey is his name and to his face I call him Daniel. He is such a sunny fellow. Even his hair shows it: it is a light yellow, the color of silk in corn. I do not know how he comes by his playful temperament because from what he has told me of his childhood, it was not a happy one. And he must scrabble for his money, unlike many who come to this house. His work has something to do with buying and selling property. He must earn a fair pile from it as he can afford me on a regular basis.

We are atop my bed one night—naked and above the linens, as it is hot as Hades—and I am slowly lighting his cigar, holding his gaze as I do it, which I know makes him think of other times I act the temptress, and gets him to smiling in that way of his. But once the cigar is lit, to make the only glow in the darkened bedchamber, we settle back against the pillows and Daniel gets on with his praise of St. Louis, which this night has to do with Opportunity. "The city had sixteen thousand people in 1840"—he puffs his cigar so as to send the smoke in rings toward the ceiling—"and now it is said to have thirty-five thousand."

I leave off the thousands, a trick to ease the calculating. "That is more than double and in only five years. That means that in another five years, we will have seventy thousand."

"Unless we grow even faster. What is to stop us?" Nothing: to hear Daniel tell it. "People from around the country, even the world, are drawn here seeking their fortune. Germans, Irish, Hungarians... "

I know now that what people call the Dutch are rightly to be called Germans. The Dutch are another thing entirely. "You do not mind the foreigners?" I ask him. Obadiah favors the native-born, I well remember. Here in St. Louis so many Irish are coming—like Ina, I well remember, who helped me on the steamboat. They seek their fortune, but also there is a famine in their homeland.

"Why should I, especially the rich ones?" Daniel twists to smile down at me. His blue eyes twinkle. "Do they not need property? Am I not just the man to locate it for them?"

"I believe St. Louis is still much smaller than New Orleans." I will always have fondness for that place and the people who live there.

Daniel waves away my words with the hand holding the cigar. "New Orleans is three times the size, but it is the rate of growth I speak of. That is where a man finds his opportunity."

Perhaps where a woman finds hers, too. I get the idea Madam Lantos is pleased with the number of gentlemen crowding our metropolis. More and more have been introduced to this house, and I, shall we say, have met them. I will not mention that to Daniel, though, as it is indiscreet to speak of other gentlemen when you are lying naked beside one of them.

"When you walk about," Daniel says, "I am sure you see the new buildings. I know you're a great one for walking. You and I should walk together."

I laugh and do not bother to cover my mouth as a lady would. Of course a lady would not be sprawled naked atop the bed linens, either. "You would be seen with me?" By now I am as well-known a doxy as Charity. Even when I walk alone looking demure as a virgin, ladies cross the street so their skirts will not brush mine, or they look through me as if I wasn't there. Perhaps they fear being a whore is catching. If they learned how much money I make, it might become so.

"Life is too short for Puritanical views." Daniel cups my breast with his free hand as if to prove the point. "Besides, I have no wife."

"There is another problem. I am not to have assignations"— that is the fancy word Madam Lantos uses—"outside this house."

"Ah." His hand leaves my breast so he can rub his thumb against the first two fingers of that hand, in the gesture of money. "I am sure I can make an arrangement with Madam Lantos. Do you know what else I desire to do with you outside these walls? Take you to dine at Planters House."

He begins to describe Planters House then, as if I have never seen the inside of it, and I do not correct him on the point. The details of that hotel are seared in my memory, as is the mocking ring of Chouteau's laughter. *You cannot even read, yet you imagine yourself my wife?*

Never have I begun an evening in this house without fearing that I should descend the stairs to find his tall, broad-shouldered frame. After all, a year ago I refused to give myself to him. I even drew his blood. He might come to this place knowing I lack the power to refuse him here. *A man is king when he comes here,* Madam Lantos says. *Whatever he wants, short of drawing blood, you give to him.* Is Chouteau the sort of man who would force the point? What would I do in the case?

A week later Daniel makes a bargain with Madam Lantos and so we have a date for our excursion. Indeed I am a great one for walking—I believe Madam Lantos is correct about its benefits— but it is dinner at Planters House that Daniel most wants. And so, on a temperate autumn night, I adorn myself in my favorite silver gown and beaded shawl for my first outing of the type since that disastrous evening with Chouteau a year ago.

First Daniel hands me up into his phaeton so that he might drive me about to admire his various properties. There is an impressive number and I sing their praises to the stars above. I find it interesting how the prices vary so from one location to the next. After he shows me one at Broadway and Olive, we proceed two blocks west, away from the river, and he tells me the values here are lower by twenty percent. Another five blocks further, they are lower by eighty percent.

Daniel brings the horses to a halt. "For this is considered out of town." Indeed it is shocking quiet here, almost like the country-side. "But it will not be so for long. These values will rise fast as the city grows. What is out of town today will be in town tomorrow."

My mind works as I hear this. This sounds like Opportunity. "I see how the value going up would make the man who owns it richer, but he doesn't really enjoy the benefit, does he, until he sells?"

"Perhaps he may rent it out."

"I see. Then immediately he can pocket the rents." The men of business always find a way to make money sooner than later. "If it is so easy to be sure these values will go up, any man can make money this way."

Daniel smiles. "Any man with money to spend. And nerve to take the risk."

"What is the risk? You say St. Louis will not stop growing."

"It will not stop, not in this favored location where the Missouri and Mississippi rivers meet. But"—he frowns—"some things do slow commerce. A bad year for yellow jack, say, or a raging fire." Daniel slaps the reins and the horses turn about and back we head downhill.

"Must it be a man?" I ask after a time. "Might not a woman buy property?"

"What woman has the money?"

"If a woman did have the money, is it legal for her to buy property?"

"She must have both money and nerve," and that sounds as if it is legal if not the usual case. Daniel casts me a sidelong glance. "Do you know such a woman?"

I giggle and say no, but I wonder if I do.

I do not look about as I step from the phaeton in front of Planters House as I am half afraid I will catch the eye of a carriage driver I questioned a year ago about the city's bawdy houses. Could they tell that now I, too, am an inmate of one such? My clothes are very fine and never do I embrace a tarted-up appearance. Yet I know I cannot muster the bearing of a true lady. Perhaps a country rube I might fool, but it ends there.

As I take Daniel's arm, I must quell the tears that rise to my eyes. Would my father's heart break if he saw me now, dressed in silver finery but a whore all the same? I do not even know if his heart still beats. It is so for my brother and sisters, too, and, yes, my mother. And of course all of them would wonder whether I still live, if they think of me at all. What a deep cut is made when you leave behind the family of your birth. The scar is always there, I think, covered though it may be by years and forgetfulness, and in my case by a strange brew of pride and shame.

Inside Planters House heads swivel toward Daniel and me. He, too, holds his head high. As if by magic he leads me to a part of the hotel I have never seen. We step inside an enormous empty room, only half lit. "*Et voilà*, the grand ballroom"—Daniel sweeps his free arm—"inspired by the Temple of Erechtheus." That is in Greece, he tells me, so here, too, as at the Courthouse, I am to think grand ideas. I will say that this chamber with marble and gilding and carvings is beyond anything I have seen before, and like Daniel I do feel a pride that this city of mine—I think I may call it that—boasts such a structure.

Tonight I will dine in the same high-ceilinged room as a year ago, but not behind curtains, which provides me a secret satisfaction. Here, as outside, I do not look about much, for I have seen a few gentlemen I know, some to a fair degree, and I feel sure they do not wish me to send them across the room a knowing smile. I feel the eyes of ladies upon me, too, for there are some here, and I believe many would move their chairs away if they could.

Fried oysters and broiled grouse are soon laid before us, along with dishes I cannot name, and Daniel tells me that we have a room upstairs for four and a quarter dollars per person per day—I asked the price; I was so curious—which includes four meals sumptuous as this one. What a friend Daniel is to so indulge me.

He eyes me keenly over the emptying platters. "You are more comfortable here than I thought you might be."

I am thinking what to say when he guesses the truth.

"Ah, you *have* been here before." He holds up his hands as if to stop me speaking. "I will not ask with whom, for I do not wish to know. Actually"—he leans close across the table—"I do wish to know. Tell me who before me would treat you to such an extravagant jaunt."

I shake my head. "Madam Lantos would not like it."

"She is not here to know." He narrows his eyes at me. "All right, then, tell me the initials and I shall guess it." Daniel does not know this is a game I cannot play. "You might as well tell me," he says, "for I shall tickle it out of you later."

I will not be able to hold it in then. "Tell no one," I order then lower my voice. "Charles Pierre Chouteau."

Daniel's eyes fly open as he settles back in his chair. "Well, I cannot be jealous of Chouteau as he could buy and sell me a thousand times." He dabs at his lips with a snowy white napkin. "By the by, he is returned from Europe."

"He has been away there?"

"And now he is returned. To stay." So there has been no danger of Chouteau appearing at Madam Lantos. But now there is. "I do not know if he will be seeing you now he is back, for there is news. He is betrothed."

I lower my eyes, as I must compose myself, and under

Daniel's watchful gaze, too, for he would not expect me, a bawd, to care one way or another whether such a renowned gentleman is betrothed. But ignorant Eliza did care once, very much. I ask a question though I am not sure I truly desire to know the answer. "Who is the young lady?"

Daniel waits until we are served again—custard pudding and more champagne—before he tells me. "Julia Augusta Gratiot."

This is not the first I am hearing that family name. I believe Gratiot is one of the rich Creole families Obadiah mentioned to me a year ago.

"This betrothal is no surprise to anyone," Daniel goes on, "as the Chouteaus and Gratiots cannot seem to stop marrying each other."

"What do you mean?" I ask, though already I know the answer.

"Chouteau's own mother is a Gratiot. Emilie Anne, I believe is her name." Daniel sips his champagne. Like all men of business, he must understand who the important families are and how they are allied with one another and how they make their fortune and who is feuding with whom. "And, if you can believe it, Julia's father carries the name Chouteau as well. It's these fur-trading families. They want to keep the money close. Julia's father is not in the trade. He is a military man—General Charles Chouteau Gratiot, Junior, is the name, if I have it right—but that is where the money comes from."

This is all as Obadiah said it would be. And the name of Chouteau's bride is Julia, an excellent lady's name, and her father is a general. I have never known one such; those seem very high-born. No doubt this Julia can not only paint and sing and read and write but do the same in French, too, and pronounce *aiguille* perfectly while never thinking to touch such an item save for entertainment.

I clear my throat. "Do you know... is she a beauty?"

Daniel leans close. "My dear Eliza, there is no chance under this heavenly sky that Julia is near the beauty you are."

I must compose myself again after that, and Daniel watches me do it, and though I have said near nothing of Chouteau, Daniel must guess I fancied him. Well, before I hated him I did fancy him, and if I were hearing this from another man than Daniel he might mock me for it, so this is a mercy the heavens are allowing me.

I cannot stop myself from saying the thing scratching at my mind like a hungry dog at the house door. "I wonder sometimes what I would be if I were highborn." If my father were a general and my mother a lady; if I knew how to read and write and eat and dress and speak; what would I be, compared to this Julia?

Daniel raises his champagne glass as if in toast. "You would be legendary. But let us both hope that being lowborn does not keep us from greatness. Or at least mediocrity."

We laugh at that and I push thoughts of Chouteau aside, and later, upstairs at Planters House—whose bedchambers I can assure Daniel I have never seen before this night—I make certain Daniel is the one to feel like a king.

The next morning when I alight from his phaeton in front of the house, he watches me hand coins to the ragged women and children gathered there. "If you make of that a habit," he says, "they shall pursue you like hounds on the track."

"Madam Lantos has already told me I am luring guttersnipes to her door." But I will not stop, for to these wretched souls I am rich as Chouteau. And though I wonder what I might be if I were highborn, I should just as well wonder what would be my fate if I had less than I do. I have beauty and my ease with numbers and *that quality that has no name.* And, I must not forget, the head on my shoulders. Without those I might be begging outside a bawdy house. And someday—for who can be sure what life will bring?— that might still be my fate.

As the days pass, I think about Chouteau and how he is returned to St. Louis. I remember the two lines of blood running down his hand last I saw him and how he would not have minded if my skirts had got caught in the wheels of his carriage.

One year later Chouteau may still be angry with me. If he comes to Madam Lantos's to have me, it might be to humiliate me, or worse.

I think about that. Really, I do more than think: I am planful about it.

It is only when so much time passes that I begin to believe Chouteau will never darken Madam Lantos's parlors that he appears.

He strides into the busy rear parlor and looks as he ever did, handsome and rich and as if he were a god gazing down upon the rest of us. He creates a certain stir among the gentlemen and even Madam Lantos fawns over him.

I sit on a sofa and feign a calm I do not feel. I am wearing my ruby-colored gown, which embarrasses me as harlots are tied to that color: it is believed to connote heat of a type desirable in our kind. Too well I remember Chouteau's words: *I might enjoy the fire in you. But there is only one way I ever again wish to see it.* Yet Madam Lantos chose this fabric, so its color is muted and, dare I say, refined.

As my heart throbs painfully against my ribs and my mind struggles to call back the details of my scheme, Chouteau and I stare at each other across the parlor. If he is surprised to see me, he does not show it. I do not know that I control my features so well. I have the idea Madam Lantos senses something between us and that Charity does too, for I feel her eyes hard upon me, willing me to look at her. I dare not. I fear risking the courage I must summon.

Of one thing I am certain: it is me Chouteau will buy this night.

Madam Lantos orders from the cellar her finest burgundy— she is always one to know when to choose the dearest vintages— and Chouteau signals that I, among all the harlots, am to be poured a glass, and I can tell the wine's quality for Madam Lantos will not allow it watered down.

The transaction is negotiated quickly and I am given the nod.

A housemaid accompanies Chouteau and me to my bedchamber carrying the bottle—heaven forbid he should be troubled—so I have a few moments more to gather myself.

I am fearful, yes, but do I truly believe Chouteau would try to harm me? Every gentleman here knows it is Eliza Haycraft who mounted the stairs before him. And harming a woman, even such a one as me, is beneath a man who ranks so high. Still, I too well remember the strength of his hold when we tussled on the stairs at Planters House.

And there is another point on my side. A whore I may be, but a country rube I am no longer. Though no lady would count it a point of pride, my experience in the bedchamber must put Chouteau's to shame. He might have been master of me a year ago, but on this night we shall see. We shall see.

Once inside my candle-lit bedchamber, I pivot before the window to face Chouteau. The housemaid sets down the wine bottle and leaves us. I lick my lips and wait for him to speak.

"*Et voilà.*" He smirks. "You look well."

"As do you. How was your time in Europe helping to run your father's business?"

For a moment, surprise erases his smug expression. He is irked, I am sure, that I know of his movements, and at the hint he is more his father's son than his own man. He gathers himself. "It was pleasurable. As I am sure tonight will be."

I say nothing to that but move to pour more burgundy into the wineglasses. I hand him one, sip from my own, and wait for him to speak again.

"I am not surprised to find you in such a place as this," he tells me. He samples his wine and again produces a superior smile. "I have friends who told me as much. You have, what shall I call it, a certain *notoriété.*" His gaze drops to my bosom, well exposed in this gown. "As you know, I have little need for a *bordel.* I have my mistresses and naturally I prefer them."

"Still, for me you came here. I will say I am flattered."

"You are right to be flattered by my attentions. You have not always been."

I incline my head. "I am not the woman I was a year ago," I tell him, and indeed with those words do not speak a lie.

He walks close and his finger lifts my chin so that once again we gaze into each other's eyes. "The true reason I am here," he says, "is because you and I have business to finish," and with that he sets down his wineglass. His gaze moves to my mouth. With firmness he pulls me close and lays his lips upon mine.

Oh, for now it is my scheme to do what I am paid to do, as I wish him to believe he has the better of me and perhaps only later find out—*mon Dieu!*—that he does not. So after a time of lightly playing, I open my mouth fully, as only a wanton would. I tongue him softly and yet with growing abandon. I breathe heavily, as if seized by passion. I feel against my belly that a strong ardor has Chouteau in its grip. Then, as if overwhelmed by uncontrollable rapture, I slosh wine from the glass I still hold down Chouteau's neck and back.

He jerks away from me.

"Oh, my God," I cry, "I am so very sorry," and I scramble about to find a piece of fabric with which to dry him.

"*Quel gâchis,*" he mutters, stepping about with some awkwardness, but he can do little to help himself as the wetness is on the back of him.

"I am so very sorry," I repeat, now rubbing his waistcoat and trousers with fabric pulled from a pillow. I bend low and hide my smile. "And I did not wish to do a single thing this night to displease you."

He throws off his waistcoat well as my ministrations. "Well, you have done so all the same."

"I am so very sorry," I say yet again, but to myself think, with some satisfaction: that makes one time. For Chouteau's quickened breathing has slowed to its usual pace and I see that his ardor has flagged.

"Allow me to repent," I murmur, and move close to run my

hands over his chest. "Your heart throbs so," I whisper before I open his shirtfront with gentle hands to kiss and lick and nibble his exposed flesh. Onto his neck I move my mouth, and with my hand, oh so softly, I begin to tease his groin. In time I can tell that Chouteau has forgotten the wine and is responding to my attentions. Only then do I speak again. "I told you I am not the woman I was a year ago," I murmur, my breath feathery against his ear. "I have done things you cannot imagine." I pause to let him think what those might be, if he can. "Tell me your deepest, most secret desires. Anything, anything: however scandalous. Do not fear you will surprise or shock me. For all I desire to do is give you pleasure."

I hear him swallow. Perhaps he *will* come up with something.

"After all this time"—my fingers keep moving, working their sly magic through the silken fabric of his trousers—"all this lost time, I wish to pleasure you in whatever extravagant way will most please you."

"Extravagant," he mutters.

"Would you like me to call in another girl to be with us?" I whisper.

A groan escapes him. "No."

I lower my voice still more. "A boy?"

He stills—oh, I think I have shocked him now—and I giggle quietly. "I know just the one to join our party. Such pleasure you will have! I am so glad I thought of it." I break away and spin toward the door. "She looks like a girl, and I suppose she is, but, oh, I will not tell you the secret, you must see for yourself—"

"Eliza." His voice is strangled. "I do not desire even to imagine such a thing."

I turn back to face him. "Oh, but you cannot really imagine it. You must see it with your own eyes. She is but down the corridor," I assure him, "and even if she is busy with someone else I am sure that for you—"

"Eliza." He speaks with more firmness. "Forget all that and come away from that door."

I return to him on swift feet, making a show of docility. "Oh, I am sorry." And this makes two times, for he is now gruff and frowning instead of ardent and ready.

"I wish you to take off your gown," he says after a moment.

"Oh, yes. But please take more wine. I will say I wish I had some, too," and after I press his glass into his hand I find the bottle to replenish my own. He takes a gulp and I do the same then keep my eyes lowered in a show of submission.

"I said I wish for you to take off your gown," he repeats.

"Of course, gladly," and I make a show of first pulling free my hairpin and tossing it behind me so that it scuttles harmlessly across the floorboards. Then, with as much provocation as I can muster, I comply. Bending so that my breasts near tumble from my corset, I remove my fancy boots and lace stockings. It is a task to take off my gown, but I have him aid me, running his hands over my body as he cares to, until I step away clad only in corset and pantalettes. Slowly I turn so that Chouteau can admire his prize fully in the candles' glow, my curves firm and flesh ripe, and see clearly that he is responding, for a third time, as any man would.

I draw him to my tall mirror and, with him standing behind me, bend to free my breasts from my corset. Oh, he is getting what he wants now, a full measure of it, for as he fondles me I arch my back and rub my behind against him. I feel the bulge of him, hear the quickening of his breath, and then...

I straighten and spin about. "Wait," I pant, "there is a most delicious oil I wish to find for us, from Arabia I am told, to provide you the most exquisite pleasure," and away I move toward my armoire. This makes three times and this time I have got him very close.

Chouteau is red-faced and urgent. "Go to that bed," he manages to say, and points helpfully in that direction. But I will not move so quickly.

"Please give me but a moment." I open my armoire and poke around inside. "It is close at hand, I am sure of it."

"Eliza." He steps forward to grab my arm and spin me about.

There is that strength again. I force myself not to resist but to remain pliant as a rag doll. "What do you wish of me? I seek only to please you. I know I can find the oil. The sensation is produces is so—I do not even know the word to describe it. I need look only a moment longer."

"What would please me is less talk." He is speaking now through clenched teeth. "Back to where we were."

"Oh, of course." I move toward the mirror.

"No." Again he grabs my arm to steer me toward the bed.

I bow my head and produce a beseeching smile when I turn around. "Let me help you," and I move to aid him in removing his trousers. Perhaps I am a little forceful, though, for I catch him, engorged as he is, at an odd angle.

He winces.

"I am so sorry," I tell him, "let me," but he swats my hands away. He steps back, less engorged now, I see, and I do not think happy about it. Still, I lay back upon the pillows, for he will mount me, though after a time it seems clear there is not much good to come from that. "Oh, dear," I murmur, "this has never happened before with so young a man. This is terrible."

He pushes words past taut lips. "Do not speak, Eliza."

"And I so wished to please you." Oh, I see the strain in him. "Dear me," I repeat, "I must blame myself," and at his glare I look away and shut my eyes.

A moment later I rally and try to help, or least seem to, but he has little use for my aid now. Impressive in anticipation, he is, in the moment, deflated. Still, he labors on. Finally, after a sweaty but fruitless interlude, he lifts himself from me and grabs the stained trousers tumbled on the floor.

"I am so sorry," I tell him as he dresses with jerking motions. "Be assured no one will hear a word about this from me. Not one of the girls here, or any gentleman ever. I know how to keep a secret."

Chouteau looks as if he is about to spit fire. He flees my

bedchamber without another word. I throw on a negligée and run to the landing to hear him gallop down the stairs.

I have learned a thing or two about men this last year. Starting and stopping and starting and stopping may be fine for a mule pulling a gig along the street, but it is not so good for a man in a bedchamber. And, so it happens, humiliation in that place is not the province of women alone.

I remain at the landing, my ears perked, and though the house is noisy at this hour, I hear the front door open then slam shut, giving all the paintings on the walls a mighty rattle. I believe, at last, Chouteau has left us.

Chapter Thirteen

"This deed made and entered into this twenty eighth day of July in the year of our Lord eighteen hundred and forty six by and between James Gillespie of the City and County of St Louis and State of Missouri party of the first part and Eliza Haycraft of the same City County and State party of the second part... "

— Book D4, Page 4

— Recorder of Deeds Archive, St. Louis, Missouri

I STAND ON LAND SHIMMERING UNDER ST. LOUIS'S HELL-HOT SUMMER SUN and look down at my high-button shoes—dusty through my own fault from standing in the dirt—and wonder how I might feel if I actually owned the house that hulks upon this rectangle of earth. I might feel, I think, rich as Queen Victoria herself.

Daniel stands beside me, blue eyes squinting in the glare. He points again to the two-story frame house, which has little to recommend it. "Remember," he says, "it is only the house available for purchase."

"Not the lot." I am clear on the point. "It is Dr. B.G. Farrar who owns the lot. And a James Gillespie who wishes to sell the house."

"Yes. Gillespie has leased from Dr. Farrar the portion of the lot on which the house stands."

It is a large amount to keep in the head. One name is familiar, though: that of Dr. Farrar. I do not know him intimately, shall we say, but by reputation. He is famous for being first to settle permanently in our city to practice medicine and so is called Father of the Profession. Many speak of him with reverence.

Daniel removes his hat to wipe sweat from his brow. "Let us take shade in the phaeton," he suggests, and I agree immediately as I know very well that blond Daniel cannot abide the sun as can I.

The horses whinny and stomp as we near—they are ready to be off and telling us so best they can—but I wish to admire this spot a spell longer. "It would be bold of me to do this thing," I tell Daniel as we settle in the phaeton, "very bold indeed." How many women buy property, after all?

"Boldness is part of the appeal," Daniel says, "to you and me both."

The great appeal to me, of course, is to step up in the world. If I wish to be another Madam Lantos, *more* than Madam Lantos, I must have my own house. After near two years with her, I have come to understand that while Madam Lantos has her own house, she rents our stone mansion: she does not own it. This feeble structure at which I now squint, looking as if it might topple in a strong wind, is no match for that mansion. Still, it would give me a bawdy house of my own, and if I am able to purchase it, too, I will also enjoy its increased value over time. No, it is not in the best neighborhood and no one would call it fancy, but if it were either I could not afford it.

"Let us go to Vauxhall," Daniel says, "and enjoy a beer."

I am all for that scheme. This is one tradition the Germans have brought to St. Louis that I approve.

Soon Daniel and I are two of many people settled at rough-hewn tables nestled beneath the shade of chestnut trees. Before us are set steins of frothy beer. Daniel raises his as if in toast and speaks with false sternness. "As we toast, Eliza, you must gaze into my eyes and never for a moment waver."

"I am happy to do it, but why?"

"Because the Germans believe that if you look away during a toast, for even an instant, you will suffer seven years of unhappiness in the bedchamber."

"Oh no!" I cry in mock horror. "Especially for one such as myself, that would be unfortunate, indeed."

"I should not like it, either. Let us toast"—he raises his stein higher—"to the chance that you will, before the month is out, conclude a purchase of property."

We clink steins, gazes unwavering, and sip. "I hope I am not putting a hex on it," I say, "toasting before the thing is done."

"I was careful to say 'to the chance' that you purchase property. And you are right: until the ink dries on the deed, it is not done."

I am seeing a problem: I cannot read what will be written on such a deed. Nor am I able to put my signature to it. This I must admit to Daniel and hope he does not think much less of me. And I must trust him about what is set down on the deed. Yet Daniel is like Obadiah to me, though, or Chantal, or Charity. I do trust him. In a world where those like me are shunned, it is a joy to have friends like these. I do not know what would become of me without them.

Daniel sets down his stein and lowers his voice. "If you wish to buy Gillespie's house, you must present three hundred dollars in cash."

"I am able to do that." Not that it has been easy to save so much. "And of course I will pay you, as we discussed, for helping me do this." It feels strange to speak such words. It makes me feel like a woman of business, as if there is such a thing.

"I aim to serve." Daniel winks. "When first you said you desired to purchase property, Eliza, I thought it very bizarre. But on further reflection I find that it is"—he searches for a word—"modern."

It was months after Daniel showed me his properties that I broached the topic. I trembled as I did so. But trembling often stops, does it not, when finally you act? "I don't suppose," I say, "that you will tell Gillespie my plan for the house?"

"You mean that the house Gillespie built will become a cathouse?"

"A quiet and discreet cathouse. And Gillespie will always be welcome."

A WEEK later I am walking to the bank, a regular errand, under clouds low and grumbling, like sullen children. It will rain and I will be joyful for it, for I am desperate for the air to cool and for the filth on the streets to be carried off to the river where the poor fish will be the ones that must swim around it.

I am near the bank when I see those women again, the ones who forever dress in dark colors—I suppose they are always in a mourning of sorts—who speak out against one thing and for another. As is usual, today they raise their voices against slavery and for the rights of women. I agree with them on both points, but still I am not their friend and they are not mine. They know I am a trollop and so seek to reform me.

One is bold enough to come near. She is gray-haired and well-fed and has a determined air about her. In her hand she clutches a brochure I have been given before, though of course I cannot read it. That day I took it, I handed it to Charity who read it aloud to us doxies as we dined, about the *abuses and usurpations* women suffer and how they make us *abject* and how *scanty* is our pay for the few ways men allow us to work.

We all had a hearty laugh at that. And, I thought, why do these women think whores become whores? Maybe once I am rich I will take up their cause, but for now I have my independence to gain. And I wonder if I am not doing something for all women if I buy property? After all, I am not waiting for a man to give me permission.

The woman blocks my way to hand me the brochure and I take it in the hope I need not battle her. "There is another path for you," she tells me. "Factory work. Honest labor that will not sear your soul."

I try to step around her. "I am not against you, but that work is not for me."

"It is not your fault you do what you do." Again she blocks my way. "It is because men will not allow you to earn as they do. That is the problem's root."

"That is the way the world is."

"Why should women who do what you do bear all the criminal blame?" she asks me. "The men should be prosecuted as well as you."

"Then the constables could collect from both sides," I point out.

At that her mouth twists into a frown and her eyes narrow. "You must repent. God may call you at any time."

If it is not my fault I do what I do, why would God condemn me? But I don't say that, or remind her that Advent never came, which made me think my time to face Him has been put off a good long way.

"I understand what anguish you feel," she tells me, "how your soul is destroyed by what you do."

"My soul is not destroyed," I tell her and watch her eyes fly open in shock. "It is healthy as yours. And I am sorry, but I must go to the bank," and I push past her in a way that is rude—but I could not get past her otherwise—and feel her eyes on my back as I progress up the street.

Does she think the souls of the men who come to me are destroyed? I don't think so. She says women should be treated the same as men, but even she thinks us weaker. Perhaps my great whorish sin is thinking as a man would: that sex is sex and that is the end of it. At least she did not tell me that I am luring innocent men into vile acts they would never think of on their own. I have heard that more times than I can count. And when I stop laughing, it makes me angry.

I reach the bank and wipe the sweat from my brow. This is another grand building with ceilings high as the clouds and many pillars. I know that here, too, I am to feel small in the presence of greatness. What is it that is great, though? The money stored here or the men who possess the money? But for that money, even they would feel themselves small.

I am allowed inside because the men who work here know me. Of course they would not allow a woman to have an account of her own so Daniel set up one that I might use. This is another way I must trust Daniel.

Every time I stride inside, I enjoy how my heels click on the shiny floor, as if I am important enough to make a racket. I nod and smile at the men of banking. At first I did not like the idea of banking because the Chouteau family had to do with founding the banks in this city. Their hands, I am sorry to say, reach everywhere. Well, I must keep my money somewhere and I wager that even a Chouteau bank is safer than my bedchamber at Madam Lantos's. The men of banking certainly try to make it look safe with all of them conducting their work inside metal cages.

This bank does not know it, but soon I will take away three hundred dollars. I can scarce believe it; I will not trust it yet; but this means I will own property for the first time. Yes, it is a timid house, and an ugly one, but it is a house all the same, with four rooms and a kitchen back.

I think, as I walk up to one of the cages and take from my

reticule my money to deposit, that if I had not pushed Madam Lantos to pay me more than the usual, I would not have near the money I do. I believe it has made all the difference. Of course, Madam Lantos wanted to earn as much from me as from any other strumpet. Since she had to pay me a third and not a quarter of what I earned, she had to charge a higher rate for me. Now I understand, too, why she wanted only two weeks at the start. It was not just to see if I would really do the work and get along with the other bawds. She did not know if men would pay the higher rate. And if they paid it once, would they pay it a second time?

Yes, they would. And they are paying it still, even though I am growing old—now twenty-six. And so for two years now I am earning a third of a higher rate.

I have never spoken about this with Charity, but maybe this is why she is a scattergood. The expenses Madam Lantos charges are so high and Charity earns only a quarter of a lower rate, so never can she save enough money to have a house of her own. So why scrimp and save, she must think? Why not enjoy life now?

She would like New Orleans, would Charity.

I RETURN to the house to be told that Madam Lantos wishes to see me in her bedchamber. This has happened only once before, when Madam Lantos got the idea I wished to remove to Madam Hunter's. I assured her I did not. I am happy here, and I have Charity here, and I am used to life here, and I am sure I earn more here.

Madam Lantos's bedchamber is biggest in the house, of course, on the second floor, and in the rear, away from the street. She has windows on two sides, both open now to the scant breeze, with draperies so long that even tied back with tassels they crash to the floor in puddles of blue silk. The walls are papered with a print so delicate you can scarce see it—I have learned that is an elegant style—and the dark furnishings gleam from polish. Hanging across from the canopied bed is an oil portrait that Charity swears is Madam Lantos's most prized possession. It is of a royal-looking beauty with white skin, light hair curled and bejeweled, and a secret smile, as if there were many mischievous things she could tell you if she chose. There is the look of a naughty Madam Lantos about her. A Hungarian painted it, Charity whispered: those are Madam Lantos's people.

I find her in her tub, the water no doubt cool, her hair piled high, her body covered by thin fabric as she soaks. The room smells of heavenly lavender. Give a harlot a bath and she will be happy: that is what I think. It is our time to clean everything away —even what a man may have left inside us.

She eyes me from head to toe and back again. Though she is tiny as can be and lies naked in a tub while I stand full dressed before her, somehow she has a strong power about her. That is the amazement of Madam Lantos. "There you are again in the yellow," she says. "That dress is of an old style. Look at those sleeves."

"This dress is a ray of sunshine." And Chantal made it, so it is dear to me.

"The dressmaker is coming tomorrow," Madam Lantos tells me. "I wish you to order three new dresses."

Months ago she said the same, but somehow I made her forget. Oh, the cost: and when it is property on which I wish to spend my money! I force a laugh. "If a client stares overlong at my sleeves, I will just draw his attention elsewhere."

"You will order three new dresses, Eliza."

She is no longer wishing it: she is demanding it. I should stop speaking now or she might cry out for six dresses. This is one way Madam Lantos keeps her trollops in her house: they have such high expenses they cannot save enough money to do anything but stay with her.

"It is important that my girls show the latest style," she goes on, running her fingers lightly through her bath water. "That is expected of this house."

I nod and lower my gaze. Dear God, there are times I feel little more than a stray cat to be cast out if Madam Lantos were of a mind to do it. But so it must be, for now. And I can make up for this money that I must now spend. Some nights I could beat back my fatigue and squeeze in yet one more client. And some months my course runs short and I could return to work one night sooner. I am thinking that is the end of it and am turning to go when she speaks again.

"I do not like that you spend so much time with Mr. Godfrey."

My heart scuttles in my chest, as if I have leapt to the side of the road to avoid a careening carriage. "He pays you richly for my services."

"Not so richly. He does not pay me for every hour you spend with him."

"Why should he?" That is out before I can bite it back.

She straightens in the tub. A fresh wave of lavender fills my nostrils. "He is a client of this house. You met him at this house. That is why."

I shudder to think she might order me to stop seeing Daniel, now of all times. I take a breath to steady myself. Then: "Please, Madam Lantos. Mr. Godfrey will not stop coming here, regardless how many times I see him outside. And he is my friend. I have so few. And no family," I add, though that may or may not be so.

"This is what I fear. That you are in love with him, or he with you."

Of course, love is one way Madam Lantos loses her doxies. Or, perhaps it is better to say, what a girl or a man mistakes for love. I can speak firmly on this point. "I will never be one man's mistress, Madam Lantos, no matter how fond I might be of him. I will never trust that life."

"I do not care to hear the word *never*. I do not believe it when a woman says *never*." She scowls at me and for the first time I see a wrinkle mar her perfect brow. "And what of marriage? What if Mr. Godfrey were to ask you to marry him?"

I am flattered she thinks that possible but laugh because I cannot help myself. "He is enjoying life too much to marry. I expect him to put that off for years yet."

She seems not to believe that, either. "You do understand that if you marry, you and everything you possess will become your husband's property?"

I have not thought about that, because when I married—or thought I did—I had nothing. Now it is a different matter. And now I have one more reason to hope I was not lawfully married to John Haycraft, so that he may not reappear to claim my money for his own. "I have no interest in marrying," I can say truthfully.

She thinks for a moment, her green eyes trained on the water's ripples. Then: "I will not say you cannot see Mr. Godfrey outside this house. But I do not wish you to parade yourself with him as you have been doing. The gentlemen in this city must believe you are as freely available to them as ever, that you are as eager to please any of them as ever, that your body is not bound to one."

She gestures that I am to leave her and I do. I could near cry with relief. That is the end of Planters House for Daniel and me, least for now.

As DANIEL and I ride in his phaeton through the dusty streets, the sun is a hellish globe of heat and the poor horses glisten with sweat. I am wearing the first lady's dress I ever owned, the one in the color of bluebells, made by Chantal and paid for by Obadiah. I wish to honor them both on this day that I make my first purchase of property. They are the two who really taught me about the world. Without them I would never have tried such a thing as this.

In my reticule, clutched tight, I carry three hundred of the dollars I have earned, and on my chatelaine is my sheathed dagger. I do not doubt Daniel would beat back a thief if need be, but as I begin to claim my independence I wish to stand, at least a little, on my own feet. Though there is one way I cannot stand alone and I have yet to confess it. I signal Daniel to halt the horses.

"Are you frightened?" He is smiling because he knows the answer is no.

"Only of this. There is something I never told you." I take a breath. "I cannot read or write."

Daniel drops back as if my words have sucked the air from his lungs. "But you and I discuss what is in the newspaper. Just minutes ago we were talking about the drought."

St. Louis has had a shocking number of days over a hundred degrees. Crops are dying in the fields. The people who know say that 1846 is the hottest year this century. How is it possible that two years ago we had the Great Flood and now this? "I can talk about the drought," I say, "because Charity reads the newspaper to me. She is from Massachusetts and the girls there are taught to read same as the boys."

He considers this. "And so you cannot write, either."

"My brother can, least he can sign his name, because my father taught him. But he did not teach my sisters or me. He taught me my numbers," I add, because I thank my father on this day, too, so much that suddenly my eyes sting. He would hate how I earned this three hundred dollars, but I believe he would be proud of me just the same. My mother and Sarah would harrumph. My mother would say this still does not make me special. Nothing could make me special but flying to the moon on angel's wings and even that she would find a way to spit on.

Daniel shakes his head then smiles. "You are a dark horse, aren't you?"

When he explains what that means, I smile and agree that I am. Then he tells me how I will sign the deed: I will write an X in the space between my first and last names and over that X the clerk will write *her* and below the X the clerk will write *mark*. "Her mark," Daniel says, "the X written in your hand is your mark."

I must ask one question more, though it makes me feel very ignorant to do so. "How do I write an X?"

He shows me and once I understand I am ready again for the horses to move. I feel better, too, for I am not the only person who cannot sign my name. This is not a strange way to sign papers, Daniel assures me: I am not the first to do it so.

In the end there is nothing fancy about how I purchase the two-story frame house. Standing in the hot, cramped city office, Mr. Gillespie seems a nice enough man and the clerk too busy to care about either of us. The clerk writes out the deed in an enormous book covered with leather, below another deed written earlier today. As he bends to his task, he and Daniel discuss phrases like *to have and to hold the same* and *rights and privileges thereunto belonging,* which I would not understand even if I did know how to read. Mr. Gillespie signs his name and then the quill is put into my hand and, strange though it feels, I put my X in the small space I am shown. Mr. Gillespie doesn't say a thing about it and the clerk doesn't, either. Daniel smiles at me and I smile at him and then it is over.

Afterward, I ask Daniel if we might ride past the house. This is the first I will cast eyes on it when it is mine, all mine. I will sleep there one night soon, all by myself, but only on a night when I am having my monthly course, because I don't care to miss a night of work and the money I would earn.

Chapter Fourteen

"Love, pain, and money cannot be kept secret. They soon betray themselves."

— Spanish proverb

THE SUNLIGHT OF A BRIGHT SUMMER MORN REVEALS THE TRUTH, whether or not we care to see it.

Alone I stand in my bedchamber in the house of Madam Lantos. Wearing nothing but the skin I was born in, I gaze at my reflection in my mirror. Outside my window the city throbs, and soon I will dress and throw myself in among the melee, but for now I gaze at myself with wide-open eyes.

February next, I will go to twenty-seven years. Some of my skin's freshness is gone: I will admit it. Yet, because I am faithful to parasols, it is so white that one who did not know me might think me an angel. My brow is unlined, as is my mouth. My jaw is firm and as yet there is no hint of the chicken about my neck. My hair is lush and dark and my lashes still long and full. My eyes... what can I say of those? I have to say they reveal the shadow of all that I have seen. Sometimes I must work to raise in them a bright, warm light.

My body has not yet betrayed me. My breasts are high as ever and I am careful not to eat overmuch, so my stomach does not stick out, and I walk every day as Madame Lantos suggests and that keeps me firm in all the places I wish to be so. Am I still a beauty? So I am told. When I hear the word "handsome," I will worry.

These passing years are good for something. A woman must be of a certain age to open a cathouse or the powers-that-be will not take her seriously.

I plan to open my cathouse in four weeks, before the month of August is gone. I will pass just two years under the roof of Madam Lantos. Before that day, there is much to be done, and people to be told.

I worry about telling Charity. I dread telling Madam Lantos. I quiver to think of telling the powers-that-be, whose consent I need above all others.

I dress quickly to run my errand for Charity. Her birthday is on the morrow and she has the girlish notion to make ginger-bread, same as she did as a girl. She wishes me to help. Cook will allow us to use the kitchen so long as we have tidied up by one o'clock. On a day like this, I feel keenly the six years between Charity and me. Why must we waste our time and money on sweets? Yet today of all days I am happy to oblige. So before I have drunk my fill of coffee, I scurry out to purchase the treacle and brown sugar and spices that we need.

Of course, even though Charity and I are alone in the kitchen, I dare not broach the topic of opening my own bawdy house and taking her with me to do it. I believe there is a saying: the walls have ears? So instead we drink coffee and toss flour at one another and giggle at the word *lebkuchenhaeusle*, which is what the

Germans call gingerbread and which reminds me of the word *aiguille,* even though that is French, because both are impossible to pronounce.

"Mr. Zimmerman taught it to me and likes to hear me practice it." Charity winks at me. Her hair is tied back in a kerchief and she has dough on her chin and flour on one cheek. "You won't believe what we're doing some of the times I practice it with him."

"I will believe it," I say, and giggle imagining the tubby Mr. Zimmerman doing wicked things with Charity. He is one of our best German clients. We have more of them than Irish because often they come to this country with money. It is not famine that brings them here but something about the politics in their home country. I have noticed they like to buy property, the Germans—in this way I am like them—and they take great care to have clean stoops.

Charity wishes to cut the rolled-out dough into heart and diamond shapes, which takes an age, but we do it. She reads from a recipe on a scrap of paper that I can tell has been folded and unfolded many times and too often been placed near the baking. " 'Bake in a quick oven in a tin plate,' " she reads. " 'A little time will bake it.' "

I don't know what a "quick oven" is or what is meant by "a little time," but Charity must, because the gingerbread is very good, dipped in cream or dipped in coffee or not dipped at all. As we sample it and rust-colored crumbs collect on the roughhewn table, I watch her carefully fold the recipe and slide it inside her pocket. "Who wrote that recipe?" I ask, though I might already know.

She does not look at me. "My mother."

Charity busies herself with the tidying and I remember that her mother died when Charity was but fourteen. "I can imagine you making gingerbread together," I say, "back in Massachusetts. I wish you could still," and I take her in a hug, and she cries, and I think how hard it is every twelvemonth when your birthday comes around because always you get to thinking about those no longer on this earth with you.

"I took the recipe when I left," Charity says when again she can speak, "because I wanted to keep something in her hand and I didn't want *her* to have it," and I know the *her* is the stepmother who was only too happy to have Charity walk out the door never to return. Charity raises her head to sniffle one last time then speaks again, her tone defiant. "I will make these with my own children someday," and she gives the table one last swipe with the damp rag.

I must do it now. Now is good a time as any and Charity has already brought up The Future. "Come to my chamber," I murmur, "I wish to talk to you about something," and she follows as I knew she would.

I pull Charity to sit on the carpet near the window, the spot furthest from the door. I wish no one to hear us from the landing. By now Charity has loosed her hair from her kerchief and it hangs long and black about her shoulders. The same thought I had when I first met her goes through my mind and it shames me to have it because she is my dear friend but still I am thinking of her as a madam would: here is a young woman with exotic looks that I know can fascinate a man. I also know her skill with a whip and that she can play the innocent, too. Charity has what she likes to call a "full repertoire." She laughs at that, but I know it brings in extra.

"Do you need to come around? Is your course late?" Her face creases with worry. "We could go to the apothecary for a remedy."

"Nothing like that." Nothing like that has ever happened. Sometimes I wonder why. I take a breath. "I have bought a property where I wish to start a bawdy house of my own. And I wish for you to come with me." I grab both her hands. "I wish that with all my heart and soul."

The words spill out fast and maybe that is why Charity can do nothing but frown and look puzzled and repeat the word *but* with different questions attached. *But how did you have the money to do such a thing? But what will you tell Madam Lantos? But why have you never said a word of this before?*

The last is the toughest to answer. Charity is accusing me of something and I cannot say I blame her. "I did not know how long it would take to save the money," I tell her, though that is not the whole of it. "And I wasn't sure that even when I did, that I would have the courage to really do this thing."

Charity rises to her feet shaking her head. "Running your own house… That is much harder than working here. Madam Lantos works all the day long, and the night. She is never at her ease."

I am on my feet now, too. "But think how much money she makes. She has enough money to do whatever she pleases."

"So do I," Charity tells me, and I am so shocked that I cannot think what to say. "And what about when the raids come? You have not seen one at this house, but they are terrible frightening."

So I have been told. Sometimes reformers make the citizens angry and they rise in a mob and attack bawdy houses. Sometimes reformers push the police to raid bawdy houses and we are arrested and sent to the calaboose, with a trial in the morning and penalties to be paid. Afterward, though, I hear it is over until next time.

"I will pay the constables," I tell Charity, "and City Hall, too, just like Madam Lantos does, so we will be just as safe."

Charity shakes her head again. "You have been here only two years, Eliza, not an age like Madam Lantos. They won't protect us like they protect her."

I have known Charity to speak wise words from time to time despite her young age and she has done so now, I admit.

"And who do you have to protect our house?" she wants to know. "Who will be our Joshua?"

I raise a warning finger to my lips so she will lower her voice. "I will find a good man to be our Joshua." I have already spoken of that with Daniel and he is thinking on it. I move closer to Charity, but she spins further away. I do not like what she is telling me by spinning away.

"I am not like you, Eliza," she says. "I do not wish to be a whore my whole life."

"Nor do *I* wish to—"

"You do not think Madam Lantos is still a whore? She may not take a client upstairs anymore, but she is still a whore and everyone knows it."

I do not know what to say to that.

"I knew when you first came here," Charity says, "that you were one to watch. I did not know what you would do, but you would not just stay in your little bedchamber. That is fine for you. But I am not like you. I wish to fall in love and I wish a man to marry me. Like Lydia."

"Yes, Lydia did marry, but—" I stop myself.

"But what?"

I do not care to say what I really think. Lydia told us she married, but I don't know the whole of it. I also do not know that love was involved. All I know is that a small, timid sort of man who from time to time was a client here took her away—or she took him away—and off to Kansas they said they would go. It is not common for a doxy to marry, though sometimes, as with Lydia, an out-of-towner who need not explain much about his bride takes a fancy. I worry that years will pass and never will there come a day when a man offers his hand to Charity. But much as I love her, I will not be the one to give that warning.

"I wish to have children, too." Charity's voice rises. "I do not think you wish for those things."

It is not that I do not wish for them! That is what I long to cry out, what I am biting back. It is that I do not believe they are for me. They are for other women but not for me. They are passing me by. Almost I see them move past me, like ghosts that disappear into walls. I cannot trust in them anymore.

"Charity." I take her hands. She is near to crying. "Can you not find that man working at my house same as working at Madam Lantos's house?"

One tear spills from her eye. "You will try to stop me."

I shake my head. "No. I wish for you to be happy. If he is a good man, like Obadiah—"

"That is the man who was your lover in New Orleans?" I have scarce nodded when she goes on. "You never spoke his name to me before." She pulls her hands from mine. "You kept that from me, too, like you kept secret about the money you saved, like you kept secret about the house you bought. I think you keep another secret, too, about that rich Creole who came to this house last fall."

Chouteau. Of course Charity is keen-eyed enough to have seen something pass between us that night in the parlor.

"There was something with him," she is saying now, "I am sure of it, but do I hear about it from you? No."

And there is still another secret that I keep from Charity, even as I stand facing her. How I married John Haycraft, or thought I did, and how I escaped him.

"How did you even buy this house?" Charity cocks her head, confused eyes shining with tears. "You, who cannot read or write?"

I must not keep this secret, too. "Daniel helped me."

"So you trusted Daniel." Her lips quaver. "You could have asked me to help you. I can read like he can!" She is full crying now, harder than when she remembered her dead mother. "I wish you had told me, Eliza. I thought you were happy, but you weren't and you never told me. Where is this house of yours?"

I tell her, but she only shouts at the answer.

"That is blocks away! All the way across the city! I will never see you anymore when you go there," and she runs from my chamber crying, and Madam Lantos will hear about this if she isn't hearing it already, and maybe she will wonder if after these two years Charity and I are now like the girls who sleep together on the second floor and like each other best, for there are many tears between those two, and yelling, and slamming of doors.

My eyes are still red two hours later when we gather to dine in the kitchen. Charity does not spare me a glance above the roasted chicken. I see she does not have her usual appetite—I don't, either —and I do not know how I will service my clients. It is a rare man who likes to see tears flowing down the cheeks of his harlot.

Why was I so sure Charity would think the same of this that I do? I should not have thrown this at her all at one time, like a boulder from a cliff.

Why do I keep secrets from her, still? That question I can answer. I fear she will say something before thinking it through and what I have will be grabbed away from me. I cannot rest easy. What if I had told Charity about my money and she spoke of it and someone robbed me? What if I had told her about wanting to buy property and Madam Lantos heard about it and stepped in the way? It is not that I do not trust Charity. She would be careful, but she might make a mistake all the same. My own mistakes I can live with; I *must* live with. I do not want to add to those the mistakes others make.

It is the same old thing. It is myself I must rely on. I believe I will go to my grave with this feeling. It is very sad, though, because it makes even those dearest to me seem apart from me.

When I am in my chamber dressing for the evening, a house-maid summons me to Madam Lantos in the rear parlor. I am not surprised, for always Madam Lantos has her ears and eyes wide open. But I get a shock when I reach the parlor, for there is another body standing there, too. Charity.

Madam Lantos wears a gown the color of daffodils, its sleeves of the latest style. "There is a black mood in this house," she says, "because of the two of you. I will not have it."

Madam Lantos could make a dead man sit up and answer questions. Though she will try not to, Charity will tell her about my house. I must tell Madam Lantos myself, though I wanted not to for weeks still. "I told Charity some news today," I hear myself say. My mouth is dry and I must stop to lick my lips. "I have the idea to open a bawdy house of my own, Madam Lantos."

"Ha!" She laughs loud as a thunderclap. I did not think she

was capable of such a sound. "How do you think you will do that?"

There is no hiding it. "I have purchased property on Green Street. A two-story frame house."

"You have purchased a house." She is not laughing anymore. "Where on Green Street?"

"Between Fifth and Sixth."

"How big is this house?"

"Four rooms and a kitchen back."

"And what did you pay for this house?"

"Three hundred dollars, cash in hand."

I can tell I have stunned her. I think she might sink into a chair, but she remains standing. I glance at Charity, white as bed linen when the evening starts.

"You paid for this," Madam Lantos says, "with money you earned here?"

"Yes." I think of bowing my head though I do not know why I should.

"This is what you have been scheming with Mr. Godfrey?"

"I do not think it right to call it scheming, Madam Lantos."

"I do not think any of this is right, Eliza Haycraft." She spins away from me with a swish of her yellow skirts. "And you." She points a finger at Charity. "Are you betraying me as well?"

"No, Madam Lantos." Charity does bow her head. "I do not wish to go with Eliza." She stops, then: "Though she is a dear friend of mine." I see she is again near tears.

"You are wise," Madam Lantos tells Charity, "for your friend has no idea what she is about. Have you furnished this house of yours?" she asks me.

"No."

"Have you hired a man such as Joshua?"

"No."

"A cook?"

This goes on for some time as she asks about housemaids and a housekeeper and a laundress and where I will purchase food and liquor. I notice she does not inquire about the powers-that-be. Maybe she hopes I do not understand that I must make arrangements with them and thinks that will stop me.

"So," she finishes, "you have no whore but yourself and a rickety house in a faraway ugly neighborhood in which no gentleman would put a foot."

I will not tell her what Daniel said: that what is out of town today will be in town tomorrow. Already I have seen improvements on Green Street. And, where there are trollops about, gentlemen are known to journey to all variety of places.

"You may go, Charity," Madam Lantos says, and I wonder as Charity scurries from the parlor with a frightened glance at me what is to come when Madam Lantos and I are alone. Then: "You will find it is not so easy," Madam Lantos tells me, "to put in place this scheme of yours."

Of course she is trying to warn me away. "There are men enough for many bawdy houses in our city," I say. "It is growing by a leap and a bound"—this is a phrase I have heard—"and the need is great."

"If you are a woman of business as you pretend to be, you will understand what I am about to tell you."

I am forced to wait and wonder. Then:

"You may stay in this house until the week's end," Madam Lantos says.

Now I am the one who is stunned. She will throw me onto the street. Out of my bedchamber, away from Charity, removed from everything I have grown to love these two years. I thought I would have all of this until I was ready to depart.

"I would have you leave sooner," she goes on, "but I have commitments for you until the week's end and I do not wish to disappoint my clients."

She is saying, without saying it, that I am one to disappoint and that the gentlemen I service are her clients and not mine.

"Mr. Godfrey is no longer welcome in this house," she goes on. "And for these last few days you are here, I will pay you the rate at which you started and not a coin more. I will not enrich one who schemes to betray me."

She gestures for me to leave. I think she is done speaking until she says one thing more to my back. "I may not be able to stop you, Eliza Haycraft. But I will not make your path an easy one."

Chapter Fifteen

"For one man who sincerely pities our misfortunes, there are a thousand who sincerely hate our success."

— Charles Caleb Colton

— *Lacon: or, Many Things in Few Words; Addressed To Those Who Think*

— 1824

A S I WAKE ALONE OF A MONDAY, after a night huddled in blankets on the rough floorboards of my frame house, I am not at my ease.

I rise from the floor with my muscles aching as if it were years ago and I have been worked on by the man who called himself my husband. I passed the night in the larger bedchamber, thinking how strange to be in so quiet a house that at midnight I could hear from afar the constable's call: *Twelve o'clock and all's well!* I half feared someone might enter the house, so I kept my dagger near and chose the second floor to sleep so as to hear an intruder's creaky progress up the staircase. I believe Madam Lantos guessed correctly and this house is rickety, for the stairs creak so mightily they might wake Charity in her bedchamber across the city.

I will say this place has few charms to attract her, or anyone else. I so wish I need only trip down the stairs to find coffee and bread with butter. Alas, the only thing that awaits me in the kitchen back is the heel of bread I brought with me.

Today I will begin to buy what I need for this ramshackle structure. It was all I could do yesterday to remove my belongings from Madam Lantos's and bring them here in a few trips by hired gig. At least she did not heave the rest of my belongings out onto the dusty street after I first departed.

I must be exceeding careful with money. Even with three hundred dollars gone from my bank account, I have a good sum left. But I don't know what I must spend to make this a proper cathouse. And who is to say when again I will earn as I have? In the last few days at Madam Lantos's I did whisper to a client or two that I would be removing to this place on Green Street. Yet what would those gentlemen think should they appear here now?

This leads me to thinking about my first task.

I know not the hour—this house is empty of everything, including a clock—but I suspect that dour-faced housekeepers kept by bawdy houses are already about their rounds, struggling to keep the coins in their carrying bags from clinking so loudly that they rouse every pickpocket between Sixth Street and the levee. I thought I would be still at Madam Lantos's and so could follow the housekeeper, hide well behind until her work with the constable was done, and then approach him to make my own case. Things as they are, though, I must find him on my own.

Dressed in pale green that suits the season, I join the throng upon the streets. This day will be hot. Already it is as if we walk about in a furnace.

I have skulked behind Madam Lantos's housekeeper before, wishing to know how this thing is done. Of course I could not ask Madam Lantos for advice on the subject. I take myself to the usual spot but remain a distance away. It is an age before I spy the constable, but then there he is, a man neither young nor old, with a badge over his heart and a nightstick in hand, striding about as if he owns the city. I would run up to him this very second but do not wish to be seen by Madam Lantos's housekeeper. So I ignore the growling in my belly and wait for her to come, hoping she has not already. The constable does what a constable does, I suppose: talk to one person and another, rap his nightstick on his free hand, enter a sweets shop and linger there.

Finally she comes. The bag of coins passes so quickly from her pocket to his, you might think there was a crime afoot. But these are only the dues of commerce. Then she is gone.

I make my way toward the constable, my speech in my throat. "Sir," I begin, and he turns toward me, his eyes growing wide. "I am Eliza Haycraft—"

"I know who you are." He glances about as if wishing to be rid of me.

I keep my voice low. "I have been working for Madam Lantos—"

"That I well know," he says then leans close. His voice goes to a whisper. "Have you something for me?"

I do because I wagered I might need some such. I did not think, though, I would need it in the first instant. I pull from my reticule a bag of coins and, fast as a wolf snatches a rabbit, he palms it. "I have come to you," I murmur, "as I would start a house of my own."

"Why is that my concern?" Now his voice is loud and he grasps his nightstick with both hands.

A warning sounds in my head. "I wish to do everything right and proper. My house is on Green Street. And I understand that I must speak—"

"Why do you think I know anything about that?" Slap, slap,

goes his nightstick against his palm. He steps a distance away. "Move along now."

"But—"

"Move along," he says more loudly, and this time gestures with his nightstick. I know not what else to do, so I sweep past him in the direction he motions.

As I walk away, I remember the words Madam Lantos spoke to me. *I will not make your path an easy one.* I believe the constable knew I would come to him. I believe Madam Lantos told the housekeeper to warn him of me. Madam Lantos will laugh twice when she hears this story, for the Eliza who "betrayed" her achieved no satisfaction *and* her reticule is empty of her bag of coins. I did not put so many in that bag, for I am not such a fool as that, but all the same I wish I had them still.

And now what am I to do about the powers-that-be?

I turn in the direction of my house. Now I am both hungry and frustrated. Yet surely there is another route open to me. I am lost in scheming when I see not far from me, coming near, a gentleman I know. It is a client of mine, or should I say of Madam Lantos, though I have serviced him often. He is older, with a beard but no moustache, white-haired, name of McPherson. He is doughy and unremarkable but nice enough. He is alone, I can tell, so I feel I may safely grace him with a smile.

Yet he averts his head and dodges me as if I were bright yellow with fever. In his haste to steer clear, he nearly steps in a mound of horse dung big as a toad. I cannot help myself: I stop to watch him hurry away from me. He glances back as if to make certain he has put me well behind him.

Sunshine beats hard on my head. In my haste this morning, in my strange house in which I am not used to waking, I forgot my parasol. Now my skin will brown and I will look like a chestnut.

I resume walking, disquiet in my chest. All around me, things are wrong.

Yet… it does not help to dwell on that. What helps is to be planful. So I will go to the Reveille, well situated on Green Street, to drink coffee and put something in my belly. Then I will return to the house to get my parasol and set out once again to begin purchasing the things I need.

MANY HOURS later I stand in my kitchen back, gazing outside. Darkness has fallen. I can tell from my new mantel clock in the parlor—mahogany with a white enamel dial and "French move-ment"—that it is gone nine o'clock. I imagine the ruckus at Madam Lantos's house at this hour, though here all is still. Behind me, a candle struggles to cast a brave light.

Soon I realize that a man is walking toward the house across the hard-packed earth. He carries a lantern and leaves a track in the dust. He is not the youngest of men, I don't think, but he moves at a good clip. He is dressed as a gentleman. Might he be a client? I do not believe I know him. My fingers go to the sheathed dagger on my chatelaine.

He stops a distance from the house and raises a hand in greet-ing. He sees me through the window well as I see him. "May I near?" he calls out.

Least he makes a show of being kind. "Please," I call, and join him outside. I would rather meet there than allow him into my house. But soon as I hear his name, I know I need not fret.

"I am Doctor Bernard Gaines Farrar." He doffs his hat—he is bald beneath—and peers at my face. "I am fortunate to own the lot to the east," he says as he gestures toward Fifth Street, "and I heard from my tenant that after some days of disuse at this house, that it appeared a body had settled in."

"As of just yesterday I am here." I smile. "I am Eliza Haycraft. I have heard of you, Doctor, and only the best things, too."

"Ah, well." He smiles. I take him to have sixty years or so. He glances about. "May I ask... are you alone here?"

A woman alone—without a husband, father or brother to

protect her—is not the typical thing. "I do not expect to be alone for many days longer," I tell him.

If Dr. Farrar knows I am a trollop, his expression does not betray him. He nods and seems to have trouble deciding what to say next. Then: "It is simply that these are troubled times, and we have so many newcomers in our city, and there is much crime about."

"It is kind of you to worry about me, but you need not."

"Well, we are a distance from the riverfront"—that is where the saloons, gambling halls, and my type cluster—"but there can be danger, too, where few people are about."

An idea comes to me. "I wonder… is it possible you know the local constable?"

"Indeed I do. Ah!" He nods with vigor. "Perhaps it would be best for him to know you are here. I could make the introduction."

"I would rest easier," I tell him.

The smile he gives me is a fatherly one. He leaves with a vow to return soon and I think to myself, as I go back inside, that I will be getting off on a good foot with this constable who hears of me first from Dr. Farrar.

Of course, it may come as a shock to both that my plan for this place is a cathouse.

———

It is a few days later, when I am out walking, that I spy Charity. It is her rapid gait that first draws my gaze. We are both on Fifth Street, just past St. Charles, heading south. She wears an old brown dress of which Madam Lantos is not fond, for it is both old and brown. But it is comfortable, Charity told me, and a dear friend.

I wonder she is in this district, as it is some blocks from Madam Lantos's house but not so many from mine. Maybe Charity came this way to look at my property? That seems too much to hope for.

The simple truth is that I need another strumpet by my side. I wish for it to be Charity, but if it is not, I must find another. I do not let my mind linger on the fact that no client has yet crossed my threshold.

I run to catch Charity and so when I do, I can speak her name only in a breathless way. She smiles before she can stop herself. Then she remembers she is angry with me and frowns.

People make their way around us. I hold out to Charity a present. It is bulky but contained in a length of cream-colored fabric tied with lace. "I should have given this to you before I left Madam Lantos's," I tell her.

Slowly she takes it from my hand. "You have it with you now?"

"I carry it with me. When I walk." *Because I hope I will see you.* "Please untie it, as I will have to explain."

Charity cannot resist such a mystery. After she unties the lace and fabric, she sees an apple—very shiny—and a paring knife with a handle carved of walnut. She raises puzzled eyes to my face.

"There is a legend I have heard," I say, "that this is how you learn the first initial of your husband. You must peel an apple very carefully in one long strip. Then you toss the strip over your shoulder and it lands in the shape of his initial."

This would not work for me, even if I wanted a husband, as I cannot tell one initial from its neighbor, and even if I did I would not know what name it might begin to spell. But Charity would know all that. She gazes at the items in her hands. "Over which shoulder should I toss it?"

"Oh yes, that is important." I stop to think so as to tell her the correct instruction. "Toss it with your right hand over your left shoulder."

She nods. I can see she is memorizing this. Again she looks at me. "You are trying to make me leave Madam Lantos and work at your house."

"I wish for that, yes. But I wish even more for us to be friends."

She looks away as if thinking. Then: "Thank you, Eliza," she says, still not quite meeting my eyes, and I know I should say something but cannot make more words come for the lump in my throat.

Charity spins and walks quickly away, her head bent. This, too, seems too much to hope, but I get the idea tears might be coming to her eyes, too, the very same as to mine.

ON THE FOURTH morning of this strange week, with dawn's light still feeble, I snuggle beneath my new bedclothes. If I could, I would stay in this nest all the day long. That would be better than to face my troubles. At least I own a bed now, sturdily built as every strumpet needs, the foot and headboards carved of dark wood gleaming from beeswax.

When finally I force myself to rise, I feel beneath my toes a Turkey carpet woven of red, gold and purple threads, the most threadbare section hidden beneath the bed. Across the chamber is a beadboard cabinet and in one corner a chair that rocks, with a spindle back and floral cross-stitch cushion. From a needlewoman I ordered simple draperies for the windows—no crashing silk for me—and I have asked a peddler to find a tall mirror that is not too battered, for gentlemen like to make use of that from time to time.

I am careful with my money but can buy these things because I found shops that sell second hand furniture, indeed most of them on Second Street, which made me wonder if the merchants are making a joke on us all. Do I mind here or there a nick in the wood or thread loose in the fabric? Not I, with only a rustic house to fill. Nor do I fear to bargain. And since I know my numbers, shopkeepers cannot easily confuse me, though they try.

I am in the kitchen back getting coffee to boil when I hear the clatter of a carriage. My heart near to jumps out of my chest for what do I see but Daniel's phaeton. He steps out of it with a package in hand. "I knew you would come before long!" I call out to him as he ties the horses. I grab him in a hug soon as he steps inside and catch a whiff of something sweet.

He raises a small white box tied with string. "Peach tarts for my favorite tart, with pecans baked in, too." He gives me a keen eye. "I stopped by Madam Lantos's last night."

"Only to find I had quit the place."

"I was told I was no longer welcome, though why would I care to be made at home when Eliza Haycraft is no longer in residence?"

I can only hug him again then pour him coffee. We take that and the tarts upstairs to my bedchamber to sit upon the Turkey carpet, for I have no dining table yet. "What did Madam Lantos tell you of me?" I ask.

"She intercepted me before I reached the rear parlor and said she had learned of our scheme, as she called it, and she would be happy to see the back of me for now and forever." He inspects a tart before carefully biting into it.

"I wonder if I am missed." All we doxies disappear for our courses so it may be too soon yet.

"I spied someone new in the front parlor. Very toothy girl"— he wipes crumbs from his lap—"who reminded me overmuch of my roan mare."

I near spill my coffee when I hear that. "It is so wonderful to see you, Daniel. I have been"—I am not sure how much to admit —"not at my ease here."

He glances about as if he expects to see another. "Where is Charity?"

"You did not see her with Madam Lantos?"

He shakes his head so I tell him the story.

"At least I may have found a good man for you," and Daniel tells me his name is Noah Moberry and Daniel has seen his freedom license. People like to say that piece of paper "attests to his good character," though if Chantal were here in Missouri, I don't think she would get one even if she were told to. And she has an excellent character. I believe the powers-that-be insist on them because they do not wish people like Chantal to have it easy in this state. None can even come here from other states. Chantal would disapprove and I could not blame her.

I must think about such things all the day long now, for I am a woman of business, or least starting to be.

Daniel begins to tell me news that does not cheer me, about the wages I must pay Noah.

"That is higher than I thought it would be," I say. Of a sudden I am ready to admit even more. "I found the same when I talked to the Irish cook at the boardinghouse where I used to stay." I waited until she came outside and asked her what her wages would be if she came to work at my house. "She was bold about it."

I was bold, too, when I demanded certain wages of Madam Lantos. It was because I believed I could get those wages if only I stood my ground. Yet now, for the first time, I begin to understand what it is to be the one paying the wages. I remember what Charity said to me about Madam Lantos. *She works all the day long, and the night. She is never at her ease.* I understand that now.

Daniel pops the last of a tart into his mouth then reaches over to tickle me. It is not long before I get the idea how this will end. We enjoy ourselves as we always do, but I must tell him something when we are relaxing after against the pillows. "I hope you will understand that after today, Daniel, I will be the same harlot as always." For I must earn money. I have been careful, but still I shudder to think how fast my account at the bank dwindles.

"Though I would be far richer"—Daniel pauses to kiss my forehead—"I would be severely disappointed to discover otherwise."

THAT AFTERNOON, after my dining table has been delivered and its biggest notch covered by an amber-colored vase in the Persian style—least so I am told—the constable Horace Mackey appears, unaccompanied by Dr. Farrar.

We stand outside in the fading light. He is younger than I am and neither handsome nor ugly. Something about his manner tells me he is eager to carry out his duties with zeal. He gazes at me with obvious puzzlement. "You are a friend of Dr. Farrar?" His tone says he cannot believe it.

He knows I am a harlot; I can see that. "Dr. Farrar was very kind to make our introduction."

"He is a great man. He was professor of medicine at the University of Transylvania. He served with the Territorial Legislature of Missouri." Mackey is near stammering. His defense of Dr. Farrar cannot be spoken strongly enough.

"He takes his duties very seriously, as I am sure you do, too."

Mackey puffs up. "As our citizens well know, last year we were formally organized into the Department of Police, styled after the city of New York." I know nothing of the sort but will believe him. "On our night watch alone," he goes on, "we have forty-eight officers."

"That makes me feel exceeding safe," I tell him. "Which is what I know Dr. Farrar desires." I feel bold as I speak with this Horace Mackey. "I am sure you know this will soon be a bawdy house?"

His eyes widen as he nods. Perhaps he has never been to such a place, and believes he should not go, but try as he might wishes to all the same.

"I wish to do everything right and proper," I say. "I will run a quiet house and keep our business behind closed doors." The police and men of business want the same, I know, and for St. Louis to be a "boom town." That is the phrase I hear. But if many newcomers arrive in a town, they need a place to go. Otherwise wives and daughters are not safe on the streets. That is another thing people say, though I am not sure I believe it.

"There must be no thievery at your house," Constable Mackey declares. He has put steel into his voice.

I drop my gaze and clasp my hands. "Absolutely none."

"You will not be running a saloon business here?"

"I will not consider it."

"And you will admit no Negroes."

That is against the rules, too. "Never a one. Constable Mackey, be kind enough to wait a moment," and I run inside to put coins in a bag. Back outside, I hold it out to him with a smile. "For the benevolent fund of your department."

He frowns.

"There is such a fund every year," I tell him. "And I would like to give what I can, as the need is great."

He takes the coins. Whether they land in his pocket or in such a fund, I will be happy. They will serve a fine purpose.

THAT NIGHT I am spared what I feared would be my fate: walking the streets like a common trollop. I am spared only because Mr. Creath appears at my house, Mr. Creath who I know from Madam Lantos's, with his too high forehead and lank hair and breath that never smells sweet. Still, I am happy to see him and I make that plain. He is the first client to come to the house of Eliza Haycraft.

I fuss over settling him in my parlor's finest plush chair with a glass of excellent whiskey and a cigar. It is a strange thing to be alone in this house with him, no music to pave the way, no other bodies telling tales or puffing smoke toward the ceiling. Still, it is a small job to get Mr. Creath talking, and it is what I have always done to hold breathless, as if his tales are wonders to be admired no matter how many times I have heard them.

"Not so hard to find you then," he tells me.

Mr. Creath is not among those I could alert to my departure. "A different part of town than Madam Lantos's, but as you see, not so far afield."

"Charity told me the spot when I asked her." He narrows his eyes at me. "So why'd you do it? Leave the best sporting house in the city to be out here all by your lonesome?"

"Well, I'm not alone now, am I? I wish for a house of my own, Mr. Creath. Not forever to be working for someone else." He should understand that: he started his own factory after working many years for another man, as he's so often told me.

He taps his cigar against my new ashtray, made of copper with a blue and green enamel design and only one chip that I could spy in the sun. "I'll tell you this." He chuckles though I'm not sure I hear much mirth in it. "Madam Lantos is telling stories about you. What women will say about each other! I'll tell you I don't half believe it."

Behind me on the mantel my clock ticks, so loud I can hear it even over the pounding of my own heartbeat. "What is Madam Lantos saying?"

"I don't want to believe it. If I did, I wouldn't have come this far to Green Street."

I must wait patiently though I struggle not to grab him by the shoulders and shake it out of him.

Finally he speaks again. "She says she threw you out. And for excellent reason."

I remember Mr. McPherson in the street, his foot nearly steeped in horse dung he was so eager to avoid me.

Mr. Creath leans closer. "She says you're diseased through and through. That's what she says. That you're diseased the worst way a whore can be."

Chapter Sixteen

"We may stop ourselves when going up, never when coming down."

— Napoleon Bonaparte

— *Maxims*, 1804-15

I T IS ONLY ONCE A NIGHT I ALLOW MYSELF TO DO
THIS, this mean-spirited ceremony best left to the darkest
hours.

By the light of a candle, I take from the beadboard cabinet in
my bedchamber the poppet I have made, the despised item carefully sewn of white cotton and stuffed with scraps of the same,
with green buttons for eyes and thick golden thread for hair. I
have not crafted a mouth for the poppet, for I wish above all for it
to remain silent, least where I am concerned. I lay the poppet on
the Turkey carpet and hiss at it to be quiet. I hiss at it not to speak

of me. I hiss at it not to spread false tales. Have I driven a pin into the place where the poppet's heart should beat? Not yet, though I've considered it.

My own heart pounds with vexation as I return the poppet to its place deep inside the cabinet. I know not what Chantal would think of this ritual, though the tradition comes from her New Orleans and it is from her that I learned of it. I know Chantal would be angry on my behalf if she knew what Madam Lantos had done. I also know that Chantal, practical Chantal, would tell me to stop wasting precious time hissing at a poppet.

WHY IS it that when you want a place to be full of men, it is empty of them; and when you want a place to be empty of men, it is full of them? My bawdy house is empty of men, but the bank in which I stand is full of them. To a man they stand silent, and all ears, far as I can tell.

"You do not have a sufficient sum in your account," the banker in the cage tells me. His words echo off the white marble floor and tin ceiling imprinted with a design of oak leaves. "You have no more than"—he writes on a slip of paper and shoves it in my direction—"twenty-two dollars."

Why did he bother to write the number if he planned to speak it aloud? I crumple the paper into my reticule. "Then allow me to withdraw fifteen dollars," I say, my voice low. I keep my chin high, though, and will my cheeks not to flush.

He purses his lips, disapproving of the strumpet who must be so lackadaisical at her "vocation" that she has such a meager sum in her account. Finally he produces the money and I click-clack out of the bank in my tasseled shoes.

It has been two years since I wanted for money, but I do so again. The stash that gave me comfort is gone. Three hundred dollars fled for the house on Green Street. Near fifty more flowed out for furnishings. I am forced to remember what it is to have in my stomach a stone of worry. In my dreams—I should call them nightmares—I fall into a black hole that I myself dug. I look up from the pit to see faces cackling with laughter. One of them is my mother.

The problem is not so much that my expenses are high as that my income is low. Clients are few and I cannot charge for my services as Madam Lantos did. Her whiskey and cigars I can match, but not her stone mansion or men of business in the parlor. I knew that would be so, but still I thought gentlemen would appear in their usual number and, as madam and whore both, I would collect their fees in full.

But they do not appear in that number.

I have wages to pay now, too, to Noah and the cook and housemaid. All appear on their workdays whether I have one client or none at all. And the cook must purchase enough food to serve several gentlemen, for what if that many should cross the threshold? How can I prosper if gentlemen leave my house hungry? They must leave feeling like kings, every part of them sated.

Worries crash in my head like billiard balls even as I continue my smiling promenade around our city. I do it not only for health but for income too, as I wish the gentlemen of St. Louis to see that I am still about, with a glow to my skin and a spring to my step. I wish for them to ask themselves how diseased can Eliza Haycraft be, looking as she does? I wish for them to wonder, as Mr. Creath did, if perhaps Madam Lantos is lying. *What women will say about each other!*

I have thought to go to her house to yowl at her, but what good would that do? She is not one to admire a hothead spectacle or hold her tongue because of it.

I grew soft during those years with her. Never did I fret over customers; at Madam Lantos's, many were turned away and we whores tittered behind our hands. I became bold about what I could do without having to prove I could do it. Now, once again, I am reminded I have only myself to rely on.

I walk past Planters House, where of an evening I have alerted a carriage driver or two to my new lodgings. That has not yielded much, as their masters do not think of me as they used to. Gentlemen new to this metropolis must come to know me. I will do my part to make it so. But that will take time. And these days as the money flows out, not in, I am become like Chantal: I worry I don't have time.

I am walking past the public market when I see someone I know from Madam Lantos's: Frederick Norcom. He was never a client of mine, though all were forced to put up with his speeches. Now he sits in his gig berating a woman about my age who I take to be his slave. Hester, he calls her, his voice impatient.

I remember that Mr. Norcom does not live in St. Louis the year round. He and his family live also in New York. At Madam Lantos's, he spoke loudly of the military school he attended there, called West Point. He said few were admitted to that institution, but he is of the sort that believes everything he does is special and he is more intelligent than most.

Perhaps. Yet something about his short, windy person made me doubt it. Sometimes the other men rolled their eyes when he could not see and Madam Lantos tried to hurry him upstairs. Always he spoke of how a man could get rich by taking lands from the Chickasaw Indians, and the Choctaws. I remember Chantal saying the Choctaws are honest and their women chaste. I do not like that Norcom—I leave off the Mr. as I think of him now—may have made his fortune off their loss and despair.

Soon I am near my house on Green Street. Lingering beneath the beating sun is a woman I have seen before: eyes huge in a thin face, hand on her back bracing her enormous belly. Her baby will come before the new moon.

While the gentlemen of this city may shun me, the poor like me well as ever, maybe better. They know my kitchen back after midnight yields much by way of warm food. They know I will not turn a soul away. Far better it go to their empty stomachs, I say, than be wasted.

I reach into my reticule as I pass the woman. Not even fifteen dollars now.

———

THE NEXT MORNING, early, I hear a carriage clatter outside my house. It is not Daniel's fancy phaeton, I see from my parlor window, but a hired gig. And who steps from it but Charity.

She is wearing her brown dress, her old friend. I watch her help the driver wrestle a trunk out of the gig onto the ground. It lands with a thump on the hard earth and dust billows around it. I know I am like Esther peeping out from behind the draperies in Obadiah's house, but still I stay to watch Charity count coins to pay the driver. She turns to face the house, and spies me, and her eyes ask a question. I smile and gesture that I will come out to her. I have prayed for this; I have longed for this. Now here it is, and I churn.

"Madam Lantos threw me out," Charity says soon as I am close enough to hear her. "She found out I told a client or two where to find you."

"Mr. Creath," I say. "Mr. Rumbager."

"I am angry at her for doing it, and not angry, too, because it's not been the same since you left." Charity being Charity, she moves straight on to the point. "Will you have me? I know it's different now I've been thrown out. It's not like me coming with you at the start. And it will be only until I marry, which cannot be so long now. But anyway, will you have me, even with all that?"

I grab her in a hug for what else can I do? She is my dear friend and my heart sings to see her. But all the same, there are troubles at my house of whoredom. "Let us get your trunk inside before anything else," I say, and am spared telling her my sorry tale until at least we have hauled the trunk far as the kitchen back.

She looks around. I can see she's surprised we're alone. I hasten to tell her that I have a cook, a housemaid, and a man, too.

"So Noah can carry my trunk up to the bedchamber," she says with confidence.

"All three come late in the day," I add, and leave out that is because more hours mean more wages. And there is only so much work at a lightly used cathouse like this one.

"May I see the whole of the house?" she wants to know, and I can delay the bad news again as I show her. She praises more than needed, I think, but the house is comfortable for all that it is homely and I do not stint where it matters. The mattresses are plump, the towels thick, and the soap fragrant. "It is so quiet!" she cries when we're returned to the parlor, "but for the clock," and on it ticks, the mantel clock, reminding me how fast time passes and how all the while Chantal makes her needle go in and out, in and out of her fabric.

I busy myself with boiling coffee, my thoughts bubbling madly as the water on the fire. Again Charity does not do what I might have done, even to such a dear friend as her. Might I have come first without my trunk, pretending that Madam Lantos had not thrown me out? Might I have pretended that I could return to that house and tried on this visit to push for a higher wage, knowing I was wanted? Those schemes never crossed Charity's mind.

She joins me in the kitchen back, cheerful as ever. "It is a W, you know." She sees I don't understand. "The letter the apple peel formed when I threw it over my shoulder. W, as in William. That is what it must be, for what other man's name does a W start?"

"I can't think of a one," I say, which gets us both to giggling, for I do not know what letter starts any man's name.

"It could be Winston, I suppose," she goes on, "but that is too serious for me. So it must be William. And now I know it's fated I meet him, it doesn't matter where I am. Here or at Madam Lantos's."

It makes me sad to hear her speak of this William. I hope he does arrive someday to fall in love with her, but I cannot say that he will. I stop my hands from moving and force myself to look at

Charity straight on. "You could be at Madam Hunter's, too. You could look for him from there, too."

I watch her smile fade. "You do not wish me here?"

"Oh, I do wish you here. But this house is not what it should be," and of a sudden I am telling her how the money is near to gone and the gentlemen few. I'm surprised how my mind eases as I tell her this. She listens with rapt attention and does not tell me I am a fool for any of it. When I tell her why gentlemen do not come, she near shrieks with anger and for the first time I pull the poppet from my beadboard cabinet in the daylight hours.

Charity will not settle until I find a strip of white fabric and needle and thread. She sews fat black stitches onto the fabric. "Madam Lantos, it spells out," she tells me, and insists we unstitch the poppet on one side, stuff the name inside, and sew it anew. After, we both sit back on our heels and gaze at the poppet lying on the carpet, hints of black from the rough new stitches showing through the white fabric on its chest. "I wish I *were* a witch like the others in Salem," Charity mutters. "Then we could put a real curse on her."

I shiver from that. "If you stay here, Madam Lantos will tell everyone you're diseased like me. If you go to Madam Hunter's, she won't speak a word against you."

"It is you Madam Lantos most hates," Charity agrees.

"At Madam Hunter's, you would eat your dinner then wait for the clients to come." I am not full sure of this but believe it to be so. "If you are here, on many nights we must walk about and find clients and lure them here, like the trollops near the riverfront."

"We will never be like them," Charity vows.

That would be a very great distance to fall. I stare at the poppet and ponder what Charity said. *It is you Madam Lantos most hates.* The interesting thing is why she hates me so. I think it is because I have the quality that has no name, and a head on my shoulders, too. Maybe I have been remembering too much one thing Madam Lantos said to me and not another. *I will not make your path an easy one.* That is in my mind all the time. Yet what else did she say? *I may not be able to stop you, Eliza Haycraft.*

"You do not have another whore here," Charity says.

"No." I shake my head. "I waited for you."

She springs from the carpet and brushes dust from her skirts, making me think I must speak to the housemaid about her sweeping. "I hope," Charity says, "that William takes his sweet time to find me."

"I cannot pay you as Madam Lantos did," and I explain why. I must tell her all the bad things now.

"That is of no mind to me. I know where I wish to be and it is with you, Eliza."

I reach for her hand and she draws me to my feet. Her smile wavers. "I wish I had money to give you," she says. "I shall start saving from now on."

I squeeze her hand, though Charity is not Charity if she is tucking away nuts for the winter like a squirrel. We go downstairs to drink the coffee, cool now but we can ill afford to waste it. I think for only a second before I say what is at the top of my mind. "There are things I never told you." I watch her head snap in my direction fast as a fox sighting a rabbit. The rest of my words come in a rush. "First about that rich Creole who came to Madam Lantos's. And also"—I force it out—"I thought I was married once, to a man called John Haycraft."

It is all we discuss for the next few hours.

It is late September, a month or so since Charity came to me, and clients grow in number. I am feeling lighter of heart when of an evening, as I am in my bedchamber dressing for the night, Charity calls to me from the corridor. On the floor below Noah rustles about, as do the cook and housemaid.

In Charity's voice I hear a note of worry and so it must be for she does not wait an answer to enter but bursts into my chamber on swiftly moving feet. She pulls me to a window and draws aside the drapery to peek outside. The sky is full dark with only a sliver of moon. "Look." She prods me to take her place at the glass. "Coming up the street this way."

I do as she bids and my eyes alight on a group of half a dozen, men and women both, less than a block away. Their lanterns bob as they stride. I drop the drapery and step back. "Why should we care about them?"

"The one in front points at this house. And he is a constable." Charity's skin is pale as milled flour. "I saw him swing a nightstick."

I peer out again. Now the group is nearer I can see by lantern glow the face of the man in front. Charity is right: it is Horace Mackey, the constable.

"This is how it starts," she tells me, and as my mind grasps what she means by *this*, voices rumble on the street. The six have stopped. "Eliza Haycraft!" a man shouts, and raps hard on my front door, locked at this hour. "Open this house!"

A woman's voice lifts skyward. " 'Tis a house of debauchery and fornication!" and the others jeer alongside her.

Charity grabs my arm as I hear Noah bound across the parlor fast as a large man can move. My heart jabs in my chest like a trapped animal trying to escape a sinking cage. Under the ramming of a man's shoulder—so it must be—the front door rattles in its frame. "Here are committed dreadful filthy and lewd offenses!" another woman cries.

"I cannot keep 'em out!" Noah shouts, and in that moment I hear the front door give way and the rabble rush into my parlor. Females screech: the cook and housemaid?

I run down the stairs. Charity follows. Already I hear glass breaking. "Stop at once," I shout, "do not touch that!" as a man dressed in the clothes of a workingman raises my mantel clock high above his head only to smash it down upon the floorboards. "What is this?" I point my finger at Horace Mackey, trying to keep it steady though it shakes wildly in my agitation. "You are to save my house from these brigands!"

" 'Tis nothing but a bawdy house kept for filthy lucre and gain!" an older woman cries. Though her face is gaunt and her mouth lacks teeth, her eyes gleam with a fierce light.

Charity and Noah move among the mob, trying, I know, to keep them from poaching any item more. I see nothing of the cook and housemaid; have they fled?

"You!" Mackey points his nightstick at Noah's broad back. "Are you escaped from your rightful master?"

Does Mackey expect a *yes* in answer? I daresay he hopes to collect a bounty. Constables can pocket such funds and so keep their eyes open for escaped slaves.

Slowly Noah turns toward him, his head lowered. His words come out soft and mumbled. "Sir, Constable Sir, I swear to you that I am a free man."

The mob mutters as if they can scarce believe it and I will say that I am surprised, too, but for a different reason. Where is the strong and bold Noah I know? The man before me is cowering.

But... of course he would be. For don't I understand what hell the constable could bring to Noah?

"He is a free man," I tell the constable, "I know it to be true," but Mackey will only scoff at the words of a doxy. "Show me your paper," he demands Noah.

Noah can do it and I see Mackey is not happy with that. He turns his glare upon me. "I accuse you of thievery, Eliza Haycraft."

"No." I struggle to steady my voice. "Constable Mackey, you know this to be a lawfully run house." Does he forget how I cross this city to give him coins? For his eyes are cold.

"I accuse you of thievery," he says again. "I accuse you of running an ill-governed, disorderly house that is an offense to the peace and dignity of this city."

Many a bawdy house is accused of thievery when the powers-that-be cannot conjure another crime. "There is no thievery at this establishment," I declare, though as I speak I know I see before me a man who has already made up his mind what is true and what is not. "Name my accuser. It is my right to hear it."

"I have it on the excellent authority of a fellow officer," the constable says, naming no one at all, and the rabble howls in approval and I wonder if I see in this, too, my God, the hand of Madam Lantos. I remember the prophecy Charity spoke months ago. *They won't protect us like they protect her.*

"Name that officer," I demand, "I have a right to know his name," but my hope for an answer dims to nothing as Mackey steps nearer and raps his nightstick on his open palm as if yearning to use it on me.

"Tell it to the judge," he says, and the mob looses a mighty yowl. Now I know the horror will rise from here. There is nothing to stop Mackey from manhandling me to the calaboose, humiliating me down one street and up another. Then I will pass a night in a cage for the first time in my life and in the morning a judge will assess on my head a fee I cannot pay.

But that is not to be the worst of it. "You, too," Mackey says to Charity.

"I will not go!" she screams, and backs against the wall.

Mackey moves toward her, still rapping his nightstick in his hand.

"Leave her be!" I cry. "She has scarce been at this house!"

The constable only grunts for an answer and would strike Charity on the legs if Noah, brave Noah, did not step in front of her. The mob is made only more restive after this. "Take in both whores!" a man shouts, and another topples a chair. "They are a great nuisance to all decent inhabitants of this city!" that man bleats, and I hear in these phrases the so-called trials this rabble has witnessed, of bawds on parade before judges, entertainment for one and all.

One of the brigands yanks Charity out from behind Noah. Mackey grabs me by the arm. Toward the broken front door then out into the street we are pushed. Into my mind comes the petrifying picture of this rabble in my house. Noah, no matter his size, will not be able to corral them. And what will happen to him? They will beat him if they can, and, oh, worse could happen.

Behind me I hear glass shatter. "Throw that riffraff from my house!" I shout at Mackey. "They have no right to be there!"

"They are the righteous citizens of this city," he says without sparing a glance, and I would spit on the word *righteous* if I could, for that is the last word to describe what is happening here.

The night is a monster that will not let me sleep. The morning brings a judge who repeats the phrases I heard from the rabble. "Did keep and maintain a certain common bawdy house… " "Evil disposed persons of evil name, fame and conversation… " "Being in manifest destruction, ruination and subversion of youth… " Thievery is alleged but not proven, for it cannot be. The accusing officer is never named, for the same reason. On these trumped-up charges the bawd Eliza Haycraft is assessed a fee of eighty dollars and Charity half that.

Of course we cannot pay. If we were not whores, to the work-house we would go. As it is, they will release us with the penalties on our heads. They know how we will earn the money to pay: plying the vocation they arrested us for. That is the strangeness of this world we live in.

It is not a mercy to be freed, for there is but one place to go and that is the house we were forced to quit. Charity cries when we enter, but I do not, for tears are gone to me. What pains me most severely are the dresses sewn by Chantal's hands: the yellow, the bluebell, and the jade. Destroyed they are, shredded, their beauty only a memory. The trunk Obadiah gave me, too, is now broken and useless.

What survives, though, is the poppet, lodged in the depths of my shattered beadboard cabinet. That night my own hands build a fire in the hearth and I toss the poppet atop the flames and watch it burn until it curls in onto itself and is no more.

ONE MONTH LATER, it is Frederick Norcom who buys my house on Green Street. Daniel cannot find a buyer who will pay the sum I did, for after the rabble had their way with it, the house is even more ramshackle. The three hundred dollars I paid becomes the two hundred fifty dollars Norcom pays.

I am a woman who bought property, but an excellent example I did not set. In just four months I lost a good part of the value. That is what can happen when a buyer must of a sudden sell. And it was not Norcom I was hornswoggled by, either. If it was anyone, it was Madam Lantos.

It is on the twenty-third day of November that I put my X on the deed that sells the house to Norcom. Some weeks later I see Norcom's slave Hester walking, in her arms a babe with the same café au lait skin as Chantal. I do not long wonder how Hester got her baby: I wager she had to put up with Norcom. When she stops to look in a shop window, I do the same and hold out a coin. She looks surprised but takes it and I smile at her babe and ask the name. Priscilla.

I have heard tell of another babe in the world. Chouteau has celebrated one year of marriage with his bride. Already he is a father, to a girl they call Emilie Anne, the same name as his mother.

I remain on Green Street but remove to a boardinghouse, Charity by my side, and Noah, too, for he made it through the raid with his body and his freedom intact. Charity and I salvage what we can of our clothes and furnishings. I pay Charity and my penalties and once again start anew.

Has Madam Lantos defeated me? I will not admit it, even now.

Chapter Seventeen

"The mass of men lead lives of quiet desperation."

— Henry David Thoreau

— *Walden; or, Life in the Woods,* 1854

ONE SPRING PASSES, THEN ANOTHER. On this day the irises twist their purple and yellow faces toward the sun and I wonder how they find the strength to do it.

Charity's hands still over the pillowcase she is removing. We are in the boardinghouse, in my bedchamber, pulling linens for the laundress, a task that for strumpets never ends. "How many more times," she says, "will we hear those bells toll?" She turns toward the window, open to admit every somber knell along with the breeze. "I hear them and think to myself, there is another one, there is another soul left us and gone to heaven."

I won't remind her some might go in the opposite direction.

"And if it's not those"—she is near tears now; her face is crumpling in that way she has—"it's the clatter of the wagons." The two go hand in hand: bells toll the dead and funeral wagons carry the corpses from church to cemetery.

It is late in the forenoon of a day too lovely to think of the cholera, though we must because it is all around us. The newspapers say near two hundred succumbed just the week last. "No one can know how many more times the bells will toll," I say. "Better those who are gone are quickly buried, their pestilence put in the ground."

There is no arguing that. Charity nods. She carries the linens from my chamber with shoulders slumping as if the world's weight is upon them. I would close the window to the melancholy tolling, but nothing so simple as that can dull it.

Daniel has told me the scourge's symptoms with gusto, in the way men do when they wish to proclaim they will not catch a thing. So I know the disease loosens the bowels first then invades the stomach. If eyes sink into the head and fingers and toes turn blue, the sufferer best prepare to meet his Maker. Even Daniel pales at stories that some perish within hours: children, too. In the morn they are playful and cheery, after noonday shriveled and stone cold dead.

Miasmas are the problem, most say, so it is best to avoid the night air. Do not eat pickled foods for they excite the system. Others say not to rage or cower, for either may cause you to fall prey. I never believed sauerkraut caused it, though many point an accusing finger at the Germans, and some at the Irish, and many at the Argonauts en route west to seek their fortune in California gold.

It is as it always is: as plague takes hold of our city, the rich flee for the country while the rest of us stay put and suffer. I have seen that excellent man Dr. B. G. Farrar bustle about the riverfront tending to all who need him, no matter they live in a hovel.

I am not one to believe it, but churchmen say the cholera is

Divine Wrath on us sinners. We are paying for our city's crime and intemperance and us trollops plying our trade, and on the Sabbath, too, when saloons and beer gardens stay open and the *Republican* risks damnation to publish a paper.

Passion pulses despite the disease in our midst, or maybe because of it. Is St. Louis become like New Orleans? For all seem to live for today. Our bawdy rooms see a goodly number of clients; here I do not draw the richest so my clients stay in town. These days it is not only Charity and me who make up our band of bawds but two others as well. And Noah Moberry still works for me. I am happy he will do it despite what happened at that cursed house I purchased. Here rooms will soon empty and I've half a mind to find new strumpets to work inside them. I could use a girl to play the timid virgin, to rouse even the most apprehensive gentleman to manly feats beyond his wildest imagining. How any man thinks he could encounter such a female within these walls is beyond me, but we all know that at times men will believe what they choose to. And if I find one such, well, my bank account will grow stouter still.

Though I can scarce believe it, it is five years gone since the night I flung myself into John's canoe. A lifetime ago it seems and now I strain to remember John's face, or my father's. My littlest sister Minerva I cannot even imagine: she would have twelve years now. Is she at all like the impish girl of seven?

When I think of my family, tears do not run as they used to. My family seems lost to me as petals tossed upon the river. I will say that Obadiah and Chantal are embedded in my heart. Sometimes, sometimes, I allow myself to dream of boarding a steamboat to see them again. What keeps me from such a voyage? Perhaps the fear they are lost, too. I shudder when I hear how cholera swamped New Orleans. There are so many dead that corpses are thrown into pits. No bells for those.

But for Charity and Daniel, I feel myself alone in the world. I am without kin and no longer young by anyone's measure.

"'TIS A MIGHTY DIN," grunts Mr. Lynch.

It is the evening of the spring day and he is atop me, is Mr. Lynch, a man of middle age with more girth than mirth about him. I hear the far-off commotion well as he does—it's loud enough to raise the dead—but I thought it best not to distract the man at such a moment as this. He is forgetting what he is about, though, as he raises his head and cocks it as if to listen.

"Fire bells," I say, though as I pay attention I realize that is only the half of it. Much shouting, too, and wind battering the half open window like an avenging angel hard upon us.

Mr. Lynch heaves himself off me. "On the north levee, from the sound of it."

"This morning I saw a fire on one of the steamboats." I had braved the plague to go out and provision. I rise from the bed as well, and right my corset. "Mattresses aflame. Some tossed right in the river."

"Christ Almighty." Mr. Lynch is staring out the window toward the river and I am surprised to see upon his face a strange orange light.

I join him at the glass and am struck dumb. This is no mattress fire: this is hellfire across near half our levee. "I think"—I hate even to speak the words—"many steamboats are ablaze."

"Could be the lot of them." Mr. Lynch grabs the jacket he tossed on the chair and is down the stairs before even his trousers are buttoned. It is not the usual thing for a man to leave his strumpet before he is satisfied, but Mr. Lynch is the proprietor of a warehouse and like as not it stands on the levee.

I spin again to the window. On this floor I am high enough to see the flames, writhing like living things. It is a strong north wind feeding them; I can feel it. I am blocks away, but even here my skin heats from the fire's power. I press my hands hard against my chest as if that will keep my heart from stampeding like a frightened horse. I remember Obadiah telling me of fires in New

Orleans that destroyed much of the city, but those were in the
century last and surely nothing like that could happen again? Not
in these modern times. And what is the world come to, that on top
of the plague we now have this?

Charity's man must be fled as well, for she is come to my side
at the window. "How did so many boats come to burn so quickly?" she cries.

"Obadiah told me once steamboats are nothing but pine and
paint." I turn from the window. "Come with me." Something is
pulling me outside and I soon learn I am not alone in the feeling.

It is as if the city entire is out, children, too, dogs yelping,
swine running amok, all of us madly careening down one street
and up another. As Charity and I flow with the mob a few blocks
north to Cherry Street then downhill toward the levee, I see,
above the warehouses that stand between us and the river, flames
eating the steamboats alive. Oh, those glorious white palaces, now
nothing more than tinder for a thunderous fire. Sparks and
flaming cinders dance in the night sky, their partner the whipping
wind.

At Cherry and Main there is a foundry, and a fireplug, too. In
place are hose reel wagons from the volunteer companies, and
their horse-drawn engines. Firemen are pumping into a hose that
runs down toward the levee. I grab the arm of one man I know;
now is not the time to remember how. "What in the world
happened?" I ask him.

He nods, his eyes squinting against the smoke. "It started on
the *White Cloud*. We thought we had it down then the wind spread
it south to the *Edward Bates*."

"Then her crew let her loose!" the older man beside him cries.

"Or fire burnt through her moorings. Any rate, once the *Bates*
was loose she lit up the next boat then the next after. Watch yourself now," and he is back to wrestling with the hose, a snake fat
with water and a mind of its own.

Around us people shout the names of the steamboats torched
one after the next, all moored and helpless as the wind and the

river's current crashed the flaming *Bates* into them, one floating pyre lighting the next. The *Boreas Number Three*. The *Prairie State*. The *Mameluke*. The *Alexander Hamilton*.

"A man is saying there are more than twenty steamboats afire!" Charity cries, and what about the barges and flatboats, too? Through the smoke I cannot even see her clearly though she stands not far away.

A roar rises from the levee. "It's the bales!" I hear that man's yell above the rest, and my heart sinks, for I know what is happening though I cannot see it.

On the cobbled levee lies everything the warehouses do not hold: bales of dry hemp and piles of lumber soon to be loaded and shipped. It is the old mayor, I think, who said those should be moved, but that was last year and who in this busy city listened? There the bales are still; I saw them this very morning.

Charity is clutching my arm, her grip tight. Tonight no one minds us harlots: not amid this horror. All as one we citizens shudder as flames tower over our levee, shooting for the moon. On Cherry Street behind the warehouses, we can see the north wind push the pillars of flames to the right, toward the south, as if with mighty arms. That is where most of the city lies.

And why does my nose now smell grease fat? It is as if—how can it be—a giant hog roasts on the cobbles. That is what shouts from afar soon tell us: barrels of bacon and lard are on the levee among the hemp and wood. Those must be what explode now, with great booms that make the ground shake.

You need not look long to know this orange monster will not keep to the levee, not with the freakish wind, not with embers flying about like crazed insects. It will reach its greedy arms across the city. Men are dousing the warehouses along the levee, but that can't stop it, I don't think, and seconds later there is another hue and cry as flames pierce the roof of a warehouse not on the levee at all, but, I fear, on Main Street. "My God," I mutter, "that could be at Main and Green."

Just up Green Street, too few blocks from the warehouse now

aflame, our boardinghouse squats. There, helpless as the steam-boats, are stashed the pathetic belongings Charity and I salvaged two years before—clothes, furnishings, whatever small treasures we still possessed. I try not to imagine flames licking that struc-ture—dilapidated it may be, but it is still my home. My God, I do not know how I will bear it should it fall to ash.

I must see how bad is the fire at that warehouse. I pull Charity toward Green Street even as she moans in my ear. "If this fire leaves the waterfront... "

I dare not give voice to that fear. For all around us are build-ings of wood. The shanties, filled with women and children? Those poor souls can barely survive within those hovels. What are they to do without them?

"Look!" Charity points uphill. "We could do that, hire a dray and get our things from the boardinghouse."

That is what people are doing, mostly shop owners I wager, piling wares on a dray wagon and paying a driver a dear fee to drag it uphill to safety.

Before I can think on that, a man runs toward us. "The fire's on Locust now!" he shouts, and that means the middle of the city, and I see flames out the roof of another building in the distance.

The heavens allow us one mercy. The warehouse near Green Street is saved. I am enjoying the tiniest relief—dare I hope our boardinghouse will survive?—when a mighty explosion sends Charity and me to our knees. A horrified roar rises from the river-front, where cinders rain like wicked hailstones. "It's the *Martha*!" people are yelling, "kegs of gunpowder belowdecks on the *Martha*!"

What could blow next? I dare not imagine what else lurks in our city or on the steamboats. There is no time to think anyway, there is only frenzy, as hundreds of men are fighting this fire now, I see all around me, not just firemen but citizens. I hear shouts of *bucket brigade* and that is something women could do, that Charity and I could do, much better than standing agape in helpless panic.

I grab her hand and push south through the throng toward

those shouts. It is a craziness around us of yelping people and crying children and bucking horses and loaded drays, men of business rushing from buildings with sheaves of papers in their arms, saving what they can. The thought comes to me: where might Daniel be? We are close, I realize, to his office.

We find a bucket brigade on Locust Street, which draws water from the river and sends it uphill. Beside us is an Irish lad of ten or so who cannot hand me a bucket without sloshing water. I do not know how much time has passed when I glimpse Daniel's blond head not far away. I shout to him and the Irish lad does the same and finally Daniel's eyes spot me. He runs to us, hair wild and face and shirt streaked with dirt and ash. "Your office?" I pant. My eyes sting from the smoke; I can scarce keep them open.

"I got out what I could." He sets himself between the boy and me and grabs the passing bucket. "Hid it behind your place, near the privy. I pray that'll be safe," and I am surprised if he means it for Daniel is not a man to drop to his knees. Then: "Dray drivers are charging fifty dollars a load. Can you believe that?"

The Irish boy screams that he cannot—" 'tis a kingly fortune!" —but tonight I know that anyone who can pay it, will.

Daniel lowers his head near mine. "It's everywhere, Eliza, it's blazing by Elm and Spruce now, walls of fire," and I know he is telling me this because I cannot see it from where I stand. That is where the best part of the city is, where my beloved places are, where Charity and I lived for years. It is where Madam Lantos lives.

"So far south?" I hiss. "Are we to lose all?"

"It's everywhere," he repeats, "and now the problem is water. Fireplugs are running dry." His next words petrify. "They may explode buildings to try to put a halt to it. Deprive the fire of fuel."

"I never heard of such a thing! Using what?"

"Kegs of gunpowder."

I remember the *Martha*. The shudder of the earth when she

blew as if the ground had split open to spew out the Devil himself.

"They've sent men and wagons to the Arsenal," Daniel adds, and I know that is where the gunpowder would be. "They'll cover the kegs with wet cloth."

I close my eyes. Wet cloth only between the gunpowder and these flaming cinders dropping from the sky. I pray God to save those men.

Daniel steps back from the brigade and once again the Irish lad sloshes my skirts. "Keep at it long as you can," Daniel urges, "it's the Liberty and Union companies by the Cathedral I wish to help again," and I realize the fire must be far uphill as Third Street. I squint to watch his white shirt disappear in the smoke as he rushes toward Walnut—will I ever see him again?—and I wonder if I am wrong, if he *is* a praying man, least on a night like this one.

It is not long before Daniel proves right. Cries arise that hoses are down to a trickle. The men who run the city fear the Cathedral and all south will burn. There is only one thing to do, the thing Daniel told me: to explode the buildings that stand in the fire's way. Somehow that may make this terror stop. The captain of the Missouri Company—Targee is his name—says they must do it. It is the most terrifying task I ever heard. A man must hoist a keg of black powder onto his back, never mind the balls of flying fire all around him, and race with it inside a structure, where he is to leave it off and run, fast as his legs will carry him, before the building explodes at his back. Who has the courage for such a job? Targee does, people are shouting, but only if his wife will let him. He has run to his house on Fourteenth Street to beg her leave to do it. I can just as easily ask what woman would say yes as wonder what woman would say no.

Our buckets stay full, Charity and mine, for the river will never run dry and we wish to do what we can, but my arms and back tremble from the long work of it, and when in time men come to take our places, we let them. I lean against a brick building, Charity in a crouch beside me. It is hours we have been out. The morn cannot be far off. I am exhausted to the depths of my soul. The Irish lad is fled, looking for his mother, and I wish I again saw Daniel's white shirt in the throng, for I fear for him with all my heart, him blocks away in the thick of it, where people shout that it is worst and hopeless and all is lost.

Then I hear it, and feel it, from my feet to my head, a thunderous roar, and people shout that a building has been exploded. Targee's wife must have given her leave. Another boom follows, and another—they are making quick work of it—and now I crouch like Charity, helpless to do more than pray and tremble. People yell that it is not just Targee running with gunpowder strapped to him but other of his men in the Missouri Company, too. "Phillips Music Store next!" boys run and yell. I know it, on Market Street and Second, for there was a time I dreamt of a piano forte for the Green Street house and Phillips had beautiful instruments on offer.

Another blast shakes our city. Charity groans, a mound beside me, and I wonder how many more explosions I can stand. I don't half believe it, but in time, across the river, I glimpse a faint light. This time it comes not from the blaze but from that ball of fire we call the sun. Dawn will follow even this heartrending night, and whether we want to or not, all in this city will be forced to look at what this fire has wrought.

I expect another explosion; I wait for one; but it does not come. People are not running now, but lumbering about. I expect more commotion, but of a sudden it is quieter. There is a different murmur on the breeze, for now the wind is quelled. People are saying the explosions did what they were meant to. *The fire is dying.*

And: *Targee is dead.* The captain perished in the last blast, people murmur, at the Phillips store, not out quick enough. He showed enormous courage. And now his wife—I hear her name is Sarah—will have a lifetime to remember the permission she gave and all he did to save the rest of us.

Around us is hell come to earth. I help Charity to her feet and lead her through the rubble to our rooms.

Do I SLEEP? I cannot keep my body from it. I drop onto my bed and for some hours at least escape to a place where there is no fire and no devil wind and no screaming and no blasts. We are the lucky ones, Charity and I, for we have beds on which to rest and when we wake we can boil coffee and put bread in our mouths and find water to wash our faces.

I will walk after I eat. I must see what is left of this city. What is gone and what is left. Charity will not walk with me. She is numb and can only sit.

When I am walking, I wonder. How did St. Louis draw such misery unto herself? As I walk block after block, smoke rising from the small fires that still burn, everywhere it is the same: crumbled walls of brick and charred wood and ash. It is as if the city is become nothing more than a hearth. On the river bob burnt wrecks of steamboats. I hold a handkerchief to my nose, but that does little to banish the smell. How long will the reek linger? How long will the memory linger? Until I am dead, I am sure of it.

As I walk I am not alone. Others tread with careful feet among the ashy leavings. Horses trot and whinny, wagons attached, as if all were the same as yesterday. I wish I would see Daniel, but I do not. I do see the Cathedral, though, its spire intact. He helped save it and I pray doing so did not end him.

There is no thinking that leads me across the city to the place I used to live. I do not send my feet there but do not stop them from going, either. I do not wonder what I will see, for I see the same everywhere: block after block the same.

And when I arrive at the place I did not know I was going, I see a woman I did not know I had set out to see. She is wearing a pink gown fragile as a rose petal, though it is streaked with soot and ash. Madam Lantos.

Chapter Eighteen

"When a man is a favorite of Fortune she never takes him
unawares, and, however astonishing her favors may be, she finds
him ready."

— Napoleon Bonaparte

— *Maxims*, 1804-15

SHE IS A STRANGE SIGHT AMID THE RUBBLE, is
Madam Lantos. Though her hair is tumbled and her face
streaked with dirt, still somehow she does not look
slatternly.

She stands half a block away, by the stoop to a burnt-out building; even amid all that is lost she will not sit on the stoop and soil
her skirts more than they are already. One of her girls, with no
such scruple, crouches beside her. Felicity is her name, I think. She
is light-haired and solid as Lydia used to be; I have learned it is

valuable to a madam to have one such in her employ. Felicity is rent by sobs Madam Lantos seems not to hear. Madam Lantos is dry-eyed and wearing a look that tells me her mind is working.

She is not far from the stone mansion, but I know without walking past that it is gone. All in these blocks is gone, even, I must think, the item Charity believed Madam Lantos would save first if sparks flew: the oil painting of the queenly woman with the mischievous smile who looked down upon the rest of us.

I think of the poppet. I think of how my own hands threw the poppet onto the hearth fire and watched it burn.

I walk nearer, passing grime-stained people who seem more asleep than awake. Stunned they are, as am I. Madam Lantos turns her head and spies me. We have seen each other in the streets these last years but exchanged nary a syllable.

"Come to crow?" she inquires. "And aren't you about it quickly." There is malice in her words but not in her voice, that lulling voice, which floats over the debris that yesterday were this city's most gracious dwellings. "I have heard that all north of Locust Street is untouched, should anyone care to put a foot there."

The fire has not improved her opinion of the still-standing blocks where I reside. "I hope," I say, "that no one in your house suffered injury."

"Not *there*, but I cannot speak for what they met with after they left."

I can imagine the mad scramble at Madam Lantos's house as gentlemen learned of the fire, most in their cups, all with enterprises, mansions, wives, and children to save, and there they had been, blissfully entwined with a harlot while the levee and the city blazed. "I am sorry"—I don't know how best to say it—"that your house burned."

"The house stands, in a fashion." She will do her best to show I can get nothing right. "It is everything inside that burned."

I think of the yellow kitchen with the trestle table. In the bedchamber that I loved, I remember the armoire with the painted vine-and-flowers pattern. Oh, and Madam Lantos's blue silk draperies, and her gowns of taffeta and moire and faille, and her piano. Her piano. All dust now. Still, her eyes are dry. And if ever they are not, no one will see it.

"You know of Captain Targee?" she asks.

"That he is dead? It is very sad."

"Not that he is dead. We all know that. That his head has been found, near a full block from Phillips Music Store." She says it with relish to make a show of her bravado. Felicity says nothing, though it has distracted her enough that she has ceased crying.

"What will you do now?" I ask Madam Lantos. "Where will you go?"

"Oh, I am thinking I shall go to Planters House," and I don't need her to look away to know she is lying.

"I do not believe you have a plan to go there," I tell her. "And even if you did, no room could be had. They are all bid up by now and let just the same."

I know from walking these blocks that Madam Hunter's house is burned, too. There are this morning many trollops without a home, but I am not one of them. Even before I lay my head on my pillow this early morn, I told the mistress of my boardinghouse that I wished to rent the rooms coming empty. I paid three months' rent for them, at the higher rate she haggled out of me. Rents will rise with so much destroyed: she understands that well as I do. Whoredom may have taken a nap last night, but it will rouse with vigor in the weeks to come. Though this is a bizarre time for it, I feel stir within me a strange excitement.

"As you have nowhere to go," I tell Madam Lantos, "I will offer that you come to my boardinghouse." I do not trust Madam Lantos, but I believe I am her match now. "Felicity as well," I add, and the strapping bawd raises her head with a light of interest in her eyes.

Madam Lantos tsks. "You are a whore who pays too much for a dilapidated house and loses it a month later. A whore the constables will not protect, who after all this still thinks too much of herself."

"You know much of my business"—I need not wonder why—
"but about much of it you are wrong."

"It is because of me you have that dress on your back,"
Madam Lantos says, "those shoes on your feet."

"For two years you profited from me. And when I would not
stay with you, you did much to try to stop me. Yet here I stand."

"You stand because of all you got from me," she says, but her
repetition lacks spirit. She hates that this fire robbed her of all and
me of nothing. Yet that is what happens in life, even to those
powerful as Madam Lantos. The great wheel spins.

Madam Lantos caused me true harm, with the raid and with
her lies. Most of the gentlemen from her house have not come
back to me and I must think it is because too many believed her.
No, some would not put a foot on Green Street. But some, I am
sure, would gladly tumble again with Eliza Haycraft if only they
knew there was no harm in it. Well, now all gentlemen must come
to Green Street for their sporting houses, or thereabouts, for the
nicer parts of the city are no more.

Felicity rises to her feet. "I'll come with you."

"You are wise," I tell her. And once clean, fed, and rested,
Felicity can go in search of the strumpets I believe most desirable.
They can come to my employ now.

Felicity comes fast to my side. I turn my back on Madam
Lantos to walk back the way I came. Though her feet will drag, I
wager she will follow.

I AM on my back and Daniel is above me, proving in excellent
fashion how alive he still is. It is Sunday, three nights since the
fire, and here we are with full abandon tempting God to rain
down yet more wrath on our city.

After, we lie quiet and talk of the thing we cannot stop talking
about. By now I know how wide the Burnt District spreads. Over
four hundred buildings are gone, most of them businesses. More

homes are destroyed than my mind can grasp. Not as many died as I feared. Three from the *White Cloud* and one poor soul on the levee after the *Martha* exploded. Five were found in the city's ruins.

Yet there is news to cheer the soul. The city will give Sarah Targee her husband's position as a weigher so she and their children will have an income. The insurance companies survive and most all say they can pay what is asked of them. And the banks say they have cash to lend, as their safes still stand. I know that to be true of my bank as I went there to make certain.

Daniel strokes my arm and I close my eyes from the gentle pleasure of it. "Were you frightened at the Cathedral?" I ask him. Daniel was so close to the fire there that he might as well have been a rabbit on the spit.

"I was afraid. There is a joy, though, in being one in a number, doing your part for all."

I felt that, too, passing the buckets in the brigade. And for me there was as well the joy to be seen and not scorned. We are quiet, then: "I wonder what Madam Lantos plots," I say.

"What makes you think she plots anything?" He laughs even as the words leave his lips. "I wonder you took her in. Does she not have friends to help her?"

"She is not the sort to have friends." To have real friends you must tell them the bad things. You must unwrap the scars and show them. I understand that now. I rise on my elbow to stare at Daniel's face. "You are not just my friend but my dear friend, Daniel," and I would say more if tears were not coming.

He leans forward to kiss my forehead. "And you are mine." When he leans back he makes his voice light. "I wager Madam Lantos schemes something."

"Well, I scheme, too. Besides Felicity, I have collected two new tarts." Several strumpets Felicity brought by the boardinghouse I would not take. One was over melancholy. Another I feared was of the lazy kind. That will not do.

Daniel moves to come atop me again. I understand if today of all days he feels more alive than usual. "On any day," he says, "I will take one Eliza Haycraft over one Madam Lantos *and* one Madam Hunter."

―――――――

It is only days later when Madam Lantos comes to me wearing triumph on her face. In her rose-petal dress she strides inside my chamber in the boardinghouse and juts her chin the way I like to think is mine. "I am coming to tell you," she says, "that I am leaving."

"Are you going to Planters House, then?" Rude, but I cannot resist.

"Better than Planters House." She does not care to look direct at me as she lies, so she glances at her nails. "One of the many gentlemen I am pleased to call a friend will assist me in establishing a new house."

Madam Lantos may not have friends, but that does not mean she is unacquainted with gentlemen who would profit from her labors if they could. "Which gentleman is that? I wonder if I know him."

Her eyes return to my face. She will not answer that, probably for fear I might try to stop him. "So the time in which you may enjoy your"—she glances about as if seeking a polite word—"ascendancy will be short."

"Short perhaps, but sweet."

She spins away but does not quit my chamber. With her back to me she speaks again. "Do not think your piddling assistance is reparation for betraying me."

"I offered you help from the kindness of my heart. It does not surprise me you do not recognize the feeling."

One more swish of her skirts and Madam Lantos is gone. Until the end of my days, I am sure, she will plague me.

―――――――

IT IS a Monday in July when I hear news that much saddens me. It is early in the evening and the heat still wraps us in a shroud as Charity and I walk along Green Street past the Reveille café. Business is brisk and so children aplenty linger outside, palms outstretched. I daresay many are orphans of the cholera: despite our hopes, that plague rages. It is only because we must provision that Charity and I risk the deadly air.

I am handing coins to a mob of ragamuffins and Charity is urging me to be done with it already when I hear a patron of the Reveille speak the name *Farrar*. My ears hear what I wish they did not.

Dead he is, of the cholera. As I saw with my own eyes, the good doctor was using all his hours tending to the afflicted. When first he himself was sick it seemed he would fight it; he improved; then, in hours, it took him. I remember when he came unbidden to my house on Green Street, eyes kind. He was an important man, and a busy one, but he worried for me.

IT IS NOT the first time I attend a burial in this fashion—in fact, it is the only fashion in which I have ever attended a burial—but it is the first I do so for a man I did not know as a bawd would.

I hired a gig for Charity and me to come to this place called Bellefontaine where Dr. Farrar will be buried. It is some five miles north of Green Street and almost as if we are in the countryside. Here is another way our metropolis changes: the men of business no longer wish to spare land in the city for the dead. They prefer now to bury them further afield and in the meanwhile create a peaceable retreat. I've heard tell the idea comes from Paris, but I wonder if that is just the *famille Chouteau* spreading a tale that pleases them.

In black from bonnets to boots, we hold ourselves a distance from the gathering, trees giving us shade and a hiding spot. The hour of a man's interment is not the hour his widow need learn of the whores he knew.

Charity whispers beside me. "Dr. Farrar had more than a few sons."

"One daughter, too." All huddle round the widow, she veiled in black net. "And look how many treasured him," I add, for it is a crowd gathered at the gravesite, heads bowed, hats doffed, all, I'm sure, filled with memories of Dr. Farrar yet wondering alongside when their own day will come to fall to dust.

At this noonday hour, though, the bereaved are assaulted as much by sun as by grief. One man, taller than most, dark, with unruly hair that droops low on his forehead, turns his head to the right and catches my gaze across the space that separates us. He is my age and not a Farrar, I don't think, as he stands apart from them. His eyes on mine are steady and not, I believe, disapproving. We stare at each other for some moments before he returns his gaze to the ground at his feet.

Charity tugs me into the trees' shadows. I made the mistake of drifting into my own thoughts and allowing a ray of sun to light upon me. Does that man know of this whorish tradition of attending a burial in secrecy?

The prayers go on for some time and then men must lower the doctor's casket into that yawning rectangle where he will forever rest. I think the world is never more silent than when the first clumps of dirt fall upon the casket. Even birds hold their song. As the earth upon the casket mounts, I hear an ill-concealed wail, from elsewhere a sob caught in the throat. I bow my head then motion to Charity to follow me away. I do not wish to intrude upon this scene, when those who love Dr. Farrar best must turn away from him one last time. They must leave him to the unforgiving earth and sun, then to the night and rain and snow that will someday follow. It pains even me, the acquaintance of a moment, to leave a good man thus.

We are embarked upon our return to the boardinghouse, a march of some two hours, when one carriage then another pass us on the road, headed toward the city. Our black skirts suffer from the dust raised by their wheels and horses' hooves, and even with my parasol above my head I think it will be a hundred times that my handkerchief wipes the sweat from my brow.

"Least the country air must be good for us," Charity remarks.

A carriage slows beside us then rolls to a stop just in front. From inside leaps the dark-haired man who gazed at me. As I look at him now from a lesser distance I see that though he is dressed as a gentleman he is not garbed as the highest sort. Still, I like the look of him. And there is a lightness to his eyes, as if they are made of amber. He nods at Charity then addresses me. "May I offer you ladies a ride to the city? It is a distance from here and the day is hot."

Does he not know we are the opposite of ladies? I am surprised Charity does not chortle at the idea. "That is kind of you," I say, "but we will not trouble you."

"You would not in any case and especially not as friends of Dr. Farrar."

Still I hesitate, as I like to do things for myself.

"Oh please, Eliza," Charity says, with irritation in it, and then to him: "If really you have seats for us, we would appreciate it."

He gestures to the carriage. "I can seat four and it is only myself returning."

Charity whispers to me—"we might fair melt before we make it all the way back to Green Street walking"—and she is closing her parasol and preparing to step up into the carriage when of a sudden she stops. "Please, what is your name?" she asks the man.

He frowns, then: "Richard Bonner."

"Oh," and disappointment crosses her face. He is not named William: I know that is the cause of it. She gathers herself quickly, though, and steps up to the rear seat of the carriage, a rockaway if I am not mistaken.

Mr. Bonner looks at me with puzzlement. I will not be the one to explain. I move to join Charity on the rear seat when he speaks again. "Please, will you ride in front and do me the favor of conversing? You will be sheltered from the sun," and that cannot be argued as the overhang of the roof will shield me.

I should do as he asks. It is a favor he is giving us, and perhaps he is lonely, and I am sure the day made him melancholy, as it has me. "I would, but I will not like the wind in my face, least once we are nearer the city."

"If your concern is cholera, you need not be."

Does he not know of the miasmas? Or does he dismiss them, as do people who believe themselves superior to the rest of us? It is the latter. "I believe it is not the air that worsens the plague," he says, "but the unsanitary conditions in the city."

I am prepared to dislike him when he adds something that much improves my opinion. "Since I have no intention that we ride to Chouteau's Pond and swim there—and I would rather we call *that* a cesspool—I am sure you will be quite safe."

I of all women must smile at a man who puts the words *Chouteau* and *cesspool* so close together. It is years since the so-called Pond drew bathers and artists. And Mr. Bonner is not the first I hear express the view that the city's many sinkholes and caverns, filled with scum not only from people and animals but factories and slaughterhouses, too, are a pestilence all their own. "Which do you think is worse?" I ask him. "Chouteau's Pond or Kayser's Lake?"

"Where is that one?"

"Biddle and Tenth."

He thinks for a moment. "Perhaps we could ride past both and compare."

"In the carriage and from a distance, of course."

"If there are more cesspools you care to examine, and have the afternoon free, we could do a ranking and request that the newspapers publish it."

"For the benefit of all," I say.

"Quite the public service," and he holds out his hand to help me step up, and I find myself sitting beside this Mr. Bonner in the front seat of the rockaway.

I wonder I have never seen him at Madam Lantos's? Judging from his garments he has not the wealth to afford her house, but then how to explain the rockaway? Of course I have not seen him at my place, either. Perhaps he is an ascetic, or, even more rare, a man blissfully wed.

He takes up the reins and clucks at the horses to move. "I heard your first name is Eliza, but may I ask what is your family name?" and after I tell him, and he seems not to know it, I ask how it is possible he knows not of Kayser's Lake. "I have been in St. Louis only a short time and have not made the viewing of cesspools my first business."

"I have been here some years now and still have not done a full assessment. Where did you come from, then?"

"Chicago."

"Our rival to the north." Then I have another thought. "Though I think you in Chicago regard us as your rival and we in St. Louis do not spend much time thinking about you at all." I glance at him. Now he is smiling. I see in his cheek a dimple.

"You do not lack for confidence, Miss Haycraft," he tells me.

He is right and wrong both. At times my confidence flags, but never does it abandon me entirely. Yet a saddening thought rises to my mind. "It is a strange time for you to come to St. Louis, with the cholera killing so many."

His manner becomes grave once again. "It causes misery and death in Chicago, too, though not so much as here. And that is why I came." He turns to look at me as his horses trot straight and true on this simple stretch. "I wish to help the physicians here. Doctor Hardage Lane, Doctor Wisehart, Doctor McCullough, and, of course, Dr. Farrar."

"And you would help them how?"

"I am a physician as well." So he is a man of science. I have not encountered many of those. "I am a graduate of Transylvania University," he says, "as was Dr. Farrar. I was honored finally to meet him here." There is a moment of silence, then: "How did you know Dr. Farrar?"

I hear a curiosity he cannot hide. I am not ashamed of what I do to earn my keep, but all the same I feel the urge to tell this Richard Bonner that the man he admired was not one to feed his desires at bawdy houses. "He was a neighbor of mine," I say, "and he was kind to me."

"Do you attend the burial of every kind man you know? I wonder you have time to do anything else."

"I would have plenty of time, as really it would not be so many. Did you have companions on the journey here or did you come alone?" I ask, for both my frank words and Mr. Bonner's sideways appraisal make me feel oddly revealed, as if I said too much too quickly.

He tells me about them—they are physicians who met with other folk they knew, and in fact this rockaway belongs to one of them, so I am back to thinking Mr. Bonner must not possess much wealth—and after all that is said, Mr. Bonner asks again about me. "Why did you and your friend come all this way alone?"

"Well, I am not alone and neither is she."

He thinks for a moment before he agrees. Of course he knows well as I do that in this world of ours, two women without a man are alone. Three are alone. I wager you need four of us to give one of us company. And women like Charity and me, who move about the world without a man to shelter and guide us, as so many would say, raise the ire of all. We are not docile as we should be. We are overbold. In the bedchamber we are boldness itself, perhaps the greatest sin of all.

"So I will ask instead," Mr. Bonner says, "why you chose to stand among the trees and not at the gravesite."

"If you have not already guessed it, Mr. Bonner, we are public women, Charity and I." I turn to look at him as I am curious what effect my words will have. But his is not a face to give much away. "One such as me could only hurt the memory of Dr. Farrar. People would believe things that are not true. That is the way the world is."

He is quiet for a time, then: "There is much about the world I would change if I could," he says, and with that ceases speaking. As silent moments pass, one after the next, I am forced to think that, like most men, he sees no point conversing with a public woman like myself.

I find that disappoints me.

WE DO NOT PASS Chouteau's Pond or Kayser's Lake or any other cesspool of note. I ask Mr. Bonner to leave us at the edge of the Burnt District—I hear grumbling from Charity as I do—but I do not wish him to view our boardinghouse. I turn to face him after I step from the carriage. "It is not only the ride I thank you for, Dr. Bonner," I say, realizing late that I should give him the respect due him as a man of medicine. "Thank you also for helping so many who are sick."

"Please keep yourselves away from the dirtiest parts of the city," he says, and I believe he might say more, but I spin away and lead Charity north on Sixth Street.

"Is his advice some you'll take, then?" Charity asks, panting after me in the heat, and I hear the tease in her voice that comes when a man handsomer than most appears at our rooms.

"He is a doctor, and not the first to say such a thing, and there's common sense to it, don't you think?" and as we walk I keep her on that topic.

Outside our boardinghouse a young woman comes swiftly toward us and all thoughts of Dr. Bonner leave me. She is dressed plainly, bone thin, pale of face and red of hair and holding by the hand a small version of herself, perhaps four or five years of age. About the elder there is agitation and I am thinking I see in both something familiar and I understand why when the young woman speaks.

"I am Bridget Carpenter," and I hear in her voice her mother's voice, "and this is my sister Anna, and our mother was Ina Carpenter."

Was. Ina. Who tended to my beaten face when I was just off John's canoe; who shared with me her family's food on the steamboat belowdecks; who shunned me when she saw I would go with Obadiah to try to make my way in this hard world. *You know what he'll be expecting.*

"My mother is dead of the plague, she is," Bridget Carpenter tells me, as her face crumples, "and I don't know what we'll do now, as my father's dead, too, years ago, and there're six mouths it falls to me to feed, and I know you're a fancy lady as my mother told me so when we saw you walk about—she said you were made for the trade, right from the start—and now I'm asking if you'll make me a bawd, too, for I must feed all of us and don't know how else to do it."

It is a pang I feel hearing this speech, and seeing the face of Ina's eldest wet as the river. I look down at little Anna, who must be the babe Ina held to her breast on that steamboat. "Come inside with us," I say to Bridget, "and I'll get food for you."

Bridget hesitates and I wonder how she thinks she'll be a bawd if she won't even enter a bawd's boardinghouse, but then she rallies and follows me upstairs. It is a rule I have, to take on only trollops who are ready and eager, who know what they will be doing but will go about it all the same. I do not judge Bridget to be such a one. And I remember too well her nerves on that steamboat. Her nails were bit to the quick then and still are. After she and Anna eat, I press money into Bridget's hand. "Find me when you need me, for I will always help you if I can. I do not believe you are right for this work," and I watch her face crumple again but for a different reason. "I will think on work for you, and I have friends to ask about it," and of course Daniel is first among them.

"I am a hard worker," she says, "I promise you that, and I have work now but it won't pay near enough," and I assure her I understand and in fact I do.

The next day I see Daniel and do ask him about it and now two of us are thinking on the problem, twice as good as one. It is as he is leaving the boardinghouse that the mistress hands to me a parcel left in my name. I unwrap the string and brown paper to find a toy carriage the size of a bread loaf.

"There is a note," Daniel tells me, and since he knows I have no hope of reading it he takes it from my hand. " 'To Miss Eliza Haycraft,' " he reads, " 'so she needs no one's help to journey wherever she might desire to go.' It is signed Richard Bonner." Daniel eyes me. "That is not a name I have heard you speak."

"He is a new acquaintance." And though I did not lead him to this boardinghouse, he found it all the same.

"I see." Daniel hands me the note and sighs. There is a sadness in his eyes and it's near never I see that in him. "You are no man's to keep, Eliza," he tells me.

And that is the truth of it.

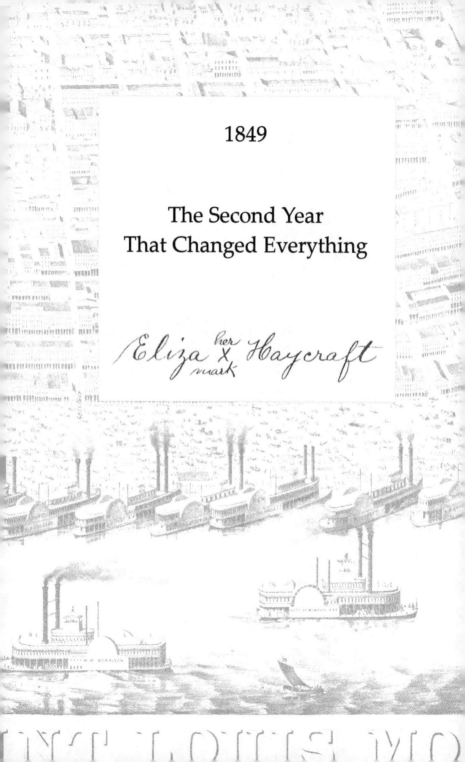

1849

The Second Year
That Changed Everything

Eliza *her X mark* Haycraft

Chapter Nineteen

"A sudden and almost unexpected wave of emigration swept over us, and we found the town inundated with breweries, beer houses, sausage shops, Apollo Gardens, Sunday concerts, Swiss cheese and Holland herrings. We found it almost necessary to learn the German language before we could ride in an omnibus, or buy a pair of breeches, and absolutely necessary to drink beer at a Sunday concert."

— Editorial from the *Daily Missouri Republican*

— June 1857

I T IS A NIGHT FOR MUCK-A-MUCKS, for I had one earlier and now here I am below another. A city officer this is, though I am not one to say which.

It is not his face I'm looking at but the pillow, for that is the way he likes things, and I know he won't be long about it. It is a release he wants, a relaxation from the day's labors, and my warm and willing flesh provides it. When he is finished he collapses atop me then rolls off and gives my rump a slap. "You are a hussy, yelping like that."

"These walls are thin"—I roll to my side and give him a smile —"and I'd hold myself quiet if I could."

He chuckles. He would rather not think how a trollop might yelp often as she lifts her skirts. Another chuckle, and he would laugh longer if he didn't wish to sleep. Off he drifts. I slip from the bed to cleanse. Near seven years a harlot and I can do what I must swiftly and in darkness deep as an inkpot, though outside the boardinghouse windows the Green Street gaslights flicker.

Through these thin walls I hear in the bedchamber beside mine the landing of Charity's whip on striped flesh. If I were in the corridor I'd hear my other tarts at their labors and their clients in their raptures. Ours is not a silent business. I don't mind the sound of coins clinking, either.

And they pile up. They pile so high that I begin to consider something that frightens me.

When my city officer is awakened and I'm stroking him lightly in the way he likes, I ask what he thinks on a certain matter, though as usual I have my own opinion. "Property prices," I murmur, "you think them on the rise?" For a time, after the cholera and the Great Fire two years back, they were not.

"There is no stopping them, not with how quick our city is rebuilt."

"Rebuilt much better, too." There is much more brick—near everything is brick now—with facades of stone or cast iron. Even walkways are brick. I wonder who is selling all this red brick to our city, for he must be wondrous rich.

I do not see a reason why St. Louis would stop growing. Not even the plague or the Great Fire kept the Germans and Irish from coming.

"Still"—my officer is speaking again—"only the wisest men

among us will know which properties he may profit from quickly."

I will not tell him a woman might make those judgments, too, for I do not wish the sad tale of my Green Street house to spill from my lips. Oh, how swiftly I lost the value from that property! That tale would make any man even more sure this is a game only they can play. Even if men make such mistakes, they are not scorned for them as I would be, I who am not merely a woman but even lower than that: a strumpet, too.

"St. Louis will only grow bigger, don't you think?" I say to my officer. "Our many factories, our location where the rivers meet, the busyness of the port, all of that will make it so?"

He agrees, and heartily.

I told all this to Richard last I saw him, but he was not convinced of it.

I AM VERY proud a day later as Daniel and I hurry south along Fourth Street toward the Courthouse, where inside we will find the recorder's office. I am amazed this castle of white stone is only a handful of blocks from the plot of land I will today purchase. I have with me the cash in hand.

"You are not afraid?" Daniel asks me. His question is serious, but there is teasing in his tone and happy light in his blue eyes.

"Oh, I am afraid. But I will do it all the same."

For my desire to be Madam Lantos, *more* than Madam Lantos, returned to me in the dying embers of the Great Fire, when she and Madam Hunter both were laid low. I saw I had a chance to have their harlots work for me. I saw I could keep my expenses low, with only the room rents and Noah Moberry to pay. So I took that chance and am seeing the reward from it. Now I wish to use my money to purchase property and put to work yet more harlots. There is no end to the need for them, not with so many men flooding our city. In St. Louis there are near two men for every woman, one of my city officers told me, and from what I see I believe him correct on the point.

When Daniel and I reach the recorder's office, I see a different clerk from five years before. He opens the handsome leather-covered book in which he writes the deeds. It is of a tremendous large size befitting such a serious business.

Soon the seller appears, a Mr. Turner Maddox, who, Daniel says, makes his fortune in lumber. I look at him across the book of deeds. I guess him to be ten years older than myself, wearing both a great moustache and an expression of astonishment. Even though he sees me in front of him, still he cannot believe that a woman is purchasing this land he is selling. He must wonder how I came to have the money to do it.

Well, if he wants to know, he had better be about it quickly, for these days I have less time than ever to show him, least in a way he would enjoy.

Finally the clerk is finished writing out the whole of the deed. Mr. Maddox signs his name and I lay down the two lines of my X, which I practiced this morning as I have not written them in years and did not want a mistake when the important moment came.

Daniel and I return to my bedchamber to, shall we say, celebrate. After, I light his cigar and we lay back among the tumbled bedclothes.

I glance at Daniel, who is puffing smoke at the ceiling. If he is trying to make rings, he is doing a good job of it. "I wish to own more properties than just the one on Fourth Street," I tell him. He stops puffing and I believe it is because I have surprised him. "What is to stop me from owning properties all over this city?"

He turns his head so his eyes meet mine. "Money will stop you."

"I have money." I pause to listen to those words rise to the bedchamber's ceiling, same as Daniel's rings of smoke. "And I make more each day. For example," and I tell him what my trollops and I earned the week prior, which I carried to the bank Monday.

Daniel's eyes widen in astonishment. "Might I become a whore, too? I promise you I would be very good at it."

He would be; I know that without thinking long about it. And there are rooms in this city, here and there, where he could ply that vocation.

Much money as I have, I do not wish to stop piling it up. For one thing, I do not yet have a house of my own so I am not yet become like Madam Lantos. I hear news of her. I have learned that a certain gentleman from Virginia was the one to put her into a house after the Great Fire. It took some months, but she found new strumpets and gentlemen found her.

Well, what else would I expect? This is her trade, as it is mine. Does she wonder—as I do—how large a trade she might grow? I think mine will not grow so large as the fur business of Chouteau's family, but it need not be so very small, either. And I would like to point out to Charles Pierre Chouteau, if ever I speak to him again, that I do not have ancestors before me who built up my trade. All my ancestors could do was feed themselves, and not always that, either.

"I will not take so many clients now," I tell Daniel. Really, such is already the case. With so many strumpets to look after, I am fierce busy. The sort of madam I wish to be does not raise her skirts as she did in her days of youth. She saves herself for the select few. And I believe it more profitable to arrange matters for my strumpets than do the whoredom myself.

I realize Daniel is staring at me with a face full of shock. "I hope this does not mean," he says, "that anything will change between us."

"Oh, no. You are my special friend and always will be."

He sinks back against the pillows—"well, that is a relief"—and blows yet another smoke ring toward the angels.

"First," I tell him, "I must have a house built on the lot on Fourth Street."

"What good is that to me?" His blue eyes dance.

I punch him playfully in the arm then have an idea. "I could pay you a share of my profits from that house if you find me a man to build it." I wish someone who is excellent at the task, who will not build creaky stairs such as I had in my house on Green Street. "A share of the profits for one year," I add, thinking on it further. "If you also help me keep an eye on the work while the house is built."

He rises on an elbow to eye me narrowly, though a smile curves his lips.

"I did not say *what* share," I finish.

"What sort of proposition is this? It worsens with every word you speak. You are a most stern harlot," he adds, and begins to tickle me.

"No, that is Charity," I tell him, and giggle, and that is the end of our conversation for some time.

It is a rainy morning in June. The parlor of the boardinghouse is empty save for Charity and me, as it is too early for our fellow bawds and too late for the other inmates. Hair loose and wearing our negligées, we sit upon a near threadbare settee drinking coffee and sharing a strawberry crumble. By the sunlight poking vaguely through the window, Charity is reading to me something from the newspaper that I can scarce believe.

"No spirits at all," she repeats. "In the entire state of Maine, from now on, no manufacture and no sale of liquor."

"That is foolishness itself." So much money can be made from liquor. Men especially wish to drink it whether they be happy or sad or in between.

"It is called"—she frowns and holds the newspaper nearer her face—" 'total abstinence.' "

"I hope city officers here do not get that idea." Liquor—not too much—so often smoothes a harlot's labors; I have long known it.

"I don't think they will." Charity speaks with confidence. I watch her eyes read the words on the newspaper, dancing back and forth like feet across a tavern floor. I suppose I could learn to read like that, for I wager Charity would teach me. For that matter, Daniel would. But I worry: could I learn at this great age, I who never sat in a schoolhouse? And how embarrassed would I be if I could not!—even if Charity or Daniel were the only one to know.

I need not read words, I tell myself: it is people that *I* read.

"That is one of the good things about a frontier town like St. Louis," I hear Charity say. "People here are not Puritans like they are in New England."

Sometimes Charity's eyes grow dreamy when she speaks of New England and at those times she calls it *home*. Other times her eyes grow cold, as if she would never see it again if she could help it. I think my eyes must be cold as river ice most times I think of Cote Sans Dessein.

"Now I see it is not *total* abstinence they want." Charity drops her arms, crushing the paper onto her lap where crumbs from our strawberry treat linger. "They will allow liquor for 'medicinal and mechanical' purposes. What could be a mechanical purpose for liquor?"

We both laugh at that. What could it be? We are still laughing when the boardinghouse mistress shouts that now is not the time for whores' hilarity as our new washerwoman is standing on the stoop and do we expect our mistress to conduct a whore's business?

I am wearing only a negligée, but especially as it is raining hasten to bring the washerwoman inside. She is mulatto, small of stature and near the age of Charity, with a face wide open like a full moon. She blinks at Charity and me, undone as we are, but she knew already we were harlots and I am sure expected no better.

It is not long after I gaze upon her that I remember her face. "Are you not the slave of Frederick Norcom?" I ask her. I do not think kindly of him, the man who would pay only a low sum for my Green Street house and who I saw yell at this woman at the public market and who I believe made her with child and not after asking first. "You told me your name once, but I am sorry. I do not remember it."

"Hester, and I am free for two years." There is pride as she says it, and though I do not ask her for it she pulls from her pocket what I know will be her freedom paper, the thing she must carry everywhere for any white person might demand she show it. If she does not have it on her person, she might be arrested, and it is so for I have seen it happen.

She hands it to me and I hand it to Charity. It is near soft as muslin, that yellowed paper, and the most precious thing Hester can possess, beside her child.

Charity unfolds it with care. Through the thin paper I see black ink from someone's writing. " 'This is to certify,' " Charity reads, " 'that negroe woman Hester and children are free, and have all the rights to go where they please, that other coloured people have. They were set free by me in January last. Signed F. Norcom.' " Charity puts the paper back into Hester's hand, where fast as can be it is stowed again in her pocket.

"You have more than one child?" I ask. The paper said *Hester and children*, but I remember only an infant girl.

"You saw my Priscilla," Hester tells me. "Two more now."

I will not ask if she got them by Norcom, but I fear that is so. And after he set them all free, Hester must feed herself and her children with no man's help, unless Norcom gave her money to do it and that I doubt.

I am thinking of Hester's four mouths to feed as I slip her a few extra of my bawd's coins.

IN AUGUST RICHARD is again in St. Louis, walking beside me along Fourth Street. The day is hot as the one Dr. Farrar was put into the ground. On this day, across the river and far away still, thunder growls like mad dogs circling. "It will rain and I will be glad of it," I tell Richard.

"You like the rain?"

"If I am inside I like it." I think more about it. "Sometimes if I am outside, too. If it matters not if I get wet."

"If it is not too cold. If it is a summer storm, such as this one would be."

He smiles when I agree and falls silent again.

Twice since the cholera ended he has returned to St. Louis, and this time, too, he says he will depart soon to go west. Not so far as California—he seems the last one to want to pan for gold—but to wild, frontier places where doctors are needed but few can be found. He stays there for some months and then quits that place to return again to Chicago. In that city is his practice, where he works beside another doctor who stays put.

"I would not like all that time away from home," I told him last time I saw him, leaving out that I must earn and where better can I do that but here where I have a steady business? In return he said something that gave me the idea he does not like to stay long in one place. That makes him like a steamboat pilot, except that in every other way he is different from those. If he were a steamboat pilot, I am sure he would have had me on my back by now. Sometimes I catch him looking at me as if he very much wishes that, but he has not done a thing about it. That makes me wonder what is he about where I am concerned.

Now we have crossed Spruce Street and are approaching Poplar. Times like these, when the sun is high, I wonder at the wisdom of red brick everywhere as we all bake from it. I stop to mop my brow and Richard does the same. "You see?" I point to make him look. "The bricklayers are at work on my house."

"It shall be a large house," Richard observes.

Large as possible, for the more rooms I have, the more harlots I can put into them. It is no mystery to Richard what I do, but still I do not like to speak of it with him. So instead I say: "It is cheapest to build now all I might ever wish to on this lot."

"Indeed, you have not left much ground to spare."

I bristle, but he is correct. "That is what most do. In this part of the city are buildings, not gardens."

He nods and smiles, but I am not sure that means he agrees with me. When we arrive at the lot I step ahead to speak to the chief man, leaving Richard behind. There are workingmen aplenty, near all of them Irish the chief man has chosen from among his neighbors.

There is much to ask the chief man, tall and skinny as a church spire, and a thing or two to criticize. This is not the first time he speaks to me and I think he begins to forget it is a woman he builds for. After some time I remember that Richard walked here with me and I turn to search for him. I need not look for even a moment for there he stands at the lot's edge. Nor need I draw his attention, for already his gaze is steady upon me.

I wave to him and he smiles. Wind whips about me and I think the rain cannot be far off now. When I join him and we turn to walk, he asks if all is to my satisfaction. "Not all, that is too much to hope for, but I am happy with it."

"The men work very hard. Long hours in the hot sun."

"They are glad for steady work. How can you be so often away from your work?" I ask, for that is another thing about Richard that makes me wonder.

"I work as a doctor wherever I go. I know what you're asking, though, and I will tell you. My father is a wealthy man and so I have some wealth, too," and I find it interesting I do not hear pride in those words as I usually would.

"Is your father also a doctor, then?"

"God, no. My father is a banker in New York. That is where I was raised."

"New York is a very grand place, is it not? Why do you not live there?"

"Because my father lives there." He turns to look at me and I see in his amber eyes something I understand.

"That is how I feel about my mother. But my father I love

truly."

"My mother I love truly. My father... I am not sure he can love."

"That is how I feel about my mother," I say again, and this time we laugh, for it seems funny we both feel this.

Richard speaks again. "I was wrong before. There is one thing my father does love and that is money."

"It is easy for you to say that if you have always had enough." I realize I am speaking sharper than I wish to. "Perhaps he has not always had enough."

"He has never wanted for anything. Eliza." Richard halts and grabs onto my arm so that I must halt, too. Around us people flow as if we were tree stumps snagged on the river bottom. "I understand what it is not to have enough. I have not felt that myself, but I understand it."

"It is not the sort of thing you understand with your head. If you have never been in the pit yourself, you do not know what it is to fall into it."

He nods. I see his mind working: he is deciding whether he agrees with me. Then: "It is simply that I do not wish to die knowing I passed my life entire doing nothing but making money." I am about to speak harshly again when he takes the words from my mouth. "I know that is a luxury not all men have."

"Not all women, either."

"I do not fault you for what you do, Eliza."

"Well, thank you very much." Perhaps it is the heat or the rain coming, perhaps it is that I do not understand what he is about, but he is irritating me now. "You spit on your father's money, but still you use it."

"I use it for good."

"I use my money for good, too. I give much away. Every night I have outside my door women and children who would not eat but for me."

"I see them. It is a wonderful thing you do. Do not be angry with me, Eliza. I am not against you."

A raindrop wets my parasol. I knew I would see Richard and was silly enough to carry a pretty parasol meant for sun. "I do not understand what you want from me," I tell him.

He surprises me then. "Nor do I. I have thought about it a great deal and I am afraid it is not a simple thing."

"It is always simple between a man and a woman." Harlots have lovers, of course. I do not, for that has passed me by. I am past thirty years and not so foolish that I still long for love, as does Charity. That is not how I think of men, not anymore. I service them and to some of them I enjoy talking—they understand so much more of the world than we are allowed to—and I have also known the rare case of a man who has become my dear friend.

"You do not think as other women do," Richard tells me, "or look as they do or speak as they do or act as they do." He is looking away from me and speaking as if rain is not falling harder upon us. "I have tried to stay away from you. But that has not worked, as here I am again."

"You need not stay away." I step nearer to him. Some around us have begun to stare. A whore's conversation with a gentleman is bound to be of interest. I lower my voice. "You could come to my boardinghouse. I wonder why you have not already done so."

His amber eyes are fiercely lit as he stares down at me. "Do not think that the fact that I have not means I do not wish to." From the way he speaks those words, and mostly from the way he looks at me, I do believe him. "The problem is that I do not care to be one in a number."

"Well, you have not a thing to say about that."

He stares at me, fierce as ever, then of a sudden laughs. I watch his dimple flash. "We will become drenched. Did we say we liked a summer storm?" and he takes my hand and leads me at a run back to my boardinghouse.

When we get there I think he may come inside with me—and I will admit I hope he does—but he does not. He stops at the bottom stair as I climb the rest then I am forced to watch him doff his hat and go.

———————

WE ARE BACK in the recorder's office in December, Daniel and I, and this time it is a property on Poplar Street that I purchase.

"What is the thing people say?" I whisper to Daniel as the clerk writes out the deed. "The third time pays for all?"

"Yes, that is the proverb, that the third time you will succeed even if you did not the first or the second."

I do not know why that would be so, but I will believe it as this snowy afternoon marks my third time to purchase property: first Green Street, then Fourth, and now Poplar. In this case I do not need a house built, for already one stands.

I do not wish to think too much of myself, but there is some-thing to admire here. Eliza Haycraft, doxy, owns two brick houses now, one built with money she piled up herself and one standing purchased with the same, and she believes these two won't be the last of them, either.

I will not long remember the name of the man who sold to me this property. I disliked both the look of him and what he muttered as he brushed past me outside the Courthouse after the deed was signed, while darkness gathered and snowflakes drifted from heaven like winter's petals.

"To think you got here spreading your legs, whore," he said, and off he strode, settling his hat on his head. He looked both ways as he crossed Fourth Street, which is a shame for I would not have minded if he had got careless and a carriage plus two had trampled him beneath its wheels.

That is the thing with some men. It is to bed us women that they want us—for some men it is all they want us for—yet never are we to profit from it? Ever in this life would a man agree to such a thing?

That question is so easy even a bawd could answer.

Chapter Twenty

"Her house was the favorite resort of troops of soystering firemen, out on a night's lark. At such times the house was thrown open and wines and smiles dispensed liberally...

"Madame Haycraft was no saint... Still there were some traits about the woman to be taken into consideration when the world passes judgment upon what it is pleased to term an abandoned life. The police authorities seldom had cause to complain of a riotous disturbance of the peace on her part, or the part of her women. Her house was known for quietness and order, having about it an air of refinement which made it perhaps all the more dangerous in a moral point of view."

— "A Noted Character Gone"

— *St. Louis Times*, December 6, 1871

O N A GRAY MORNING IN JANUARY, WHEN THE YEAR IS STILL NEW, I hear of two tragedies, one far and one near. Though Charity and I, in our night-dresses, sip coffee in the snug kitchen of the Poplar Street house—a kitchen I had painted yellow to be like Madam Lantos's of old, though never would I tell her as much—I will wonder later if these calamities bode ill for the year.

"Trains must be shocking dangerous," I tell Charity, though really I do not know. The month last, we in this city witnessed for the first time a locomotive chug away on fresh-laid tracks. It was called *Pacific* and departed from a station at Fourteenth and Chouteau on its way west to Cheltenham. I was one of many to watch it from a distance and maybe one of few to have no desire to see it closer.

But no remark can pry Charity's dark eyes from the newspaper, where the tale of an ill-fated train lies. She bends over the paper laid flat upon the trestle table so all there is to stare upon is the place where her hair parts, a line pale and wavy as a string. "It was down an embankment both cars of the locomotive plunged," she murmurs. "Aboard were Pierce, his wife Jane, and their son Benny, just eleven." Her eyes rise to mine, with sadness in them. "The boy was killed in an instant."

Franklin Pierce is to be our nation's president in two months' time. Charity told me his firstborn son died days after birth and his second fell to typhus at four years of age. Soon he and Jane will go to Washington alone as if they were newly wed but with none of that happiness, and three full doses of sorrow.

I must wonder again about God's designs when but an hour later a young Negro washerwoman I never laid eyes on before, barely sixteen I am sure, appears to collect our linens. When I inquire after Hester, she tells me with a mournful face a thing I can scarce believe. "Blakey and McAffee have her, ma'am."

"The slave traders?" We all know them: they are near the biggest in that foul business. "That cannot be. Hester is long free."

"She is not free." The girl's face is grim. "They dragged her from her public house, and her children, too. Many saw it. They're in jail now."

In the Negro jail, it must be. How could this happen? I have seen Hester's freedom paper with my own eyes and Charity has read it aloud and it is years that Hester walks free.

Hours later, Noah Moberry comes to my house to work. It is near seven years he works for me, starting at the house on Green Street. His wife is a churchgoer, he has told me, and not happy about this trade, but the work is steady and there is not much danger in it. I need his strength and loyalty more than ever, and that of his friends he has recommended to me, for still I rent boardinghouse rooms on Green Street for trollops of mine, and more work at the house I had built on Fourth Street, and still more labor here on Poplar. As of September last I own a lot and house further up Green Street, too. This brick house on Poplar is where I live, and Charity, too, for once I owned this spot I wished to be here and not on Fourth, and Charity felt the same.

I tell Noah what I heard about Hester. "I wish you to go to the Negro jail to see if she and her children are truly there."

"You do not believe it?" Noah asks.

He doubts not this sad tale, I can tell. "I do not see how it can be so."

Noah cannot visit the jail until the morrow for the night's work awaits us. But the next day, after he comes inside and brushes flakes of snow from his wide shoulders, he says he has seen Hester and she is truly in the jail, and her three children, too. "She told me," Noah says, "that you know the man Norcom."

"The man who was her owner. From long ago I did not like him." After these seven years, Noah and I speak with frankness.

"This Norcom came back to Missouri from the state of New York and sent for Hester. When she went to him, he asked for the freedom paper he wrote for her."

Of a sudden I feel tightness around my heart, as if I am watching a child toddle too close to a horse. Hester could not refuse such a request. When a white person demands that paper, it must be handed over.

"Norcom took it from her hand," Noah says, "and tore it into many pieces."

"Why would he do such a thing? Four years after letting her walk free?" It is as if John Haycraft appeared on Poplar Street and declared that I am his wife, no matter nine years have passed with us good as strangers. *She is my wife and all she owns is mine!* I could scream that he is not my husband, but things as they are in this world I would have to prove it, against the marriage license Haycraft could show. How can Hester prove she is no man's slave if she has not that freedom paper?

"Then," Noah says, "Norcom sent Blakey and McAffee to take her."

"Why would he enslave her and not keep her himself? Noah"—I lower my voice—"this means her children, too, he sent to the slave traders. And they are his own blood." What man is so wicked as to lift the yoke from his children and then put it back on them again?

Noah is shaking his head. "Only Priscilla is from Norcom. The others are from Hester's husband."

"She has a husband? Where is he?"

More sorrow crosses Noah's broad face. "Williams is his name. He is dead."

I throw my hands in the air. There is no end to Hester's anguish. "Are they fed at least? Not beaten?"

"They are well as any others in that place." I hear what Noah is telling me. All jailed there are well enough to live, for the traders want them healthy to sell. "The thing is not done yet." Noah eyes me steadily. "There is hope still."

Much as I ask, he will not tell me what that hope rests on. I get the idea it is something his people are about and not to be discussed with the likes of me, who is not one of them.

"IT IS an age since I have gone to Planters House," Charity tells me.

I watch her spin about her bedchamber, where the counterpane, curtains, and Turkey carpet are all one shade or another of pink. This is another way I am different from Charity, for in my bedchamber I favor the color jade. By the flicker of candlelight she and I lay upon her bed her best gowns so as to choose among them for her outing. I am allowing her to go, as the gentleman in question will pay the usual fees. So I am put where Madam Lantos was years ago when Daniel asked me to accompany on exactly this excursion. I understand now why Madam Lantos was not happy. Tonight I am not happy, either.

"Martin says," Charity tells me, "that Charles Dickens had plenty of nasty things to say about St. Louis when he passed through on his tour of America, but even he praised Planters House."

"Oh, yes, Dickens the English writer." I have heard talk of him in my parlor.

Charity smiles at my hard-won sophistication, though I daresay there are few words I could speak right now at which she would not smile. If I say the name Martin Terris, her face will glow like a bonfire. Mr. Terris is a client of Charity's and her age and not married and nothing to complain about—especially as he sits atop a great pile of his family's money. Will he risk that for a trollop? I will not say so to Charity, but I doubt it. I hold up a gown I favor in particular. "The burgundy?"

Charity wishes a brighter hue. "The amethyst. The neckline"— she holds the dress before her, cocking her head this way and that as she faces her tall mirror—"is extremely fetching." She will expose much of her bosom with it and in Planters House that will earn her many gentlemen's bold stares. Perhaps I will be lucky and one of them will distract her from Martin Terris. She lays the gown atop the others and walks to her armoire to search for an item there. "I thought something about Martin's name the other day." She kneels upon the carpet and pushes her head deep into the cupboard. "It starts with an M, you know."

"And what is special about an M?"

"It is very like a W." She withdraws from the armoire but remains kneeling and looks at me. "In fact, it is the same letter, just upside down. When I thought the apple peel made a W, I might have been wrong. Just as likely it made an M."

I know what she is telling me. I also know what she is asking of me. And I will give it to her for I do not have the heart not to. I go to kneel beside her and clasp her hands. "Charity, I wish you always to be happy as you are at this moment."

———

ONLY A FEW DAYS have passed when Noah comes early to Poplar Street to tell me news of Hester, who I now know to call Hester Williams. He was right to be hopeful. "She is out of the jail, and her children, too. She has sued for her freedom."

I do not wish to appear ignorant but do not understand what that means. "Who has she sued? Norcom?" I know it is possible for a slave to purchase his freedom, if his owner will allow it—as Chantal's mother did—but that is all I know on the matter.

Noah nods. "She went to the Courthouse and did it."

"How can Hester manage such a thing?"

"She can do it with the help of Reverend Jordan Early."

There is pride as Noah speaks that name. "This Reverend Early has a church?" I ask.

"He preaches at many Negro churches. He has a fruit store."

I learn this store is on Green Street and think I would like to pay a visit. For I wish to understand what this reverend and Hester have done.

Noah and I go in the gig, for I have one now—simple, with a single horse, not a phaeton like the bawdy ladies in New Orleans had. We have a groom, too, to care for the horse. Today the winter sky is clear, but the wind blusters so that it will cut through my thickest shawl like scissors.

At the shop I load my basket with apples and bananas and we are happy to find Reverend Early there. He is a young man, thin and small, but from his throat comes a large voice, which might be why he was called to the pulpit. I do not know if it is God who gives him confidence that glows like a torch. He is a free man and Noah has told me he was able to make free his wife and oldest boy, too.

I wonder if Reverend Early is one of the free Negro men in our city who can be called prosperous. I do not have to be told the powers-that-be are not happy about it; neither are the likes of Bridget. The higher-placed free Negro men often are stewards on steamboats or own barbershop emporiums or shops, like Reverend Early. Truth to tell, I feel a kinship with them. They are men, but I am white, so we both have a plus and a minus in this world that white men run.

"I have known Hester Williams for some years," I tell the reverend, "and her daughter Priscilla, too. Mr. Moberry tells me she has sued Norcom, with your help. He is not a friend of mine."

Reverend Early gestures to Noah and me to follow him outside. This is no topic to discuss amid the pears and oranges. "Frederick Norcom," he says, "will soon learn that we in the Negro community are far from powerless to help one another. Hester Williams is a churchgoing woman. When I heard of her plight, I knew it was my duty before God to help her."

I hear many things then that I never heard before. In our state, a slave who thinks he or she is rightfully free can go to the Courthouse and make that declaration. I do not know how the slave is supposed to get there, but that is another matter. A clerk writes out the statement and the slave signs it with an X, just as I sign my deeds, and then the Courthouse finds a lawyer who will push the case before a judge. Sometimes the lawyer will do it for no pay at all, which is an amazement to me and I wonder in that case how hard the lawyer labors. "And sometimes," I say, "the slave wins?"

Reverend Early looks surprised that I would doubt it, but to me it is as if a gnat bite kills a horse. "Slaves have been winning these cases for forty years," he tells me, and I hear many are declared free because their owner took them to a state where there is no slavery and then returned them to a state where there is. "Though there is a case," he adds, "of a slave named Dred Scott where the Supreme Court in this very state ignored that precedent."

"What I do not understand," I say, "is why Norcom would take away Hester's freedom and then immediately call for her to be sold."

The reverend lowers his voice as if we were in church. "I believe he is in want of money. I understand he is filing lawsuits regarding a property he owns on Front Street," and then I see it clearly.

If Norcom needs money, he can make it from selling Hester and her children. But he can sell them only if he owns them, no matter one is his own blood. Norcom is a bastard of a man, is what I think.

"I have seen the freedom paper written in Norcom's hand," I say. "A woman who works beside me saw it also, and read it aloud." I do not wish to say in front of Noah that I cannot read and hope the reverend does not ask about it. He nods but looks away and I wonder if he thinks, as any man would, that the testimony of a pair of doxies is of little use in the Courthouse or anywhere else.

He will not tell me where Hester is now or how she will earn her keep. I understand he has no reason to trust me. As if to make up for that, he waves away my coins for the fruit, leaving me with the good word that Blakey and McAffee cannot sell Hester unless the case is lost and that sad outcome the reverend does not anticipate. I am less sure than he.

It is March and so we are caught in that dismal time between winter and spring. The clouds cannot decide whether to hold back the rain or pelt it at us, so it is the worst of all: I must carry my umbrella but may never need it. It is a long walk I am doing, as I desire to feel my heart pump in my chest. Now that I leave most of the whoredom to others, I pass my evenings sitting in a parlor. And I have a gig as well, so my horse also does my walking. From time to time I hear Madam Lantos in my ear telling me I will become fat. She laughs as she says it.

It is eleven blocks to the north already I have walked so it will be eleven on the return. It is along Fifth Street I have been marching and now I turn left onto St. Charles. There is a reason for it.

Here is the property now owned by Chouteau and his wife, number 512 St. Charles Street. They no longer reside with their children at the castle of his ancestors. It is become the fashion for their kind to move into their own mansion. It is a brick structure set far back from the street yet astonishing deep, with railings of iron and eight stairs to climb to reach the front door. Shall I call it magnificent? I know Chouteau has had not just joy here but agony, too: the year last, his infant daughter died. He and his wife have a girl and a boy still—Emilie Anne and Pierre—and I hear murmurs that Julia is again with child.

I wonder if Chouteau knows I own property now, too, and not just one. Not that I measure myself against him.

I continue my promenade, and as I often do I stride past Madam Lantos's house. It is a grand structure, too, though of course not so majestic as Chouteau's. Three stories tall it stands, with a façade of finished brick painted brown and columns of a Greek style on both sides of the wide front door. She has this place because of a certain gentleman from Virginia who owns the property. I do not have a man above me who might tell me to do this or not do that. All the same, Madam Lantos has very important gentlemen come to her house. I have some, too, but not so many.

So am I become more than Madam Lantos? I cannot say yes. Not yet.

What to make of this mood of mine? I am not happy, but I am not sad. I am content but not at my ease. I am richer than ever, but I wish to earn more still. Am I free? From want, yes, from need; but I have new bonds now, for always I think of those who without me might not work or eat or have a roof above them.

I was sure when I had freedom, I would be happy as a bird on the wing. Perhaps now that freedom is something I have, I long for something else, not that I could say what it is. Maybe I would not even know it if I found it.

Not far away I see walking toward me a whore I recognize. Louisa Clark is her name and, sad to say, she is one of Madam Lantos's strumpets. I will not profess that Louisa possesses *the quality that has no name*, but I will say there is a certain something about her, like me a daughter of Missouri. Is it her tumble of honey-colored hair? Or her lips so full they look as if they might be bruised from kissing? Is it that even on a dull Tuesday she promenades with her waist corset-laced to the size of a fancy China vase? It is all these things and in a woman likely Charity's age: younger than me by six odd years but by no means young.

I meet her gaze as we near each other. Louisa smiles as if I were a gentleman she would not mind knowing better. I would not mind if she were one of my harlots. I have heard her name whispered even in my own parlors. She is a doxy who draws men to her as hounds to a beef roast. She is like Charity in that.

Oh, Charity.

"It is good to see you," I tell Louisa, "looking so well."

"And you. That is a most handsome dress."

Handsome, the wench calls my sage-colored frock. She is quick of wit, is Louisa. That sparkle lures gentlemen, too, if lightly displayed. "I hope Madam Lantos is well?" I say, though the wish is less than heartfelt.

"Extremely well. These days it is only happy tunes she plays on the piano."

I heard she has a piano again. "That is wondrous, indeed, if unfortunate for Beethoven."

Louisa laughs—that is a pretty sound, too—and we spin away from one another, whores gay as daisies beneath skies of charcoal gray.

I dare not say to Louisa that I wish her to work for me. What a rate she must command! Yet I might be wise to speak to her on the matter.

Oh, Charity.

IN MY YOUNGER YEARS, I could not have dreamed of such a bedchamber as I have now on Poplar Street. It is shocking spacious, with a ceiling from which hangs a chandelier of many crystals. The ceiling is white with a gold design stenciled upon it —an extravagance Charity suggested—and the walls are a rich jade. The draperies are ornate and tasseled and the Brussels carpet is fat and woven with a pattern of flowers. The bed's foot and headboards are carved in spectacular fashion, with velvet inserts, too, and there is a velvet settee at the foot, and more tassels on the counterpane. By the fireplace I have plump chairs where a gentleman and I might sit, with a low table between us for glasses of wine or whiskey. On the walls are gilt mirrors in the oval shape and also there is a *chiffonier* with another mirror atop it.

Daniel clutched at his heart and staggered when first he saw it. "Am I to call you Marie Antoinette now?"

"I would not mind it, and I will give you a piece of cake when-ever you do," for I know all about this queen of France from stories my bawds have told.

Daniel said it is a good thing his eyes are oft closed while he is in this bedchamber and I laughed along with him, but I do not really care what he, or any other gentleman, thinks about it.

On this April night as I dress, I take from the top drawer of my *chiffonier* the first bawd's coin I ever earned, given to me by Mr.

Lewis, the steamboat captain whose ginger-colored mustache was wide as his pilot house. From time to time I rub the coin and remember I had not a single one to my name when Mr. Lewis handed me this. Near nine years ago that was. What shall I be nine years from now? 1862. I can no more imagine that than I could imagine this life nine years prior.

It is a cheery crowd in the parlor this night. Here, too, the furnishings are plush. I have a parlor set now, carved of rosewood, and antique ginger jars, and—I am proud of these—brass cigar stands in the shape of a lion's head.

To the music of a Negro man at the piano, near midnight I am seated with Daniel, Robert Marcellus Stewart who sits in the Missouri Senate, Martin Terris—which means Charity is close at hand, gazing with lovesick eyes—and Dr. Richard Bonner, too.

Near four years I have known the doctor and still he confounds me. For a time last year many months passed and I did not see him. Did he travel through St. Louis and fail to call? One night he did call, though, and over the threshold he stepped. I saw again the ferocious light in his amber eyes when he looked at me. *I have tried to stay away from you. But that has not worked, as here I am again.*

And here he is again this year. Not in my bed, but in my parlor.

Now the conversation turns to a year ago when we had riots in this city over who could rightly vote. The women are left out, of course, which I don't cotton to. At the Soulard Market, immigrant Germans tried to stop Americans long in this country from the balloting and it was thousands who protested, with rocks, brickbats, and pistols, too. Long into the night it raged and some lay dead after.

"The Germans are bolder still," Terris says, "in their even greater numbers, and what is to stop them from the same thing in a year's time?"

"It is not just their numbers," Richard says, "but their money, too, that riles up the rest. Look how many of the new enterprises the Germans found."

"And how many they already have." Daniel taps the ash from his cigar. "Not that I mind the beer gardens and sausage shops."

All chuckle at that and murmur agreement.

Senator Stewart clears his throat and the room quiets, as oft happens with a politician. This one has an unusual look about him: not a single whisker and hair combed straight back from a high forehead. "It is a matter of some pride to me," he says, "that no state is more welcoming to the immigrant than our own Missouri. The Germans are an industrious people. What matter is it that a German housewife can buy all she needs from a shop run by one of her own without walking more than a block or two? Or read a newspaper printed in her own tongue?"

"I believe it does matter, sir!" Terris cries. "For then why should that German bother to learn English?"

An awkward silence falls. "There are many German churches, too, " I murmur, "more than a half dozen, I wager."

"That is why you are special, Eliza." Daniel raises his glass to me from across the parlor. I can count on him always to lighten the mood. "You are a bawd who counts churches."

"And will mount the stairs to enter one, too, least on Christmas and Easter. Not yet have I been smote down, either."

Laughter mounts and beside me Richard's amber eyes twinkle. It can be an odd thing to have Daniel and Richard both in the parlor, though I begin to get accustomed. I am sure one does not like the other and I am the cause of it. Now I ask Mr. Stewart a question, which I feel sufficient bold to do as I am the madam in this parlor. "Why do so many Germans come here when already they have wealth in their native land? It is not like the Irish, starving almost to a one."

It is a long answer he gives and I do not understand the whole of it—"monarchial oppression" I have not heard before—but it seems to come down to a revolution in '48 that went wrong. I learn that many Germans did not like the kings and queens and counts and dukes and tried to do something about them but failed.

"Then here they come to America," Richard says, "hoping to find a more liberal outlook, and what do they stumble upon but another aristocracy of sorts. The slaveholders."

All fall quiet. You cannot go long these days without the word *slave* spoken.

Again the senator clears his throat. "Germans do not have the same feeling in their souls about African slavery that our Creole brothers do."

Most Creoles favor the practice, I know. When the Chouteaus lived in their family mansion, slave cabins hid behind. Over twenty slaves they owned, people said, with only ten or so family members there residing.

"The state of Missouri is torn on the matter," Richard says.

Daniel frowns at him. "Unlike your own Illinois."

I think Daniel does not like that Missouri could be torn asunder by these troubles but Richard's state would likely not.

"Exactly so." Richard's gaze across the parlor is steady. "Missouri might as well be a body with an anti-slavery mind and a pro-slavery heart."

"The mind is in St. Louis," Terris says, "and the heart in Little Dixie."

Where I am from. Along the river, where most hail from the south—like my Virginia father—and near all our state's slaves are to be found.

"The mind *and* the money are in St. Louis," Daniel says, "and they face north and east."

"The Arsenal is here, too," Terris adds, and I remember Captain Targee with a barrel of gunpowder strapped to his back in the Great Fire, snatched in desperation from that very Arsenal.

Such talk goes on for some time, in somber tones, until I see Terris and Charity give each other a special smile. He raises his brows to me to say without words that he wishes to climb the stairs. Of course I collect from him first. Off they disappear,

Charity bright as the moon. It is from Senator Stewart that I next receive the signal. Daniel knows if such a luminary is in my parlor, he will not enjoy my services.

I rise with a smile. I must leave Daniel and Richard alone. I hope no crystal shatters. I feel Richard's eyes upon me as I mount the stairs before the senator. I know what he must be thinking and hide a chuckle. If only he knew.

I THOUGHT it would be a quiet night, but I am wrong. It could not be more than an hour gone when Noah is outside my bedchamber bidding me return downstairs. He leads me swiftly past the still buzzing parlor to the rear door, the one we use to escape to the privy or hand out food when the night's dining is done.

Noah whispers low. "A man stands below. He knows our private knock." And with that Noah opens the rear door.

Below the bottom step I behold a man I recognize. Oh, he is a famous man, and a stranger to this house. Yet there he stands with blood stained large upon his white shirtfront and a stricken expression upon him. Our governor.

Chapter Twenty-One

"The mendacity of these prostitutes is so notorious that no man is required to contradict anything they say; and, in many instances, falsehood stands out so prominently on the face of their letters that a knowledge of the character of the writer is not necessary to surmise it."

— *St. Louis Globe-Democrat*

— April 16, 1853

I SPEAK NOT A WORD BUT CLOSE THE DOOR SOFT BEHIND ME. Down the steps I hasten into the rear garden then deep into the night's blackness, gesturing to the governor to follow. I need not tell Noah to remain in that spot to make certain no other departs the house; he will know to do it. I pray no gentleman or whore glances from a rear window to view the moon and stars in the clear cold sky, lest they spy us instead.

It is behind the privy I scurry, where we two can stand well hidden beneath the lush branches of a catalpa tree.

I turn to face the governor. I have seen him about in this city, though he lives where the capital is, miles west. He is a shocking tall man with hair of white, I would guess in his sixth decade, with a forehead high and nose protruding. He has no whiskers but instead feathery sideburns down to his jowls. I know he is a hero of foreign battles and was in our state assembly and Congress, too, before he became governor the year last. "Governor Price," I murmur.

"Madam Haycraft." He eyes me. "Louisa Clark sent me here." I must learn how that wench knows this house's private knock. "She vowed," the governor goes on, "that you would aid me."

Sterling Price is fortunate he is governor, for most men who appear at my rear door bloodied at midnight would be chased away posthaste. "So you were at Madam Lantos's." He is a desperate man indeed, is this governor, for he pitches in the wee hours from one brothel to another, and not for the usual reason.

"A bawd died there. In the room beside mine. Stabbed," he adds when he sees my eyes drift to the bloodstain large as a cantaloupe upon his shirtfront.

My hands fly to my face. Did I know this woman? Is she a bawd I labored beside? It might well be. And I might well have been her, impaled by a man's dagger. Any of us might have been.

Again Price speaks. "We heard noises in the next room, Louisa and I, muffled sounds, a thud, a screech. Then the door opened and someone flew down the hall."

I do not know this house of Madam Lantos's yet can picture it all. "What did you do?"

"I entered the room beside ours." For a moment his eyes close. I imagine he sees the bawd again in his mind, pierced and bloodied. "The door was ajar. She was in her bed. She bled profusely from a wound in the neck." He stops for a moment, then: "I witnessed her final moments."

I do not dwell on the picture that rises in my mind. Instead I wonder: do I believe him? That he only saw this killing and is innocent of it? Many would not. Many men would think nothing of plunging a knife into a harlot's neck. Many would praise a man for it. How do I know it was not this man's hand that did the deed? This governor I see before me is a hero of war. He knows death; he has caused it.

"I moved to her bedside," Price tells me, "and bent close to her. That is why my shirtfront is bloodied. Her blood was"—he searches for a word—"spewing."

I swallow. "You know the man who was in that room with her?"

"I never saw him before tonight. He might have been a stranger to that house. He is from Virginia," and the governor's thin lips curl with distaste. He hails from that state, too, I know, so this killer was once one of his own.

I will believe this story. I do believe it. I must make judgments swiftly in this life of mine and will do so now. "And Louisa? How fares she?"

"Louisa keeps her head on her shoulders. She helped me leave the house quickly, before anyone else could see."

For once another sees: what a hue and cry. With gentlemen in the house who want not their name in the newspapers; harlots screaming; constables stomping in; Madam Lantos watching her dreams fall to dust; and the dead doxy growing cold and stiff, her eyes startled and wide, staring without seeing.

"Out the back door Louisa sent me," Price says, "and here I came. Unseen."

I know what he is telling me. I know what he is asking for. If I move fast, no one will be the wiser. It will be as if the governor had not been in a bawdy house the night a whore was left for dead and her killer fled invisible into the night.

I am shivering, both from the tale I just heard and the chilly air. "I will bring you fresh garments," I tell Price. A well-equipped bawdy house like this one has such items in abundance. "Also a washbasin. Do not leave this spot," and I abandon him to the catalpa tree.

Back in the house, Noah still standing guard at the rear door, my mind jumps from one thought to the next. I must speak to the senator in my bedchamber, for if he is still there he will wonder what I am about. He is there, watching the fire, and I tell him one of my harlots is ill and I must tend to her. He nods and I realize I am a better liar than I think myself.

I spin past the parlor; I do not know if Daniel or Richard is still there. Neither will hear this story, not from me.

Soon I hurry back outside. Price could not return with a bloodied shirtfront to wherever he is staying, for who might see him thus? His wife? A servant? A rival? Yet after I help him, he will be able to go wherever he wishes without suspicion.

I guard the privy as he goes inside. He comes out with the bloodied shirt in hand. "I will burn it," I tell him, "this very night." Maybe it will remind me of burning the white poppet of Madam Lantos. She suffered after that. I wonder if Sterling Price will, too. "You have my word that I will not speak of this matter to another soul." I gesture toward Noah. "And with my life I trust Noah's silence."

"Thank you, Madam Haycraft," and with quick steps Price is fled. Noah and I watch without a word spoken. With each passing week, the more of this strange life we share.

———

Is it lying I do in the bright light of day when the bawds around me cry over the murdered harlot and I pretend to know little about it as they do?

Every doxy has heard the news, but barely a tidbit on the topic is printed in the newspaper. It is in the parlor that Charity reads it to me. As it is a warm day, April promising summer, we have opened the windows to let in the fresh air and let out the stale. I sip coffee and watch dust mites fly as the housemaid beats without mercy at the russet-colored draperies.

"It does not say," Charity complains, "who is the man who did the killing. How could they not know what client was in that bedchamber?"

Madam Lantos knows. Yet she does not say, or least so it appears. Does that mean it was the governor? "Is Madam Lantos's name in the story?" I ask.

"More than once and not just hers, either." Charity raises the paper. "She is called 'a woman of ill fame' and of course 'lewd and disreputable' and 'a refugee from Hungary,' too, as if that has anything to do with it."

"Poor Marjorie." She is not a bawd I knew well: only one I passed with a smile and a nod. "I doubt there will be justice for her." Yes, the constables will put on a show for a day or two, but how hard will they labor to find a whore's killer? It is not as if the corpse is the untouched pink-and-white daughter of a gentleman.

"This will be a stain on Madam Lantos." Charity lowers her voice to say it. "Gentlemen's names are in the newspaper, tied to a murdered bawd in her house."

Yes. Charity understands well as I do that the worst part of this for Madam Lantos is not the dead strumpet but the scandal for the gentlemen.

Charity goes on, in a hiss. "How could she make such a mistake as to let in a man who would slash a woman's throat?"

Perhaps Madam Lantos's hands were tied. For if it was the governor who desired entry, how could she not admit him? But I cannot speak those words to Charity, for, to my sadness, again I have a secret from her. Instead I say: "Let us thank the angels she did not err this way when we were under her roof."

That seems to settle it. A few minutes pass before Charity speaks again. "There is something I wish to talk about with you," she says.

I rise from the settee. "Let us talk later. I must walk earlier than usual today." I am distressed as I depart the parlor for I do not invite Charity to walk with me. I wish to find Louisa and will not be able to talk freely with Charity in hearing. Also, if I can put off what I fear Charity wishes to say to me, I will do it.

I dress in a spring frock of a lilac color—surely no one who aids a murderer would choose such a hue?—and after a round-about stroll I spy Louisa across Walnut Street, glowing in aqua. I dodge gigs aplenty to cross to her and see she peers into the window of a cracker bakery to await me. Scowling matrons grasp tight their skirts to avoid us, but gentlemen glance our way, and not shyly, either.

"It is a melancholy day for our kind," Louisa murmurs when I join her.

"We are not dressed as if it is, but black bombazine will not help Marjorie now."

I look at Louisa and am surprised to see tears gather in her light eyes. Perhaps I was too quick to judge her unsentimental—different from so many of our type. Show most of us a kitten or play us a sad song and watch us weep. "How did this happen?" I whisper.

"Madam Lantos did not know the man." She is telling me Governor Price is not the killer. I watch her close her eyes as if to remember the scoundrel's face. "The blackguard is from Virginia" —that is what the governor told me, too—"and though known only a little to Mr. Skillern, he wished to admit him."

Mr. Skillern is the gentleman from Virginia who put in the money for Madam Lantos's new house. He is the one above her who can say do this and don't do that. How could she say no to a man Mr. Skillern wished to allow inside? Yet she is the one who suffers if a poor judgment is made.

Well. The trollops suffer, too. Marjorie suffers most.

"How fares Madam Lantos?" I murmur.

"You will never know how she truly is, even from watching closely."

I cannot dispute that. "Are you a favorite of Price?"

Perhaps she, too, values highly the discretion Madam Lantos

so prizes, for she says only: "I hope you do not mind I told him your knock."

"I mind only that you know it. How do you?"

The question scarce leaves my lips when of a sudden she says: "I must go," and away she spins to leave me alone in front of the cracker bakery, staring at Boston and soda crackers, too.

―――――――

THAT AFTERNOON I am again on Second Street, but this time I am following Charity inside the shop at Number 81. In the window stands a large black trunk of hard leather, propped open so passersby might inspect the complex fittings of the deep green interior. "Why do you wish to enter here?" I ask Charity.

She takes a breath before she speaks. "I need a new trunk." Behind her a gentleman pores over a selection of carpetbags, a clerk with a thin, waxed mustache describing their charms in low tones. "The one I have will not suffice."

My heart sinks in my chest fast as a cannonball in the river. I understand why Charity believes she needs a new trunk. Now it is just for her to speak the words and for me to hear them.

"Martin has told me," she says, "that he does not wish to share me any longer. He dearly wishes me to live in a house of my own, that of course he will provide."

The gentleman behind Charity does not pretend he does not hear. He near drops the carpetbag he is holding to examine us, trollops bright in spring colors, hoping, I am sure, that we discuss our lovers in detail and perhaps name a man among his acquaintance.

"Why are you telling me this," I ask her, "here in this shop?"

"I tried to tell you this morning in the parlor, but you would not have it. You had to walk early and apparently alone, too."

"Here in a shop you think I will not scream and cry. I may surprise you." I turn away.

She takes my arm and tugs me outside. "Martin tells me he is very pained that he must share me. Can you not understand that?"

I do not tell her I have heard much the same claptrap from Richard. "I would not mind if from today you service him and him alone, Charity. You could help me more in the parlor when he is not about, as you do already. You need not live in a little house of your own."

"But that would not be the same."

No. For Charity imagines domestic scenes, the two of them not only in bed but at table and in the parlor. Morning, afternoon, and night is what she imagines, as if they were wed. And she believes that in a few months' time, that will push him to one knee. I am not so sure.

She is speaking and I am hearing spill from her lips the arguments I myself made to Obadiah and Chantal about Chouteau. I did not believe those two dear friends when they disputed me. Why would Charity believe me now?

"You told me you would not say no," she says, "not to a good man. Do you not think Martin is one such?"

"I think Martin a good man." But that does not mean I think him a bold one and boldness is required for a gentleman to risk reputation, family, and fortune to wed a doxy.

"Then it is settled," Charity says, and I suppose it must be, for I cannot keep her by my side if she wishes to be elsewhere.

"You may always return," I tell her, "always, always return."

"I will not need to," she says, with some harshness in it. I believe I said much the same to Obadiah; I felt insulted rather than grateful when he gave me money before I departed New Orleans. Yet that became my salvation. "Shall we return inside?" she says, and steps toward the door of the shop.

I pull her back. "No, you may borrow my trunk and empty it at your house and then Noah can bring it back in the gig."

She grasps my hands. "I will visit so often, Eliza, and you will visit me, too. We will see each other so much it will be as if I did not leave."

AFTER CHARITY DEPARTS—AND she is quick about it, for with all her heart she wishes to do this thing—I am left with an empty bedchamber where there used to be my dearest friend. Richard sees I am not in spirits and proposes a picnic in Lafayette Park.

"You have not been?" He stands in my parlor on a May afternoon wearing an expression of amazement. "I live in Chicago and already have been two times."

"I work a great deal."

He arches his brows. "I do not?"

He is accusing me, without saying so, of devoting insufficient time to leisure. Well, tomorrow I will make up for it, between the hours of one and three.

We travel there in his friend's rockaway—it is become a regular thing that he goes about in it—for the park is two miles from Poplar Street and we wish to do our walking there, not in getting there. He has prepared a basket for a picnic, or more likely got someone to prepare it for him. Any rate, I have not lifted a finger.

"The park is the whole of thirty acres," he tells me as he helps me step down from the rockaway. "Do you know the man it is named for?"

Beneath my bonnet I squint into the sunny distance. There is not much about, I will say, but softly mounded earth and a tree or two. "Lafayette. He is a Frenchman."

There must be something in my tone for Richard laughs. "You do not like Frenchmen? There is a story there."

"There is, but I am not sure I will tell it."

"I wonder how many of your stories you will tell me." He eyes me. "I will tell you all of mine, but I do not know you will return the favor."

"I do not know you really wish to hear them."

"Oh, I do, Eliza. Not just the pretty ones."

He thinks I, a harlot, have pretty stories. Few would agree

with that. Yet here he is giving me that steady look of his, which prods me to believe him. "So who is this Frenchman?" I ask.

He looks away and when next he moves his mouth, he does it in a very exaggerated way to speak in a French accent so silly and thick he might ice a cake with it. "Marie Joseph Paul Yves Roche Gilbert du Motier, Marquis de Lafayette."

I burst into giggles. Richard sounds so witless I can scarce help myself. "How do you remember all of that?"

He looks wounded. "I am a physician. I have the brain capacity for it. In addition I looked it up and practiced it strenuously this morning before the mirror. Come: try it with me. Marie Joseph Paul Yves Roche—"

I try but collapse again from giggles before I get far. "I cannot remember those names, leave alone say them as you do."

"You must try again. I insist," and as I giggle I try to push my lips into the shapes his are making. It is a different thing I begin to feel as I stare at his mouth and try to mimic him and laugh all the while and can see from the light in his amber eyes that he feels the same as I.

I am hoping he will kiss me, at last he will kiss me, but instead he murmurs low. "Lafayette was a hero of our great revolution." He stares into my eyes now, not at my mouth. I know he is a great one for the history of our country and those who helped make it what it is. "America owes Lafayette a great debt."

"And we repay him with this park?"

"At least a little."

"It is a paltry payment." I glance about. "There is nothing here."

"Eliza, you are very impatient." He is teasing me, as I am sure he is not speaking only of the park. "It is but two years ago the city dedicated this land."

"And what have they to show for that time? If I waited so long between buying the lot on Fourth Street and putting improvements upon it, I would lose a great deal of money."

"You should be a city officer. Everything would go faster then." He reaches into the rockaway to pull out the hamper he has brought. "But I will ease your mind by assuring you that already a wooden fence is being erected to keep out grazing animals and soon there will be pavilions and walking paths and even gaslights."

"That is good about the fence, for I do not wish to have to push away sheep while we eat our lunch."

Indeed it is a feast Richard brought for us. Cold salmon with mayonnaise sauce, pigeon pie, sliced cucumbers, cheese, bread and butter, and strawberries, too. All eased down our throats by lemonade with port wine, which we sip while swatting lazily at insects that wish to eat, too.

I gaze at Richard, in repose on our white blanket, and think I have made a true friend. He is not like Daniel or Charity or Obadiah or Chantal, but he begins to become dear to me. I wish I understood what he was about where I am concerned.

Perhaps I look pensive, for: "Marquis de Lafayette," he says again in his funny Frenchy way, and as if I were a puppet on a string I laugh immediately. He smiles as if satisfied.

"You are very kind to try to cheer me," I tell him, "but still I am sad about Charity leaving."

"You cannot be happy for her?"

"I do not believe she will get what she desires. What most women desire."

He sits up. "And what is that?"

I will say it straight. "A proposal of marriage. A hearth. A home. A child."

"You do not desire those things?"

"They have passed me by."

He shakes his head. "I will dispute you. You are a young woman still."

"I am not young in body or soul. Thirty-three years I have in body and my soul might be older still."

"Well, I have thirty-five years, but still I feel young. My father would say otherwise, but he and I quarrel over everything so it is not of much matter."

"You are a man so you have longer to feel young. And perhaps you feel young because you are not yet wed. Unless you are already?"

"I am not. Though often I think that many young women, and their mamas, and sometimes their papas, too, conspire against me to make it so."

Oh, but I find *this* interesting. "Yet you do not fall prey to their schemes?"

"No." His gaze rests sure on mine. "For there is a woman who will not leave my mind. From the first moment I saw her, I contrived to know her better."

The park is silent but for the soft whinny of the horse. It is as if she urges Richard to say more, as I wish, too. "How did you do that?" I murmur.

He speaks in a matter-of-fact tone. "I was attending the funeral for a very great physician, and had gone there in a carriage with two friends who had every intention of returning with me, but I told them they must make other arrangements for I desired to journey back to the city with another, still a stranger, if I could."

I am struck mute by this confession, I think because it so pleases me. I like that Richard is a man who does not hide how he feels. He knows his own mind and fears not to expose it. That is uncommon.

"This woman is a great beauty." Now Richard is speaking softly. "But, I am amazed to say, that is but one of her charms. So, though I sometimes try, I cannot devote my full attention to another."

"Do you truly try to attend to another?" I realize it pains me to think it.

"Last year I tried a great deal." Perhaps that is why I saw him so little then. "But it all came down to the same thing."

"You should not wait for this woman." I tell him this because I feel I must. "For, like Martin Terris to Charity, I believe she will not give you what you desire."

He smiles. "I have not told her what I desire. Shall I tell her now?"

Yes. It worries me, but I think it best I hear it. "Please."

He leans closer across the white blanket. "I desire time with her. I desire her company. I desire to hear what she thinks. I desire to hear her stories."

"Is that all?" I murmur.

Now his voice goes almost to a whisper. "It is but a start."

"And what about"—I will say this straight, too—"her whoredom?"

"I am making my peace with it. Though it is a struggle." He sets his face in a mock expression of sternness. "But is it not good for the constitution to struggle? I tell myself it is."

"And"—this is the last thing—"what about home and hearth?"

"They can wait." He smiles. "They can wait a very long while."

He does not kiss me then, either, though I think the very heavens are crying out for it. I would not have thought it would happen so, but it is when I introduce to Richard the word *aiguille* that at last he lays his lips upon mine. We are standing close to one another beside the rockaway and the horse is staring at the road as if telling us it longs to depart for home.

"*Aiguille*," I say to Richard in my funny Frenchy way, and he repeats it, and I say it again. *Aiguille*. This is the same game I played with Chantal, but it is different playing it with Richard.

Oh, it is different.

He leans very close and it is some time he spends staring down at me. I think perhaps I am lost in his amber eyes. Like a sea of gold, they are. Then, at last, he bends down and kisses me.

It is not like John Haycraft. It is not like Obadiah. I will say it is not like any other man. And for me, that is saying a great deal.

Chapter Twenty-Two

"The Nebraska bill has passed the Senate as it came from the House, and Nebraska and Kansas are now territories under the Constitution. The Missouri Compromise has been swept away, and one of the great break-waters of slavery agitation is thus torn down to let in the sea of angry fanaticism upon the constitution and the country. What the future has in store? what are the elements of coming strife? what the dark clouds of conflict that float up from the South and down from the North may portend? none can yet say—but in all the obscurity we have yet one watchword that will always rally the American people—that is, "the Union, it must, it shall be preserved."

— *St. Louis Globe-Democrat*

— May 29, 1854

"WHAT NUMBER IS IT NOW?" I murmur these words to myself though I near the Courthouse with both Daniel and Charity walking beside me. It is the last day of June and, for those with no business to attend, made for lying in the grass with your face upturned toward the sun. I cannot recall when last I did such a thing. "I believe this is the seventh property I will purchase." I think but do not say: *So it will be the sixth I own,* as always I will have the failure of the first Green Street house.

"Who would believe such riches belong to a hussy like yourself?" Charity cries with cheer in her voice.

Who, indeed? Truly, with all of this, could my mother still shout at me that I am not special but like all the rest? It must be, for still I can hear her in my mind.

"And to think," Daniel says, "I stood beside you, Eliza, for your first purchase of property."

I can see that irks Charity still, for she throws him a glance with annoyance in it. I wish I would see more happiness in her, but neither Daniel nor I is the cause of its absence. I take her arm. "This is a first in its way, for it is a woman I buy from. A widow by the name of Catharine Wochner."

"The trustees of Catharine Wochner," Daniel specifies.

"I believe it comes to the same thing," and try to convey by a look that I wish him to be particular kind to Charity.

He rolls his eyes, but being Daniel, obliges. "You look especially fetching, Charity, in that pink. It is a coral pink, is it not?"

"Coral as if I were part of a reef in Oceania." She swishes her skirts. "Not that I shall ever adventure to such a place to see it for myself."

"Today," I say, "is not a day to think of what we will *never* do but of what we *will* do," and I race for the Courthouse in the hope she will give chase and her spirits will lift like a feather in the breeze. Thus it is winded we arrive in the city office to witness the

long deed written out and to affix my signature—rather, my mark
—upon it.

The Wochner family has sent a lawyer for the business and as
he is of little interest, Charity peers at the book of deeds as this
one is entered, murmuring over the phrases. Finally the clerk
reaches the end. "You are to put your mark there," Charity tells
me, and points, and I do it, and she smiles even more widely
than I.

"It appears there is no use for me anymore," Daniel snivels as
we three depart the deed office.

He made the remark in a joshing way, but all the same there is
something different about Daniel of late. He is less in my parlor.
He is less in my bed. From time to time I see a distance in his
gaze. "Will you join Charity and me for apricot pastries?" I ask.
"Your favorite," and he gives me the answer I knew he would.

"I cannot, as I have too much work to attend," and he pecks
me on the cheek, and away he strides. So it is Charity and I who
head to Poplar Street. It is there I still live, and in the same house,
too, though for some months now I own two more properties in
that place—they are called *adjacent*—and thus possess what
Richard calls a *compound*. I remain in the same bedchamber in the
first house, as I went to such trouble and expense to outfit it just
so. Charity and I go to the yellow kitchen for the pastries and I
hope we are quick about eating them as I have more tasks to
accomplish than I can count on all my fingers and toes.

"It gladdens my heart you let me come with you today. I want
for company," Charity confesses.

I knew it already. We pull out the bench to sit at the trestle
table. "Martin is still little about?" I ask.

"Always he is working. And when he is not, he is with his
family." Now we are out of Daniel's hearing, complaints spill
from Charity fast as water from a cracked vase. "I think," she
finishes, "his mother must have no friends to talk to."

I will ask another question though I fear already I know the
answer to this one, too. "What think you of his mother?"

Charity will chew her pastry thoroughly before she speaks again. Then: "I have not met her yet." And it is a full year Charity lives in the little house Martin Terris provides. "Nor," she says, "have I met his father or a cousin or a chum. Do not speak a word about it for already I know what you think. He has introduced me to his dog."

Dickens. Named after the English author who wrote nicely about Planters House, or so Charity told me. Yet, lest Dickens is a very special dog indeed, it cannot alert Martin's parents to what their son is about. I wonder if they know all the same.

"I do not fear Martin tires of me," she says, "and need not explain to *you* why I feel so. But all the same I worry he sees no reason to change things between us."

I am wondering what to say to that when Louisa enters the kitchen. I will say she is lovely in her negligée, with hair cascading, just roused from bed.

It is no surprise to Charity that Louisa is with me. It has been thus for six months, since I am queen of the city's harlots by reigning over a *compound*. Louisa is one to wish to be at the best house and now that is the house of Eliza Haycraft. Of course Charity is gone from here now, so there should be no ill will between the two, but all the same there is a chilliness to how Charity greets Louisa and in return a superior jut of the chin, as if Louisa judges Charity has put a foot wrong in a way she herself is wise enough to avoid.

"You are celebrating the new Fourth Street lot?" Louisa asks, now with coffee in hand. "You are to be congratulated, Madam Haycraft."

Louisa may no more call me Eliza than years ago I could call Madam Lantos by her given name. It is a very pretty one, I learned some time back: Evaline.

"I knew from the first *Eliza* was one to watch," Charity says.

"Well, I will leave you two to your gossip," and out Louisa sweeps.

She is one to say a thing that irritates, but always it has truth in it and always it is said sweetly. I must fight to box her in lest she become too much a handful. Still. She draws Governor Sterling Price to this house. And where the governor goes, other high muck-a-mucks follow. This is a loss to Madam Lantos, for in years past it was to her house they would flock. Now it is to mine, for who wants to go to a house where a throat was slashed among the bedclothes?

Far as I can tell, Price did not suffer from his near brush with a bawd's murder. Some tattled he was at Madam Lantos's that night, but for them he had a ready reply: *I will not dignify such tripe with an answer.* Perhaps I will say the same when next I am called into court and charged with running a bawdy house "contrary to the form of the Statute." I will see if it serves me well as it served him.

Charity rises from the bench. "I must get back," she tells me, and I know why: Martin might pay a visit to his little house. He must not find it empty of his mistress, for what if he should wonder what is the good of keeping one such if she is not there waiting when he wishes her to be?

———

"THIS WILL QUIET the national agitation over the slavery issue." Governor Price speaks with confidence in my parlor crowded with gentlemen and strumpets, all mute but for him, for who would speak over the highest leader of our state? "Surely no man can dispute the value of *that*."

"Hear, hear," mutters Robert Stewart of our Missouri Senate. Louisa steps away from the governor's side to top off Stewart's whiskey, as she is attentive to all in state office.

"I hope your words prove prophetic, Governor," another man says, and I am glad he spoke in a mild tone for I know he is one to judge Price—and Stewart, too—dead wrong on the matter at hand.

It is the Kansas Nebraska Act all speak of, and I believe I

myself could recite its provisions, as in the month since it passed Congress it seems there is little else to discuss. It makes those two places territories, but that is not the shock of it: *that* is that the people who live there, and they alone, will decide whether to embrace the slavery practice. No longer will it be Congress to decide. This means that our Missouri Compromise is flung out the window like the contents of a chamber pot.

"Three cheers for the Little Giant!" a man cries and the huzzahs rise high. He speaks of Stephen Douglas, senator from Richard's own Illinois, who pushed this famous law over all the obstacles in its way.

Daniel leans close to whisper—"Maybe I would do better if I, too, were shorter than Napoleon"—and I titter behind my hand.

"Mark my words," another man cries, "the Little Giant will land in the White House 'ere long."

"But will he get his northern route for the transcontinental rail-road?" another wants to know.

For it is that desire that began it all. If tracks are to be laid all the way to California—and through Illinois, too, as Senator Douglas wishes—Kansas and Nebraska must be settled territories. For who will invest in a place where they cannot stake a legal claim to land?

"But why should the eastern terminus of the transcontinental be Chicago?" one man shouts. "Let it be St. Louis!"

The cry rises. *St. Louis! St. Louis! St. Louis!* My house shakes from the roar.

"Mark *my* words," Daniel whispers amid the ruckus, his face uncharacteristic solemn. "The slaveholding states won this time. But for the Union, this bill is a disaster in the making."

"YOU WOULD BE WISE," Reverend Early tells me with sternness, "to make this your last excursion until Monday's balloting is finished."

It is Saturday afternoon and I am in the reverend's fruit shop with my basket full of the plums and peaches he has on offer. "You worry what happened last time will happen again?" I ask him. Two years ago Germans newly able to vote tried to keep Americans long here from the balloting. It was a melee that followed, with deaths and a tavern fire.

"I fear it will happen again and worse this time." The reverend is younger than me, but as he frowns creases line his brow. "You do not read the *Republican*?"

I will not tell him I cannot. Still, I am better informed than most women given the hours of conversation in my parlors.

It is a seat in Congress up for balloting Monday, the seventh day of August. The Democrat Thomas Hart Benton holds it now, but it is our former mayor Luther Martin Kennett who seeks to take it from him. Kennett is a Know Nothing and there is much spirit among our citizens in his favor, all those who think our city has too many immigrants who take too many jobs and grasp too much power. Add to that the free Negroes—who take jobs, too— and they feel squeezed on all sides.

I will admit the Know Nothings confound me. They are called such because, if someone asks what they think on a matter, they reply: *I know nothing*. They are a group unto themselves, with their own secrets. Who can understand them?

Reverend Early speaks again. "These Know Nothings warn so often and so loudly of a so-called 'foreign rebellion,' they will wish to see it happen. I will close this shop that day and may board it, too."

I wonder if I should do the same? For I have six properties to protect. I am not allowed to vote, of course, so we will have no need Monday to don my best garb and march from one tavern to the next exchanging views.

With all this political talk, I realize I am near to leaving the shop without asking the question I came here for. "Is there still no news on Hester Williams?" Already one and a half years have passed since Frederick Norcom tore up the freedom paper he wrote for her.

Reverend Early straightens as if about to deliver a speech in the Courthouse. "The lawyers for Frederick Norcom are expert at stalling matters. Will you believe they have the audacity to demand that Mrs. Williams be delivered to their client to be dealt with as his slave?"

"I know Norcom so I can believe it."

"He remains at a safe remove, I believe, in the state of New York." The reverend narrows his eyes as if he were gazing at the miscreant himself then turns a grim gaze on me. "These, Madam Haycraft, are troubled times. I advise you to remain indoors Monday," and though most often I am like to disregard a man's instructions, these I may heed.

It is not long into Monday, a day hot as a hare on a spit, that I begin to hear a ruckus. I stand in the parlor, still a tumble from the night's revelry. The windows are boarded so I survey all by candlelight. Rings on tabletops I see, and heaped ashtrays, and cushions that need airing and plumping both. But it is a distant shouting that grips me. Then, I am sure of it, I hear a pistol shot.

I spin to find Louisa behind me, in her negligée but with eyes alert as if a full measure of coffee is already down her gullet. "Dress," I tell her, "then rouse the others and tell them to do the same." This is not a day for harlots to lie abed. In her bare feet Louisa scampers away.

The day prior I had my houses on Fourth and Green streets also boarded, like these on Poplar, and instructed those who mind those properties to be keen-eyed today. I hurry to my adjoining houses and climb to the upper stories. With my voice loud—"Up! Dress now!"—I beat upon the bedchamber doors.

Finally, with my doxies stirred, I stop and listen. There is a fracas in this city: it is not close but nearer than it was. I step out onto Poplar Street. People are milling about and not in the ordinary way, but stopping and talking, to strangers, too. I am bold about it and approach two men with the look of shopkeepers about them, though they are garbed in their Sunday-go-to-meeting best for the voting. "Please," I say, "what have you heard is happening?"

"A judge put a delay to the balloting in the Fifth Ward," one tells me. That is where the Irish live, more in hovels than houses. "Of course all got restless standing in the sun with the line growing longer and no end to it, so the pushing and shoving started and one got stabbed and now here we are."

"Get yourself back inside"—the other points to my front door —"and keep your foreigners out of sight if you know what's good for you. That's who the mob'll be searching for," and his fellow grunts in agreement.

I do not hesitate; I return inside. There will be a melee: for weeks now all have been readied for it. And when there is one such, no one is safe, for though it may be foreigners the rabble seek they will content themselves with hussies if need be. And if I know a mob, they may do worse than beat us.

I have a few Irish girls, of course. What brothel doesn't? No Germans, for they're not as like to need the coin. I wonder whether to warn my Irish girls in particular and decide not. All that will do is panic them out of their heads.

I am scarce back inside my house when it is spindly, frizz-topped Bridget who appears at my door, and who is with her clutching her hand but her sister Anna, now ten. The little one has gone from red hair to wheat-colored but her face shaped like a heart stays the same. And so do her eyes, huge and blue as a summer sky.

"I feel a sinner to bring Anna to this den of fornication," Bridget tells me. She narrows her eyes at the bawds walking about behind me, as if that will keep their vice a distance from her ever-lasting soul. "But it is our city I'll be fighting for today and I need Anna safe and have nowhere else to take her."

Already I knew Bridget ran with the Know Nothings, I guess forgetting she and her family entire came to this country from across the sea. But they came years ago, which is what makes them resent those who come now. I watch her let go of her wee sister's hand and give her a push. Anna half stumbles inside, eyes bulging. She hasn't been here for a year or two and never with trollops milling about and staring back at her as if she were a songstress on a stage.

I spin about. "Tessa, Mary, take Anna upstairs and show her your dresses and jewels," and nothing could move Anna or the hussies faster. I turn back to Bridget. "What do you mean, fighting?" I hiss.

Quite a bit is spewed at me then, talk of "preserving our institutions" and how so many try to "Germanize St. Louis" and don't I know we must "beware the illegal vote?"

"Don't go getting yourself killed," I tell her, and it's not just Bridget I'm worried for but Anna, too, and myself, for what will I do if it's Bridget's blood gets spilt?

"You'll be thanking me later," Bridget predicts, and departs, and I watch her melt into the throng, sure of her righteousness.

I am not one to take a side—that's bad for business—but St. Louis would not be the boom town it is without immigrants. Maybe it's this life I've chosen makes me think this way, but I favor letting people be who they are and do what they do.

The city fire bells begin to peal not long after, a warning to all. I stand upstairs, where I allow the windows to be full open to let in the scant breeze. Dozens are running along Poplar Street howling loud as banshees and armed with axes and brickbats, clubs and pistols. From time to time, I pull my doxies back from the windows, warning them not to show themselves for fear they draw attention or take a pistol ball. Is this tumult near Charity's house, too? I wonder. How frightened must she be? No part of me believes Martin Terris is with her; no, he is shut up with his parents, I would wager good money on it, protecting what his family owns, not what he rents on the sly.

It is pounding on the front door I hear late in the afternoon, when the brawl is still loud as ever. Who do Louisa and I find there but Daniel. We pull him inside quick and again bolt the door. He stands in the foyer clutching the banister, puffing from the work of running through the streets in this hell-hot nightmare. Covered with dirt he is, and with a gash on his cheek and blood running down one hand, too. When finally he can speak: "The fighting is hand to hand," he tells us. "The mob is grown to a thousand or more."

For a moment I cannot say a word. I try to imagine *a thousand or more*. Then: "That is much worse than two years ago," I murmur.

"Many shops are being despoiled," Daniel says, "German ones, mostly, windows broken, merchandise carted off, clerks beaten bloody."

"Where are the constables?" Louisa cries.

"From the windows we have seen not a one of them," I mutter.

"They are absent," Daniel says. "Their numbers are nothing compared to a throng like this. There is talk the mayor will try to mount a resistance, but I have little hope for it."

"Come," I say, and take his hand. I will bathe those gashes and get whiskey into him. "I wish you not to leave again and not just for your sake, for I want a man in this house tonight."

We reach my bedchamber and Daniel collapses onto a chair before the hearth. "You are in a pitiful state, Eliza, if I am the best man you can find for a night like this one. Where is Richard?"

Oh, I would not mind him here. "He is in the wild somewhere God alone could find him."

"Tonight that wild is more placid than here." Daniel winces from my first gentle touch of wet fabric to his skin. "Thank you for this, but I must be gone after."

"Whyever so? When you just got here and amid all that rabble?"

He is quiet for some time. Then: "Probably I shouldn't have come. It's just that I'm not used to it yet."

"Daniel, you are speaking in riddles." It must be that I press the fabric too hard against his skin, for again he flinches.

"All right, I may as well tell you, though it seems a strange time for it." He holds my hand away from his forehead and meets my gaze, though I can see it is with reluctance. "The truth is, Eliza, I am to be married. A few months hence."

I cannot help it. I must sink onto the other hearth chair.

"Her name is Alice," he tells me. "Her mother is a friend of my mother's. I've known her all my life, you could say. She's a sweet girl, I will tell you."

There is only one thing to say to this sort of news and I summon the breath to say it. "Well, Daniel, that is wonderful. I am sure you will find every happiness."

"I am near forty years of age, Eliza. Already I am late for matrimony."

"You need explain nothing to me."

"I shall be around less. But of course if you wish to purchase another property, I will help you."

He says that now, but when this Alice realizes he is friend to a doxy? He will never walk into that deed office with me again. I rise to pour tots of whiskey and force brightness into my voice. "To your joy," I say, "and to Alice's," and I push from my memory that wondrous moment eight years ago when we clinked our beer steins to toast my first purchase of property. *He was your friend for years*, I tell myself, *and you must take your happiness from that*, and that will be quite a trick if I can manage it.

By the time his gashes are cleaned and we slide back the bolt to venture outside, it is full dark. People are about, but not many. Daniel kisses my forehead then strides away without a look back.

Oh, my spirits are dismal as I lie abed. It is not, I know, that I wish to marry Daniel. I do not. Truly, I do not wish to marry any man and lose the independence I have fought so to gain. But somehow I expected years to pass and Daniel's life to remain the same. How foolish was I! And how can Daniel, of all men, wed the "sweet" daughter of his mother's friend? Finally I sleep, because I am too exhausted not to, and in the fragile light of dawn I have something to distract me: hope that the fracas is over. But soon it begins again as if there had never been a stop to it.

"There's to be a foreign takeover!" a bedraggled man shrieks at me as I tread onto Poplar Street. "Mick reinforcements are coming on the river!"

He might be right or he might have taken leave of his senses. How am I to know which it is?

I spend hours making myself busy in my house then of a sudden hear a man outside calling *Eliza Haycraft! Eliza Haycraft!* I peer out a second-story window onto Poplar Street. It is a stranger, a workingman, dirtied and bloodied. "Here I am," I shout down to him. It is a strange thing, but I have fame enough now that common folk know where to find me, and not just for a handout, either.

"There's a woman calling for you on the levee," he hollers up at me, "near the foot of Locust Street. Needs your help, she's saying, and I say be quick about it, for it's a wicked mess down there and she's taken an injury so cannot move," and, his message delivered, away he flees.

I throw up my hands. It must be Bridget and now she needs rescuing and I'm the one to do it, she demands, though I'm the very same who warned her off this enterprise. And how am I to fetch her if she cannot move? There is no hope for it but to take the gig, so I must risk my horse, too, and hope she doesn't buck in the wildness around us.

For it is wild: the same noisy brawl as yesterday, with shots ringing out and city fire bells again pealing. On my own street are shop windows broken and wares tumbled onto the pavement. It's screeching and running and stealing and tussling people are doing, with no purpose but mayhem. And into this I must brave, to save the skin of Bridget Carpenter.

I tell Louisa what I am about. Already I'm wearing my oldest frock, though the horse and gig will draw attention just the same. I run to the shed we use as a stable. Of course the groom is not about and anyway I couldn't fit both him and Bridget with me in the two-seater.

I strap my horse to the gig and set off. I slap the reins to urge the horse to go swiftly, to discourage any who might think they can snatch her from me. It's not my first time driving but strange enough my nerves are atremble. I will say that streets clear when a horse and gig come fast pounding.

I keep my eyes on the road but still see it everywhere, the looting. At more than one German shop, the rabble is tearing the lettering off the windows, as if it's them who own the place now and not the rightful proprietor. And still there is not a constable to be found.

Down onto the levee I ride. We may have a melee, but it's a day for business, too, with boats arriving and departing same as ever. Here are horses and drays and gigs and freight stacked upon the cobblestones. An able body might leap from one pile to the next without touching the stones themselves. And down the levee there's brawling aplenty.

I slow the horse to a walk and keep my eyes peeled when I reach the foot of Locust Street. It's easier to find those who aren't moving than those who are and that'll be Bridget with her damnable injury. It's a man and woman sitting on the cobbles my eyes are drawn to, though her hair isn't red like Bridget's but dark like mine. The two are leaning close like a private pair, but when her gaze catches mine she sits up straight as a chairback and he might as well not be there.

I will say everything else fades away for me, too. For there on the levee is a woman I have not seen for ten years full passed, a woman I must squint at for some moments even to recognize.

It is my sister Sarah.

Chapter Twenty-Three

"I hope I am over wary; but if I am not, there is, even now, something of ill-omen, amongst us. I mean the increasing disregard for law which pervades the country; the growing disposition to substitute the wild and furious passions, in lieu of the sober judgment of Courts; and the worse than savage mobs, for the executive ministers of justice…

"Whenever this effect shall be produced among us; whenever the vicious portion of population shall be permitted to band in numbers of hundreds and thousands, and burn churches, ravage and rob provision-stores, throw printing presses into rivers, shoot editors, and hang and burn obnoxious persons at pleasure, and with impunity; depend on it, this Government cannot last."

— Abraham Lincoln

— "The Perpetuation of Our Political Institutions: Address Before the Young Men's Lyceum of Springfield, Illinois"

— January 27, 1838

I T COMES BACK TO ME THEN, SARAH'S FACE ON THE MIDNIGHT BLACK RIVERBANK, pale and twisted with surprise as John's canoe carries me downriver fast as you like it.

I bring the horse to a halt and watch Sarah prod the man beside her to help her to her feet. Against him she leans with one foot raised above the cobbles. "Get me over there then," she tells him, gesturing to me, and I step down from the gig for I know not what else to do.

The two hobble nearer. "So somebody did get you here," she says as she nears. She peers at my face then throws out a laugh that's more like a cackle. "You're a famous one now, aren't you? Even back in Callaway County. Notorious, some might say. Eliza Haycraft."

I listen to her draw out those two names of mine, the rough-looking fellow beside her doing the same. There was never a softness to Sarah when she was young and there isn't one now she's old. Not so far from forty she is and the years hang heavy. Her hair is dark like mine but streaked with gray and she's skinny as a pitchfork and I don't know where I'd find time to count her wrinkles. Her garments are country poor and, I don't think I'm wrong about it, an odor rises from them. Her dark eyes still glimmer with a sharp light. I remember that too well. She's one who'll see everything, even what you don't show her.

"How long have you been here?" I ask her.

"Got here this morning, on the steamboat."

"You came by yourself?"

"The better to get reacquainted," and in her eyes' gleam I imagine the schemes she's contriving. *You're a famous one now, aren't you? Even back in Callaway County.* "Lift me in then," she tells her fellow, and the man tosses inside her tattered carpetbag. My horse neighs and shakes her head as if in protest.

"Wait a minute," I say, and step between Sarah and the gig.

Down the levee the rampaging goes on. I cannot take long about this one way or the other.

"What do you mean, wait? You're my sister. And it's a rotten blow I suffered when this mob got me trampled." She raises one foot as if to show off her wound through her clodhopper. Then: "And I know it's a kind one you are," she says, in a different, wheedling sort of voice. "I was just telling this fellow how kind. I was telling him I know you'll take pity on a sister fresh come to this city that's having its own share of troubles."

"That she was," he tells me.

Sarah would rather ride atop a blazing locomotive than call me kind, but I don't have it in me to forsake my father's daughter on this levee with brawling about and her come up lame to boot. "You I'm leaving," I tell the man and step back to give him room to raise Sarah inside my gig.

I wish it was Bridget he was lifting, for her I know how to handle. Every other one of my sisters I've missed over these last ten years, and I've cried for every other one of them, too, but if I had my choice I'd pass into heaven or hell without ever again seeing Sarah in this life.

I don't wait for the two of them to make their goodbyes and the horse must be of the same mind, for I barely touch the reins before she turns to go back the way we came.

"You'll be knowing where to find me," Sarah shouts to the man with a wave.

If he'd get her off my hands, I'd tell him myself. "Safest way to go is fast," I say, and off we set at a pace the hounds of hell would envy. Sarah falls back and her hands clutch the seat for purchase. It is the road I must watch as my mind moves even faster than the gig's wheels. What will Sarah have to say to me? About my father and mother? My sisters? John Haycraft? Who's dead and who's alive? The ones I loved and the ones I didn't I pushed from my mind all the same, because I never thought I'd see them again or even hear tell of them. Now I will. Really I'll hear what Sarah wants to tell me, for she'll spew lies if they suit.

And though I can't say exactly what it'll be, already I know she brings trouble.

We race through the streets. People run hither and yon and it's screaming I hear in the distance and more than one pistol shot. I glance at my sister. She's silent, her features pinched, and why wouldn't she be? She's never been in a city before, I wager, and it's into a melee she comes. That should raise kindness in me. But all I can think is that I'll have to shut her inside with the rest of us and what stories will she tell of me, to anybody who'll listen?

It is a mercy the horse, the gig, and we two make it back to Poplar Street in one piece. The horse I return to the shed and a bucket of water; I will tend to her later. The crippled Sarah I must aid now: I must suffer my arm about her shoulder and hers about my waist and her carpetbag dragging on my free hand. And we must make our plodding way to the front door of the house as the rear is boarded.

It is Louisa who draws back the bolt at my pounding. She cannot keep her eyes from growing wide at the sight Sarah and I make as we lumber over the threshold. "This is my sister Sarah," I tell Louisa. Somehow I don't choke on those words, which I never thought I'd speak again.

"Well, well," Sarah murmurs beside me, "aren't you the fancy one now," and I hear her mind work as she takes in my foyer, with the Brussels carpet and grandfather clock with mahogany inlay. "I heard tell of it," she mutters, "but wouldn't half believe it till I saw it with my own eyes."

I deposit Sarah on a stuffed chair in the parlor. More bawds swarm. I hear the word *sister* hiss from one to the next. From what my doxies know of me, I might have fallen from heaven to earth full a madam, with never a family in between. And if they did picture relations, I wager it's not this they conjured. "This is my sister Sarah," I announce. "She'll be staying with us for a spell." I don't wait for a comment. "You'll be hungry," I tell Sarah. "Tessa, put together a plate."

The food goes down fast and the small beer even faster. I try to think where to stash Sarah once she's eaten. The shed? I've half a mind for it. She can't climb the stairs in the state she's in. There's a small room off the kitchen that could do. She must bathe first. That'll mean the tub in the kitchen and my strumpets toting in the water, since we've no housemaids about.

Am I less charitable than I should be? Oh, I could be accused of that. Would Obadiah think I should give her a hand up, as he did me? If he knew her nature, he wouldn't think so. In the case of Sarah, it is as if I feed a snake. I will be lucky she doesn't bite me and I know she'll try. All the same, I remember my first time in the city and the shock it was to me. I should remember that time and only time will get her accustomed. And I should forgive her smell: I was hardly fragrant when I stepped out from belowdecks.

"There are many from the family who might've come with me," I hear her tell Louisa. "Eliza and I have a big family, especially with all the young 'uns now."

From the parlor Sarah sets her eyes on me as I stand in the foyer. Do I imagine it or do I see glee in Sarah's eyes at my disquiet? I must remember how I used to hide my feelings from her. I had my ways back then and must remember them anew.

"But I came alone," she tells Louisa. "This time."

"MAMA'S DEAD," Sarah tells me.

It is evening and we are alone in the parlor, lit by a lone candle. Sarah is bathed and has poured down her throat more than one tot of whiskey. I am bathed and sober as a pine tree. If it pains Sarah that the parent she loved most is in the ground, I see no sign of it. Does she see pain in me? It is there, a pang. But wait: already it might be gone. "How long ago?" I ask her.

"Four years or more."

My mother is dust. I believe we are the better for it. I know what I wish to ask now, though the answer frightens me. "What of our father?"

"Married again. Not long did it take him. To a widow in Osage County."

He lives still. He breathes. "Is it there that he lives?"

She nods. "After the flood."

From Osage County, just across the river from Callaway, my father knows what I am about. *Notorious, some might say. Eliza Haycraft.*

"He never wants to see the likes of you again," Sarah tells me. "He calls you an abomination."

She is lying. I need not see the glint in her eyes to know it. That is not a word he would use. He would be shamed and would wonder how poorly he raised me. It is possible he wishes not to see me. That, I will say, cuts deep. But such a word he would not use. And I will believe that somewhere, somewhere in him, he carries pride about me.

"I'm not saying I agree—" she begins, but I interrupt.

"What of Visa Ann?" That sister I love best, that sister who seemed almost a daughter to me, with eleven years between us.

"Married when she was fifteen, to Benjamin," and Sarah need not speak the last name for me to know it's Babb, of that family that hails from Tennessee and is rich enough to own slaves.

"They married when she was so young?" I can guess why.

"Had her first babe that age, too, and four more since."

Visa Ann was but thirteen when I leapt in that canoe and we all saw already that Benjamin had his eyes on her. The Babbs were ever a high-placed family in Cote Sans Dessein. I wonder if a pistol had to be pulled to make them do right by my sister. They might have had wisdom enough to want her in their clan. "What of Asa," I ask, "and our other sisters?"

That takes time to tell. Asa is wed to a Sarah Chambers, heavy with their first child. Lucinda married in '45 and lives in Osage County, too, and not just with her husband and two daughters but Nancy and Minerva, too, for they wish not to reside with our father and his wife who is not their mother. I am grateful to Lucinda and her husband for putting a roof over our youngest sisters. It does not surprise me she would do such a thing, for she was always one to understand how a body felt, almost as if she felt the same herself.

"There's one you don't ask about," Sarah says.

John Haycraft. "What know you of him?" Neither of us need speak his name.

"He never set out to search for you." She is telling me he didn't love me, as if that will distress me. Does she forget I am the one who left? She would rather I be the one abandoned. "Some years back he got it into his head to leave."

That is no surprise. "Where to?"

Her eyes shift away from mine in a way that tells me she doesn't know. "He would take a keen interest"—her gaze roams my parlor—"in all this."

If he were my rightful husband, the law says he could claim it. That is what Sarah wishes to remind me of. Now I will take *her* to a topic she will not like. "How have you made do these past years?"

She shrugs. "You know what folk do where we come from."

"You made do well enough to get steamboat fare."

"I wanted to get away, so I did. Guess I'm like you that way."

I say nothing to that. As if she is like me in any way but the blood that flows through our veins. Upstairs I hear my doxies, visiting from room to room. It is another night without whoredom. A client who ventures past will see the front doors boarded and know to return another night. Bored doxies will do what they always do. Gossip. Titter. Tear pretty pictures from magazines. Try on each other's clothes. Anna is up there with them. Still there is no Bridget.

"Why did you come here?" I ask Sarah.

She shrugs again. I see fatigue in her now, from the journey and the liquor. "For years you were good as dead to us." Her words are flat as a coin. "Then we started to hear about someone who came from our parts but went to St. Louis and became a famous whore. Eliza Haycraft."

Now she draws out three words. *Whore. Eliza. Haycraft.* She does this all the while she wishes to lay her hands on my whorish riches. I rise. "You know where your room is." It is by the kitchen. My trollops have squeezed in a better bed than Sarah ever slept in before.

"That room is small, but it is a real kindness you're showing me letting me stay in it."

I say nothing and turn to mount the stairs.

It is a good thing my bedchamber windows are full open, for if they were not I would not have heard Richard whistling to me from the street below. In my night shift I stand at the window and wave that I will let him in. Oh, it is a special joy for him to return! —especially after the news from Daniel. I put a finger to my lips to urge him to be silent as he can while walking his horse and gig to the rear shed. Most of all I wish not for Sarah to awaken.

Though it is deepest night, it is still warm. Insects buzz about taking their pleasure and stars hang bright as if tossed in great handfuls from angels' buckets. Richard and I tiptoe through my sleeping house as if we were thieves. Once again I am glad that in all my houses I made certain the stairs do not creak.

It is a long kiss we share when we reach my chamber. Richard smells of a long voyage and places far away. "I tried to get here yesterday," he whispers, dropping kisses on my neck. Already he has pushed my shift to the floor. "I worried what might happen with the voting."

"That is not the worst of it," I murmur, and say a thing or two about Sarah.

But he does not care to speak of my sister. He wishes for a tot of whiskey and a full measure of me. Now he is lying with me— and it took him years to get to it—he wishes to do it always. And, I will say, I wish the same, for his hands and lips on every part of me. It is a different thing with Richard, even than it was with

Daniel, and I cannot put words as to why. Maybe that we were friends before all this started; maybe that no coin passes between us. I know only that my heart lifts when he is about and sinks when he is not. I do not wish to think on it more than that.

When we are lying quiet atop my bedclothes, I tell him things he has not heard before, about my family, those I loved and those I didn't. He will believe me when I tell him Sarah is trouble, maybe because his father is the same, though in a different way. "I want her nowhere near me," I murmur.

"You need not have her near you merely because she is your sister. She will be able-bodied soon."

"It is as if she brings with her a dark cloud that sets itself atop this house and puts all in shadow."

"Are you not too harsh? Perhaps over all these years she has grown kinder."

"She pretends to be kind. I do not trust it." I sigh before telling him something that will surprise him. Why do I do it? I believe because with this man I wish to throw secrets to the side. "Years ago I was wed. Or thought so," and I explain. "I was a fool to do it." I am lying on Richard's chest so cannot see his face. All the same I can tell from his silence that he is thinking.

Finally: "If I saw Haycraft," Richard says, "I would throw him in the river."

"I would help you do it."

"You worry he will be next to come here, after Sarah?"

"What if he is?"

"You worry he will try to take from you what you have?"

"What would stop him?"

"You would stop him." Richard rises on an elbow to gaze down upon my face. "You are not the woman you were, Eliza. There are people called investigators. If Haycraft should come here and lay a claim, you could hire one and find out what you need to know to fight him."

Richard is telling me I am a muck-a-muck. Like a rich man, I have just to think a thing to do it. I do not judge it easy as that, but

I see the point he makes. Haycraft is not a muck-a-muck: I would bet my life on it. And even years ago he could not handle me. What makes me worry he could handle me now?

Richard whispers more things I like to hear. "Maybe Haycraft has not come to St. Louis already because he is dead. Or maybe the wife in Kentucky still lives. Or he has married another woman after you, whether the Kentucky wife lives or not."

"He might have wives lined up like oxen to a plow," and we must both stifle our laughter at that.

"Or maybe," Richard says, "he went to California to seek his fortune."

"He is too lazy for that." I think for a moment. Then: "I wish Sarah would go to California."

"If you are right about her, she is likely to go back where she came from as soon as she knows she cannot pick you dry."

Chapter Twenty-Four

"Never praise a sister to a sister, in the hope of your compliment reaching the proper ears."

— Rudyard Kipling

— "False Dawn," *Plain Tales from the Hills*, 1888

A T LAST THE RIOTING EBBS. When it is full morning light and all are arisen, Sarah sees Richard come downstairs. I can tell she understands that he descends from my bedchamber. She gives him as thorough an inspection as he gives her foot and ankle. "You will be past that hobble in a few days more," he tells her.

She shakes her head. "You don't know the pain of it."

She wishes me to think it will be a month before she is whole again. Instead I will believe Richard's diagnosis.

He turns to me. "I saw postings that the City Council holds a public meeting today about the rioting. Do you wish to come with me?"

"I cannot. I must see if there is damage to Green Street." I am worried about my property in that district, which I know has suffered more than hereabouts. I feel my sister's eyes upon me as Richard and I part.

"Handsome he is," she murmurs. "As was Haycraft."

I stand beside her as she sits in a stuffed chair and enjoy that I loom over her. "What will you do when your hobble is gone?"

It takes her a while to say it, but finally she does. "I will find a place with you here, as it should be between sisters."

"And what do you imagine you will do here?"

"I'm not made for strenuous labor. This and that."

"There is no this and that. There are bawds and the housekeeper—"

"Housekeeper then. That's a right job for me."

I must hold back a snort. As if my sister is near as meticulous as a proper housekeeper should be. "Then there are the cooks and housemaids," I say. "Also Noah and the groom."

She narrows her eyes at me. "You're a bawd. So that's what you do, then?"

"I am the madam. And I run it all." I lean close and speak low. "Tonight the house will be open. I advise you to stay inside your room and mind your tongue." I turn to leave her. It is but a few days more I will allow her to sit about while others bring her food and whiskey. I am like to be loose with the cheap liquor, though, as I like her best sleeping.

The groom is back, but I prefer to drive myself about. It is a release to pound through the streets and I wish to go fast today, too, as there is still wildness in the air. On Green Street between Fifth and Sixth, in the very place I first owned property, I am shocked to see smashed up many barrooms and boardinghouses I know to be Irish. I ride further uphill to the place I now own. It is some time I spend there with my trollops and the woman who runs it for me. This place did not suffer from the rioting. I will thank the stars I did the same as Reverend Early and had the properties boarded before the voting began.

That afternoon Richard returns to tell me the Know Nothings were the loudest to speak at the public meeting. We sit in my chamber with a breeze wafting in. "The Know Nothings were in high spirits," he tells me, "as you would expect, for their man won, and handily."

"Luther Kennett to Congress then." This I must commit to memory.

"The Know Nothings," Richard says, "now call themselves the party of law and order."

"Wasn't it their own did most of the fighting?"

"The very same. It is the Irish and Germans who suffered nearly all the damage. Their saloons and boardinghouses, churches, and the German newspaper office, too."

I can tell Richard is not surprised. He sees how many deny the thing right in front of them if it suits what they wish to believe. I tell him I saw with my own eyes how many Irish places were destroyed on Green Street and that I am worried about the little house where Martin Terris has put Charity.

"When I return to my boardinghouse I will drive past there," he tells me.

That is a reassurance. "In all this, how many dead?"

"Half a dozen, it is said. No one is sure as some are carried away when they're hit and who knows what happens afterward?" He pinches the place between his eyes. He is pained more than most, I think, by men wounding each other with no need to do so, as he sees close the horror of it. "Most of the dead were stabbed or received pistol balls. Scores were injured."

"I do not see what will stop the fighting in this city. So many who are long here are against the immigrants—"

"And against the Negroes, too, free and slave." Richard takes my hand and kisses it as if it were a precious thing. "There will be more fighting. That is why we must treasure every peaceful day."

When at last Bridget appears, before the house is opened for the night, she tells such a different story about the rioting I wonder we can both live in the same world. "We saved the city from foreign corruption," she tells me. She glows like a saint in a picture on the church wall. I need say nothing in reply for Anna pitches downstairs to throw herself into her sister's arms.

I am in my bedchamber dressing my hair for the night when I think how it must now be said that I am become more than Madam Lantos. It is all the properties I own and the rents I am paid without lifting a finger. It is all the strumpets who work for me. It is the governor coming to my house and not just him but more muck-a-mucks than I can call to mind. It is Richard saying I can hire an investigator if John Haycraft lays a claim. It is that far away, people know my name. It is a strange thing: I longed for this and now I have it. It is not because the angels handed it to me, or because a man did. It is that I made for myself this life, day after day.

Still, I worry. I worry I will be alone. I am a woman without a husband, without children. I have a family still, I learn from Sarah, but what of them? We are strangers. Ever again will we feel like blood? My whoredom stands between us. My riches stand between us. The years we spent apart: they are between us, too.

I have my friends but know I could lose them. Already Charity feels far from me. She keeps secrets and I do the same. With Daniel, of course, it will never be as it was. Then there is Richard. I cannot allow myself to depend too much on him. He says it will be years he will not think about hearth and home, but am I to believe it? He could tell me tomorrow he is thinking about them and then where am I?

I give myself a shake. What good does it do to think of these things? I will think of tonight's business and let that be the end of it. We have so many in the house—I am pleased to say Daniel is among them—that I need turn some away. Amid the hubbub I take him aside to tell him of my sister, hidden away.

His blue eyes go wide. "Is she mad as a loon?"

"Mean as a badger." I do not tell him I have put with her a

bottle of whiskey. It shames me to have done so for I know it is her weakness, but how else am I to quiet her? I cannot have her in the parlor among the gentlemen.

Deep in my heart, I feel a pang for Sarah. She does not have the head on her shoulders that I do, nor a hint of the quality that has no name. And when she is in liquor, she is like Haycraft: there is a wildness about her. How is a woman like that to make her way?

But she will surprise me. That night passes, and the next, and again another, and she remains in her room quiet as a corpse. She does not drink all the whiskey and in the morn rises when I do and begins to hobble about and get her own food. *Are you not too harsh? Perhaps over all these years she has grown kinder.*

The next night is another busy one. We have Mr. Creath, the first gentleman to come to the house of Eliza Haycraft, the one to tell me of the lies Madam Lantos spread. We have Mr. Stewart of the Missouri Senate, in my bedchamber when the governor stood outside wearing the blood of a murdered trollop. What would one man of politics give to know that about another? Oh, the secrets I keep!

It is hours later, when the house could not be more full, that I hear a shrill sound I suppose I must call singing. It flows from Sarah's room. The man at the piano, who raises a brow at me from across the parlor, changes to a new melody and plays raucous as he can. Still I hear her above it.

Oh, it is a drunken sound, and not a quiet one, and I begin to see gentlemen look at one another and frown. Strumpets titter or lean toward gentlemen to spill the secret in their ears. *Her sister. That is Madam Haycraft's sister.* Then, I wish it were not so, the sound grows louder. I believe there is only one way to explain it. Sarah has opened her door.

I wish to be first to get there, to slam the door and close her inside, but I am just outside the parlor when I see it is Mr. Stewart of the Missouri Senate in the corridor walking past Sarah's room. I see his face as he looks inside. I cannot put words to all the surprise there, but he has seen enough to stop walking and to throw his open palm against his chest as if to keep his heart inside.

Then I hear my sister's voice. "You'll be wanting some of this, won't you, mister?"

From the slurred sound of it, on this night Sarah has drunk the whole of the whiskey bottle. I push past all who stand in the corridor and run toward her room.

Sarah steps into the corridor. Naked she is, naked as the day she was born, her dark hair a bird's nest, and all can see the whole of her, and it is not an alluring female she is but a drunken slut. She grabs Mr. Stewart's cravat. He reels back but cannot loose himself. "I'll be making it worth your while," she mumbles, "better'n my sister could ever do."

I reach her and grab her arm to yank her away. Back inside the little room I push her then slam shut the door behind us. Out in the corridor is a jolly ruckus, what with whoops and laughter and ribald comments flowing toward Mr. Stewart. All are having a gay time at Sarah's expense, and at mine, and didn't I know it would be so with my sister in this house?

I spin to face her. She has a night shift somewhere; I gave her one of mine. I find it puddled on the floor. "You're not so hobbled now," I mutter, the two of us tussling over the shift. Finally I get it over her head and pull it down over her body. "You should've stayed inside like I told you."

"I did the other nights." She can scarce speak for the liquor she's downed. "You don't want the competition, now do you?"

I am sorely tempted to slap her but will not do it. This tale will grow taller still if that sound flies from this room. One sister slapping another, both whores: didn't you know it? Instead I edge her close to the bed and push her, gentle enough, so that she tumbles back upon it. In time she sleeps. And why wouldn't she, for she's drunk near a bottle of spirits? Is that her sin or mine? Both, I wager. And tomorrow she will suffer. Oh, she will suffer. How her head will pound.

That will be the least of her troubles.

———

I WAIT until Sarah wakes and has not only a good measure of coffee down her gullet but eggs and bread, too, before I tell her what will happen now. While she sits at the trestle table in the kitchen, I tell the cook to leave and the doxies, too. Even now I try not to shame her before them.

"My groom will be driving you to the levee," I tell her. On the table I set a small fabric bag. Inside it coins clink. "In there is enough for steamboat fare back to Callaway County, and more besides."

She lifts the bag as if to weigh it. "You're kicking me into the gutter?"

"I'm giving you passage back where you came from. And provisions sufficient for the voyage. Bedding, too."

"Wounded I am and you're kicking me out?" Her voice is rising.

"You move around well enough."

"You're a mean one! Kicking out a sister!"

What I could say to that! Instead I force out: "I didn't ask you to come. And you will do better in Callaway County. The city is hard. And there is nothing for you here."

She rises from the bench and leans over the table toward me. "I'll tell everyone what a mighty bitch you are."

"They'll be surprised to hear it." I turn to leave.

"Bitch!" she screams at my back.

I don't stay to listen.

———

PERHAPS DANIEL, too, wishes to believe nothing is changed between us, for a few weeks later he invites me for a walk. Of an afternoon we are strolling along Locust Street, same as ever, and have stopped at Broadway to gaze at the corner structure there, a grand building of three stories made of brick and stone. It is meant to be the new Mercantile Library. "I have something to tell you," he says.

"Oh, no." I tilt my parasol to look up into his face. "More than what you've told me already?"

He chuckles. "This has nothing to do with my pending nuptials. It has to do with your sister and I do not think it good news. She is at a brothel on Green Street."

"So she did not return to Callaway County." Am I surprised? I cannot say that I am. "I gave her more than enough money to do it."

He grimaces. "Well, you will not want to hear the rest of it."

"It is bad enough she is still in this city. What worse could there be?"

"We could walk there to see," he tells me, "or we could gaze upon this building. It shall be one of the best libraries in the country."

I begin to step along Broadway. It is but three blocks more to Green Street. "I am not so interested in this library. What good is a place where only men may buy a subscription to read the books?" I could not read them, but many other women could.

Daniel leads me to the brothel where my sister might be found, in this district where much is broken and pockmarked from the riots. Here the trade is not kept to nighttime but plied all the long day. Trollops painted bright circle us both.

It is not at them I stare, though, but at the rough pencil drawing in the brothel window. It is of a woman facing away and bent half over, leering over her shoulder, her gown hiked so you need not guess much at what lies beneath. There are words written all around her figure. "What does this say, Daniel?" I ask him. For even this simple thing I cannot read, leave alone a book in a library.

" 'Here only, in the wicked flesh,' " he reads. "This is the part you will not like. 'Sarah Haycraft, sister of the famous whore Eliza Haycraft.' "

"She calls herself Sarah Haycraft?" When she is rightly Sarah Harper?

"Sarah Haycraft," he repeats. "I knew you would not like to have your name writ on this lewd advertisement."

I do not, and doubly so for a reason Daniel cannot guess. He does not know I stood before a judge to be wed. It shames me still that I was such a fool to tie my life to Haycraft's. Naturally Daniel thinks Haycraft is my family name and so my sister carries it same as me. I could confess all to him or I could go inside and hunt for my sister. It is a blistering August day and already I am cranky. "I am going inside," I tell him. "Thank you for telling me this, Daniel, but do not trouble yourself to wait for me," and inside the hovel I go.

At this establishment where the whoring goes on in the sunlight, as if we were all animals in the barnyard, I ask myself if these bawds are really so different from me? I am not sure of it. I find one who breaks a smile when she sees a coin in my hand and tells me where my sister is when I proffer another.

I knock on the door of the chamber said to be my sister's and push it open when I hear a grunt as reply. Sarah is lying upon a mattress on the roughhewn floor. In a corner is piled her carpetbag and garments. It is my night shift she is wearing and she reeks of whiskey.

"Sarah Haycraft?" I say. "That's what you're calling yourself?"

She struggles upright then the glint in the eye appears. "And why not?"

"Because it is not your rightful name. That is Sarah Harper."

"You're one to talk about what's rightful. You who'll throw your own flesh and blood into the gutter." She eyes me then cackles. "You don't like it, do you?"

I can't deny that. I have made that plain.

"She said you wouldn't," Sarah says.

"She? Who is she?"

"Madam"—Sarah squints as if struggling to remember—"Madam Lamb, I think it was."

"Madam Lantos?"

"That's the one." Sarah smiles. "The very one who thought of it. 'Use the famous name,' she told me. 'Use the name that'll bring 'em flocking.' "

I stare at my sister. Somehow Madam Lantos sniffed her out. I wonder: was it Mr. Creath told Madam Lantos I had a drunken sister from the country come to town? He is one who would know for he was at my house that night. And wouldn't Madam Lantos delight in the news.

"I will tell you again," I say. "There is nothing for you here. Go back to Callaway County," and I do not bother to count coins from my reticule but walk forward to spill them all onto her mattress.

She eyes them then me. "Thank you kindly," she says in a mincing voice. "But I think I'll stay."

I spin on my heels and walk out. What is the good of fighting my sister? What is the good of rising to anger in front of her? As I stride down the shadowy corridor I feel in my back a thump that knocks out my breath and throws me forward. I must clutch a wall to keep from falling. A clodhopper lands near me. Sarah threw it at me, I know she did, and its mark it did hit.

I straighten and keep walking.

"I AM glad we did not purchase the quill with the crow feather," Charity tells me. She sits at a writing desk in the parlor of her house, placed before a window so that I view the back of her mustard-colored dress from where I sit. "The crow feather makes an exceptional fine line, but the goose feather suits for the purpose."

"And is less dear."

"What misers we are!" She giggles, for no trollop is that.

Charity and I are returned from the stationer's, where we purchased not only the quill but an inkpot, too, and paper for writing letters, and envelopes. Not just one envelope, either, because perhaps a correspondence will arise. I sit in a stuffed chair and hope a breeze will come up. All the windows are open and the front door, too, to admit it if it does.

I grow fond of this house, though I try not to for I do not like it for Charity. Still, I smile at the fireplace ornamented with painted vines, and the window seat in the bedchamber—Chouteau had that, too—and cozy kitchen where Charity bakes sweets of a quiet afternoon.

There are too many of those. It makes me remember the months I lived in the house of Obadiah. But Obadiah returned every night and Esther and Matthew were about and sometimes Chantal, too. There were breathing bodies about me and even then on occasion I was lonely. For who will be your friend when you live in the little house where a man hides you? Not the wife next door.

Charity poises her quill over the paper. "Dear Visa Ann or dearest Visa Ann?"

"Dearest." It is to Visa Ann that I will write—that Charity will write for me—not only because I love her best but because we hope a postmaster might most easily find a member of that prominent Babb family. We know not an exact address. I doubt Visa Ann can read, but surely her husband can? Or one of her kin is able?

"How about this?" Charity gazes toward the ceiling as if reading words suspended there. " 'I so hope this letter will find you in the best of health, and happy, too. I have missed you with all my heart.' "

"Yes. Very good." Soon I hear the quill scratch. Into the inkpot the quill dips, then *scratch, scratch, scratch.*

Again Charity speaks as if reading. " 'I have seen Sarah and she has told me so much news of my dear family. I long to see you all.' "

I do not know that I long to see them all. Some, yes, with all my heart and soul, like Visa Ann. But also I am frightened to see them, and beside that I feel I should see them, and also I am very curious what it would be like, and perhaps we will make a happy family now my mother is gone. Also: *I long to see you* sounds like the sort of thing a body writes in a letter. "Very good," I tell Charity.

Dip. *Scratch*. Dip. *Scratch*. On it goes for some time.

"You are excellent at this," I tell Charity.

"It is not because I practice by writing to my own family." She turns to face me. "Shall I write at the end that it is your friend Charity who writes this letter for you and then you put your mark on it same as you would a deed?"

That is what we do, and when we are done and the letter is in the envelope and has a sort of address on it, Charity hands it to me with excitement on her face. "What a wonder if they send a letter back to you! Or if they come to St. Louis!"

"I cannot imagine it."

"I have asked them to write to you on Poplar Street."

"Maybe they will." I think of something else. "Maybe you will come back to Poplar Street to live there again." Charity begins to shake her head, but I do not quiet. "You need not say goodbye to Martin. But your life will be more lively there." I do not say the other thing I think. *You will not meet another man who might marry you while you live here. But you might if you live there.*

"You do not understand that I am happy here," she tells me.

It is not that I do not understand it. It is that I do not believe it. "It is two years you are here. More than two years."

There is no hope for it. She will not hear of it. And so we part less happy than we would have been had I kept my mouth shut.

WILL I ever understand how time passes so swiftly? It is like river water. Ever it keeps flowing. You may dip your hand in it but never can you arrest its current.

More than a year passes and no letter comes from Visa Ann. Perhaps she is of the same mind as my father, if Sarah spoke the truth about him, and believes me, her whore of a sister, to be an abomination. Perhaps she—a wife, mother, and country matron—wishes nothing to do with me. Perhaps she tossed the letter so carefully writ by Charity and me into her hearth fire. Or perhaps she never received it.

Sarah remains about, like a blister on the toe. No longer is she at the brothel on Green Street, I hear; no, she plies her trade from boardinghouse rooms on Almond. Who am I to turn up my nose at that? Still, I would she were Sarah Harper and not Sarah Haycraft.

It comes to be a drizzly Tuesday afternoon in November of 1855. Daniel, now wed to his Alice, is come to pay a visit—a chaste one. We sit in amiable silence before the hearth fire in my bedchamber, sipping coffee. Finally he speaks. "I have something to tell you, Eliza."

This must be the reason for his visit. Alice is with child, I suppose?

"It has to do with Charity," he says, surprising me. "How is she?"

"She remains where she is and I am not happy about it." Three full years now and still Martin Terris is not down on one knee.

"Here is the thing. I walked past Madam Hunter's the other evening and saw Terris enter."

I should not be shocked. I am not shocked. Still, I am saddened for Charity. "So now," I say, "I must decide whether to probe her on the matter." Then another thought comes to me. "*You* were not at Madam Hunter's."

He shakes his head. "No. I was walking past."

I lean forward and tap his knee. "I am very glad *this* place you still enter."

"Always, Eliza," he says, and laughs. It is a happy sound that will forever cheer me.

IT IS A MONTH LATER, during the season when the holly is hung and the goose fattened for the Christmas table, that of an evening a frenzied pounding calls me to the bolted door on Poplar Street, as the house is not yet open for the night. A motley crowd stands in the circle cast by the gaslight, all strangers to me.

"It is your whore of a sister Sarah," a woman cries. She misses a tooth or two. "She's stabbed her man, she has, stabbed him till he's dead."

Chapter Twenty-Five

"The 'rush' of murders, suicides, etcetera, which have been chronicling by wholesale for the past week or two, is now over.

"Let's all rest and take courage. Lay down your nightcanes, citizens, rid yourself of bowie knives and revolvers, for we are going to have a little quiet once more."

— *Missouri Democrat*

— December 14, 1855

"SHE'S AT THE CALABOOSE," a man tells me. "Saw the constable walk her there with my own eyes."

"More stumbling than walking, I'd say," another puts in, and all laugh and agree with that.

I will believe Sarah was drunk enough to stagger and I will believe she is at the calaboose—for we strumpets too often land there, especially those who ply their trade in Sarah's district—but why would I believe she killed a man? And, really, what do they mean by "her man?" I do not know she has one such. I give out coins to all the reaching hands before me, as I daresay that will move them along faster, then shut the door and lean my forehead against it.

The evening promises to be a busy one. Much draws gentlemen to my parlors these days, not just the strumpets or the festive season: there is fighting in Kansas—since the Kansas Nebraska Act, it is endless—and hence a great deal to discuss. Those for and against slavery battle there once again and this time it was a murder that caused it: a pro-slavery man slew a free-soil settler. More than a thousand of our own Missouri men rushed to aid the Kansas militia, for the slavery side, along the Wakarusa River. Nothing brings men to a cathouse like news their own are fighting somewhere, and in this case some stand for what our Missouri men do and some stand against it. It is as if this fighting in Kansas will settle the slavery question for the nation entire. I don't know about that, but there is one thing I have learned: fighting stirs the male blood in more ways than one.

I would stay put in my parlor. I do not wish to go to the calaboose to learn if this tale about my sister is true or tall. And why, oh why, has Sarah stayed in this city? She does not live her life to torment me, but still she vexes me so. There is no hope for it. "Noah?" I call, and run about to find him.

Into the gig we go, racing through the dark night, cold air biting my skin through my thickest shawl. "I will make quick work of it," I tell him when we reach the calaboose, though I do not relay the nature of what I am about.

I do not care to think on the night I passed years ago in this calaboose built of stone, when my first house on Green Street was raided. I have heard stories that some part of me believes: one that a man was thrown into a cell and when the jailers finally remembered him, the rats were having a feast. I come often enough to this place—one strumpet or another needs my aid—that soon as I enter I hear a man call my name. He is one who knows my face.

"You'll be wanting to see your sister then," he says, and so I know for sure she is here. This too tall young man, who is a constable and wears a uniform to prove it, leads me to a cell. Huddled on the floor is Sarah, not alone but with other women, tears on her cheeks, muttering to herself, and though no one speaks a word my mind tells me I am right to fear the worst. She raises her head. I see her mind work and eyes narrow the moment she knows it is me.

"She's tight," the constable beside me says.

She rises to her feet and lurches forward to grip the bars of the cell. "Samuel Hudson is dead!" she screams at me. "He was my man and now he's dead!"

"Who is Samuel Hudson?" I ask the constable.

"A smoulder by trade, lived in a boardinghouse on Plum Street. Stabbed through the right breast, he was, with a knife of eight inches."

Eight inches makes for a long knife, a knife made for butchery. I imagine it in my sister's hand. I imagine it plunging into a man's chest.

"A mortal wound," the constable says.

"Are you so sure of it?" I ask him. "Are you so sure this Hudson is dead?"

"The coroner has.seen him, examined him on the back table of Clexton's barroom. He was carried there from the street where he was felled, near dead already."

"You cannot be sure my sister is the cause of this," I tell the constable.

He looks down at me from his great height. "People say she stabbed him."

So said that crowd at my door. Yet that does not prove a thing. "Someone saw her do it?"

"People say she did it," he repeats.

I think of something else. "This Hudson could be a stranger to her."

"What woman howls so for a stranger? And she calls him her

man. Says it oft enough. That and more tell us we're right to be sure of it."

That and more. I look away from the young constable. The light may be dim, but I do not wish him to see in my eyes what I think on the matter. "I would speak with her," I tell him.

He gestures to her. "There she is, for the talking."

"I would speak with her alone."

He won't allow that. "There she is," he says again, and motions to the sobbing wreck that is my sister.

I step nearer the cell. The other inmates, doxies from the look of them, have their ears perked and their eyes upon me. They know who I am.

"He beat me!" Sarah cries as I step closer. Her cheeks are wet as river rock. "Sam Hudson beat me!"

"Hush." I lay my hands over hers that grip the cell's bars as if they'll save her from drowning. My sister reeks, truly: I do not know how the others in this cell can bear her.

"Don't you be giving her anything," the constable behind me warns.

"Do not talk to the constables," I murmur to my sister. "Can you remember that? Do not talk to them. I will pay for an attorney for you." I did little to aid her before, God save me; I will now.

"Don't know that I need a thing from you," she mutters. Then louder: "And I'll say what I please." I watch her throw back her head. "Sam Hudson is dead!"

I never saw such agony from Sarah. I cannot remember when last I saw even one tear on her cheek. She is so in liquor she does not give a care that I see her so. I wonder if that might be her way out of this? How can a woman so full drunk be said to know what she is about?

"That's enough," the constable says behind me and I will agree with him.

I loose my fingers from my sister's hands and step back from the cell. I do not look back as I follow the constable away. It is ten years I give coins to the likes of him, and city officers, too, but all the money in St. Louis may not be enough to make them forget this eight-inch knife and what they say my sister did with it.

Noah does not ask what I came for when I climb into the gig beside him. He scarce touches the reins before the horse steps lightly toward Poplar Street. Now I do not mind the icy wind on my face but take pleasure in it. Only those of us who are free can feel it.

"I DID NOT MAKE my sister what she is," I tell Richard, "but I did nothing to turn her away from her nature, either."

It is the next morning. Richard and I stand in my parlor cocking our heads at the spruce tree, tall as me, purchased from a peddler. Does it stand straight or does it not? Who can tell for sure? This is a thing Queen Victoria and her German husband have come up with to celebrate the season: a tree such as this to be decked with bits of foil and ribbon and candy. Before yesterday I decided to do it, too. Now I wonder why I bother.

"You are a magician, then," Richard says, "that you can turn a woman away from her nature?"

"I myself gave her whiskey, to quiet her. Now look what it made her do."

He says nothing. I know he is thinking liquor did not make Sarah stab a man. I do not know how she could have done it otherwise.

Though truth to tell, I do not know what to believe. She may have done it. For all my life I have known Sarah to show meanness. When she is in liquor, the meanness grows. Yet I think another thing, too. In this world of ours, it might have been a man to cut down Sam Hudson but be an intoxicated whore to get the blame. A few coins slipped to those who saw the knife fly and suddenly all might cry that the drunken slut is the guilty party.

"I told her I will pay for an attorney," I tell Richard. "If I had placed her in one of my houses, kept an eye on her, would this have come to pass?"

"It might still have."

"Or this Sam Hudson might still breathe. My sister might still be free. I am the one who doles out food and coins to strangers, yet I would not do more than that for my own blood? What does that make me?"

"You knew she was trouble. And you are not your sister's keeper."

I think that is a phrase from the Bible though I am not one to know. "I must find an excellent attorney to plead her case." Now I am a muck-a-muck I can pay for one such. "I have one client in particular who could advise."

Richard nods. That does not mean he agrees, but he is not one to fight me when my mind is set. "There is another thing I worry about," he says. "That Sarah does not keep her mouth shut in front of the constables."

"I worry the same. Drunk or sober, she is one to boast." *I stabbed a man. And the knife was long. Eight inches.*

Richard sighs before he speaks again. "This sordid tale shall be printed in the newspapers, Eliza."

"It would be even if she were not my sister." It is not so common for a woman to be accused of murder. And this murderess has a famous whore for a sister. *Notorious.*

"Are you worried"—he seems not to know how to ask it—"are you worried your houses will suffer?"

I have thought on the matter. "Some gentlemen will not come to my houses after this. Most will not care. Those who know me will have seen I kept my sister far from me." They might think me heartless for that. But it is not for our hearts that men seek out harlots. I think sometimes they forget we have hearts beating in our chests, same as their wives and daughters.

"You are not responsible for what Sarah did," Richard says again, and I try not to be impatient with him but I am. I wish to feel all the hurt I should feel, for throwing my sister to the side, for a man knifed in the chest.

"She screamed that this Sam Hudson beat her," I tell Richard. "I know what it is to be beaten," and I tell him things he never knew about John Haycraft.

All he can do at that is set his jaw and clench his fists and think again, I know, of throwing Haycraft into the river.

"I must remember, too," I say, "and I should have remembered before, that Sarah is my father's daughter same as I am." I must stop for some moments after I say that, but soon I can begin again. "He loves her, same as me. And if I help her now, after tossing her aside before, if I help her now with all my heart and soul, maybe he can forgive me for what I did and for what I am."

"You do not need forgiveness for either of those," Richard tells me, but I will not listen.

"I BELIEVE the very same carriage goes past again," Charity tells me.

I watch her stand at the front window of her little house and peer at the dimming street, where snow falls and swirls and finally settles in uneven mounds. She wears a green frock the color of a forest; I well remember it. What I cannot recall is the last time I saw her in a new garment. What did Madam Lantos say to me, those long years ago? *That dress is of an old style. Look at those sleeves.* It was my fault I was behind the fashion then. For this now I blame Martin Terris.

"How would you know which carriage goes past?" I ask her.

Her face turns toward mine. Have I seen sadder eyes? "What have I to do but stare out the window?"

"Come away from there." I move forward to tug on her arm. "Let us finish that letter."

"Yes"—she will let me pull her away—"you are right. We must get it written." Charity moves back to the writing desk in her parlor, where she has half composed a second letter to my sister Visa Ann. Will this one reach her? Did the last? I do not know but believe I must try to tell my family about Sarah and how else am I to do it?

Charity tells me before she pens them the phrases she will write. *Sarah is accused of murder in the first degree. Her trial will be the month next, commencing on Thursday, the twenty-fourth, at the Criminal Court here in St. Louis. I have found an attorney to plead her case, and will pay him in full, and all agree he is an able counsel.*

"Please write also," I say, "that I am helping her best I can."

Dip. *Scratch.* Dip. *Scratch.*

Now I am looking out the window and see there is a woman marching through the snow to Charity's door. The phaeton she climbed from waits on the street, hot breath rising from the horses. I am wondering what could be this rich lady's business with this house when comes a fierce rapping on the door.

"Who could that be?" Charity sets down her quill and I follow her to the door for of a sudden I am uneasy.

On the stoop is a slim, well-garbed woman of more than fifty years, a beauty in the way a woman can be at that age if her life has been of leisure and the bones of her face are of the best kind. She juts her chin and surveys us both. "I am Mrs. Josephina Terris. Which of you is the whore sullying my son?"

I yank on Charity's arm to pull her back. This Mrs. Terris might clutch a bottle of acid in her gloved hand to throw at our faces: I have heard of such a thing.

Charity can cock her chin, too, when provoked. "I am Charity, and I love your son, and he loves me, too."

"That is a pretty speech, but I believe not a word of it, not even your name," and I catch my breath at that, and maybe Charity does, too, for that name is the one Madam Lantos gave Charity and she would not have it otherwise. "I have put aside my revulsion," Mrs. Terris says, "at speaking to the likes of you, for I will not allow another year to begin with my son under your wicked thrall. You have bewitched him. But at last I have thought of just the potion to set him right."

"Your son has a mind of his own," Charity says.

"And a good mind it is, which is why I am certain he will make the right choice. You know his dog Dickens? Well, my son will find out this evening that Dickens is no longer in the house with us, and never will be again, unless he gives you up. It is you or the dog."

"What have you done to that sweet creature?" Charity cries. "Martin loves Dickens!"

"And so he will choose the dog over you." Mrs. Terris leans closer. "I advise you to return to whatever cathouse you came from. And mark my words: I will come again should I need to." She throws a glare at me, too, then spins and departs.

Charity sets her hand on her chest as if to keep her pounding heart in place. "That is the carriage I saw going past time and again."

"She was deciding whether to stop here. Come," and I pull Charity back another step so I might shut the door.

Charity's face is white as new snow. Now I have another secret to keep: I am glad Mrs. Terris has done this thing. It is near three years that Charity is in limbo with Martin Terris and he, who is in paradise with everything he wants, would not do a thing about it until pushed. Well, now he is pushed. I lead Charity to a stuffed chair. She drops into it and I kneel on the carpet before her.

"Do you believe it?" Charity asks me. "What she says about Dickens?"

I think for a moment, then: "Am I right that Martin lives with her and his father?" That would be the usual way until he marries, and maybe after.

"Yes. And Dickens lives there, too. She could have put that poor dog someplace," and Charity's face crumples. It is some time she sobs and when a woman is doing that, what can you do but wait? "Martin loves me," she tells me finally, and I do not dispute it.

"It is years you have been in this house, Charity, and it would not be so if he did not love you."

I do not speak the word *but* yet Charity hears it all the same. "You think he will choose Dickens over me."

"It is not just Dickens. It is all his friends and family, and his family's fortune, too. Also, I wish *you* to do the choosing." *I'm the one who'll do the leaving,* John Haycraft told me. Men ever think they should decide these things, but I hold a different view.

"How can I leave him if he loves me?"

"He must love you enough to do the thing that is right for you, Charity." *Not leave you in this house staring out the window while on the sly he takes his pleasure at Madam Hunter's.* "Come back to Poplar Street. There are many gentlemen about, more than ever. You do not meet them here. You will meet them there."

"I am too old for them now."

"You are young and still a beauty." I say it with fierceness. "Your heart is so warm you can fill a whole house with the joy of it. And you can bear children still."

She turns wet eyes to mine. "I know it is too long Martin has waited to make a proposal to me. I am not such a fool I don't know it."

I reach for her hands to clasp them. I say nothing and wait.

Finally, finally, she asks what I have longed to hear. "Have you room for me on Poplar Street?"

"Of course I do. I will put two bawds together in one bedchamber and make one open for you." The two I think of like each other best anyway. And I have long known that two bawds in one bedchamber is a service for which gentlemen will cheerfully dole out extra.

"HAVE YOU AN OPINION," Richard asks me, "which is the better carriage maker? Bostwick or Osborn and Dougherty?"

We are sitting in the plump chairs before the hearth fire in my bedchamber, drinking tea as if we were lady and gentleman and not harlot and lover. It is afternoon of the last day of the year 1855, near dark enough already to be night. I wish to bid to this year *adieu* though all the same I dread what the next will bring.

"Is Osborn and Dougherty," I ask him, "the shop at Fifth and St. Charles?" That is the location of Chouteau's mansion, with the eight wide steps leading to the front door. Many feet climb those stairs for Chouteau and his Julia have three children now, adding a boy. I remember, too, the girl who perished an infant.

"The very same, at that corner."

I could tell him I believe that shop is better because Chouteau would not reside near any but the best carriage maker, but that would be a silly reason. "I purchased my gig at Bostwick because they had a good one on offer, but I believe Osborn and Dougherty is also a fine merchant. Anyway, does your friend think it time to replace the rockaway? Perhaps," I tease him, "you have used it too much."

"I have used it too much and as I will live in St. Louis from this time forward, I believe it time I purchase my own carriage. Well, more a gig, a simple thing."

I set down my tea. "You will do what?"

"I will come to live here, Eliza. I have thought on this and set my mind to it." Now he sets down his tea as well. "I can practice medicine here as well as Chicago. I can travel west to practice from here as well as I can from Chicago."

"But you love Chicago."

"Always I shall love it. But perhaps"—he gazes at me with amber eyes—"I do not love Chicago above all else."

He is silent after that, and so am I, and I am left to wonder what he might love above all else. That is not a word we speak between us. In this life of mine that is not a word I dwell upon. It is a word for storybooks and those do not do me much good, either.

"I am pleased with my boardinghouse," he says, matter-of-fact as he picks up his teacup. "May I use your shed here for the horse? I will need that and the help of your groom, too. I wish to take good care of the horse."

"Of course." I will not have him give me money for that. I do not wish money to pass between us.

"There is one more thing I wish to tell you. You will not like it."

What else could Richard have to tell me on this snowy afternoon? Already I am dumbstruck. But not because I dislike a word he has spoken.

"I worry," he says, "about the rising trouble in our country. It is quieter now but only because the winter is severe. When the troubles worsen, and I am sure they will, I daresay the danger will be greater in Missouri than Illinois. Illinois is firmly in the north. Missouri is caught between north and south."

Yes. That problem of heart and mind: Missouri's mind looks to the north but its heart beats for the south. "Would you not rather be where the danger is less?"

"Not if you are where the danger is more."

There he is again, saying a thing straight out. So I will do the same. "If you do this for me, I think you do too much. What if you are not happy here?"

"I am doing it for you but for me as well. And if I am not happy, I will have only myself to blame."

He says that now. "But what if—"

"Eliza." He is shaking his head. "I will not worry about if this and if that. What will happen will happen. We cannot be sure of anything, times what they are. And while I know you will not need my help if the worst happens, if I am close I can give it all the same."

I do not need to ask what the worst is. I know already. There is danger all about us. Some I see with my own eyes and some I only hear about. Bawds slashed to death among the bedclothes and their killers run free. Negroes hung from tall trees until their breath is gone. Men taking pistol balls when a mob goes amok. Our Missouri men fighting Kansas men, yesterday's neighbors.

Then there is my sister Sarah. She is accused of taking a life and soon will have to face the weight of that before judge and jury.

I leave my chair to kneel before Richard and take his hands in mine. I kiss each one in turn. "It is the last day of the old year. I do not wish to think of danger."

"No? Shall we save that for the first day of the new year?" I see a fresh light in his eyes, flashes of gold in the amber. "How about Abraham Lincoln, then? Shall we speak of him? An Illinois man."

"He walks about and makes speeches. I have heard of him." I lean forward to brush Richard's lips with one kiss and then another and that is enough to make us both forget, at least for a time, Missouri and Illinois and all the men in both of them.

"It's a funeral I'm going to then?" Sarah mutters.

I am in the calaboose, sitting beside her on a rough bench, laying out the garments I have provisioned for those days she will sit before judge and jury. She must not enter the Courthouse clothed in her usual rags. As I do this, trollops watch and listen with interest, a different troupe than I saw before. "You are to look somber," I tell Sarah, "serious as a churchgoer." That is what the attorney advised. I believe he is able. Everything he says has much sense to it.

The dress is dark and made of wool, as befits the season; there is a cape of black and also a mourning bonnet, also black and with a veil of crepe. My garments will be much the same. I, too, must hide the bawd within me for those days.

"I'll look like a crow," Sarah says. There is no liquor in her now, after these weeks in the calaboose. That is better but hardly a salvation.

"You will look like a respectable woman who would not do what you are accused of."

"*You* never ask if I did it." She cocks her head at the bawds around her. "They ask. But not you."

That is because I wish not to know. From three days hence, when I sit in the Courthouse, I will not be able to keep myself from knowing. "You would be wise to act like a respectable woman who would not do what you are accused of."

"I'll act as I choose," she tells me, and I wrap up the garments to take them away until the morning of the trial, for I cannot trust Sarah or any of these harlots to leave them be.

Chapter Twenty-Six

"THE TRIAL OF SARAH HAYCRAFT FOR THE MURDER OF SAMUEL HUDSON: The prisoner at the bar… is but without many marks of a handsome woman. She seems to be but little concerned about the character of the evidence brought against her, sitting quietly with her eyes for the most part downcast…

"Whether resigned to whatever fate the law may have in waiting for her—whether weighed down by an expressionless grief, or whether stubbornly or silently defiant… we are totally unable to even guess."

— *Missouri Democrat*

— January 25, 1856

I T IS A DAY THAT WILL CHANGE THE COURSE OF MY LIFE, but still it is drear as any other January day, the sun feeble, the air cutting, and the snow on Poplar Street pockmarked with manure from dogs and horses where it isn't streaked with grime from drays and carriages.

I have one joy, though: Charity beside me. She has quit Martin Terris at last. I would not believe it until she allowed Noah to carry her trunk into the bedchamber beside mine. I am sure Terris finds consolation in wet kisses from Dickens and a trollop or two at Madam Hunter's. It is mine to comfort Charity and I do it best I am able, as my spirits sink lower each day we march nearer January the twenty-fourth. We are frightful close now.

"There's a pair for you at the front door," a housemaid tells me mid afternoon, "they won't enter," and she rushes past with her mind on half-done chores. I open my door to behold before me a face I have not seen in a dozen years—though in a fashion I see it every day in my own mirror; still, it is a face I have never seen thus, as a woman and not a girl.

My heart stampedes like a horse gone mad. "Visa Ann."

"It is you, it is you"—she is stammering the words—"I can scarce believe it."

Yes, I can see it, I can see my sister Visa Ann as a mother—of five babes!—her figure rounded but hair light and full and eyes bright. She is still a beauty. That is why Benjamin Babb set his eyes on her—and not just his eyes—when she made fifteen years. Is she not now twenty-four years old, the very age I was when I flung myself into that canoe? How different our lives have been. Has she been happy? I look at her now, clad in the rough black wool of the country matron, and hope and pray nothing has darkened this sister's gentle spirit, loving as a dove.

I move to grasp her in a hug, but she steps back—I am shocked; she won't have it?—and I am feeling that stab when I hear from the street below a man's voice sternly speak her name. I think it must be Benjamin, but no, it is my brother, Asa.

It is not wonder I see in his dark eyes, wonder that we two are staring at one another again after these long years, but coldness, as if river ice pumps through his veins. He will never be a handsome man—he is too like our father and Sarah for that—but I have seen him frolic like any rascal and yet now he stares at me as if I am Wickedness itself and he must bear that awful truth about his own sister. I swallow, step back and wave my arm to welcome them into my foyer. "Please, come inside. It is terrible cold out here."

"We will not step inside such a place as that," Asa tells me.

He might say more if Visa Ann did not speak. "We are on the way to our boardinghouse but stopped to tell you we have come."

Now I see there is a hired gig on the street, two carpetbags inside, and a driver who could find the house of Eliza Haycraft. *Notorious.* "I'm so glad you have come," I say, and mean it. "And so long a journey. How many days?" They must have come by coach: steamboats cannot always ply the winter river and the railroad, even if they were so bold as to take it, does not reach Callaway County.

"Five days," Visa Ann says, "slower for the snow," and she might say more but for the driver raising his voice.

"Let's get to Mrs. Mudge's then," and to me: "Mrs. Mudge's on Market Street," saying it in a way makes me think he is daring me to defy him, and I know he is the one who thought of that place and coins will go his way because of it, so I will keep my mouth shut though there are plenty other boardinghouses better.

"You received my letter, then," I say to Visa Ann.

"Two of them," and her gaze is steady as she says it, and I know she is telling me that when it was me writing for myself she would pass it by, but now it is our sister on trial she will journey here. Am I stabbed again? I might be. Well, I did not journey to see her, did I? And I am the one who journeyed away in the first place.

"I will follow you to Mrs. Mudge's," I say, "in my own gig."

"No need for that," says Asa.

"But it is years we have not seen each other and we cannot part so soon!"

"It is because of *you* we parted at all," Visa Ann says. "It is because of *you* and no one else."

I cannot say a word to hear Visa Ann speak so, this sister who leaps fast as a doe from a quarrel. Yet now I see tears spring to her light eyes and her lips quiver and I reach out for her again. "Visa Ann," I murmur, but my brother will shout loud enough to rouse Lazarus.

"Sister! We have stopped long enough," and I believe he might even mount the stairs to get her though that would mean stepping nearer to me, but he needn't for she turns to descend on her own.

I watch them get into the gig, the driver sneering to see a famous whore dismissed by her better relations. Visa Ann will meet my gaze as they roll away, but Asa will only stare straight ahead. Charity is behind me when I turn around and her arms will take me. It is some time I sit in the parlor and cry, the pocket doors shut for the first time I can remember, to keep out curious eyes. There is no end to drama when a Harper sister comes to town and now there is a brother come, too.

"I left without a word to Visa Ann," I tell Charity, "and she is the one I loved best, with my father."

Charity is crouching at my knees. "You had no time to say anything."

"All these years later, all they know is I left." They do not know why, the many reasons why.

"They will know more now they're here. They would not make such a hard journey, and in winter, too, if they did not wish to see you again," and I hope it is not just her soft heart speaking but Truth itself.

I FEEL many eyes upon me as I mount the Courthouse steps under clouds charcoal gray like ash in a hearth. Am I the one on trial?

There is a way I might be, for I am the sister of the accused murderess and a whore besides, so I am Sin itself cloaked in black bombazine.

Richard is beside me, and Charity, too, and amid the throngs on the street I saw Daniel. As promised, he waited for me to pass and raised a hand in greeting. He is sending me courage, I know. Of course he cannot attend—I full understand that—and also I wonder how many bodies can fit in the Criminal Court? My sister's case draws a mob outside and won't it be the same within? What could be more enticing a spectacle than a bawd on trial for murder?

Asa will not sit beside me—he will not sully himself—and Visa Ann will stay with him. I understand that. They have allowed me to speak to them from the stoop of Mrs. Mudge's, though Asa will not let me speak to Visa Ann alone. Even if he would, I wonder what difference it would make. If Visa Ann must pick a side, it is the side of the brother who never left her and never will. For now at least, with larger matters before us, I accept all without another word spoken. I understand and accept all but for what I see from my sister Sarah.

How must her heart pound as she waits to be brought here from the calaboose! At dawn I carried her garments to the jail-house and would have helped her dress if she'd let me. No, she would be sullen and do it alone, or maybe she asked the help of her fellow inmates. I do not know for she cursed at me to leave and so I did.

I am inside the cold white Courthouse now, grand as heaven's greatest palace, meant to make us feel small and doing so ably. Yet it is not God's power I feel but the power of men, men who are judge and jury, not a woman among them, men who may never lack a coin but will sit in judgment upon a woman whose pockets are ever empty, men who might dally with strumpets yet speak loudly against them, men who would not recognize desperation but will freely opine on a woman always near it. That is the world we live in, the world I must hope will save my sister.

I do not need Richard to push our way through to the court-room, but he does it all the same, suffering sneers for the trouble he takes for the likes of Charity and me. Charity clutches my hand as if she might drown should I let her loose. This large chamber that makes up the Criminal Court is split in two, the parts separated by a carved bank of dark gleaming wood. On one side are we who can do nothing but listen and tremble. On the other are those who sit on a throne or behind a large desk to testify and argue and judge.

We sit, Charity on my right and Richard on my left. Richard squeezes my hand. He knows what Mr. Goodlett, the attorney, has warned me. *You will hear things you wish not to hear about your sister.* And: *She does not make this case an easy one.*

Richard is silent, but Charity will whisper, and poke me, too. "There, across the way behind us, I see your brother and sister."

I turn to look. Yes. I nod at them and they nod back. Asa does not meet my gaze for long. Perhaps his eyes might fall from their sockets if he does.

"I don't see Mr. Goodlett," Charity murmurs. Now she is looking where the lawyers will sit.

"He will have last matters to attend." Perhaps he has found another witness who will take Sarah's side? They number too few now.

It seems an age we must wait, but at length Mr. Goodlett does enter the Court, and then the prosecuting attorney, too. Mr. Goodlett is a portly man with a mass of white hair it is a wonder he can put a comb through; the state's man is short as Napoleon but quick to walk. There is a way he makes me think of Obadiah though I do not wish to have any good feeling about him. Was it just a moment ago the Court was filled with shuffling and chatter as people settled themselves?—for now it is church quiet. The jurors enter with not a smile among them. I probe their faces. What am I looking for? Kindness. Sympathy. If it is there, I cannot see it. Then...

Sarah.

She enters the Court with her head high, gazing at no one. If she knows she has blood relations in this chamber—who loved her once, God help them—she doesn't show it. If there is warmth in her heart, she well hides it. She wears everything I gave her, the mourning bonnet, too, and looks more a respectable woman than I have ever seen her. Her features, though, are set in hard lines; why can she never soften them? I glance at the jurors. They stare with frowning faces. I do not think they take a liking.

We rise to our feet for the judge. I cannot stop this now: it will happen regardless what I do. If I shriek and faint, they will carry me out and proceed. If I wanted to stop this, I should have begun when I spied Sarah on the levee. That would have been the time. Now it is too late and I must wonder how we Harper sisters have come to this sorry pass.

What I must do is make myself cold to this, listen to it but not let it touch me inside, as I did when John Haycraft would use his fists on me, as I did when so many men did so many things to me so I could earn my keep. I will do the same again now. I will listen to what people say but will not let the words go deep.

Well, it is one thing to think of the phrases I would hear in this Court and another to hear them. *The State of Missouri versus Sarah Haycraft... Murder in the First Degree... Feloniously, willfully, deliberately, premeditatedly, and of her malice aforethought did make an assault... She the said Sarah Haycraft with a certain knife of the length of eight inches did thrust, strike, cut, stab, and give the said Samuel Hudson one mortal wound...*

There is more high talk before the first witness is brought. Ann Williams is her name; she shares Sarah's boardinghouse. She might be my age but looks hard done by; yet she has a softer face than my sister can manage.

Finally we get to *the day in question*. "She first came to my room at seven that morning," Ann Williams says.

"And did you notice anything about her?" the state's lawyer inquires.

"She'd been drinking."

There is a ripple among us. That is a shocking early hour for liquor or else Sarah drank throughout the night.

"She wanted fifty cents," Ann Williams says, "but I wouldn't give it to her, so she put on her sun bonnet and left. Four or five that afternoon she came back, in liquor, and wanted something to drink, but I told her she'd had enough and to just sit down. She wouldn't do it, though, she said, until she saw Sam Hudson."

The lawyer stands wordless before the jurors. I believe he wishes them to take their time imagining my sister on the hunt for the man who would soon be dead. "Sam Hudson," finally he repeats. "And what did Sarah Haycraft do then?"

"She showed me the knife hid in her stocking," Ann Williams says. Gasps echo about the Courtroom. The woman speaks again. "She said to me, and to my dying day I won't forget it: 'If I go for the damned English son of a bitch, I will bring him.' " She looks to the judge. "I'm sorry to speak words so plain."

She is assured she should continue to do so. And when she opens her mouth again, I shudder to hear the whole of what she has to say.

" 'If I go find him, I will bring this,' Sarah told me, and I knew she meant the knife for she was pointing to it, and then she said, 'And if I find him and he don't make up with me, I will kill him.' "

There is a brouhaha after that and the judge bangs his gavel and all are told with great sternness to be quiet or different arrangements will have to be made. I shut my eyes and listen to the roar until I think to open them again to look at my sister's face. And wouldn't you know I don't see a human thing writ there? Not a flicker, not a regret, not a trace of a tear. She stares ahead as if made of stone and I wonder at that moment if she might be.

Even after all that, the state's lawyer isn't done with Ann Williams. Was there not an incident involving Sam Hudson a few days prior? "She'd fallen down the stairs, had Sarah," Ann

Williams says, "and asked for Hudson, and I went to go find him."

"And did you find him?"

"I did. And he told me in terms certain he would not come with me for he wanted nothing more to do with Sarah Haycraft."

"He was not so fortunate as to have that wish come true, though, was he?" says the state's lawyer to the jurors, and Mr. Goodlett leaps to his feet to object and I'm glad at last he has found a thing he might object to.

It is Mr. Goodlett's turn to ask the questions and he pries one good word from Ann Williams. "What was the condition of Sarah Haycraft," he wants to know, "when she left your boardinghouse room that afternoon of December the eleventh?"

"She did not know what she was about," Ann Williams says, and Mr. Goodlett will try to make much of that, I know, and the intoxicating liquor that caused it.

I do not know why I should wish for women to testify for the next two say nothing to help Sarah. Not long before the stabbing, Mary Pelve saw my sister "pursuing right after" Sam Hudson down Poplar Street. And Susan Johnson testifies that Sarah on that day was "staggering drunk."

"She stopped in the alley off Poplar between Second and Third streets and she took a dirk knife from her stocking special to show me. I'll tell you what she told me, too," and the state's lawyer won't keep her from doing it. "She said Sam Hudson's life should be hers before morning."

Another hue and cry. I turn to look at my brother and sister. Across these rows of rowdy citizens, Visa Ann will meet my gaze, and for a moment, just a moment, we are sisters again, the same heart beating in two chests. But Asa opens his mouth and again her eyes move away from mine and I lose her.

There is time for all to leave the Courtroom for a meal; I am surprised such a matter is interrupted. In the afternoon there are fresh words spoken that I judge even more calamitous than those I heard in the morning. William J. Clexton, burly as a roustabout and the man who carried Hudson's bleeding body to the rear of his barroom, saw my sister not long after. She told him she had killed Sam Hudson.

"There was another man there standing," Clexton says, "and he says, 'But you did not mean to do it?' and Sarah Haycraft tells him that if Hudson had stopped to talk to her, no, she would not have killed him."

It is the arresting constable we hear from last, R. P. Banning. He has an earnest look about him and is a man I would not mind on any other day. "I found her at Columbus Coffee House and asked what she had done and she would say nothing to me. I told her she must follow me to the police office. On the way I told her she had a right to tell me all about it."

I shut my eyes. Did she not also have a right to tell him nothing?

"She said she had cut Sam Hudson with a large knife," the constable says, "and said after cutting him she threw the knife on the ground."

It is at the jurors that the state's attorney stares when he asks the question next. "Did you tell her Sam Hudson was dead?"

More than once, the constable says. "The first time I told her Hudson was dead, she said if he was not dead, if she saw him again, she would kill him."

There is more tumult after that, and the judge bangs his gavel to stop it, but he does so only thrice for I think after all this he has become too tired to bang more.

OUTSIDE THE COURTHOUSE in the glow of a gaslight, I wait for Visa Ann and Asa amid the latecomers departing the trial. Richard and Charity have gone on before me; I do not wish my sister and brother to suffer a second whore and a man happy to abide the same. Finally I see them, eyes downcast and not a word passing between. They look beaten as I feel. "May I walk with you," I ask, "to Mrs. Mudge's?"

Visa Ann looks to my brother to decide. I know it is the way of most women, but I wish she would speak for herself. To my surprise my brother nods and I fall in step beside them. After a time I speak. "It was worse than even I imagined. I was fool enough to hope Sarah had not done this thing. Now I can only wonder if she knew what she was about. Yet no one, not a soul, steps forward to say they saw her stab Hudson. Saw it with their own eyes."

Asa stops walking. I do the same, and Visa Ann, too. My brother looks me full in the face. "Sarah is the only one who says it. She says, I would kill him, I did kill him, and if he wasn't dead I would do it again to make sure I killed him."

"Yes, that is exactly it, Asa." When did I last speak my brother's name? I could almost cry to hear it come from my mouth. "If Sarah did not say she stabbed him, who would? It is as if Sarah is the witness against herself."

Visa Ann throws up her hands. "Why did you not send her back to us? You could have paid for her to come back a hundred times."

I am about to say that I gave her more than enough money to return when my brother speaks. "No, Visa Ann. You cannot make Sarah move a foot she will not move on her own. She is stubborn as a cow in a barn. You can light it afire around her and push her in the rump to move, but she'd sooner roast than do your bidding."

I would say something if I could, but now words are caught in my throat, same as the tears there.

My brother walks again and we sisters step in line. "Sometimes a body surprises you," he mutters, almost too low for me to hear, but I hear all the same and know that now it is me he is speaking of, his sister who went away to become a whore and surprised everyone, even herself. "And sometimes a body will do same as she ever did," he says, and I know now he is speaking of Sarah.

From then we three are silent. They allow me to walk with them all the way to Mrs. Mudge's and I allow myself to think that maybe, maybe, we are brother and sisters in our hearts still.

———

IT IS no surprise what the witnesses of the next morning say, those put forth by Mr. Goodlett, for he alerted me to the only case he saw before him: Sarah Haycraft does not know what she is about when intoxicated. Elizabeth Garretty, gray of hair with a face pinched as if she just sucked a lemon, says the very thing. So does a thin, dark-haired policeman name of John Cherocombe, who believes he is Wisdom itself about women.

"The defendant is different from other women under liquor," he tells us. "When drinking, and I have seen it often enough, the defendant is a braggart, talking of who she can whip. I don't think she is as sharp as what some women might be."

"You come to this conclusion," Mr. Goodlett says, "from conversations you have had with her?"

"I do. And when drunk she has frequently told me as a policeman things which she would not if sound in mind. She—"

"Ah ha!" Mr. Goodlett stares with meaning at the jurors and raises a finger high in the air. "You say you found the defendant *not* to be of sound mind, from those many conversations you had with her?"

"She has told me things on herself such as would warrant her arrest."

"That is an astonishing thing!" Mr. Goodlett cries. "What sort of things has she told on herself?"

"Well, there was a time she told me she broke into a certain house and smashed up the furniture. And upon enquiry I found out what she had said was true. I therefore think she is different from other women what I have seen drunk."

"Assuredly so!" Mr. Goodlett slams his hand on the wood railing between him and the jury. "No woman of sound mind would do what you describe."

The state's attorney will not leave that point to stand. He calls again Mr. Clexton, keeper of the barroom. "I saw the defendant every few days," he tells us, "at my house and other places and never saw any evidence of insanity."

"Never saw any evidence of insanity," the state's lawyer repeats. "And when under the influence of liquor?"

"The same as any other woman except then. Then she was a dangerous woman, liquor made more so than some others."

Mr. Clexton is freed from the stand and there is much whispering then, with the lawyers up close to the judge and the rest of us left to wonder. It is some time before those two return to stand behind their tables. Then: "The defense rests," Mr. Goodlett says, and I gasp and hear the same all around me, for that seems scarce a defense at all. Surely there is more to put forth on my sister's behalf? But there must not be, for now the jurors are instructed on what *willful* means, and *deliberate*, and *premeditated. Intentional, not accidental; thought of in cool blood, that is, not in a heat of passion;* and *thought of before hand, any length of time, however short.*

There is more instruction, and I numb from the details of it, but then something is said to perk my ears: *Although you may find defendant to be weak in mind or even partially insane, yet if she had her mind sufficiently to know she was doing wrong in killing Hudson and could control her action in regard to that matter, this constitutes no defense…*

No defense. Richard reaches out to squeeze my hand.

The jurors are handed the case and we who are watching are handed our own sentence: to wait.

How long does it take the jurors? It seems an eternity but is only a few hours. In the Courtroom we take the places we know too well. Is there air enough to breathe? I am not sure of it. My heart palpitates. My mouth dries.

The jurors return. They have no eyes for any person in that chamber; they have eyes only for the floorboards upon which they tread.

I swallow. If I thought God listened to a whore's prayers, I would say them.

The judge asks if the jurors have reached a verdict. One man rises to say they have. What do you find, the judge asks? *We find the defendant guilty*, the man says, *guilty of murder in the first degree.*

There is no commotion now. There is only silence.

The judge turns toward my sister. Hath she anything to say?

She does not.

So it is the judge again who will speak. *It is therefore considered by the Court that the said defendant be taken from the Court to the place from whence she came, there to remain until Friday, the eleventh day of April next, thence to be taken to the place of execution, and there between the hour of ten o'clock in the forenoon and four o'clock in the afternoon the said day, to be hanged by the neck until She be dead.*

Chapter Twenty-Seven

"Sarah Haycraft is to be hung at St Louis next Friday, for the murder of her lover. She manifests perfect indifference to her fate. Recently a person visited her while at dinner and remarked, 'Well, Sarah, they give you enough to eat, it seems.' 'Oh, yes,' she replied. 'They are fatting me up to kill.'

— *Buffalo Daily Courier*

— April 10, 1856

"SARAH CANNOT BE MADE TO SUFFER THIS JUDGMENT ALONE," I tell Richard as I stand in the aisle beside the Courtroom seats. If I could sprout wings and fly to the calaboose, where already Sarah has been led away, I would do it.

But the sight of Mr. Goodlett threading his way to me through the throng keeps my feet from moving. "I am very sorry, Madam

Haycraft," he mutters when he is at my side, "but I warned you this case would be difficult." He raises a hand to forestall me from speaking. "I could ask the Court to set aside the verdict."

"You can do such a thing?"

"There is not much hope for it." He is alerting me, again, to all going wrong. "But I can argue a point or two."

"Do it then. I will pay you to do it," and I spin away from him for I feel the same as I did moments before: I must go to my sister.

Asa, Visa Ann, and I are brother and sisters again when we meet outside the Courthouse, in a circle with our hands clasped. That I am a whore matters less now another sister has been deemed a murderess and to the gallows she will go. My mind fills with a fresh horror: who will tell our father the fate of his first-born?

Now the worst has happened, at the calaboose no constable tries to keep us from Sarah. This time one will lead us to a small chamber where we may huddle: cold and ill lit with a foul damp dripping down the walls, its comfort is meager. And is it a sneer I see on Sarah's face when finally she is brought 'round to join us? It might be. She stands apart as if blood did not bind us together.

"Mr. Goodlett told me he can ask the Court to set aside the verdict," I tell her. She makes a scoffing sound: she has seen enough not to rest a hope on it. "I have told him I will pay him to do it."

Visa Ann says again the thing she cannot stop saying. "Your money would've been better spent to return our sister to Callaway County."

"You blame *her* for this?" Sarah says.

"More than one played a part," Asa says, and I know it is me he speaks of, well as Sarah, and though I have thought the same for weeks, on this night I have had enough of it.

"More than once I gave Sarah money to take the steamboat back," I say. "Enough and more to spare. She would not do it."

"She would never have come to this place at all," Visa Ann says, "if you did not come here first."

"You led the way," Asa agrees.

"I did what I had to do to gain a measure of freedom in this life." My voice, rising, echoes against the walls of stone; it is as if we are fallen down a well. "And though you want me to be, I am not sorry for it."

"Freedom from what?" Asa wants to know. "From your husband lawfully wed?"

"Not so lawfully wed," and I tell them what John Haycraft told me that last night, of the wife he had already, stashed in the state of Kentucky.

Still: "It is not up to a wife to quit her husband," Asa tells me.

My patience has gone thin as the soles of a poor man's shoe. "John Haycraft was not my lawful husband. And even if he was, if a man turns out to be a dog I say you can rightfully quit him and be done with it."

Visa Ann gasps, but Sarah cackles loud as a rooster at dawn. "So you were a fool to marry him! Same as Mama always said."

"I was a fool." I will admit it. The Harper sisters will be found guilty of more than one charge on this day. "But not fool enough to pay for it with my life entire."

It is footfalls we hear in the distance, coming nearer, then the clang of an iron door. The footfalls grow dimmer and again we are alone.

"You could have told me," Visa Ann murmurs. "I was old enough to understand."

"When I had a way to get a letter to you, I should have." Ten years ago, Charity would have written for me. But I was struggling then and did not wish a soul in Callaway County to know it: not John, not Sarah, and not my mother most of all. "I am sorry for that, Visa Ann." I was near a mother to this sister, with so many years separating us and my mother laden with one newborn babe after another. A wretched mother I turned out to be. "And to you, too, Asa, I am sorry."

"You don't apologize to me," Sarah says.

"You took joy in what Haycraft did to me."

"You made a whore out of your own sister," Asa tells me.

"I did not!" My voice is a shriek. "She did that on her own. But I will tell you I didn't stop her."

This time Visa Ann makes the sign of the cross.

"What else is a woman to do in this world of ours? Tell me that." I stare at Visa Ann then at Asa, silent both. "I hope and pray you teach your daughters to read. They should learn their letters and their numbers, too, same as any boy. And if you need a teacher to make them do it, I will pay for it, and joyfully, too."

"You lord it over all of us, your whore's coins," Sarah mutters, and I would tell her what I think of that but for my brother shouting over me.

"You should be on your knees thanking your sister, Sarah! You would have no defense at all without her money that you spit on. All your mouth can do is boast and suck on a liquor bottle. You have good as done this to yourself."

"Well, you'll get your wish now," Sarah sneers, "for not another sweet drop will pass my lips before I hang," and she marches to the bars that lock us together in this dungeon and shouts for a constable.

"We will send a minister to your side," Asa hollers after her when she leaves us, "for God to save your eternal soul," but Sarah will only guffaw, and I wonder as I hear her stomp away if even God will find the patience to help her.

I HAVE HAD ENOUGH of the Courthouse—oh, I have had enough of it—when a day later I hear from Noah that after three years, finally Hester Williams is to appear before a judge and say why she should be declared free of Frederick Norcom.

"Where has she been all this time?" I ask Noah, "and her children, too?" but he will not tell me.

"She will go before the judge tomorrow," is most all he will say, but for adding that I might attend the proceeding should I wish to.

He doesn't think I will, but that night I explain to Richard how Hester's case came to be. I am in my chamber dressing for the evening, though it feels a false thing to drape my body in silk and adorn my neck and ears with gemstones. "Norcom let Hester be free for years," I tell Richard, "before he tore up the freedom paper he himself wrote for her. He has been fighting over property and I believe it was to get money that he claimed Hester back, and her children, though her first-born Priscilla is his own blood."

Richard sits before the hearth sipping whiskey. "What the devil happens to that poor woman should she lose?"

"I wager Blakey and McAfee get hold of her again, to sell her. And Norcom gets his money."

"And forevermore she has a mark on her head for daring to sue her owner."

I shudder at that. "And if she is sold, who is to say her Priscilla will go with her, or her other children?" For if Hester is remade a slave, so will her children be. And they will go to whoever buys them.

The afternoon next Richard accompanies me to the Courthouse as he does not wish me to go with Noah only as company. I cannot remember another time I have found myself among so many Negroes as I am in this Courtroom. It is a strange feeling. Many glance at me with suspicious eyes; I wonder how many are Hester's fellow churchgoers, who would wish to keep the likes of me far distant. Even Noah's wife is one such; Noah will sit beside us, but she will not. Reverend Early is kind enough to greet me with a nod. I am a doxy so my testimony is of no use to his side, though I would gladly wag my tongue against Norcom if I could. "I do not see Norcom," I whisper.

"Like as not he won't come here," Noah murmurs. "Defendant never testifies, and not the petitioner, either."

"Who will speak then?" Richard wants to know.

"Independent parties who know the case," Noah says. "At

least Hester had only one owner so she knew who to sue. If you've had a whole line, you must say all their names to break the chain of title, so called."

In a moment I understand. How do you remember those names if you cannot write them down? Hearing Noah thus, with all the knowledge he has, I am reminded that he moves in a world of free Negroes whose lives I barely understand.

As I sense a ripple across the chamber, Noah adds one last thing, in low tones. "Don't you be surprised when Hester's side says she was assaulted by Mr. Norcom. That's required to be said in these cases."

Hester is the source of the ripple: I see her now. She is my age but looking older, with her cares so deep; she is garbed right and proper for this place, her expression stoic but strained with fear. The judge appears then, and both attorneys, and the high talk begins. *Hester Williams versus Frederick Norcom, case number one hundred and nineteen...* All are silent when Norcom's attorney speaks, yet when it is the turn of Hester's attorney, this Courtroom might be a church on Sunday morn. Are those around me congregants? For they call out praise and agreement as if it were the Lord Himself doing the judging.

I learn Norcom enslaved Hester in North Carolina and Mississippi before her time here. He has a few parties affirm his claim, but Hester's side can say a thing or two. There is the claim of assault Noah said we would hear. Also: what of the freedom letter, that so many saw and read? And did Norcom not write that letter in New York, where there is no slavery practice?

When it comes time for both attorneys to make their final speeches, it is Hester's who could break a heart. How sweet is the freedom Norcom snatched back from Hester, he says, and who can hold someone a slave who has lived on free soil and so has as much right to freedom as you and I?

The judge does not take long to decide: Hester Williams and her children are to be "liberated and entirely set free from said defendants and all persons whatsoever, if any, claiming under them." The last words are lost in cries of joy and relief that rise to the ceiling and beyond.

I clutch Richard's hand. This is not like the case of Dred Scott that is so much talked about. Here, here there is hope.

———————

BUT THERE IS none to be had for my sister. Mr. Goodlett comes to Poplar Street to tell me so, with new-fallen snow melting on the brown shoulders of his coat. We stand in the foyer and I take the coat though I can tell the attorney will not stop long. "The judge will not set aside the verdict?" I ask.

"There is one thing more we might try. And that is to appeal to the governor for a pardon."

"The governor?" Sterling Price? The very muck-a-muck whose bloodstained shirt I burned in my hearth three years past?

"Especially as this is a woman to be hanged, there is a chance of it." Of course he must then say something contrary. "Though the evidence against your sister makes a strong case against her."

"Would a pardon make it as if Sarah had not done this thing?"

"Exactly so."

I am astonished. What power does our governor possess! Mr. Goodlett wishes to draw up the request forthwith, and argues forcefully for it as there is not much time left, but I insist he wait to hear from me again.

———————

"HOW," I ask Richard, "can you take so much joy in snow?"

It is morning, earlier than I am usually about for the brightness of the day roused us, and we are walking through deep snow along Cedar Street, or should I say I am walking through it and Richard is ahead of me kicking it into the air.

"It is perfect white," he calls back. "I believe before our walk is done, angels will descend from heaven to dip their wings in it."

He spins to face me then twists his face into an expression of astonishment. "My God, I see one already!"

I cannot help laughing, though my heart is heavy. The only thing that could truly lift it Richard is powerless to give me.

He comes near and holds out his arm so I will be snug against his warmth. "Mr. Goodlett," he says, "may yet pry a pardon out of the governor."

I have not told Richard that Mr. Goodlett has not yet asked the governor for such a thing for I intend first to argue the case with Sterling Price myself, using a plan of attack Richard could never guess. Yet night after night passes and the governor remains absent from my parlor. "And what would Samuel Hudson's family say," I ask Richard, "to such a pardon?"

"They would not like it. But many of us do not like paying for one life with another." He squeezes me closer. "I know you were sad to say goodbye to Visa Ann and Asa."

I bid them farewell on the coach the prior forenoon. "I wager they will never again see Sarah in this life. And I wonder when I will see them again."

"When the weather is fine. When it will be a joy to journey by steamboat and so they will bring their broods here to meet their Aunt Eliza."

"It is a wonder to me, but they may do the very thing." I can pay for them to do it, and in staterooms, too. "I think Benjamin Babb does not mind having his wife's sister be rich as me." I could tell Visa Ann did not think much about it before she told me Benjamin said she should reply to my first letter. "Especially as I have no children to take my fortune when I quit this life."

"Not yet do you have children." He eyes me with an arch of the brow.

I say nothing to that. Yes, he is a physician, but Richard may not understand how strange it is that a woman who has lain with so many men has reached thirty-six years and never had a new life quicken in her belly.

He bends to whisper in my ear. "Shall I say it to you again? Happy birthday, Eliza."

"Thank you. But I am not happy to be such a great age."

"To me the remarkable thing is that you were born on the fourteenth day of February."

"Do you mean," I say, "because it is become the day of valentines?"

"The very same."

"It is a holiday the stationers made up. Sharp clever of them, though."

"Eliza, if I did not know your soft heart, I would think you a cynic. Shall I not give you your present, then? I warn you, it is from the stationers."

We stop walking, for in snow so deep one cannot walk and do anything else. Richard pulls something from the inside pocket of his overcoat. It is a card covered with lace and tinsel and drawings of cupids and hearts. And there are words, too, written in a hand that must be his.

I feel Richard's eyes upon my face. I inspect the card for some time then hold it tight against my chest. What is the miracle? That I need not read the words for tears to flood my eyes.

Richard takes my face in his hands and kisses me. "There is that soft heart again; you cannot hide it," and he kisses me more and I wonder should I tell him I cannot read what he has written to me?

I will not tell him. I do not want him to think less of me and cannot be sure that he won't. I hand the card back to him. "Please keep it safe in your overcoat."

"Safe from what?"

I wait until he does what I ask before I bend down to scoop snow into a ball and throw it at his chest. It hits only his arm, as he dodges to the side, then he proves how much better he can throw by scooping a ball that lands square on my chest.

There is much flinging of snow after that, and giggling and racing about and grunts of disapproval from passersby, and it ends with me lying on my back in the snow with Richard above me. I beg for mercy, which he refuses to give, but I would do the same if I were in the position.

He stares down at me grinning, but there is something in his eyes that is serious, too. "This is why I desire that a portrait be painted of you, Eliza, as I wrote in the card. So I may forever remember how beautiful you are in this moment."

IT IS mid March before Governor Price appears in my parlor. Few can remember a winter hard as this one and so he travels little between our state capital and here, despite the lure of Louisa. Oh, it is a mercy to see him, for my sister's remaining weeks number only four. If Price did not tower before me now, tumbler of whiskey in his hand as he orates to gentlemen and trollops, I would be the one forced to shiver a coach ride to Jefferson City, more than a hundred miles west.

On this night it is the South Price wishes to speak of, how "obscenely" it is "economically subjugated" to the North. "How much of this nation's manufacturing capacity is set in the South, I ask you?"

"I'll say a quarter," Richard calls out, and he is near howled out of the parlor until Price shouts it is even lower than that: eighteen percent.

"A Southern man," Price booms, "reads books published in the North, puts a Northern-made pen to paper pulped in the North, rides his horse atop a Northern saddle, and even clothes his body with fabric woven in Northern mills!" Mills in places like Lowell, Massachusetts, where Obadiah would send Louisiana cotton. Earning a pretty fee for his trouble.

"Why does King Cotton not render the South rich?" someone yells, and all quiet to hear our governor answer.

"Southern states that grow cotton keep only five percent to manufacture at home." A Virginia man, Price shakes his head at the lunacy of it. "Twenty-five percent goes north and seventy, *seventy* percent ships abroad." Price points his finger around the room to each man in turn and raises his voice to a shout. "Most on Northern vessels sailing from Northern ports!"

There is a commotion after that, but I can tell Price has had enough adulation from a crowd of gentlemen. He is ready to enjoy it in private from his favorite trollop. Louisa gives me only the briefest of nods as she precedes him up the stairs. She knows what I am about.

It is swiftly I must excuse myself, for I wager the governor will be an impatient client this night. I know Richard wishes me well as I climb the stairs to Louisa's bedchamber, though he cannot guess all I am about to say. My knock is quickly rewarded with an open door. Louisa slips into the corridor as I enter. Price, standing beside the bed with only his jacket removed, narrows his eyes at this switch of harlots. I see he does not like it, but I will not be insulted he would rather bed Louisa than me. My cares are greater than my vanity. "Louisa will soon return," I assure him. "There is a matter I wish to discuss with you. I beg you leave to do so."

His sigh is heavy, but he nods. In this chamber as in mine, plush chairs hunch before a hearth fire. I pour him whiskey and take one myself. He suffers to sit beside me. "I expect you know," I say, "that my sister Sarah has been convicted of murder and sentenced to be hanged."

He looks away. "I understand the jury arrived swiftly at its verdict."

"My sister was baptized the week last. Every word she speaks"—here, I will say, I exaggerate—"is full of penitence and remorse."

"And the victim lies in his grave, regretting in his last breath that he ever knew your sister."

"I hope he regrets, too, that he beat her." Price scoffs, but I go on. "Dead he is, yes, but I believe him to have been not a good man but a heartless villain."

"If all our scoundrels are to be stabbed in the chest, we shall lose half our men." He looks me full in the face. "What is it you desire from me, Madam Haycraft?"

"I desire you to pardon my sister." There: I have said it. "She is a woman of high passions, to be sure, but in love, full intoxicated, and in dread fear of her man quitting her. I beg you"—I lay my hand upon his arm—"I beg you, Governor, pardon a woman who could not control the emotions a powerful love raised in her."

"To read what in the headlines?" He struggles to keep his voice low. "That I will subvert a just verdict to appease a notorious whore with a murderess sister? What shall be written of me then?"

"That our governor understands female frailty." I wonder I do not choke on these words. Yet I have one chance only to save my sister's neck. "That our governor is wise enough to see that such a woman should not pay for her weakness at the end of a noose."

"And when next I face election?"

"In these turbulent times, voters will scarce remember such a small matter as this. But I will. And be forever grateful." I speak now with the greatest care. A bawd risks her business entire to use a gentleman's secrets against him. "Perhaps I can continue to forget what happened in the past. Perhaps Louisa can as well. So long as we have no attack of conscience, that a woman was stabbed in the neck and her killer left free to roam."

I watch the governor's eyes grow wary. I force myself to kneel before him. "I beg of you, sir. You are my sister's last hope." I kiss both his hands then rise to leave, and remember as I quit Louisa's chamber what I vowed when I departed Planters Hotel with Chouteau trailing me, his hand bloodied by my hairpin: that never again would I beg a man for anything. Who would believe I would break such a promise for my sister Sarah?

Though, as I gather myself on the stairs before I return to the raucous parlor, I must wonder if I don't do it for myself, and for the love of my father.

Is this the same bench in the calaboose on which Sarah and I sat the eve of her trial? Then, doxies behind bars watched us sit—they will again; a fresh set of them—while Sarah and I fingered the garments I had made for her. "You look in health," I tell Sarah when she is brought 'round to me.

"They feed me well enough. Can't see what the sense of it is."

"Asa and Visa Ann are safely home. I received a letter saying so written by Caleb." Visa Ann's eldest, now with ten years.

Sarah says nothing to that. She looks toward my boots as if I might be hiding something beneath my skirts. "Didn't you bring something for me? By this point I wager they'd allow a bottle."

"I do have something for you." Why does my heart pound? It is as if I run a race. No, perhaps that I have won a race. "Excellent news, Sarah. You will not be hanged. The governor of our state so decreed it. I asked him to do it and he agreed. He commuted your sentence." It is not a pardon, but it is a great mercy all the same. "Your life will be spared."

She frowns and half rises. "What? I am free to go?"

I motion her to sit again. "Not free to go, but you will not be hanged. Do you understand? You will live. You will go to prison instead. The state penitentiary, in Jefferson City." Will I visit her there? Now there is a question.

"For how long?" Her voice rises.

"It is a sentence of twenty-five years. Not your life entire. I begged the governor to show you mercy and he has done it."

"What kind of mercy is that? Twenty-five years?" She rises to her feet. Now she is screaming. "I'd rather be dead! Hang me by the neck before you lock me in a cage for twenty-five years! Constable!" Away she turns, shrieking. "Constable!"

It is a ruckus in the pen after that. One of the strumpets hollers to me. "Talk to the governor for me, too, why don't you, dolly? I'll be one to thank you for it!"

She might be, but my sister will not.

1860

The Final Year
That Changed Everything

Eliza her X Haycraft
mark

Chapter Twenty-Eight

"UNCERTAIN JUSTICE ... The history of our judicial tribunals furnish us with almost daily evidences of the uncertainty in the administrations of law and justice, and of the defeat of its ends by the interposition of wealth and power. Our readers will recollect the case of Sarah Haycraft, who killed a young man named Hudson, in St Louis, some time since, and was tried, found guilty, and sentenced to be hung... Her sister, who has immense wealth, obtained by the vilest means, spared neither pains nor expense to clear the murderess... Influenced by we do not pretend to say what, Gov. Price commuted her sentence... "

— *Alton Weekly Telegraph*

— April 17, 1856

I T IS ON A SNOW-BRIGHT AFTERNOON WHEN THE YEAR IS NEW that Noah puts to me a question it will take me some days to answer.

He begins with a different query that requires of me no thought at all. "Do you remember," he asks, "Hester Williams?"

We are standing in front of the Poplar Street house as I wait for the groom to bring 'round the gig for the day's errands. "Of course. She sued to be free of Norcom after he tried to make her again his slave." The same for his own daughter, though he did not recognize her as such. "Have you had news of Hester?" It is more than three years since she won her case and I do not know what became of her and her children since.

Noah steps nearer. "I remember you worried about her." He makes his voice low as if confiding a secret. "And now I know of others who need help as much as she did. Would you be one to provide it?"

"Me? What could I do?"

"I, and others like me, can do most of it, if you will do just one thing."

I find myself frowning. Noah has not answered in a straight way, which makes me worry he hides something. "And what is this thing I could do?"

"You could purchase a family owned by a slave master in this city. Six in all, a man of twenty-five years, four women, the oldest with some forty or fifty years, and a boy of seven."

For some moments I am too shocked to speak. Then: "Noah, you know I am not one for the slave practice."

He nods gravely. "I do not ask you to use them as slaves or keep them for long," and he tells me how their owner plans soon to sell them, sending them hither and yon to whatever slave masters buy them. "They will be separated," he says with urgency, "unless they are sold together to one person."

"And you wish that to be me." The gig clatters to a stop in front of us. The groom gives me an expectant look and indeed I do wish to board and go on about my business, for I do not care to hear more on this topic.

Noah must sense it, for he steps between the gig and me, surprising me again with this boldness so unlike him. "You remember my wife is a churchgoer. That is how she comes to know of this family. They are fine people, hard workers who do anything the master asks."

"Then why does he wish to sell them?"

Noah shrugs. "Who can know the man's mind? But their hearts will break if they are taken from one another. All their lives they have been together. Think how one is a boy of seven, another a girl of fifteen."

I know what she might suffer, if she hasn't already. I think of Hester and what Norcom must have forced from her and the babe who came after. I think also of Hester's despair, and her children's, if they had been separated. Yet: "Six in all," I murmur. "The cost would be—"

"Thousands." Noah eyes me steadily. He knows I can lay my hands on an enormous sum when I so choose. "I know your good heart," he tells me. "And with time, we will pay you back."

I can guess who he means by *we*: the same people, like Reverend Early, who helped Hester. Noah, I realize with some amazement, must be one in their number.

"So," he finishes, "it is a loan I ask for."

That is to make it seem less in my mind. Still: "What am I to do with them? I do not need their labor."

"You would think of tasks. And you don't need to keep them for long."

"Again you say that, but what do you mean?" I am irritated now. Noah is so persistent with this thing that I do not care to do! Still, despite my harsh tone, he remains unmoving before me. "If I am not to keep them, where are they to go?"

He hesitates. Then: "Leave that to me."

I see it clear before me. "You wish for them to be free." I wait for him to deny it and what do I hear? Not a word. And oh, I have heard whispers of what Noah's people might do to help their own: talk of a railroad, but one without rails or joints. "That is not something I will mix in, Noah. There is too much risk in it. And not just for me, but for you, too. It is very, very dangerous for you."

In the year just ended, the highest court in the land said yes again to the fugitive slave law, so called. Anyone caught helping a slave to become free, whether Noah's color or mine, might have to pay the steepest price. There was heated talk of it in my parlors, and as always our Missouri men split on the question.

"It is for me to decide what I do," Noah tells me, and of course it is so. "I know your good heart," he repeats. "From the first day I knew you, you were handing out coins. And it never mattered the color of the hand held out."

"That is a different matter," I hiss. "There is no risk in that. This would show me to be on one side and not the other." I look past Noah to the groom, but his attention is lost to a pretty young thing batting her lashes in his direction.

"No one need know how you came by this family," Noah says, "or what happens to them after they leave."

"You speak as if it is possible to keep secrets in a cathouse," but soon as the words leave my lips, Noah gives me a knowing look. Too well he remembers the governor arriving bloody at our back door. Who else in this metropolis knows about that? Yes, it is a secret that together Noah and I keep these long years.

I push past Noah—"I will think on it," I tell him, "but I promise nothing"—and I clap my hands at the groom to catch his attention. But there is nothing for it. He is staring after the girl wearing such a silly grin that I am only annoyed further.

THE MORNING next I wonder why I bring up the topic with Richard because even before I do, I know what he will say.

We sit alone at the trestle table in the yellow kitchen drinking coffee. It is just dawn and far too early for my bawds to be afoot—I am still in my peignoir—but already a loaf of new bread is out of the oven. I am content to slather a warm slice with butter and enjoy it while staring at the newspaper Richard holds up between us. Such a thing is not his habit.

Indeed soon he lowers the paper. "I'm sorry, Eliza. That is rude of me." He smiles his slow smile and there is apology in it. "I was reading about the railroad system in this country. Can you believe we have thirty thousand miles of track?"

Just what I desire not to hear about: railroads. As if I need a reminder of the matter ever on my mind in the last day.

"Only a quarter of it in the South," he goes on when I say nothing.

"It is the sort of thing our governor was telling us last year." I remember Price orating in the parlor, the night I asked him to spare my sister.

"Yes. How in so many regards, only a minor fraction of the nation's economic might can be found south of the Mason-Dixon line."

North versus South: that topic we can never escape. "Noah wishes me to buy a slave family," I hear myself say, and the story spills from my lips. Richard listens, rapt. "I would be buying slaves," I finish, "only to free them."

"From the sound of it, Noah and his people would be the ones to free them. Or try to, at substantial risk to themselves." Richard's tone is mild. "Perhaps you do not think it a worthy cause?"

"Worthy it may well be, but still, think of the trouble it could bring me." I know that argument will not go far with Richard, so I try another. "And Noah says I must do it quickly so the family does not go to auction and be separated. But how often must that happen? Am *I* to take it upon myself to stop it?"

"Only this time. And then in due course these six would be free. Think what an excellent thing you would be helping to do, Eliza."

"Already I do enough good," I tell him. "Think of the coins I hand out, and money to this institution and that one."

"Yes, you do a great deal of good already." He sips his coffee and eyes me over the cup's rim. "And you certainly might have trouble if you do too much."

"Do not mock me, Richard." I lean closer as someone scuttles along the corridor behind me. "You know I am not one to try to change the world."

"Noah is not asking you to do that. He is asking you to help him change six lives. And that is a great thing all in itself."

"And so I must bid for them at a public auction? Make a spectacle doing so?" There are words I do not say. *Show Eliza Haycraft is one who will buy slaves? And later make people wonder where they disappeared to?*

Richard furrows his brow. "Noah knows who the owner is. You could go to him and make an offer. In private."

"He will wonder how I came to know he wishes to sell these six."

"Tell him you hear many things in your parlors and it so happens you need a goodly number of fresh hands to work at your houses. If your offer is generous enough"—Richard shrugs—"he will not ask many questions."

I fall back in my chair. It is so simple to Richard. He is not one to worry if everyone sees he is for one side and not the other.

———

A FEW DAYS LATER, it is one of those times when I wish a man's words would leave my mind. Yet I remember too well what Richard said to me, and Noah. Nor can I forget that Noah is not one to ask for anything. And this one time he does ask for something, I must wonder if it is because his wife asks for something.

In the end I am always one to think for myself, and so it is on my own power that I go to stand before the slave master who wishes to sell and bargain to buy from him Rebecca, Patty, Betsey, Mitilde, Lewis, and Grafton. It is as Richard said it would be: I make a generous offer, proffer the cash, and the man's questions are few.

I leave it to Noah and the groom to collect the six and bring them and their meager belongings to Poplar Street. My doxies, I can tell from their glances and whispers, cannot divine why this group should appear in my parlor of a snowy afternoon, but I had taken care to contrive a tale. The hour prior I whispered it to the cook, knowing it would leap from her lips to every ear in the house. *A client of this house for many years gambled too hard and was forced to sell his property and all the servants with it. Madam Haycraft did him a good turn by making work for these, and taking in their child, too.*

"That is what I wish you to tell any who ask," I say to Rebecca, the matriarch, thin as a belt but with a look of iron about her, and though Noah says she is but five years older than me, I would have guessed her to be fifteen more.

She will only narrow her eyes at me, so I speak again. "And I will pay for your labors," and to prove it I give to each in turn a small bag with coins. Yet I wager this will prove nothing to them and who could be surprised? How could they trust I am not the same as the man who owned them this morning, even if Noah told them so?

I smile at the boy, the only one to poke his nose inside the bag. "I hear your name is Grafton?" I say to him and he raises surprised eyes to my face as if he cannot believe I would address him.

Before he can form a word, his young father, a wiry man I know to be called Lewis, speaks in his place. "He is my son with my wife Betsey." Unlike Rebecca, Lewis will meet my gaze, and steadily.

"Well, Lewis"—and I look at Betsey, too—"I do not expect your boy to do any more than the simplest chores, chores right for his age." I turn to Noah. "Have you explained that they will be not at this house but instead on Fourth Street?" It is quieter there, with fewer workers, and away from my sight.

"I will take them there right now," Noah says, and since I know that the woman who runs that house is prepared for them, I nod, mouth a quick goodbye, and quit the parlor. For I do not wish to dwell on this thing I am helping to do, or the trouble it could bring me. And the more I think on it, the more I tremble at the trouble it could bring Noah.

It takes some while, but the next I hear of the matter is when Noah repays to me, in full, what I paid the slave master. And then one day he tells me that the six are gone. I ask no questions and vow to think on it no more.

I will find, of course, that it is not so easy.

"I AM desperate to walk about outside and see it for myself," I whisper to Richard.

Whyever not? Outside my parlor is music and revelry while inside are far fewer than the usual gentlemen. I would worry but for one reason: the election about which there has been such a brouhaha occurs on the morrow—at long last it will be settled!—and so tonight people parade the streets calling out praise for this candidate or that one. I do not doubt this parlor will bustle later, but for now the raucousness is more outside than in. I wish to be part of it.

Richard leans close. "I am delighted to go with you on the condition we search for Lincoln's parade."

"That is fine, but we must search for Douglas's, too, and also for those for Breckinridge and Bell, for if I am seen at one I must be seen at all." Then who can say where my allegiance lies? Better for business if no one knows for sure.

It is much to keep in the head, the views of these candidates for president. Lincoln heads the Republicans and so wishes not to extend slavery into the new territories. Douglas is the Little Giant, so called, who pushed through the Kansas Nebraska Act that has caused blood to spill for seven long years. He says he heads all the Democrats, but really he heads only those from the North because those from the South have picked their own man, called Breckinridge, who now sits as our vice president. Last is Bell, who wishes to pretend slavery is no issue at all.

Richard sets down his whiskey. "The Rail Splitter first," and I well know that is Lincoln's nickname, to make people forget he is a lawyer and think of him first as a humble workingman.

I leave Louisa to preside over the house: Charity must abide that from time to time or I will have rebellion in my ranks. Once outside we have not walked far when I see a parade of men before me, bearing torches high aloft. They have more than one boisterous band to accompany and banners with words writ large upon them. Richard grabs my hand and steps faster, dragging me along. "Lincoln's men!"

What a crush of bodies we must push through! All are out—men, women, children, too—almost as if this were again the Great Fire. This night, too, I feel I witness something monumental.

The torches wind through the streets like a massive snake afire. The din of the bands and shouting of the crowd echo off the brick walls of our city and make my ears ache. "They head to Center Market," Richard tells me, and so there we go, to find a bonfire that lights all from Market House to Eighth Street. Stands draped with patriotic colors are erected for speakers—"One for German orators and one for American," Richard says—and how can I be surprised? The Germans are out in their numbers and they are all for Lincoln; the slavery practice is the last thing they will cotton to.

I could not say who the speakers are, but all orate in words fiery as the torchlight. *Fellow citizens, we may as well, this night, if we have not already done so, open our eyes to the dreadful fact that the Union of these States is in imminent peril, from the deadly struggle between Northern and Southern sectionalism, which has already almost rent the nation asunder...* After a time of listening to such phrases—

my nerves rattling at what they mean—I tell Richard I will go find Douglas's people. He will go with me and soon we discover that oh, they have a mighty crowd, too, at Lucas Market.

These men also have much to shout about, how each state has *the right to mold their own domestic institutions* and how the North, when it comes to slavery, has become *aggressive, overbearing and defiant*. We walk to see the Breckinridge and Bell parades, too, though by now my head pounds. Do I see faces I know in every crowd? Yes, and some see me, as I wished them to.

Finally I tell Richard I would go back, for I long to remove my corset and sip warm milk with nutmeg. Is this how it feels to be a woman of forty years? I have had enough of *the greatest contest since the formation of the Union*, especially as we women have not a thing to say about it. We turn toward Poplar Street, arms linked. "Should we wager, then, on who will win?" I ask Richard. "Already I know you will go for Lincoln."

"He is helped by the splintering of the Democrats into two camps, yes. But can he win one hundred fifty-two electoral votes? I am not sure of it."

"He will win this city."

Richard smiles. "You speak with confidence, Eliza."

"Well, half the people in this metropolis are foreign-born and they do not like the slavery practice. And most of those men who have come here from other states came from free states."

There is a matter, though, that I will not give voice. What of those Southern states that threaten to secede if Lincoln becomes president? Are we to believe it is talk only and in the end they won't do it?

WILL there come a night when I sit beside a governor in my bedchamber and need not pinch myself to remember I am the same Eliza Haycraft raised in a cabin with mud packed between the logs to keep out the cold?

Perhaps I should pinch myself on this frigid November midnight as I sip whiskey and chat with Governor Robert Marcellus Stewart. Despite what most who visit this house assume, this is all I ever do with this Mr. Stewart who served in the Missouri Senate, the very same who waited in this chamber while secretly I ran about in the dark aiding the blood-soaked man who was governor before him. "Are you surprised at Mr. Lincoln's election?" I ask this governor. He is a striking man, ever a bachelor, with fine garments and light-colored hair combed back from a high forehead. Some call him eccentric. There is a story that once he rode his horse up the stairs into the governor's mansion.

"Well, our state most assuredly did not go for Lincoln," he says.

No, Lincoln came in last in our state. So many in the countryside are all for the South. "Those from the South hate Lincoln so," I say. I have heard Southern men mutter that he is secretly a mulatto, or a cannibal, or hides a tail and horns. Perhaps all three?

"I worry for Lincoln's safety." The governor leans close. "Some even whisper that President Buchanan might be kidnapped so as to install his vice president in the White House and keep Lincoln out that way."

"Vice President Breckinridge!" The South's own man, who won most of the states there. "What think you of the man who will follow you as governor?"

Stewart narrows his gaze as he stares into the hearth fire. "Claiborne Fox Jackson. Do you know what he did when the territory of Kansas was voting for its legislature? He and his fellow slave owners led ruffians from our state over the border to stuff ballot boxes for the pro-slavery side." His eyes slide to mine. "At gunpoint. Yet Jackson stood for governor declaring he does not wish Missouri to secede from the Union."

"So it is impossible to believe him." Could Missouri secede? What then?

"I will tell you this. I wish for our state to remain neutral, but she must stand in readiness to protect herself from plunder, come from what quarter it may."

He departs some time later. Of course I collect the usual fee, though what did Governor Stewart receive for his payment? The same as ever: amiable conversation and a kiss chaste as one sister might give another. I do not know what this governor longs for, but for some years now I have believed that I cannot give it.

CHARITY WISHES to make cookies of gingerbread for the Christmas holiday and of course I will help though I have warned her I am in no mood to do more to celebrate the season.

"You do not care to purchase a tree to decorate?" she asks me. Across the kitchen trestle table she stands, flour plentiful on her cheeks.

I thwack my rolling pin at the dough, particular stubborn this morning. "I will not stop you should you desire it."

She is silent, her head cocked, then: "I wish I understood what it means, the secession convention they will hold in Charleston." It seems we cannot go long before returning to this topic. "Yes, I understand what it *means*, but how does South Carolina propose to do it?"

"Well, they wish more states to join them." I pound at my dough. It will not lie flat and submit, much as South Carolina threatens not to submit to Lincoln as president.

"If there is war," Charity says, "I believe the Union shall win in no time and then the South will be proved idiotic."

"Charity." I lean closer to her. "I wish you not to speak your opinion so freely. I have told you so before."

"There is no one but you in this kitchen to hear me. And I know *you* believe same as I do."

"We must hold our tongues." I am hissing now. "What if Missouri goes the way of South Carolina? We are a slave state, after all. It could be dangerous for us, and this house, if people know we are on one side and Missouri goes for the other."

Charity gives me a steady gaze. "People already know which side *you* are on. For everyone knows Richard is a Lincoln man."

"Do I not have a head on my shoulders to think for myself? The point is that both sides must be happy in this house. And Richard knows that."

"I wonder how long that will make *him* happy," and with a superior arch of her brow she bends again to her baking. She is same as ever, Charity, since she quit Martin Terris, now four years ago: lovesick from time to time, strong in her views, and ever cheerful. When Terris married, I was relieved to see she despaired for only a short while. I wonder: will her William ever come? I love her enough that I hope he does, even if he takes her to California.

It is just before the night's rush when Richard appears at the house with a friend I am at first delighted to see, before I am shaken to my boots by what both he and Richard have to say.

"Bernard." I smile and take his hands. I believe Bernard Gaines Farrar, Jr.—dark of hair with piercing eyes—to be wise as his doctor father, and Richard agrees with me even though the younger labors in business and not medicine. "I will offer you tea and gingerbread," I begin to say, but both chuckle at that and head for the decanter of whiskey. Why do I pull the pocket doors shut when we reach the parlor? Something tells me I will hear words best kept in confidence.

Richard keeps his voice low. "Bernard will begin organizing the men in this city who share our views." My face must show my shock, for: "It is not too soon," he adds, and since all know what South Carolina is about, I suppose it must not be.

I look to Bernard. "How do you mean to organize such men?"

"We must take every man's measure so we know on whom we can count. Those we trust, we will arm. Those we arm, we will begin to drill so they will understand how to work in efficient units."

Drilling in our city, as if St. Louis were an armed camp. "If you do such a thing," I say to Bernard, "you make clear on which side you stand."

"Soon," Richard says, "making clear a side will be required of us all."

I believe it is me he thinks of when he says that, but I look to Bernard still. "Should not Missouri try to remain neutral? That is what Governor Stewart says."

"I do not believe that will be possible," he tells me, and Richard nods in agreement, and we all know that in mere weeks Governor Stewart will be able only to suggest what Missouri do.

I will express another idea, though I know it sounds desperate. "Even if Southern states do secede, would it be so bad simply to let them go?"

Richard and Bernard exchange a look. I am sure they think that women, we soft women, will too soon abandon our views if that means we keep from spilling our sons' and husbands' and brothers' blood.

"The Union must be preserved," Bernard says simply, the same sentiment I have heard shouted from speakers' platforms, and there it is, the single idea from which men like him and Richard and Lincoln will not stray.

Bernard does not linger long and after he is gone I pull Richard upstairs to my bedchamber. Barely a moment passes before I push out wishful words. "You will leave this drilling, I am sure, to younger men."

He will snort at that. "You believe that with forty-two years I am good only for the rocking chair?" He cocks his brows in a comical way. "Though perhaps my memory does begin to fail me, for did I not bed you, and in a most rollicking manner, just the night last?"

"I hope you will do the same tonight." I do not say: *And every night for a thousand years*. "But remember that Bernard is full ten years younger than we are."

"And already twice a father, so with responsibilities greater than mine."

"I hope you do not allow your long friendship with him, or your admiration for his father, to pull you further into this. Remember, you are a physician, meant to heal men, not pump them full of rifle balls."

"Eliza." He takes my hands. "Did George Washington tell his men he had more than forty years and so would leave the revolution to them?"

"You are not a military man, or a general."

"No, thank God. But I have a conscience all the same and when matters are so urgent I must do what I can." He pulls me toward the chairs before the hearth. "Do you realize Washington died only nineteen years before I was born? Alexander Hamilton, only fourteen. Thomas Jefferson died when I was a boy of eight."

I do not see the point so remain silent.

"When I was that boy," he goes on, "I thought the revolution that founded our nation happened impossibly long ago. I came to realize it was not long at all. Some of those men trod this earth the very years that I did. Never did I imagine that I would be called upon to defend the Union they made, but now I am and so I must."

I argue all I can but must abandon my case with one final line. "It is because that damn Lincoln is an Illinois man."

"You must stand further back from the looking glass," Charity tells me, "to see the whole of the gown."

We are in her bedchamber and I am trying to admire the gown the dressmaker just sent. It is of burgundy velvet and perfectly suits the season. Yet in these trying days nothing makes me full happy, not even the beauty of this garment.

"How many at tonight's dinner?" Charity asks.

"Only ten," and that is because Governor Stewart will be our honored guest and he is that rare politician who prefers to dine among fewer. Every December a madam such as myself will host holiday dinners to indulge her most important muck-a-mucks. I will maintain the tradition though my heart is not in it. And since I must find a moment to take our governor aside, truly I will not be at my ease.

I feel Charity's eyes on me from across the chamber. "Try not to worry about your father," she murmurs. "I am sure the next letter will say he is improved."

He is in poor health, the last letter said, and Visa Ann believes it is because of Sarah. The penitentiary wardens report her unwell; she lacks spirit; she might go for days without eating. I remember what she hollered at the calaboose. *I'd rather be dead! Hang me by the neck before you lock me in a cage for twenty-five years!* Five of those years have passed. Have I seen her even once? Yet of late thoughts of her fill my mind. "Can you believe Visa Ann has borne nine babes?"

"She could bear still more," Charity says.

"All my sisters could, and Asa's wife Sarah, too." Asa is the father of three girls now, and Lucinda and even Minerva have a boy and girl each. That makes sixteen nieces and nephews for Aunt Eliza. It is good I know my numbers.

I have paid for my relations to come to St. Louis on the steamboat, above decks, and for boardinghouse rooms, but save for Visa Ann and Asa, and even them sometimes, I feel they look at me like a freak at a fair.

And one is steadfast in refusing to come. My father.

THAT EVENING, when the sumptuous dinner is through, Governor Stewart rises from the dining table, sends me a look I recognize, and makes a small bow. "May we all partake of the season's joys best we can," he says, and to raised glasses and wishes of good will, ushers me toward the staircase.

If he were a different man, I would soon be on my back. With this one, I can pour us tumblers of whiskey and ease into my chair before the hearth. "I daresay you will miss your post, Governor."

He touches his glass to mine. "Tonight, Eliza, you may call me Robert."

Is it ease I feel? It might be. We chat of this and that before I push myself to ask if he recalls the case of my sister Sarah.

He eyes me. In the hearth fire I hear one log tumble into another, shooting sparks toward heaven. "This is your sister who is in our state penitentiary?"

"Governor Price was so kind as to commute her sentence. Still, she does poorly."

"I expect few thrive."

"She has been there five years. Robert, I will ask you for this favor plainly," and from the very chair where I begged the same of Governor Price, I ask that he pardon my sister. "It is for her that I ask you, yes, for she is in ill health. But it is also for my father." For a moment I cannot speak. "He declines and my family tells me it is because he so worries about her, his eldest child."

"I daresay he worries about his other daughter, too."

"If he does, he does not show it." I hesitate, then: "He will not see me."

The governor sighs. "It is near thirteen years since my father died, in New York where I was born. I know what it is to feel a distance from one's father."

I wonder if he speaks of miles or of something else. Might his father, like mine, find something to disapprove in his child?

"Eliza," he murmurs, "you have always made me comfortable in this house. Never have you asked questions of me, where others might well have done."

"It is not mine to ask questions. It is mine to make the friends of this house happy as I can make them."

Stewart gives me a sad smile. "Happiness is elusive for some of us." He leans forward to pat my knee. "I will do it, Eliza. I will pardon your sister."

My heart thumping, I leave my chair to kneel at his knees. "Robert, there are not words enough to thank you. For years I did not even think of raising this matter with you."

"Why now?"

"Because it is my sister's last chance. And perhaps my father's, too." I kiss both his hands. "I will be bold, for I have one request more to make of you."

———

"Why, Daniel," I say. We sit in the parlor of a chill afternoon, December near done, and I hold up what he has brought me by way of a Christmas present: satin gloves in forest green with tiny flowers embroidered in ivory silk. "I adore them. But you should be buying more gifts for Alice and your boy. Not me."

"I enjoy it. And remember you are still a client of my firm."

That is so. For Daniel, despite his marriage, has been stalwart at my side at the deeds office: three times in '57 alone.

"I cannot believe," he goes on, "that Governor Stewart pardoned your sister."

Soon as I could, I sent a telegram to Visa Ann. I am sure when *that* was put in her hand she was sure I was dead, and perhaps her husband rejoiced, but I believed the news too momentous to reach her in a simple letter. And the sooner she would know, the sooner my father would, too.

"It is extraordinary"—Daniel eyes me with keenness—"that the pardon requires Sarah to quit the state of Missouri now and forever."

"Yes." I sip my wine. "The governor insisted on that condition."

And that is all I have to say on the matter.

Chapter Twenty-Nine

"WHAT EUROPE THINKS OF US: In truth, the people of Europe are lost in surprise at the very idea of a disunion party receiving any support from even a fraction of the great intelligent American Democracy...

"The prodigy of a nation like this, of late so great, so prosperous, and seemingly so perfectly organized, suddenly to their apprehensions endangered and threatened with dissolution, is to them portentous and almost incredible...

"So far as their voice may make itself heard, they call upon us to repudiate Secession and preserve the Union, as the sole means of perpetuating our own prosperity, and saving our national character from the scorn and pity of mankind."

— *Missouri Democrat*

— February 22, 1861

"LOOK AT THE MEN CROWDING TO GET INSIDE THAT TURNER HALL!" I cry as Richard and I ride past in his gig. I spin about to look back at the redbrick structure before which dozens of Germans throng. With snow melting under a January sun, one might think our city hadn't a care in the world, but I know better. "Why is it so busy on a Friday forenoon?"

"All the Turner Halls are busy." He lowers his voice. "Men are organizing as Home Guards. And drilling."

There must be a dozen such Turnvereins, so called, in our metropolis, where Germans banquet and debate and even exercise. "I'm glad," I say, "that Governor Jackson isn't here to see this." As of the week last he sits in Jefferson City as head of our state and feels free to fly his true colors. For what did he say at his inauguration? That South Carolina is to be praised for seceding and Missouri will "stand by the South." Then he called for a state convention to consider secession. By all this, he makes plain what he desires.

It frightens me that many in the South are shocking bold. Already Mississippi and Florida followed South Carolina into secession. In Alabama, Florida, and Louisiana, Southerners seized Federal arsenals, and in Alabama and South Carolina forts and bases. What else will happen by the time Lincoln rises to the White House? That will not come until the fourth of March.

"You have seen what transpires at Berthold Mansion?" Richard asks me.

I well know that place. Bartholomew Berthold is a fur trader who married a Chouteau—but of course—and then built a magnificent pillared mansion with deep porches on both its floors. That corner of Fifth and Pine streets is not on our route, but now I wish to ride past all the same.

"This is where the Minutemen drill," Richard murmurs when we arrive there, and he slows the horse.

"The side for the South."

"Can you believe they have the audacity to name themselves after those who fought in our great American revolution? They think our Union is now the tyrant."

I say nothing to that, as I am busy trying to pick out faces I recognize among the men who strut about. I know many are Creole, like Chouteau. "Already they are armed." Flashing in the sun are their pistols and revolvers.

Richard slaps the reins. "Well, we are, too, if you consider our wooden weapons." My face must show my shock, for Richard laughs. "For practice only. Come, while we are at it let us look at something to buoy our spirits."

After a time I see ahead of us men marching and realize these are for the Union side. "These must be the troops from Kansas," I say, "newly arrived."

Richard chuckles. He is one to enjoy when I tell him things I know and must wonder where I learned them. "Yes, these are troops the War Department sent to guard the Arsenal."

"I hope they will have more than weapons of wood to do it." I am cheered as Richard and I ride about the city, but it is not a gladness that lasts long. To go back to Poplar Street we ride past Berthold Mansion again and this time men are cheering and discharging their weapons into the sky. A crowd has gathered to join the gaiety.

Soon we learn why. Alabama, too, has seceded.

ON THE SUNDAY two weeks later when Louisiana secedes, the sixth state to do such a thing, I take my walk alone. I think well when I walk. I set out and soon make the right turn onto Fourth Street.

What do I know for sure? Only that it is past time to pretend our nation will not have a war. All I wonder is on which side Missouri will fight. Well, another thing I wonder, too: what should I do to prepare. This is a time to be planful.

Richard has his drilling, pulled into it by Bernard, though he needed no encouragement. Daniel drills, too. He is not so ardent, I know, but tells me he wishes to do his part. Those who work for me are full occupied, as we are busy as ever. Should I be ashamed that I prosper even as war approaches? Then I ask myself: would a *man* of business feel ashamed? He would scheme to profit even more.

There is one thing I believe strongly. Now is not the time to buy properties but to hoard money. I must be content with the ten properties I own.

I walk and I think and my mind keeps going to the same thing. What can I do but what I have ever done: keep my views to myself and run my business? Of course my bawds are a worry. Time and again I tell them they must not show they have taken a side. Most understand, but what will they do when we are in the thick of it?

And what view do I take? Oh, I am for the Union side, not thinking with Richard but with the head on my own shoulders. I do not have much of an opinion about the rights of the states, but long have I been against the slavery practice. Perhaps it would be different if I never left Cote San Dessein, where slavery seemed not to be wondered at. Then I never would have met Chantal. How knowing her has changed me! How could I hear her wisdom and feel her warm heart and think it right and proper she be a slave? And Noah, too, I have learned from, and Reverend Early, and Hester Williams, and many others.

I am a woman of business, too, and believe our city's strength comes from its ties to the North. That is how we prosper and where our future lies.

I cannot imagine what will happen when the two sides rise in battle. Oh, God does not listen to the likes of me, but still I pray for Richard. I fear he will thrust into the fray with all the vigor he possesses.

Still, in the face of all this, I am not such a coward that I will shut my houses and flee. Where to go if I did? If our state does rebel against the Union, surely we will see fighting on our own ground. Well, I will board up. I know how to shoot my pistol and the dagger on my chatelaine is good for something. I am not brave, but always I have told myself I can do what I must when the time comes.

I have asked Charity if she wishes to return to Massachusetts. That is so far north it will be safe from fighting. But she would only hug me and ask who does she know in Massachusetts after these long years?

Is Obadiah in Massachusetts or Louisiana as the bugles of war sound? Oh, and Chantal... If she lives, she must fear so for herself and Honorine. What will become of free Negroes now, or of the slaves who cannot choose for themselves?

There are so many questions with no answer.

One looms large in my mind. Where is my sister Sarah? Of course my family does not blame me that she was forced to quit Missouri in return for her pardon. This I add to the secrets I keep. Still, there are better places than Missouri now, and in my last letter to Visa Ann I told Charity to write exactly that. After all, some in our state flee for the Colorado territory or Oregon or California, far from the battle lines. Does not Sarah have a touch of the adventurer? She did come to St. Louis. I hope this idea reaches my father's ears and offers him comfort.

I WATCH Richard's face twist into a frown as he stands in the foyer of the Poplar Street house while I descend the stairs to join him. "Do you have a dead husband lying about somewhere? For it looks as if you wear widow's weeds."

"This garment is not black but midnight blue, so called, and it suits the dullness of the winter day."

He does not stop frowning. "That may explain the garment but not the veil."

There is no fooling Richard. "If we are to watch this Nathaniel Lyon parade into town at the head of fresh Union troops, I do not care to be easily recognized."

"Ah, I see. You might be taken for a patriot. Well, you could jeer half the time so as to confuse all onlookers."

I have reached the foyer so walk close to him and look up into his eyes. I do not see anger there, or disappointment, but both might be coming. "It does me no good to throw for one side or the other."

"So you will continue to pretend you're neutral?"

"I will continue it today. I cannot say what I will do tomorrow." He looks as if he might interrupt so I go on. "It is wise to watch and wait. I am hardly the only one to do so."

He bends close to whisper in my ear. "I'll alert you if you turn yellow from cowardice."

Richard does not often anger me, but he begins to now. "It does not make me a coward to protect my houses and those who work inside them. I do not wish them destroyed should one side or the other decide to hate me."

He sighs then takes my hand and kisses it. "Why fight about a few weeks or a month? It won't be long before we must all show where we stand."

The lines are drawn more clearly every day. Now there is a Confederate States of America. It has a constitution and a capital city and a man who will soon be its president: Jefferson Davis. I believe it no accident that his inauguration is set for two weeks before Lincoln's.

Richard holds out his arm but cannot resist one last jab. "Perhaps I should walk ten paces in front of you or ten behind so none see us together?"

I take his arm and step forward. "So what is there to know about this Nathaniel Lyon?"

As we walk through the city's bustle, I learn that Lyon is Richard's age, Connecticut born, and never wed. He is ever a military man and many count in his favor that he slew Indians in great numbers; his temper is said to run hot.

I am not in that camp and neither is Richard, but still: "He wrote many fervent essays for Lincoln," Richard tells me, "and is said to be a member of the Wide Awakes, so called because of their vigilant defense of the Union."

I know them already. "Those young men who accompany Lincoln about, yes. They carry torches high aloft and wear capes to catch the oil that might drop."

"The very same. I am also told Lyon does not always respect the chain of command but does on his own what he judges best."

"And now he must protect the Arsenal." Yet another federal arsenal has fallen, in Georgia. But none under threat is so mighty as our Arsenal here, with more weapons and ammunition than any other west of the Mississippi. So often I have heard it discussed in my parlor: thirty thousand muskets, fifty tons of gunpowder, field pieces, siege guns, cannon ammunition, and machines to make more of all of it. "That Lyon is put there shows how much the Union trusts him," I say, and now I hear the pounding of booted feet to the tempo of a drum.

"They shall march to the Arsenal," Richard murmurs, and I know that is three miles south of our city, on a plateau above the river. "Come"—he tugs my hand—"let us try to get in front of them," and we quicken our step.

We are not alone in coming out to witness this spectacle. In time we push our way through the throng to a position in front of the marching troops and I lift my veil to see Lyon clearly.

I do not know that I would pick him for a great military leader. Yes, his eyes are blue and piercing and there is great purpose to his stride, but he is not so tall, his hair is unruly, his whiskers are reddish and wispy, and his face is fierce weathered. "He makes a parade on his arrival in our city," I whisper to Richard, "yet he is unkempt." His long-skirted Army coat is faded and its brass buttons dangle loosely; his trousers are wrinkled; and his cavalry boots are scuffed and scarred.

"So long as he keeps the Arsenal for our side," Richard says, "I do not care that he looks a ruffian," and I cannot disagree.

It is fortunate I got a good look at Lyon that morning so as to recognize him when he appeared on the stoop of my Poplar Street house that night. Given his motley appearance—unchanged from the forenoon—Noah denied him entry yet was wise enough to summon me for a second judgment. Now I can greet Lyon pleasantly and with his title, too. "Captain Lyon. Good evening."

He frowns at me, two of his men on the stairs below. I see the silver flash of revolvers on all of them but am become steeled to that sight. "Madam Haycraft, I take it," Lyon says. "Your Negro man barred my way in."

"That is because you are a stranger to this house." I step back and wave a welcoming arm. "Though I am delighted to make you our friend." It befits the status of my house to have this prominent military man plead for entry, yet all the same I wonder that on Lyon's very first night supposedly guarding the Arsenal, here he is a'whoring. I will be interested to see which of my doxies he wishes to bed. I suppose he is of such a rank that if he requests me, I must accede? How will Richard feel about his Yankee hero then?

But: "I'm looking for someone I'm told is here," Lyon says. "No need to come inside if I won't find him. Bernard Gaines Farrar."

I hesitate, for it's not typical to assure one man he will find another within the confines of my cathouse.

"Is Farrar here or not?" Lyon demands.

"He is in my parlor," I allow, and Lyon pushes past me with his men behind. In the parlor several gentlemen scramble to their feet at the sight of the captain, though not all, and I suspect Lyon's keen eye is taking note of who does what. Richard and I exchange a glance and I know he could not be more pleased at this turn.

Introductions are quickly made and I can tell Bernard is gratified that Lyon grasps his hand with vigor.

"Heard about you," Lyon says, and would say more if another man did not push forward. Lyon will take a stein of beer and a cigar lit by Louisa, and the way his eyes widen when he sees her makes me think he's made his choice of strumpet if it comes to that.

"How soon do you expect us to knock back the rebels, Captain?" one man calls out.

"More like the other way around," another shouts. "Yanks don't have the stomach for battle."

"A lady's thimble will hold all the blood that'll be shed!" hollers still another.

This goes on while Lyon downs his beer and puffs fiercely on his cigar, pushing out smoke as if he were a steam locomotive. Then: "Not sure I think like the rest of you. This war is like to be tough and long. I certainly expect to expose and very likely lose my life. We shall rejoice, though, in martyrdom, if need be. Farrar, follow me," and off Lyon strides the way he came, Bernard wide-eyed at his heels.

There is no end to the back-and-forth after that, of the strengths and weaknesses of each side. Yes, near all the nation's firearms are made in the north, but it's the militias in the secesh states that are now strongest, as the federal army is scattered through the West and the few serviceable navy ships sail in foreign waters. All can agree on one thing, though: the importance of not just our Arsenal but of St. Louis and the whole of Missouri.

"Here where the Mississippi and Missouri rivers meet," one man intones, "Missouri could be a dagger pointed at the Union heartland."

"Or," Richard cries above the huzzahs that follow, "the base from whence the Union could thrust south into the heart of the Confederacy!"

"We must also take into account our machine shops and foundries," Richard tells me later as I lie in bed beside him.

"Those are of paramount importance. As are the richness of our agricultural land and deposits of iron and lead."

" 'Our,' you say. So now you are a Missouri and not an Illinois man?"

"I have sufficient loyalty to split between the two," and after these ten years I know Richard Bonner to be a loyal man indeed.

"Why did Lyon come to this house looking for Bernard?" I ask.

"He heard about the organizing and wanted to meet him sooner than later."

"I must wonder," I murmur, "what kind of leader Lyon is to say he's very like to lose his life. Who wishes to follow such a one?"

"He does not seem a leader to paint a pretty picture," Richard says mildly.

I would say not. *Rejoice in martyrdom*, indeed. I shivered to hear those words and will help my housemaids clean the parlor with great thoroughness tomorrow to expel the stink of them.

ON TUESDAY, the fourth of March, Charity comes running to find me at my usual morning place in the dining room, counting coins into cloth bags as madams of bawdy houses must every day do. "I have been out walking," she pants. "There is something afoot at Berthold Mansion. A jubilant crowd gathers there. And this is the very day of Lincoln's inauguration."

I will not give voice to my fear. Did Lincoln lay his right hand upon a Bible only to take a pistol ball? We have all heard rumors the government would put sharpshooters about to prevent exactly that. "I will finish this and walk there with you," I tell her, and now I am rattled it will take me twice as long to count correctly.

I began to breathe easier two weeks before when the Electoral College voting in the Senate went as it ought. The Southern states did participate and electors did not change their views. It was a surprise to many when Vice President Breckinridge watched over the counting and made it go right, even though he is the very man the Southern Democrats put up for president against Lincoln. Some feared he might declare he'd lost the electoral certificates and so a new plan would have to be made, maybe one that made *him* president. But in the end he did his duty.

Charity and I are near out the door when Louisa comes along behind us, radiant in an apricot-colored gown. Alongside her in our workaday gray and beige, Charity and I look like rotting fruit next to fresh. "I will walk with you," she says.

I watch Louisa and wonder, as I have before, where her heart lies. It shows her canniness that I, who live beside her, cannot be sure. It is years she remains the favorite of Sterling Price and I believe they are as thick as two thieves. I will say that though Price is a Virginia man, he speaks loudly for the Union side. He does not cotton to Lincoln, though: in the election he put his vote behind Stephen Douglas of the Northern Democrats.

"Let us be quick about it," I say, and lead the way to Fifth and Pine. Oh, there is a throng there, Wide Awakes and Minutemen both, striding among those gathered to argue their points and hand out their pamphlets.

"This is the first I see the two sides together," Charity mutters, and with pistols and revolvers loading down waists, I cannot say I like it.

"Oh, but look!" Louisa cries, and now I see Minutemen along the porches brandishing muskets and fixed bayonets. "They're at all the windows, too," she says, and by now insults are flying and a scuffle or two is breaking out.

"It's not safe to linger here," I say, "for brawling will start soon, if not worse."

"Worse," Louisa says, and I see what she means, for a band of men who must be from the Union side tries to mount the mansion stairs. Down come the Minutemen's bayonets, pointing at the men's throats. Constables try to step between, shouting for all to disperse, but this mob will have none of it.

The pushing and shoving grows to a rare frenzy and we three

are caught in the pulsing mayhem of it. I have had enough. I raise my voice above the ruckus for Charity and Louisa to follow me.

That night, safe again on Poplar Street, I hear two fine things. No blood was shed at Berthold Mansion. And Lincoln has been sworn in as our president.

Chapter Thirty

"In your hands, my dissatisfied fellow countrymen, and not in mine, is the momentous issue of civil war. The government will not assail you. You have no conflict, without being yourselves the aggressors...

"We are not enemies, but friends. We must not be enemies. Though passion may have strained, it must not break our bonds of affection. The mystic chords of memory, stretching from every battle-field, and patriot grave, to every living heart and hearth-stone, all over this broad land, will yet swell the chorus of the Union, when again touched, as surely they will be, by the better angels of our nature."

— First Inaugural Address of President Abraham Lincoln

— March 4, 1861

"**D**ANIEL," I SAY, RIDING IN HIS GIG OF A CLOUDY FORENOON, "now *you* are driving me about to witness Union troops marching to the Arsenal. All is lost if even *you* suffer from war fever."

"I will be the last man to be so afflicted. This I am showing you because of how I admire it." He halts the horses then turns to me. "Though you must keep your knowledge of this ruse to yourself."

"You say that as if you mean it."

He declares that he does—though such seriousness is unlike him—and so I promise. He gestures toward the troops, who make a ruckus marching in tempo to numerous drums. "These are newly arrived," Daniel says, "don't you think?"

"Well, of course. They come uphill from the river and look where they head."

He lowers his voice to a whisper. "Overnight they quit the Arsenal in covered wagons to be deposited halfway to Jefferson Barracks. In morning's light they make a return march."

I think for a moment. "To make all believe Lyon has got rein-forcements?"

"Exactly that. Lyon orders this time and again. So who can say with any certainty how many men he has inside those walls?"

"Sharp clever of him." I gaze at Daniel. Now a father of a boy and a girl, he is lean and blond as ever though a wrinkle or two lays claim to his face. "So I must call you," I say, "one of Lyon's admirers."

"I will admire any man who uses his wiles to get us through this madness." He slaps the horses' reins and we jerk into motion, turning back the way we came.

"I will tell you this, Daniel. I breathe easier since our state convention." For the delegates voted against secession. I dared not hope that Missouri would go with her brain and not her heart.

"That damn Governor Jackson didn't get what he wanted. But that hardly puts an end to the matter."

"You cannot mean it. Now Missouri will not become a confederate state." As Texas, too, has now done, making seven states that have seceded.

"This is war, Eliza, or soon will be. What men vote at conventions won't keep the South from trying to claim us."

I believe Daniel is right about that. I see him much less often than in his bachelor years, but always I am keen interested to hear what he thinks. I have long known I am more like to share his views than Richard's. Daniel and I take the world as we find it. We do not care to struggle to change it.

Ten days later, I am in my bedchamber with needle and thread repairing the hem of my sage-green gown. I use a needle with a double eye, which Chantal would approve. As she taught me, I have laid in two stitches and am pulling through the thread when I hear someone bound up the stairs and along the corridor. Soon my door is flung open by a panting Richard.

He looms in the doorway. "At half past four this morning, the militia in South Carolina fired upon Fort Sumter."

My needle stills. "Does that mean—"

"Yes. The South has begun the war."

I see on Richard's face what I feel in my heart: disbelief. It is as if I have been gazing at a tree during a lightning storm, knowing all the while it will be struck, and still I am shocked when a bolt sets it aflame. My hands fall to my lap as Richard shuts the door. "So this happened at Fort Sumter," I say. That Army post guarding the harbor of Charleston has been under discussion for weeks in my parlor. "That is where Lincoln wished to send food so the men there would not starve?"

"It has been ill supplied for some time. South Carolina wanted the troops to evacuate instead, leaving the fort to them. Now they pound it with artillery."

I feel a tightness in my chest. "Have supplies got inside there?"

"No. High seas kept away the supply ships."

So the men inside are near starving. How well can they fight? I see clearly that the South Carolina militia saw a chance and took it.

"There is something else, too," Richard says, "which you must tell no one."

There is much promising of this kind of late. I nod.

Richard leans close and speaks low. "Captain Lyon schemes to remove weaponry from the Arsenal."

Now we have gone from South Carolina to Missouri. I push my mind to what Richard is telling me and understand it quickly. If weaponry is removed, the Arsenal will not benefit the Southern side so much even if it falls. "But how to do such a thing without everyone seeing? All eyes are on the Arsenal now."

"You know Governor Yates of Illinois is firmly in Lincoln's camp. Yates could ask the War Department to order that some Arsenal weapons go to him."

"Yes, I see the sense of it."

"Springfield, where Yates sits, is but a hundred miles away. It is where Lincoln himself has his family home." Richard sets to pacing. "Lyon has already written a letter to Yates asking him to make such a request, for ten thousand rifled muskets. Now the question is how to deliver a missive of such import." He spins to face me. "I offered to do it myself."

"What?"

"Who knows Illinois, and the routes there, as I do? But dammit, the task has been given to Bernard."

Relief floods through me, though I know enough to pretend I feel nothing of the sort. Also, I am not the kind of hysterical woman who judges this a dangerous journey. It is but into friendly Illinois. Still, if Richard desires to do this, he will desire to do other things, likely more perilous. I struggle to think of something mild to say. "Well, Bernard Farrar is a fine man for the task."

"Lyon trusts him more than me. But I ache to go, Eliza! And to Springfield, for our cause! Especially now, as the war begins."

I do not like to think of this war as *our cause*. Those words demand more than I wish to give.

"All this has resolved me to a course of action," Richard tells me then and I do not like the sound of that, either. "I will quit my boardinghouse rooms and move to barracks at the Arsenal. Bernard is already there."

"But, but"—I am sputtering now—"you are not mustered into the Army."

"Many are not mustered who serve already. There is not time for such niceties. If I am at the Arsenal, Lyon will see more of me and come to trust me faster. My mount of course I will take, but may I leave my gig here?"

"You may, of course, but this is foolhardy. You put yourself at risk at the Arsenal. The South might attack it at any moment."

"That is precisely why it is the place to be." Richard looks at me as if I have taken leave of my senses. "Eliza, must I repeat myself? It is not enough to believe in a thing. What is required is to take action on its behalf."

Why is that required of you? I wish to shout. Instead I bite my tongue, for loud as my voice might go, still Richard will not hear me.

ON SUNDAY CHARITY reads to me from the newspaper that the flag of the Confederacy has replaced the Stars and Stripes above Fort Sumter. After thirty-three hours of bombardment, the Army surrendered.

On Monday no one needs a newspaper to hear the new thing that has happened. It is shouted on Poplar Street; I am sure it is shouted across the nation entire, in the Union and secesh states, too: Lincoln issued a proclamation calling forth seventy-five thousand militiamen, for ninety days of service.

"Lincoln wrote that the rebellion is too powerful to be suppressed otherwise," Charity says. She has returned from her walk and is spinning about the sun-streaked parlor as other doxies laze around in negligées awaiting dinner. Agitated Charity is. She cannot stop her new habit: wringing her hands.

As I do not wish my trollops to worry overmuch, I make my voice light. "Probably Lincoln schemes for a quick end to it, a fierce early punch. For ninety days is not so long."

"It is the Confederacy that landed the first punch," Louisa says. "At Sumter."

Oʜ, there is another man on the Union side Richard is devoted to, and his name is Francis Preston Blair, Junior. He is an attorney and sits in Congress for our state and hails from an important family of lawyers and newspaper editors tied to Lincoln himself.

Of a dreary forenoon I am in a coffeehouse purchasing pastry and there Blair is striding about shaking men's hands, as politicians do. I will say there is something commanding about him, that he dresses in dashing fashion, and that he is handsome, my age with sweeping dark hair and moustache but no other whiskers.

"There is something else to know about him," Richard tells me that afternoon in my bedchamber. "He, too, studied at Transylvania University. Law, in his case."

"As if you need another reason to admire him."

"Now he is returned from Washington City, he meets with Lyon. But let us not talk about Blair. Come," and Richard takes my hand to lead me downstairs. In the parlor, propped against a sofa, is the portrait he had painted of me.

It is hard to fathom that such a thing exists—a portrait of a strumpet!—but indeed it does. It is an oil, and a very pretty one, and I believe I would think so even if I were not the subject. It was painted by a woman, too, Sarah Miriam Peale, for soon as I heard there was a woman portrait painter I desired she be the one Richard choose. I like her very much, and how she posed me in a way that was not vulgar, and believe that even though I am a trollop and she an artist we could be friends in this world where few women make their own way. Still, I turn to Richard with trepidation. "What is this doing here?"

He tells me what already I have guessed. "I have quit my boardinghouse rooms and brought this here for safekeeping. You well know how I treasure it." He lifts the oil and holds it in front of the painting already hanging above the hearth. "Shall we put it here? Or"—he strides across the parlor and displays it there—"is this better?"

"I wish you to set the portrait down so we can talk about this harebrained scheme of yours to move into the Arsenal."

He does not set down the oil but instead holds it in front of yet another painting. "I have done it already so there is nothing to discuss."

So that is that. Richard lives his life as he chooses and I do the same. Yes, he does things I ask of him and I do the same. But always I could do the opposite. And so could he. "Well, I do not care for the oil to hang in the parlor," I tell him. "It is too much of me, hanging on the wall and sitting in a stuffed chair both."

Richard sets down the portrait so he can take my face in his hands and kiss me. "There is no such thing as too much of you, Eliza. If I did not need sleep, I would stare at you the night long."

In the end, Richard and I stow the portrait in my armoire. I do not wish that it hang in my bedchamber, either, for it will remind me he is in peril at the Arsenal.

When Charity learns it is there, she has but one thing to say, with a sigh and a shake of the head. "And to think, Eliza. You are the one who doesn't believe in love."

A FEW NIGHTS later Richard is fired with such satisfaction I wager we could see to mount the stairs to my bedchamber without a candle. I have not even had the chance to inquire why he is not at his barracks when he begins to speak. "Finally I have done something of worth, Eliza! Today on behalf of Blair himself I took a telegram across the river to be sent to Washington City from there."

"You did what?"

"I took it across the river, yes, to Illinois, for we can trust a telegraph operator there. We know him to be sympathetic to the Union side." Richard spins about the chamber as if he were a child's top. "This came after Blair's meeting with Lyon. It was a telegram to the War Department, to ask them to order Lyon to swear in the regiments Lincoln wants from Missouri."

"Because Governor Jackson won't do it." Oh, I heard in my parlor what Jackson wrote in a telegram to Lincoln: that the president's request for troops was *revolutionary, inhuman, diabolical,* and I do not know what else. "Richard, that was an important telegram."

"Yes."

"And *you* were the one charged with ensuring it was sent."

"Yes. I implored them to dispatch me, as I did the week last. This time they agreed and now I have done it I will be trusted even more."

He does not wish to speak after that but instead do what men with war-fired blood desire to do, and I have no objection but for the fact that when we are spent, swiftly does he quit my bed to return to his barracks.

———

IN THE NEXT DAYS, more than one frightful piece of news comes to my ears. Virginia secedes, the Southern state with the most people and the greatest industry.

"And," says Charity, eyes wide above the newspaper as we sit at the trestle table in the kitchen, "Virginia sits right beside Washington City. Secessionists will be able simply to look across the Potomac if they care to see Lincoln."

After that, secessionists in our own state of Missouri seize Liberty Arsenal, far away west on our border with Kansas. No, it is not near so mighty an arsenal as ours here in St. Louis, but now the Southern side has taken *that* one, is it not even more certain they will aim at *this* one?

Charity leans close to whisper. "Do you know what Mr. Buehler told me the night last?" Oh, Mr. Buehler, who faithfully followed Charity here from Madam Lantos's. "That Governor Jackson will call our own state militia into training camps. There is a law says he can do it."

I am sure Mr. Buehler heard this at his Turnverein, where he drills even though he is too ancient even to hold a musket steady. "If Jackson wants militiamen trained," I say, "it is not for the Union side." I drink hot coffee in a kitchen warmed by baking, yet still I feel a chill. For there is Richard at the very Arsenal we fear for, each day seeking a new task to aid *our cause.*

The week next he is triumphant, telling me the War Department has given Captain Lyon authority to enlist regiments at the Arsenal. We are riding about in his gig of a sunny spring afternoon, for unless the horse is a secesh spy it is a safe place to speak freely. "Now, Eliza," he says, "though it is not mine to take credit, a full two thousand men have joined us at the Arsenal."

I gaze at Richard's profile, proud as a silhouette stamped on a coin. "So fast? I cannot believe it, not with how Lyon likes to put on a show." In the last days I have heard neither drums nor marching feet.

"Men were instructed to come singly, by the river path and the water gates, in darkness, if they could. And to gain entry, each man had to present a card with one word printed upon it." He gives me a sideways smile. "Saxton. In German that carries the meaning of swordsman. Of course many of these men are German."

Well. Captain Lyon seems more than happy to carry out a fine scheme. Even, I am soon to find out, one devised by a strumpet.

Chapter Thirty-One

"I do not see how a war is to be avoided. Under quack management it may be long and bloody. Yet I have no apprehensions about the final triumph of almighty truth, though at the cost of many unnecessary sacrifices. But let them come. I would rather see the country lighted up with the flames of war from the center to its remotest border than that the great rights and hopes of the human race expire before the arrogance of Secessionists. Of this, however, there is no danger. They are at war with nature and the human heart, and cannot succeed."

— From a letter written by Nathaniel Lyon in early 1861

"I COME TO TRUST WHAT MR. BUEHLER HEARS AT HIS TURNVEREIN," Charity murmurs to me of an afternoon as we stride past Planters House, overrun by the secesh side just like Berthold Mansion. "He told me," she goes on, "that Governor Jackson would call up the state militia. And so he did."

Between lashes of the whip Mr. Buehler has relayed to Charity quite a few tidbits that proved correct. Now these men called up by our scheming governor are camped six miles west of the Arsenal—do I wonder why?—in Lindell Grove. Some even begin to call it Camp Jackson.

That night, after Mr. Stewart and I decamp to my bedchamber —for though the former governor is gone from his post, he pleases me by remaining a client—he tells me something alarming has happened close to home. We settle before the hearth, though on this temperate night we need no fire but open windows and a breeze instead. With an impatient hand he brushes back his light hair from his forehead. "A captain of our state militia managed to lay his hands on munitions here in St. Louis and transported them to Jefferson City."

"To our capital? Do you know why?"

"There is a worry Jackson will push the legislature into granting him special powers. That is easier to accomplish at the point of a bayonet." His thin lips twist. "The blackguard wishes to be more a king than a governor."

"What think you of the encampment at Lindell Grove?"

"There is but one thing to think. Jackson plots an attack on the Arsenal." It is some time now that Mr. Stewart and I speak frankly, but still I startle at his directness. "Yes, it is legal under our state constitution that the governor call up the militia *for training purposes*." He jabs thrice in the air, one for each of those last words. "But does any thinking man believe training is Jackson's purpose?"

"Did he not call up the militia for six days only?"

"Exactly so, Eliza. If our scoundrel governor plots as I believe he does, he will act swiftly against the Arsenal."

HOURS LATER SOMETHING wakes me from my slumber and I rear up in bed with a cry for in the shadows I see hulking the shape of a man.

"Hush"—Richard rushes forward—"hush, Eliza, it is only me," but though he tries to soothe me, my heart flails against my ribs and my breath comes fast as steam from a boiling kettle. "I am sorry to frighten you," he whispers, "but I have snuck away from my barracks."

"I can see that, but why do you crouch beside my bed?"

"The better to gaze at you. Come, you are full awake now," and as there is no disputing that, he throws back the blanket and pulls me to my feet. "Let us sit and enjoy a tot of whiskey."

Now I am waked I see something to bother me: the doors of my armoire are ajar. I walk closer. "I am sure I shut those before."

Richard pulls me from there, too. "All is fine. Come sit," and I join him at the hearth and light a candle as he pours from the decanter. "Let us toast," he says, "to a quick rout of the South," and as we clink glasses and whiskey burns down my throat I realize there is something different about Richard. It is in the way his eyes meet mine then dart away.

"What has happened?" I ask him. "For I can tell something has."

"It is just that"—it takes him some time to say it—"Lyon is strong in his belief that the Arsenal soon will be attacked."

"I heard the very same tonight from Mr. Stewart."

"Would you believe Jackson sent a message to Lyon that he would set up forty men on the bluff south of the Arsenal to practice building fortified positions? Of course Lyon smelled a rat and sent a message back that if anyone so much as dug a spade into ground near the Arsenal, he would salute the enterprise with the music of whistling shells."

Even as my heart shudders—*the Arsenal soon will be attacked*—I chuckle. "Lyon can be colorful with his words."

"I am told it is all the Shakespeare he reads. Anyway, Lyon also heard today—from a Union spy, no less—that the steamer *J.C.*

Swon comes up fast from Baton Rouge loaded with armaments sent by Jefferson Davis. At Jackson's request."

The Union side would call that treason. "And is the *Swon* meant to land here at St. Louis?"

"In but a day or two. And it contains stolen weaponry, Eliza, poached by the rebels from federal stores in Louisiana. Not only muskets but siege guns and cannon, too. Enough to break the walls of the Arsenal."

I imagine the *J.C. Swon* with its unholy cargo plying the Mississippi. "Perhaps the boilers will explode. Then so much for those stolen armaments."

"You could wish for such a thing? Men who have committed no crime labor on that vessel."

I will not tell him that indeed I could wish so, for I see before me a guiltless man who puts himself in the way of harm. I leave my chair to crouch at Richard's knees. "Bernard Farrar must be safe back from his mission to Springfield."

"He is, but how do you know?"

"*You* know more of Lyon's business when Bernard is about." I take Richard's hands. "This fighting business comes close now."

"I would that it stayed far away. But that is not how wars are won."

No. Wars are won only when men kill one another. They are lost that way, too. "Will the militia at Lindell Grove be the ones to attack the Arsenal?"

"It is easy to think that. But it would be better to be sure." He leans close. "Imagine if the weaponry on the *J.C. Swon* makes its way to Camp Jackson. In that case, the governor and his men are caught red-handed conspiring with the rebels. Yes, already we can guess what Jackson does. But that would be proof of it."

"You are saying, then, that Lyon would be sure of an attack coming."

"Just as important, he could justify taking action of his own to head one off."

At that, my heart takes flight. "So an attack does not happen? That is possible?"

Richard smiles. "With Captain Lyon, anything is possible."

"Stay with me tonight," I ask him, and he will, but only for too short a time.

I SEE it the next day as I walk on Poplar Street, the sleek barouche all in this metropolis spot so often, with white-haired Old Peter up top loudly chattering away as if every citizen need hear his descriptions of this and that shop or frock or carriage and two. Inside sit Congressman Frank Blair's wife and her mother, who long ago lost her sight and so desires the ancient driver's regaling. Hasn't she nodded off, the old woman dressed in widow's weeds? For her head hangs and sways with the lulling motion. It is impossible to tell, though, whether she is asleep or awake for her veil is thick as a shroud. I nod at the younger woman whose face points in my direction but know not why I bother. The eyes of a lady like Appoline Blair look right through a strumpet like me as if I were made of air.

It is when I am returned to the house that an idea fills my head. It is a poppycockish notion to be sure, but still I sit in the parlor and think about it and when I am done doing that and still think the same as when I started, I summon Noah. "I wish you to go to the Arsenal," I tell him, "fast as you can, and when you get there ask for Bernard Farrar. Ask if he will please come to this house to talk to me. It is urgent, Noah. I know not to waste his time. Please make that clear to him as you are able."

I confound Noah with this strange request, but out he goes to the gig and soon I hear it clatter away at a speed I approve. I hardly dare hope Bernard will come, but a few hours later, when my doxies are afoot in their negligées, he appears. As he tries not to gape, I lead him upstairs to my bedchamber, where I shut the door and spin to face him.

I grasp his hands. "I thank you for coming, Bernard. It was not lightly I requested you." I keep my voice so low that he must bend close to hear me. "I have an idea how our side might get a good look at Camp Jackson," and I force myself to relay it though I fear I sound the most ridiculous ninny.

Yet when I finish he does not race from my chamber tossing choice words over his shoulder. Instead he paces the Brussels carpet, staring down at the floral pattern. Finally he raises his dark gaze to mine. "I wish you to present this idea to Captain Lyon himself."

"What?"

"At once." Already he stands at my door with his hand upon the knob. "I have come on my own mount so let us have Noah convey you back and forth."

"Back and forth where?"

"To the Arsenal, of course."

MORE THAN ONCE I have ridden past the Arsenal, but never did I dream I would enter it. Now troops crawl all over it; I hear its walls are mined to explode should Minutemen try to penetrate it; and somewhere inside lurks Richard, who might well be punished severely for speaking over freely to a trollop.

The Arsenal sits on a flat plot upslope from the river, with hills at a distance. Surrounding it on all but the river side are limestone walls twice as high as me and fierce thick. On the river side is a fence no one would scoff at and what I know is called the water gate, with room aplenty for a vessel to land.

Inside the grounds—for that is where I am now, Noah and me brought through by Bernard—are a few trees high as the sky and more structures than I guessed. Two large ones stand out: each of two stories, built of stone with roofs of slate. Must these hold the armaments so precious to both sides?—least those Lyon has not had spirited away.

I must quit Noah and follow Bernard into a smaller building. I am taken to a chamber with nary a window and the simplest of table and chairs. Not long am I there before Congressman Blair appears, and then, in a rush of stomping boots and bellowing voice, Captain Lyon, mussed and bearing a look of impatience. He slams shut the rough door behind him, leaving a trio of men staring at wood. Lyon squints at me then glares at Bernard. "This had better be worth my while, Farrar."

"Captain"—Bernard looks from Lyon to me—"this is Madam Haycraft, whose acquaintance I know you have made."

I watch Congressman Blair arch his brows.

"Madam Haycraft," Bernard says, "please relay to Captain Lyon the ploy you described to me earlier." He lowers his voice to a near whisper, which causes all to lean close. "Which would allow our side a tour, if you will, of Camp Jackson."

Those words snap Lyon's head in my direction.

I raise my chin, try to ignore the wild thumping of my heart, and tell myself that if this war hero judges my scheme a poor one, I am none the worse for offering it. I nod at Blair. "Near every day, Congressman, we here in St. Louis witness your barouche criss-cross our city with your wife and her mother inside and Old Peter up top. It journeys all about and none of us think a thing about it."

"What of it?" Lyon demands.

"Well, why not have one of your men dress in the garments of the Congressman's mother-in-law"—I hear Blair scoff—"and put him in the barouche instead, thick veiled like she is, with Mrs. Blair there, too? Old Peter could drive around Camp Jackson and your man could see what goes on there and, as it is such a usual thing, no one would make a fuss."

There is silence for some moments. Then: "That is a prepos-terous ruse," Blair says. "And an extremely dangerous one."

Lyon says nothing. Instead I believe I see the wheels of his mind turn. "Of course it would be me," he then says, "and not one of my men to be so disguised. I must see what goes on there with my own eyes."

"You are considering this?" Blair says.

"With all due respect, Congressman," Bernard says, "I thought the idea had merit, which is why I brought Madam Haycraft here directly."

"Captain," Blair says, "you must not risk your life for this folly."

"I'd be done for if I were found out," Lyon says, "bayonetted through by those rebel zealots," and he spins on his worn heels to pace the small chamber.

"I will not allow my wife to participate in this scheme," Blair says. "It is unthinkably dangerous and she is a wife and mother of four."

"How about Old Peter?" Lyon asks. "Is he free or slave?"

"Long freed. But I shudder to think—"

"What about the barouche?" Lyon asks. "And the horses?"

Blair shakes his head. Then: "Of course, Captain, I will give you the use of all."

Lyon stops pacing to glance at me then at Blair again. "Is Madam Haycraft about the size and complexion of your wife?"

"What?" I cry. "I did not—"

"Is she or isn't she?" Lyon turns his gaze on me. "Does Mrs. Blair go out veiled, like her mother?"

"She does not," I say, "and I do not see a resemblance between us."

Bernard says nothing, for which I thank him to the depths of my soul. I am sure he thinks, as I do, that Mrs. Appoline Blair and I are not so *very* different, if you ignore that she is a lady and I a doxy. Yes, she is younger, but we are of similar size and both possess dark hair. Of course her locks are dressed more severely than mine, and, if I may say so, her nose is considerably longer and her features less graceful. "I am well known in this city," I point out. "Many recognize me. No one would mistake me for the congressman's wife."

"Maybe not if they did a side by side comparison," Lyon says, "but we're talking about a passing view. What do you say, Blair?"

I jut my chin as the congressman conducts the sort of assessment of my person that I have many times suffered from a man. In the prolonged silence I speak again. "May I remind everyone that I did not offer myself for this scheme. If it is unthinkably dangerous for Mrs. Blair, it is unthinkably dangerous for me."

"You are not a wife and mother," Blair says, and he would say more, but I will not hear it.

"That does not mean I am to be cast to the wolves. I am a daughter and an aunt and a sister and a friend. I am also a woman of business who gives a great deal to this city, to our institutions and the poor alike."

There is silence after that, finally broken by Lyon. "Well, Madam Haycraft, you keep your wits about you. I can't say that about everybody I meet. Not"—he nods at Blair—"that your wife lacks bravery."

"She most certainly does not. But she suffers already enough depredations. Our house on Washington Street is stoned so often now that I am sorely tempted to move her and all of my family far from town."

"Most of us do not have the luxury of quitting this city when it becomes a danger," I tell him, and believe I hear Lyon snicker. I turn my gaze to him. "And you, Captain, have no reason to trust me. Especially not on an adventure where you could lose your life."

"You're not going to squeeze out of this on that basis. I trust you well enough. Farrar does and Bonner, too, though that's a different matter. Anyway, you're not going anywhere until the thing is done." I begin to sputter, but that does not keep Lyon from talking. "One more thing. I'd lay good money on you knowing how to keep a secret. Any madam worth her salt knows a lot she never tells."

Just when I do not care to be trusted, I am. "I have not said I would do this thing," I remind Lyon.

"Madam Haycraft, I need a woman in that barouche to make it look the same as every other day. What other woman could hold her own and have menfolk who would allow it?"

What can I say to that? Always I tell myself that I can do what I must when the time comes. And in this world of ours, near all women must answer to a man. And then there is Eliza Haycraft, who has made her life so she doesn't have to.

Captain Lyon moves close and locks his gaze onto mine. "If we lose this Arsenal, I fear we lose this state, these rivers, and who knows what else to the Confederate side. Ever had anything more important laid before you? And for what little it's worth, if you do this you'll earn my eternal admiration." He steps away and speaks over his shoulder. "Blair, follow me. You need to talk to Old Peter," and the rest of his instructions are lost as out the two men stride, leaving me behind with Bernard.

———

"Now I'm a prisoner here?" I say to Bernard. I see the shock on his face that I know is mirrored on my own.

"Same as we all are, Eliza. And you heard the captain. Now that he's considering this, he won't let you leave and risk that word of this ploy slip out." He shakes his head. "I did not imagine it would come to this. And for that I am sorry."

"I knew Lyon was one to latch onto a fine scheme." Now I am the one pacing. "I did not know how fine a scheme he would think this to be. And I hardly thought I would be pulled into it."

Bernard lowers his head into his hands. "Richard will throttle me."

"It is not his to throttle you," and I watch Bernard's head snap in my direction. "It is my life to be put at risk and not his to decide if I risk it or not." Bernard is agape to hear me speak this way. Richard may be used to it, but most men are not.

"Why did you not go to him first," Bernard asks, "but to me instead?"

"Because I judged you could get the idea to Lyon faster. And I believed there was no time to waste."

"We are woefully short on time." He frowns and I wonder if he is thinking of the *J.C. Swon* hurtling upriver, her bowels laden with stolen cargo. Might she even now be landing here?

"I would talk to Richard," I tell Bernard, "if I can."

"To help settle your mind on what to do?"

"I will settle my own mind, Bernard."

"Yes. I should grasp that." He gives me a small smile and moves toward the door. "I know where Richard might be. I will seek him out."

I am left alone but not unguarded. One young soldier outside the door, I can see, has been told to mind me.

It is not long before Richard heaves into the chamber, astonishment on his face. "Well, it must be true, for here you are. As it is, I cannot half believe what I am hearing from Bernard. There is some scheme afoot that *you* are pulled into?"

Some scheme. So Bernard has not confided the particulars to Richard. I suppose that means I must do the same. "In fact," I tell him, "the idea was mine."

"What the devil?"

I believe Richard might explode from shock. "I am surprised to tell you that Lyon himself judges the idea a fine one. And he asks me to undertake it with him."

"But Eliza, any undertaking in wartime could go wrong a thousand ways! Lyon should not attempt to drag an innocent woman into whatever this is."

I doubt if the word *innocent* comes to any man's mind where I am concerned. "Well, if I may say so, this enterprise does not pose *that* grave a danger."

Though, I suppose, Old Peter could slip up and put a word wrong. Or a gust could blow the old woman's veil off Lyon's face. Or a soldier could realize I am not Blair's plain-featured wife. *I'd be done for if I were found out,* Lyon said, *bayonetted through by those rebel zealots.* And me, I am sure, they would wait to kill until they'd had their fill first.

I turn away from Richard as more of Lyon's words rattle in my head. I know a military man is meant to speak in grand style to prod his men. Well, now such a one has spoken in grand style to me.

Richard turns me around to peer at my face. "There is another thing I cannot half believe, Eliza." His voice is soft. "What I fear you are thinking."

I raise my eyes to his. "The thing needs doing and I am the best one to do it. Lyon was canny to say he would admire me if I joined him. Can you imagine that? That a harlot could win the admiration of such a man?"

"You are not a mere harlot." I do not know if Richard could speak more fiercely. "I hate when you speak of yourself that way."

"I speak the way the world does." For then, what words does that leave the world to hurt me? Yes, my heart is harder to those jabs than it once was. But still, from time to time, I reel under their blows.

Between Richard and me silence falls, though beyond these rough walls I hear the marching and shouting of daily life in the Arsenal. Closer I almost hear turning the wheels of Richard's mind as he tries to think of a new way to persuade me to his side. Finally: "Are you not the one," he says, "who told me a thousand times you must not reveal which side you are on? Now you propose to work right alongside Lyon."

"It is meant to be a secret scheme, Richard. Very few will ever know about it. I must ask you: would *you* not admire me doing this thing? Helping the Union side?"

"*My* admiration you earned the very day I met you. Hiding in the shadows to attend the burial of a man you admired. After walking miles in the sun and dust to get there."

"Oh, Richard." I must smile then. "You forget. I hired a gig for Charity and me to get there. And I attended that burial for me. *I* wished to honor Bernard's father. Always, always the things I do are for me. Even handing out coins is for me." For who will hate me then? And really, what if they do? I need no one's say-so to do good as I see fit. "Much of my life I have done what I must. Now I may do what I choose, least some of the time. And I would do this for the very Union, the cause for which you risk your own life. Please"—I stop him before he can speak—"do not tell me it is not a woman's place."

"I am too wise to say *that* to you, Eliza."

"I will say something more." I lay my hands on Richard's chest and look up into his eyes. "How many risks has Noah taken, to save his own?"

Richard shakes his head. "We will never know."

"Well, this is very small, compared to that. And who expects a woman to put herself in danger? No one. Not a man, not a woman. I will tell you I like that, too."

You have that rare quality that has no name. Maybe—I'm not sure I believe it—that is not just what I see in the mirror.

Richard throws up his hands. "You are no Confederate, Eliza, but apparently you are a rebel all the same."

"I do not do this to be contrary. I do this because Lyon asked if I ever had anything more important laid before me." I see that look in Richard's amber gaze then, when he knows I will do what I will do. "And I have not."

Chapter Thirty-Two

"The commencement of civil war in St. Louis will be the signal for Illinois to assail our river frontier at a hundred different points; for Iowa to pour her legions across the Northwestern border and annex all of Missouri north of the Missouri river; for Montgomery and the organized Abolitionists of Kansas to burst like a tornado on the Southwest and keep it clear of everything portable, negroes especially. Taking Missouri out of the union will be no theatrical ceremony, but a task as hard as the removal of mountains without faith...

"Ah! Mr. Claiborne Jackson, we would not be surprised if the grim vision of the gallows and the hangman proved averse to your slumbers... "

— *Missouri Democrat*

— Early May 1861

THE BONNET MRS. APPOLINE BLAIR SAW FIT TO SPARE shows years of wear and indeed is of an old style. Immediately she conveyed to Bernard when he went to fetch it that she did not care to have it returned. I doubt she knows much about the proposed scheme of *reconnaissance*—I have learned yet another word—but I am sure that if she did, she is too much a lady to have said in so many words: *I will not so much as look upon that bonnet after that bawd has worn it.*

It is an overcast Thursday forenoon as I stand in the grim Arsenal bedchamber in which I passed the night, gazing out the lone window that allows a narrow view of a dull rear corner of the grounds. Richard is long gone from outside my door, where he stood guard the night through. He feared both that the Arsenal might be attacked from without and that I might be from within.

Last night I was brought a meal on a tray and the same this morning. Did it make me think of my night passed in a calaboose? Oh yes, and of Sarah's many. How often in those midnight hours did she imagine a black sack dropped over her head, followed by a noose, followed by the falling away of the floor? I will say that in the night's fitful length my mind conjured more than one assault, though never did it get far, for always I jolted awake panting. I feel a strange new kinship with my sister. I wonder: is it possible Sarah is dead and cackles to me from the grave? Does she expect me soon to join her? If so, is it to Hell I am to go? Well, perhaps my heroism on this day will send me in a happier direction not oft open to strumpets.

Bernard told me this morning that the *J.C. Swon* docked on our levee yesterday. In the hours when the owl keeps watch, spies for our side witnessed a caravan of drays roll up to the steamer. With Minutemen sneaking about, it was onto those drays that the cargo was unloaded. Can you believe the crates had the word *marble* written upon them and the barrels the word *ale*? Where did those provisions go?

That is the very question Captain Lyon seeks to answer.

How my doxies must wonder about their madam! Noah will have told them I was seized of the desire to see Richard at the Arsenal and once there took ill. I hope all will forget they never before saw me ailing. And since it is better to hew close to the truth when spinning a lie, I will not be caught out should someone have spied my gig rolling onto these grounds.

I hear rapid footfalls approach. The door opens. It is Lyon, his arms full of black bombazine, an enormous bonnet of the same midnight hue, and more. He deposits all on the table beside the bonnet I may now call my own. "I trust you're rested?" he inquires.

"Well as I can be." I eye his stash, which must come from the ancient Mrs. Alexander. My frock of mouse-gray has been judged sufficient drear for this mission. I would hate to die in my most unremarkable garment, but so it may well be. "I don't suppose, Captain, that you will trade your larger bonnet for mine?"

"Not on your life." He looses a grim chuckle. "But I am hoping you will button my gown all the same. I am told it is wide enough to accommodate."

"That's a mercy."

"There's no indication Jackson plots to attack the Arsenal this afternoon," Lyon tells me in an amiable tone, and I know what he is really saying: our masquerade will proceed. If he had any reason to conclude an attack was in play, he would put his efforts into defending the Arsenal.

"Jackson would've been wise to attack the Arsenal in January, when it was easy to take as a lamb."

"Once more I'm glad you're on my side, Madam Haycraft." Lyon's tone is dry. "They will lunch soon at Camp Jackson and the parade of female visitors will begin."

"I heard tell the wives and sweethearts pay a daily call."

"It is quite a jolly scene for an encampment." I hear the derision in his tone before Lyon squints at me with fresh attention. "I'm grateful to you for riding in that barouche with me. I believe there's a fair chance this scheme of yours'll succeed."

A night has passed, but still he calls it a scheme of mine. All will do the same should it fail, but I wager legend will render it Lyon's scheme if it succeeds. "I hope the chance is more than fair," I tell him. "I have lived long enough to know that few pay much mind to an old Negro and two women with the look of matrons."

———

With every nearing of footfalls to my door, my heart leaps like a cat after loose yarn. Will this visitor bring the summons to my fate? Or will it be Richard, appearing once more before I go? With near desperation I wish for him, but in vain, for the last to visit is a young soldier come to collect both the garments and me. He leads me into the yard and the bright sunshine that tries but fails to persuade me that I will survive until nightfall.

It is another small building I enter, and another small chamber, and this one is filled with a pacing Captain Lyon. His face has a grim set about it and of a sudden it comes full clear to me that he and I, and Old Peter, will indeed do this thing.

Lyon raises a cigar to his lips and puffs. He spins on his heel and strides away then puffs again. Only when we hear the clatter of a carriage does he exercise his voice. "Finally. There it is." He stomps to a window to peer into the yard. I expect to see the fancy conveyance of the Blair family but instead my gaze falls upon a barouche whose best days are behind it. It is pulled by two nags and on the battered box up top sits a young coachman wearing simple garb. Despite the May sunshine, he has the leather hood full raised, as if the weather were too poor to bear.

"That will take us to our meeting place," Lyon tells me, and I understand then that we cannot risk passersby viewing the Blair family barouche exiting the Arsenal. Lyon tosses the cigar out the window and bends to shove the bottoms of his trousers into his boots. Off comes his collar and over his head flies the bombazine gown, which might be a tent for all its cascading fabric. If this were another day I would laugh, but as I button him I am somber as a widow.

He sets the enormous bonnet on his head. With the black veil that falls from its wide brim, the thing covers him well as a shroud. I half hope he will declare he cannot see and so this must end our masquerade, but instead he throws back the veil, stomps across the room, and pulls from a cupboard not one revolver but two.

"One is for me?" I ask.

"My trust in you does not extend *that* far," he mutters, and then I understand that he will not risk being shot at close range by a trollop who turns out to be a secesh hothead. I watch him twirl each of the revolvers' chambers to his satisfaction. "If we meet trouble"—he sets down the revolvers to encase his hands in Mrs. Alexander's black lace mitts—"the other side will meet it, too. Now put on Mrs. Blair's bonnet and tell me: is it true the old lady is mute as a button and only nods when called to? And how does she sit? Prim and stiff?"

It is more than one question I answer as we cross the yard toward the tumbledown gig, driven, I must think, by one of Lyon's men. There is no ceremony as we climb inside and roll from the Arsenal's grounds. It is not far we go, only to a quiet street near the limits of the city. Behind a decrepit house overrun by shrubbery waits the Blair family barouche, a beautiful shimmering black, pulled by two grand horses of the same ebony hue. Up top is Old Peter, silent for once.

Old Peter grins wide when he spies Lyon and I can tell that already they have met. Yet as I near I see disquiet in the old man's eyes, same as he can see in mine. I reach up to grasp his hand. "We'll have a story to tell," he murmurs to me and I nod and smile, though even should I live to tell this tale, will I? Or will I take it to my tomb like the other secrets I carry, pebbles in my boots?

Into this barouche I climb. Do I tremble? No, it is as it ever has been: when the moment comes to act, I raise my chin and cease to shiver. Old Peter directs Lyon where to sit, with me beside him, both beneath the cover of the leather hood, full raised to mask us best it can though still leaving us to the open air. Lyon sets the revolvers on his lap beneath a blanket. The horses whinny and stomp, I am sure half undone by us strange people, this strange spot, our barely checked agitation.

Old Peter clucks to the horses and the barouche rolls forward. From beneath the black veil, Lyon speaks. "I think it's past time I call you Eliza," he says, and I know those will be the last words he utters in this carriage unless we meet, as he calls it, *trouble.*

WE DO NOT IMMEDIATELY commence the drive to Camp Jackson but instead conduct a tour of city streets, Old Peter jovial as ever, chattering—does he ever stop?—and waving to all who salute him. I keep my gaze straight ahead and my chin high, the better to appear the high-placed wife of a congressman. A time or two someone will call to "Mrs. Alexander" and Lyon will allow a tilt of the head. Beneath the bombazine, does his heart thump like mine? Does Old Peter's?

After a time our merry driver speaks words of note. "Am I right to think you have a hankering to ride past Lindell Grove, Mrs. Alexander? To enjoy those fine spring blooms in the meadow," and we roll uphill from the city, the bustle ebbing as we near the limits of the metropolis.

Bernard described to me our likely scheme: to drive the perimeter of the grove, itself the shape of a rectangle, the long sides Laclede Avenue to the south and the Olive Street plank road to the north, and the short sides Garrison Avenue nearer the river and Grand Avenue uphill.

As we see the pretty meadow before us where Governor Jackson plots his mutiny, I wonder if the hearts of the straining horses beat any faster than my own. The grove is ordinary enough, dotted with trees bestowing shade on long grasses frolicking in a light breeze. Soon it is on Laclede that we ride, uphill toward Wesleyan Cemetery, rolling past another gig or two coming down, which gives Old Peter something besides prairie flowers about which to wax. Then, spread across the meadow, it is tents I begin to see, in small clusters and large groups, some among trees and some in the open, some with flaps lifted and others with flaps closed. Men—all from the first and second regiments of our state militia?—stride about or loll in the grass, some in a uniform of belted sack coat and trousers. Are those uniforms the blue of the federal army? Oh, yes. But others are gray, the color the secessionists begin to favor. What are we to judge of that? And what of the men wearing simple garments from home?

Beside me, Lyon edges forward. I do not see his mitted hands, for they lie below the lap blanket. Do they clutch his two revolvers?

Outside the barouche, it is many weapons I see. Lying across the meadow upon long stretches of canvas are pistols and revolvers, muskets and rifles, cap and cartridge boxes, stacked tidily. And men carry rifles topped with spiked bayonets. Are these weapons pilfered from the federal arsenal at Baton Rouge, I wonder? Might they be newly unpacked from the *Swon*? Does Lyon see something that will let him know?

Oh, it is even more a bustle as we continue uphill, and I am happy to see that there are other carriages to distract. Must that be the headquarters tent we roll by? For it is large and well positioned, and yes, its flagpole flies the Stars and Stripes. Old Peter must like that view, for he comments on the wind whipping the nation's banner of red, white, and blue. Men's eyes follow us as we ride past, idly curious, and those of women, too, for they are here in their numbers, chatting, laughing, as if our city had not a care. Do those wives and sweethearts, mothers and daughters not see rifles piled near their tasseled shoes? Do the weapons not remind them that their menfolk are in this meadow to do more than picnic?

We turn right onto Grand Avenue, at the uphill end of the

grove, and soon turn right again onto the plank road, downhill. Oh, and now I spy something that must keenly interest Captain Lyon, hulking in a stand of trees. Cannon, all in a row. Unloaded from the *Swon*? *Enough to break the walls of the Arsenal,* Richard said. And, if I am not mistaken, that brass contraption 'neath the flagpole is a saluting gun. Yet Lyon betrays no agitation. He remains unmoving as a figurehead on a schooner.

Still downhill. "Mrs. Alexander!" a trio of beauties calls. Decked in pastel finery and arrayed on a white blanket, they wave from beneath their parasols. They are looking to us, I can see, to amuse themselves and their menfolk. Then: "Mrs. Blair!" they call. My heart jabs against my mouse-gray bodice as Lyon and I both tilt our heads as grand muck-a-mucks might do. Old Peter, the best showman of us three, laughs and calls out wishes for a fine day then goes on to describe the beauties' frocks to "Mrs. Alexander" in detail Chantal herself would have envied.

Now we near the bottom of the grove. Has Lyon seen enough of this damnable place? Through that veil I hope he does not wish to count the troops or the armaments, for if so we will be riding till nightfall. But I am forced to accept we will conduct another tour, for instead of continuing straight towards the river Old Peter leads the horses into a right turn onto Garrison Avenue. When we reach Laclede, I am sure we will turn right once again to climb uphill for another tour of the perimeter.

The horses are very near Laclede when of a sudden I hear Old Peter shout. "Whoa! Whoa!"

"Halt!" I hear a man holler in front of us. "Halt here!"

Old Peter yanks the horses to a stop and they whinny in distress. The barouche careens dangerously on the uneven road and Lyon and I are tossed about before we can right ourselves. I hear a thumping sound on the carriage floor. My eyes catch a flash of silver. Then I see why. Lyon has dropped one of his revolvers. It lies in plain sight beyond his skirts.

A young but stern-looking bearded man in a uniform I cannot call Army blue appears below Old Peter, to the left of his box seat.

Without a thought my booted foot captures the revolver and tugs it beneath Lyon's billowing skirts. My heart hammers as the meddlesome soldier frowns up at Old Peter, his eyes suspicious, his right hand cradling the bayonetted musket at his hip.

"What do you take this camp for?" he demands. "The proper place for a spring excursion?"

"Rightly so!" Old Peter cries then chuckles as he so often does. "Why, we are just enjoying a ride to see the prairie flowers in the meadow."

It is not just the first soldier now. Others approach, and women, too, though they stay at a remove. More than one soldier takes this chance to glance inside the carriage, a finer conveyance than most. A few stand mere feet from Captain Lyon. I lick my lips for I find my mouth has gone dry. *I may have to speak. Lyon cannot. We will be found out if he is pushed to.*

I do not know how, but I feel the air thicken between Lyon and me. Very slightly he lowers his head and pivots his body toward the center of the barouche. I lay a gentling hand on his knee. "It is just a moment's interruption, Mother," I say in a lilting tone.

"Who," demands the bearded soldier of Old Peter, "gave you permission to ride about this encampment?"

"Why"—now I hear a stammer in the old man's voice—"I'm mighty sorry to say, sir, we didn't think about something so serious as that on such a fine example of a spring day."

"You should've thought about it!" another man hollers. "The Blair family in particular should have permission before riding about *this* encampment!"

"The Blair family?" I hear a voice or two repeat.

Now. Now.

I do not allow myself to think. I half rise—yes, the revolver remains hidden beneath Lyon's skirts—and push my bonneted head forward. I lower my hand over my brim as if I cannot bear even the slightest sunshine to light upon my delicate skin. "Young man," I call to the soldier, mimicking the fine ladies I have heard over the years, "I admire your strenuous performance of your duties. But my mother some time ago began to tire and I must beg your leave to depart this meadow. Old Peter, finally do as I say. Turn left on Laclede and take us downhill toward home," and I pull back and drop upon the seat.

"Yes, Mrs. Blair!" Old Peter cries. He slaps the reins and clucks at the steeds with vigor. They leap into motion and we roll forward. I avert my face from the left side of the carriage, where the officious soldier is forced to step back, and coo at "my mother," though I wonder I find the breath to do it.

Oh, we might be shot at, or stopped some other way, but the angels must be on the Union side for nothing of the sort happens. Old Peter takes us at a cracking pace downhill while Lyon keeps his head lowered and raises no objection.

Old Peter wears a grin wide as a sunflower when he returns us to the battered barouche. I wish I could sit with him and reminisce, but that must wait for another day, for after shaking Old Peter's hand Lyon will return posthaste to the Arsenal, taking me with him. Once there he whips the bonnet from his head and surprises me by taking time to hand me down. That does not make him a man who will linger over praise. *Excellent* is all he will say; though his gaze, blue as a summer sky, tells me he speaks the word truthfully.

Still, for another night more, my life is not my own.

———

IT IS after nightfall when Richard finds me. I am returned to my Arsenal bedchamber and much easier of mind than I was the night prior, though I long for my own house. Richard sweeps me into an embrace that lifts me well off the floor. "Tell me all, tell me all," he insists, once he is done kissing me.

"First tell *me* why you did not wish me well before we departed."

"I was kept away. I am sure Lyon feared I would make off with you somehow. And believe me, I considered all the ways I might. Now tell."

I do not make more of the escapade than there was, but the tale does not suffer in the telling.

"I am sure your tone is considerably more dulcet than Mrs. Blair could ever produce," Richard says.

"And I am sure I will never know. Now I must wonder if this scheme was worth it. Did Lyon see what he needed to?"

Richard lowers his voice. "He saw enough to judge that seven or eight hundred men are at that encampment. And he is far more certain of the armaments there." Richard pauses and I wonder if he, too, knows of the cannon, enough to make mincemeat of the Arsenal walls. "And, I am surprised you did not mention it, he saw signs bearing the names of the two main thoroughfares, Jefferson Davis and Beauregard."

I will not say that *my* seeing those signs would have done little good. "Well, how can we believe in the Union loyalty of those men if they name their avenues after secesh leaders?"

Richard nods. "It will boil over tomorrow, Eliza, and Lyon will not let you go until then. I believe he will demand that Camp Jackson surrender."

Chapter Thirty-Three

"You are openly in communication with the so-called Southern Confederacy, which is at war with the United States, and you are receiving at your camp, from the said Confederacy and under its flag, large supplies of the material of war…

"It is my duty to demand, and I do hereby demand of you an immediate surrender of your command… "

— From Captain Nathaniel Lyon

— To Brigadier General Daniel Frost,

— Commander of Missouri's First Military District

— May 10, 1861

I T MUST BE HAPPENING AS RICHARD SAID IT WOULD, for the following dawn I witness a fair bustle at the Arsenal. On the slice of ground I can view from my bedchamber window many soldiers are afoot, striding about with grave faces and great purpose. And more than what I see is what I hear: the stomping of booted feet, the snorts and whinnies of horses, gigs rolling about, commands shouted across the yard, and unnerving descents into near silence.

I am glad a soldier brings me a meal on a tray, for otherwise I might think I am forgotten in this chamber. Still, he can tell me nothing of my fate. And though I tremble with nerves, I eat. I will need my strength, for what if Lyon does demand the surrender of Camp Jackson? Will they give it, or fight? Or what if the men of Camp Jackson attack this Arsenal first? If any such events transpire—as my eyes, ears, and head on my shoulders tell me they will—it will mean Missouri men fighting Missouri men. It will mean war on our own ground. With me in the melee.

The next time footfalls reach my door, it is Richard who flings it open. "Come," he says, and grabs my hand, asking only after we quit the chamber if I have my belongings and not waiting an answer. "My mount is there," he says when we make the yard, and points somewhere, but he must drag me along for my eyes fasten upon the hundreds of soldiers forming parallel lines. Armed with muskets and bayonets fixed, they fill the cartridge boxes on their waist belts with ammunition. Striding among them, reddish hair wild in the wind and papers stuffed in his pockets, is Captain Lyon. I would think him a wreck, and no leader, if I did not know him better.

When we come to Richard's steed, tied to a post, he hoists me atop then follows himself. "I was given leave to free you," he tells me as the horse spins into motion, "but I cannot spare the time to get you to Poplar Street," and I can do no more than grab onto his waist for Richard is not timid in the pace he sets departing these grounds. And do I understand why he is in a hurry? I believe I do, for holding him so I find that he, too, is armed, with a revolver holstered on his belt.

Oh, it is the same pandemonium outside the Arsenal, for here are more regiments lined up, again hundreds of men, these, too, carrying bayoneted muskets. "They will all march to Camp Jackson?" I call to Richard's back.

"They and more," he shouts. "Units are forming into columns across the city, armed like these and commanded by Union men."

All will see these extraordinary assemblies. And they will hear about them, and prepare for them, at Camp Jackson, six miles from here.

Behind us—we have not got far—bugles blare and drums beat and voices rise in command. Then boots begin to march in rhythm to the drums. Richard swings the horse about and stops: this he wishes to see, and so do I, for whenever has our city witnessed such a demonstration? It is Captain Lyon at the head of the first column, atop a magnificent dapple-gray stallion. And as he rides into battle his buttons are not only properly in place but polished, too. From his waist belt hangs a dragoon's sword and, yes, two revolvers in holsters. I must think they are the same faithful friends I knew yesterday.

I watch Lyon's troops march past. "These regiments will make for thousands of men, won't they?" I ask Richard. "Against the eight hundred camped?"

"Lyon wishes to overwhelm," and again Richard turns the horse about to gallop downhill toward the city. But soon he must slow the steed to a walk, for these streets are as crammed with citizens as those uphill teemed with soldiers. Men, women, children, too: all are out in their numbers, excited and panicked both. Many wish to go to Camp Jackson to witness whatever spectacle will unfold there. Whole families are on the move—as is every sort of conveyance, from drays to barouches to buggies. Men stream uphill, too, bearing pistols and knives and rifles. I get the idea most desire to battle for the rebel side.

Richard has fought through the throng a fair distance when he leads the horse into an alley and brings him to a halt. "I must leave you here," and he dismounts before pulling me down after him. "It will be dangerous today—"

"For you more than me, for I do not intend to plunge into the fray." I point at his revolver. "What will you do?"

"I will join Lyon's men. As a physician."

I scoff at that. "Easy to say until you are shot at."

He bends close. "Lyon believes that Frost"—I know that name: Daniel Frost, the brigadier general who commands the camp—"a West Pointer like him, will see these men and armaments and be wise enough to realize there is no hope for it. If he surrenders promptly, we will not see bloodshed."

"Can there be much chance of that? With passions so high?"

Richard looks away and I can see he shares my doubt. "Frost sent a messenger to Lyon this morning, but the captain refused even to receive him."

"Then how angry must Frost be!"

"Even if he is angry, that does not mean he will be reckless. Not with the lives of eight hundred men."

"But if Lyon sends a note demanding surrender, Frost might refuse to receive it, just as Lyon did. Then what?"

"Then Frost will take up his field glasses and count the artillery pieces our side will have set around his camp. And he will see as well the thousands of Union men with bayonets glinting in the sun."

I can imagine it. "And if Frost chooses to attack the Arsenal?"

"Lyon left a number of companies there, under strong command, and blocked the roads, and put sharpshooters on roofs." His face softens into a smile as he gazes down at me. "You have become quite the military strategist, Eliza."

"It did not take Captain Lyon to make me so," I tell him. Running cathouses is not a military operation, but it makes for a complicated enterprise all the same.

Richard laughs and grabs me in a kiss. "I well know what you are capable of," and though I have not had enough of kissing him back, he releases me and leaps back onto his saddle. He bends low for one last word. "Whatever happens today, Eliza, many will be angered by it. I wish you to be careful."

I tell him I will be and mean it. After his horse bounds from the alley, I step into the fracas of people and conveyances. Have I ever before seen such pandemonium? Well, yes, though never in this city have we been split in two camps as we are now. I do not long for the Great Fire, but I might yearn for those simpler times when we had a single enemy and fought it as one.

"Damn the Dutch!" a man shouts. "Damn the Dutch!" Others take up his cry, women and children, too, and then I see, marching along Tenth Street in the direction of Camp Jackson, a unit of Home Guards. Oh, they will be out in their numbers, and they are mostly German and fierce for the Union side, and I can see from here they are armed. Many in our city will not like that.

"Our glorious lads at Lindell Grove will never surrender!" a woman shrieks. Huzzahs rise from the crowd. I turn to run to my house fast as I am able, for I have much to protect from what may well become rabble by nightfall.

CHARITY IS in the parlor so spies me soon as I push open the front door of my house. "Do not try to tell me you have been ailing"— she rushes to my side—"for I shall never believe it," and despite her stern words grabs me in a ferocious hug. "You are not dead after all," she mumbles into my hair and I pull back.

"You feared I might be?"

"I did not know what to believe! You are always here and suddenly you are not." She releases me but clutches my hands. I realize she is trembling. "Are you ill?" she asks me.

"I am absolutely fine."

"And Richard?"

"He is well, though he rides out with Lyon's men. As a physician."

She lets out a shaky breath. "I am so very glad you are back, Eliza. I have been so worried."

It unnerves me that she feared so for my life, though she was not far wrong. "Well, as you see I am in one piece."

"Such rumors flew in the parlor! That the Union side got you, or maybe the Confederate: no one could be sure." I feel a grim satisfaction at that. "Where have you been?" she demands. "Have you been at the Arsenal?"

"I have—"

"Then you know more than I do what goes on today."

"Well, I can tell you what I have seen." I describe the show Captain Lyon puts on, his columns of well-armed troops marching along our streets, even on Market, our busiest avenue. "There will be fighting at Camp Jackson and maybe at the Arsenal, too, but perhaps that will settle things for now." Hearing that, her dark eyes are frightened as ever. "It's all right, Charity," I tell her, and as I squeeze her hands I wish that it will be. Everything I see and hear makes me believe that this city, this state, is at a precarious pass. "I also fear there will be a melee later, so we must get the houses boarded, and quickly. Now tell me: is all well here?"

I put on a brave smile, but Charity can manage only a weak one. "Well, you will learn you are not the only one who can run a bawdy house, for everything is fine, though we nearly had a murder for I am ready to put a rifle ball through Louisa, with all her airs and pretensions."

I am glad to see a flicker of Charity's usual spirit. "Is Louisa upstairs?" I turn for the staircase. "For I might send her to Green Street—"

"You will not find her there, or anyone for that matter, for everyone but the cook and a housemaid have taken the streetcars to Camp Jackson."

I hope they will be safe there. I will not say so to Charity, frightened already. "Well, that means I must do what I need myself."

"You have me to help. And the groom."

"I must get the other properties boarded," I say, and spin toward the rear door. "I will tell the groom to help you do the same here. I am sure Noah will come soon," I add, though I am not sure, for on a usual Friday already he would be about. And with this rebel mood that grips our city, free Negroes face even greater dangers. Last month Jackson's people took control of our mayor's office and police board and now arrest what Negroes they can, or banish them from the state.

Charity shouts after me. "I will do it, but you have not told me all I wish to know and I will hear it."

"I will tell you all when I am able," I call back, thinking that the day *when I am able* may never come.

————

As I DRIVE my gig pell-mell across the city, I am reminded of the day near seven years past when I rode to the levee thinking I would find a hobbled Bridget and instead came upon my sister Sarah. Oh, the distressing months that followed! But I saved my sister's neck, did I not? And still *I* live and breathe. Would I have believed when I jumped in John's canoe that I would live such a life as I have? Never. Yet years pass, full of more surprises than I could ever fathom, and somehow above them I ride. But I am not so arrogant as to believe it will be ever thus.

A few of my properties are as far north as Green Street so across the city I go. The streets are not busy, for all are drawn to Camp Jackson, but despite that lure not a one of my houses is empty. Yes, many of the doxies are out for the show, but not the well-paid trollops who run these establishments for me. They know not to abandon the property on a day there is bound to be trouble. It takes us hours to put up the boards, but we do it with skill for it is hardly our first time. To be a madam in St. Louis is to be ever prepared for calamity.

It is near the six o'clock hour when finally I climb back into the gig and take up the horse's reins. She whinnies in a way tells me she is eager to go. I know why, for the rising commotion in the streets is no longer distant but close, and much hails from that secesh part of our city around Berthold Mansion and Planters House. I must ride past there to get to Poplar Street.

Is it a triumphant ruckus I hear from that quarter? I perk my ears to listen. Oh, I don't think I imagine it: the shouting makes for a wrathful sound. *Whatever happens today, Eliza, many will be angered by it.* I will keep away from those blocks, and so I do, but still it is not long before a crowd engulfs the gig. The men are red-faced and loud—the smell of liquor cannot be mistaken—and more than one woman is sobbing. With the horse stopped I bend low toward one young woman, dark-haired like me, her features twisted with fury. "What happened?" I ask her.

"Where've you been?" she screeches. "You don't know what that devil Lyon did? He surrounded Camp Jackson illegally, he did, and forced our boys to surrender, and even when they did everything he demanded, his damn Dutch lined them up like cattle then aimed their muskets at the rest of us!"

"The damn Dutch shot our people dead!" a light-haired boy cries.

"People died?" I ask her. "People who were just watching?"

"Women and children!" a man hollers.

"And brave men from the camp, too," the young woman tells me. "With no provocation! Lyon should be strung up for it, you ask me, and if we have to take matters into our own hands to do it, we will," and she spits upon the ground.

My horse creeps forward, eager for her shed as I am for my parlor. I suppose I must believe what I am hearing, though I do not wish to. Why would Lyon's troops fire on citizens? Their fight was with the militia at Camp Jackson.

Far away a shout becomes a chant. "Hurray for Jeff Davis! Hurray for Jeff Davis!" And then another cry rises from the multitude. "Old Pap! Old Pap!" I know that nickname, and who carries it: Sterling Price.

Now there is a tightness in my chest and no denying it. Why do I hear Price's name in the same breath as Davis's, the man who leads the Confederate side? Price has spoken loud against secession. He has not wanted Missouri to join that tribe.

All the same I hear how those around me cry his name: with reverent breath, as if he were their greatest hero. Well, he was, wasn't he, in the Mexican War, even rising to brigadier general. And though Price is a Virginia man, Missouri took him to its heart. He sat in Congress for our state and of course was our governor, too.

I hear one thing and another shouted all around me and make out that Price means to stand outside his hotel—Planters House? —and give a speech. Oh, but he would not speak at *that* place unless—

But that cannot be.

It is an angry mood about me, fiery and wild, as if a thunderstorm has come to ground. My horse and gig are like a length of wood caught in the river's current, dragged where it will go. We head mostly where I wish to, closer to Poplar Street, and I surprise myself when we have the chance to turn away from Planters House, but I do not take it. I let the horse be led along the route she's been moving, for now I desire to see and hear, with my own eyes and ears, what Sterling Price is about.

He *is* there, I can see from where I pull my horse to a stop: he is standing upon the marble steps of Planters House. Of course he is not new to me. He has been in my parlor more times than I can count, and he has lurked, too, in my rear yard with bloodstains on his shirtfront. Still, it is a very different thing to see him thus, erect and proud, a multitude gathered at his feet awaiting his every utterance, hushing themselves so as not to miss a syllable.

I cannot catch all he says, for I am too distant and some of his words are lost in cries and huzzahs, but I hear phrases enough to understand. *Armed body of troops discharging terrible instruments of war... Defenseless spectators... A more reckless act has never been committed... An outrage... An affront to Missouri's sovereign rights...*

I can guess what this means. Price is not with the Union anymore. This still powerful man has gone to the rebel side. Whatever happened today at Camp Jackson has made him throw his allegiance to the Confederacy.

This is not good for the Union side. Though Price is our governor no longer, still he is beloved in this state. I watch him, face red with fury and righteousness, right arm raised in defiance. Even more I watch those around him, their eyes filled with awe, as if he were a god and not a mere politician.

Oh, and who do I spy at the front of the adoring crowd, wearing a gown of purple I know too well, her expression more rapturous than I have ever seen it? Yes, it is a woman in my own house, a trollop in my own employ.

Louisa.

YET THERE IS lightness in my heart hours later, long after darkness has fallen, when banging upon my rear door reveals Richard standing there. Though he is streaked with dirt and blood, he is unhurt and whole. I pull him inside and together we bolt the door against the tumult without.

For it is a full riot, no surprise: people running and screaming, shattering glass, firing guns. We hear many shriek that the Dutch, reeking of sauerkraut, will run rampant in our city, but they are not the ones rampaging now. No, those who take the Southern side are mounting this fracas.

I do not care that my strumpets stand about watching. I grab Richard tight as I can, without speaking. If I knew a word to say, I would say it.

"I am glad you are still in your corset," he murmurs into my hair, "for I fear your heart might escape your chest otherwise."

That he teases me gives me the strength to release him. "Your horse—"

"Is safe in the shed with yours."

"The Arsenal?"

"Is full to bursting with our state militia, now Lyon's prisoners. Those who pledge allegiance to the Union will be freed on the morrow. The captain needs me no more tonight."

If I had my way, I would make it ever so. "Will you eat?"

"Please. And drink, too," he says more loudly, and produces a smile.

"I will pour you whiskey," Charity says, running into the parlor, "so long as you tell us what you know," and so he does, between bites of bread and cold meat, though I can see he is exhausted to his bones.

Much we have already heard, and close it hews to what the dark-haired woman told me. Seeing the force raised against his camp, Brigadier General Frost surrendered instantly, to the groans of his militia. Lyon took possession of the grounds and allowed Frost to march at the head of his men to the Arsenal, between columns of Lyon's troops. The citizenry would not watch this calmly, though: brandishing brickbats, knives, rocks, revolvers, and shotguns, they jeered, shouted, pushed, and surged.

"Shots were fired," Richard tells us, "and no one can say with certainty who discharged their weapon first. Captain Blandowski, commanding one of Lyon's volunteer regiments, early took a pistol ball and I do not believe he will survive it."

"Citizens died, too," Charity murmurs. "Women and children."

There is a ruckus outside, but the parlor is silent. Then: "Near thirty dead," Richard says, and I can guess from the blood on his shirtfront and clouds in his eyes that some he tended. "A few of Lyon's men shot into the crowd. They would have been better to fire into the air, yes, but they feared for their lives, and reasonably so. It is a most lamentable thing," and I see that Richard can barely summon the strength to speak.

"Come upstairs." I rise and take his hand. He needs no further urging. I reassure my trollops that all will be well, though I myself am not persuaded. It sounds as if it is a battlefield outside those boarded windows. When will it end? What will we see in the morning light?

Louisa has not returned, though I do not concern myself much with her. She is one to rise above the fray. She might well be safe at Planters House, guarded by a battalion of Price's own men.

I help Richard wash. Soon he sinks down among the bedclothes. "Now that Lyon claims Camp Jackson," I say, "does he know what was unloaded there from the *J.C. Swon*?"

Richard rises onto an elbow for a moment more. "More armaments than I can name, Eliza, and of a certainty from the federal arsenal at Baton Rouge. Mortar bombs, shells, canister shot, cannon—"

"So Lyon was right. And this was a victory for him." I say it and ask it both.

On the bed, Richard nods. "A victory, but a costly one. And now we have lost Price to the rebel side. I shudder to think what that will mean."

Chapter Thirty-Four

"Everything was changed. There was no life on the river; the many steamboats were laid up at their wharves, their fires out, the singing, cheery crews gone—they, empty, swaying idly with the current. As we drove through the deserted streets we saw only closed shutters to warehouses and business places; the wheels and the horses' hoofs echoed loud and harsh as when one drives through the silent streets late at night.

"It was a hostile city and showed itself as such."

— Jesse Benton Frémont

— *Souvenirs of My Time*, 1887

— Describing St. Louis in the summer of 1861

I AM SOAKING IN MY TUB, IN WATER BLISSFUL COOL TO COMBAT THE AFTERNOON'S HEAT, when Charity flies into my bedchamber brandishing a newspaper. "They say it is a rout," she cries, "at the battle near that Virginia river called Bull Run."

"The rebels deserve to be—"

"No! *We* are the ones routed." She flutters the newspaper before my eyes to show me it is the *Republican*. " 'Total rout of federal army,' " she reads. " 'Six batteries lost by federals. The carnage was tremendously heavy on both sides and on ours represented as frightful.' "

"How can that be?" I spring from the tub and wrap myself in a towel. The time for lollygagging is over. The only thing certain during these sorry days is that all pleasure is fleeting—battlefield triumphs and cool baths. "The last I heard we had a victory."

She holds up the newspaper to read more. " 'A series of events took place in the intensest degree disastrous. We were advancing and taking their masked batteries gradually but surely, and driving the enemy towards Manassas Junction, when they seemed to have been reinforced.' "

That evening in the parlor I sit with Robert Marcellus Stewart, our former governor. "It is a most alarming setback," he tells me while around us arguments fly. Should Lincoln replace the general commanding the Potomac area, and if so who should be the new man be? "Now it is the Confederate side that is heartened," Stewart murmurs. "Now *they* think they might quickly end the war."

"Tell me what goes on in our state capital," for I am sure this man still has spies in Jefferson City. "I know the state convention declared itself our new government and took away all Jackson's powers." I do not know if such a thing is full legal, but in wartime I suppose no one worries overmuch about that.

Stewart allows himself a satisfied smile. "Lyon has done an excellent job of slapping down our rebel governor."

"Brigadier General Lyon now." Lyon earned that rank after Camp Jackson then proved he deserved it by making sure the Union took control of our capital city. Then he drove our secesh state guard—now headed by Sterling Price—from the town of Boonville. To this day they hunker in the southwest corner of our state, chastened. Still, Price desires to swing Missouri to the Confederates and will soon scheme some cunning maneuver or other. If only Price were still on the Union side!

"Jackson and Price still wield far too much power," Stewart mutters. "This drubbing of Union forces at Bull Run is whipping the rebel side into a frenzy. Price is wise to bide his time at Cowskin Prairie. The men on those farms are leaping to join his militia as fast as they are able."

I understand those men because I suspect my father and brother are very like them. I keep my voice low as Stewart's. "They wish to kill themselves some Yankees while they still can."

MORE THAN A FEW days pass that I do not see Richard. Often as not when that happens, he is telling me without telling me that he plans to leave soon for some godforsaken outpost. Finally, on a sunshiny Thursday forenoon, he appears in my foyer. One who does not know him well as I do might not notice the stiffness of his smile or that his eyes dart from my gaze. I do not need another clue to know he will journey somewhere, but he gives it to me all the same by suggesting we make a picnic at Lafayette Park.

"You cannot refuse me," he says, "for already I have a full hamper in my gig."

I have no intention of refusing him but protest all the same, as I am grumpy knowing I will not like what he has to tell me. Is there not need enough for physicians right here in St. Louis? "Does it make sense to picnic there?" I ask him. "I believe new-formed regiments are camping all about." Of course there must be troops somewhere. The Arsenal is much quieter now Lyon and his regiments are gone to Springfield, about a hundred miles from Price's militia.

"There are encampments at Lafayette Park," Richard tells me, "but they are federal troops so we will not mind them. Nor they us."

I wager he is right and soon have my bonnet and parasol in hand. "Where will you be journeying, then?" I ask when we have scarce ridden even a few blocks.

"How do you know I'm going anywhere?" He throws me a sidelong look of surprise. "Can I hide nothing from you, Eliza? Not that I wish to. Anyway, let us discuss it after we enjoy our picnic," and I do not object as I like that he used the word *discuss*. Perhaps this will be one of those rare times I can change his mind.

Lafayette Park is not as it was years ago, for now stone mansions of the most impressive sort rise on its surrounding blocks. Might I buy a plot and build one for myself? I suppose. But this is no place for a cathouse: it is too far from the city center. And yes, there are troops camping, so many that I wonder we will find unoccupied greensward on which to sit. A trio of young soldiers halts our progress, but after they inspect our gig and hamper and hear Richard reverently speak the name of Brigadier General Nathaniel Lyon, they are welcome itself.

"Have you seen him?" the youngest wants to know. He is wide eyed with hair the color of corn silk.

"We have *both* seen and met him," Richard says, and now they regard me, too, with obvious fascination.

"I cannot wait to fight for him," another pipes up to say, but the blond soldier speaks over him.

"My eyes would pop out of my head if *I* ever saw him. They are sore already from the sights in this city," and we are waved along to picnic wherever we wish.

"You remember our first picnic?" Richard asks once we have settled on a shaded spot and laid upon a white blanket our croquettes and cucumbers, cherries and lemonade.

"It is where you first kissed me. It took you an age to get to it."

"I have made up for it since, most ably." He smiles my favorite smile, slow and lazy as if he has all the time in the world. "As I recall, you were trying to teach me to say the word *aiguille*."

I must laugh, for now he is speaking in his funny Frenchy way. "You still cannot say it correctly."

"I am not trying to say it correctly. I am trying to say it in a way that will make you laugh. I am doing *that* most ably, too."

"You made me laugh back then by saying all the names of Lafayette."

"Ah, yes. Let me see if I can summon them again to mind." He pauses, then: "Marie Joseph Paul Yves Roche Gilbert du Motier, Marquis de Lafayette."

I do not know if that is correct, but it hardly matters for I am bursting again with laughter.

"There is another French name we will all have to learn now," he tells me, "but it will not be nearly so interesting. John Charles Frémont." Richard speaks the name in his Frenchy way, but his face has gone somber.

"He has already arrived. You don't like him?" Lincoln has put this Frémont in St. Louis to command the so-called Western Department, setting him above Lyon, which I will say does surprise me.

"Better to say Frémont *finally* arrived. He dillydallied to get here." I watch Richard chew on a piece of grass. "Bernard doesn't like him. He believes Frémont is jealous of the attention paid to Lyon."

The *Whirlwind in Pantaloons*, some call him. And the Home Guards so many here despise are called *Lyon's Flying Dutchmen* elsewhere. At least so Mr. Stewart tells me he reads in newspapers from New York. "Well," I say, "this Frémont must have been a hero somewhere or Lincoln would not have put him in the position."

"He was. And I suppose he will redeem himself in my opinion if he gets Lyon the men and provisions he needs."

"I don't think we need worry overmuch about Lyon."

"Lyon may be a military genius, Eliza, but no general can battle without soldiers and materiel. I am told his troops are short of such necessities as shoes."

I straighten hearing this. "How is that possible?"

"Too easily," and Richard explains that Lyon chased Price's regiments to the southwestern part of our state expecting to find more provisions in Springfield than he did, which left him and his tired, hungry men severely disappointed. Worse, Lyon has thousands fewer troops than Price, who musters more each day. "Remember," Richard says, "that Lincoln's proclamation in the spring called for Union men to enlist for ninety days only. Soon their releases will begin, unless they reenlist."

"And what man will wish to do that if his belly is empty and his feet unshod?"

"And his pocket empty of coins, too, for the troops have not yet been paid." Richard is silent, then: "I am sure those men lack medicine as well, Eliza. That is why I must go there."

"Go where Lyon is?" In my shock I come close to tumbling my lemonade. Somewhere on the frontier: yes, that I expected, not for Richard to join again with Union troops. "Why would you do that?"

"I would go with Bernard, in a group of men, some others physicians like me." He speaks slowly as if I will not understand otherwise. "Bernard has been waiting for the opportunity to speak to Frémont, to plead for all Lyon needs. That chance may come today. Then he will be ready to depart."

"Well, Bernard is Lyon's aide-de-camp. He must go where Lyon is. But for you it is different."

"I am not obliged the same way as Bernard, no, but Eliza, you understand my duty to the Union side. Surely those troops need medical help."

"All the same, I do not like it. You propose to go to a place where any moment a battle might break out."

"You worried the same thing when I was at the Arsenal. Believe me, no battle is imminent. Lyon will not fight if he is ill supplied. And Price may have troops in good numbers, but he knows they are green and lack order. The two sides will be at a deadlock for some time."

How often will Richard and I quarrel thus before this war is over? "Have I any chance of persuading you not to do this thing?"

He smiles his slow smile. "Perhaps I should say yes, for then you might try."

"You are a scamp," I tell him, but that does not land a man in my bad books. "Well, I suppose you will not be gone long and Springfield is not so far."

"It will be a slow journey if we take a wagon train loaded with supplies. And so I very much hope." He reaches across the blanket that separates us and tilts my face toward the sun. I will say I do not mind his inspection and smile at him throughout. "Every day I am there, Eliza, I will long to come back to you."

"Then be quick about it. And let us hope that John Charles Frémont"—now I am speaking in the funny Frenchy way—"fills fifty wagons to supply Lyon's regiments so you need go only once and be done with it."

IT IS the day after Richard's departure when I enter my favorite milliner's—for even in wartime a doxy must have bonnets to protect her face from the sun—and who do I encounter inside the shop but Louisa. She turns her head at the tinkle of the bell and, bold as she is, meets my eyes with a steady gaze.

I walk toward her and eye the bonnet of blue crepe in her hands. The few other women in the shop look away and pretend they are not in the company of strumpets. "Should you not be searching for a bonnet in gray?" I ask in a low tone. "Madam Lantos might throw you out onto her stoop if you return to her house with one in blue."

"Do not take it as a sign that I care to return to *your* house, Eliza."

So the hussy will speak my first name now I am no longer her madam. "Just as well, for I do not have bedchambers for trollops who quit my employ with scarce a moment's notice. Beside, I know you are more at your ease under *her* roof."

"As is"—she lowers her voice—"the man who used to be your most important client. Brigadier General Price."

Indeed I have not seen Price in my parlor for two months, since he switched his loyalty to the rebel side. Still, I will not let Louisa pretend she is enjoying his company and his coins. "No doubt he *would* be at his ease at Madam Lantos's, *if* he were anywhere near this city."

Louisa looks away. "Well, I suppose we have all had to choose our side."

I doubt that Louisa or Madam Lantos would make their choice so plain if they had a say in the matter. Long ago as '44, Madam Lantos told me I must not speak on the slavery topic with clients. Yet with Mr. Skillern from Virginia her house's owner, it is not up to Madam Lantos what goes on. So her doxies will sit in bright sunshine on her stoop doing needlework on uniforms of gray.

"I have long known," Louisa says, "what your side is."

"Like Governor Stewart, I prefer to stand on neutral ground."

Louisa scoffs. "Pretend all you will, Eliza. But I know how distraught you will be when General Price carries the state of Missouri to the Confederate side," and off she flounces, the blue bonnet abandoned on the counter.

IT HAS BEEN years since I visited Daniel's office on Chestnut Street, but a week later I have an excuse to do it. I tell myself that is why I mount the stairs to his second-story establishment and not that I miss his company.

He leaps from behind a desk piled with papers and pecks me on the cheek as if I were his maiden aunt. Oh, I must smile when I recall what we used to do. "To what," he says, "do I owe the pleasure? Is there a property you have in mind?"

"There is no chance of that." I seat myself near an open window but blessedly in shade. "I prefer my money in property than in bank accounts, Daniel, but these times are too uncertain."

"Not too uncertain for *you* to earn money, I hope."

"Oh no, my houses thrive." It is wartime and the blood of men is fired. I have soldiers aplenty at my cheaper houses and gentlemen mobbing my Poplar Street compound. Rich old men may speak of battling, but they do not decamp to join regiments. "I have come to ask if you hear what I do: that tenants are saying they do not have money to pay their rents."

Returned to his chair, Daniel sighs. "I hear it every day. And of course we should expect it, as commerce with the South goes to naught. You could gallop your horse up and down the levee as if it were an open track."

I have heard it discussed in my parlor. Steamboats plying the rivers must be plated with iron to protect them from pistol balls fired from the banks.

Daniel frowns. "Tell me about the property you bought from Mr. Schuabel. Do you not have a tenant there?" and we pass pleasurable time chatting of Daniel's properties and mine.

"How is Alice?" I ask when that is done, and though he is careful to look away, still I catch the light in his blue eyes, of happiness and satisfaction.

"She shows her spine," he tells me. "Before Camp Jackson, I considered sending her and the children to the country, with my parents. But she wouldn't go. She would rather stay here, despite the danger."

"To be with you."

He accepts that with a nod. "Now, of course, they're safer here. You have heard how in the countryside ruffians are attacking farmers pell-mell?"

"And many people are just giving up their land, to go back south or flee west." Property prices must be falling fast as a brick from a window. "I worry about my family, especially when weeks pass and I receive no letter."

"Don't worry too much, Eliza. Things as they are, the mail routes are disrupted. And of course as Price and his men went west, they cut as many telegraph lines as they could."

I throw up my hands. "Does Price think of everything?"

"He thinks of too much for my comfort." I note a new keenness in Daniel's eyes. "How is Richard?" he asks.

"Gone to Springfield with Bernard Farrar and others, though they didn't get near the provisions they wanted from Frémont." I'm square in Bernard's camp now, displeased with that man who replaced Lyon.

"Richard is there now?"

"I don't know where he is." If he sent me a letter, it went the way of Visa Ann's.

Daniel gazes out the window then turns to give me a smile. "Of course there's no need to worry about a man as capable as Richard."

"You amaze me, Daniel." I lay my hand theatrically on my chest. "I don't think I've ever heard you pay Richard a compliment before."

"He stole your heart, Eliza. That alone makes him a remarkable man."

———

OF AN EVENING in the first week of August, Mr. Stewart and I sit before the hearth in my chamber sipping wine and enjoying the breeze through open windows. "There are," he says, "fearsome developments."

I suppose I must hear. "Such as?"

"Troops from both Arkansas and Tennessee"—that is become a secesh state, too, along with North Carolina—"have come onto our Missouri soil in the southwest where Sterling Price is. And many are trained men, Eliza: Army troops that defected to the Confederacy."

So now our side has trained them, they turn tail to fight for our foe. "I know they plot to take over our state from there. But Lyon intends to fend them off."

"Exactly so. Yet that is more difficult if Price draws up offensive orders that Jackson solicits rebel states to help mount."

"Well, does not Lyon get help from other Union states?"

"He does not even get help from Frémont."

My heart is cold as stone as I hear this. "What is wrong with Frémont?"

"I cannot tell you. He seems to hide in that mansion of his and consult only his wife and an advisor or two." It is the Brant residence Frémont rents, I well know, one of the finest houses in our city, made of marble and claiming the whole of a city block. "Rumor has it he paid six thousand dollars to rent it for one year and has three hundred guards. I do not know how many missives and messengers Lyon sent him, but I hear many cannot even get past the sentries. And I believe it because I could not myself. Apparently Frémont did promise help to one or two but then failed to deliver it."

"Lyon is not one to sit and wait for help." My heart thuds in my chest, stone against bone.

Stewart says nothing to that, for we all know it.

It is dreadful, what I hear in the week that follows, and from men who would know, men who were with Lyon but counted out their ninety days then made their way back home to our city. One afternoon there is a ruckus at a tavern I often pass and I linger outside the flung-open doors to listen to war talk flow out like the contents of chamber pots. *We knew Price's men were on the march... More rebs than you could count... Lyon saw it plain, and me, too: the rebs were readying an attack... I got out in time and who wouldn't?*

I know who wouldn't.

LYON IS DEAD.

It is a Tuesday when I hear it, an afternoon so hot it is as if Satan propped open the doors of hell to let out the air. The news fills our sweltering city.

It was the Battle of Wilson's Creek that got him, called the Battle of Oak Hills by the secesh side. It was long in coming, Price's men facing Lyon's. And when it was over, what general lived to seize the battlefield? Sterling Price.

After hours of fighting, ever among his troops, Lyon was sitting upon his horse and took a pistol ball in the heart. There is a story—I don't know that I believe it—that as a soldier caught him while he fell, he muttered: "I am killed."

Lyon is dead. I walk the hell-hot streets where the red brick bakes under the sun and struggle to believe it. I picture Lyon marching into St. Louis at the head of his regiments. I picture him in my parlor eyeing Louisa. I picture him in the small chamber at the Arsenal listening to my scheme to tour Camp Jackson, squinting at me with eyes that say he will doubt every word until he himself can prove it true. And I picture him outside the Blair barouche when our masquerade is done, handing me down. I feel the rough skin of his warrior's hand. *Excellent*, he says before he strides away. Even now I hear his voice.

Lyon is dead, but the men who lived are streaming back. Wounded, many are, put in wagons at the battle site then in trains to return here. There are so many, people say, they will fill our hospitals to bursting.

I rush toward Poplar Street, errands undone. Sweat leaves trails down my back and legs. I stop to dab at my face with a handkerchief for I do not wish Richard to see me so, not after these long weeks. If Lyon is lost and men are coming back to our city, he will be among them. He will come back fast as he is able.

But it is not Richard at my house when I return. It is Bernard, and I will say I am startled to see him. He is in my parlor, wearing the Union's navy, his back to me as he looks out the open windows. I do not think I imagine it: he is slow to turn and face me. When he does and his dark gaze settles upon mine, I realize how hushed is this house. Even Poplar Street is quiet. Only a dog runs by, craning toward the sky as if chasing birds it cannot hope to catch. In the kitchen, pots clatter, and upstairs someone walks along the corridor, but inside this parlor where I have passed many a raucous night, it is silent.

Bernard clears his throat. "Eliza."

"You are back. You look well," I tell him, though to my eyes he looks tired. Still, though I am glad of his return, something stops me from moving forward to take his hands. "Richard is upstairs?"

Slowly he shakes his head. "He is not upstairs."

"Did he come back with you?" *Tell me he did. He is simply occupied with some piece of business he will soon finish and that is why it is you here and not him.*

He hesitates, then: "Richard is not with me."

That is not what I wish to hear. Bernard's voice is hoarse. Is it because he is so tired?

Again he clears his throat. "Eliza—"

"Do not speak a word more."

Bernard steps forward. It is he who takes my hands. In one I still clutch my sodden handkerchief, wadded hard as a pistol ball. Bernard seems not to mind. I stare down at our clasped hands. I would look down and not into Bernard's eyes for I do not care to see what lurks there. Once I see, all will be changed. All will be changed. He waits for me to speak and finally I do. "What has happened?"

"There was a battle at a place called Wilson's Creek."

"I have heard about it."

"You heard Lyon was lost."

I keep my eyes lowered. I nod. It is just an hour ago I heard the news, but it is almost as if I do not care about Lyon anymore.

"The fighting was fierce, Eliza."

"Richard was not supposed to fight. He was there as a physician, to give medicine and tend to the wounded."

"Yes. And he did so, most ably."

I see Richard with me at Lafayette Park. *It is where you first kissed me*, I said. *It took you an age to get to it*. He smiles his slow and lazy smile, my favorite, as if he has all the time in the world. *I have made up for it since, most ably.*

"No man could stay apart from that fighting, Eliza," Bernard murmurs. "It was"—he cannot seem to find the words to speak of it—"a hideous thing. Some now call that place Bloody Hill."

I think to myself that I will not look into Bernard's eyes at the very moment that I know I will. Finally I find it within myself to raise my head to meet his dark gaze. Not amber. Never again will I see amber.

"Eliza," Bernard says, "I am so very sorry."

"You are telling me—"

"I am so very sorry, Eliza. Richard was killed."

I nod. Richard is gone from me, gone from this earth. All, all is changed.

Bernard speaks again and I struggle to listen. "Lyon believed he would stun Price if he attacked by surprise, as both knew he was severely outmanned. Our men were well fired to fight, as finally we did get a caravan of food and supplies. But I will tell you, Eliza, before we marched"—Bernard shakes his head—"Lyon told me he had a presentiment that he would not survive the day. Still, he went ahead."

Of course he did. Going ahead is in his bones. Still, I wonder if Lyon erred this time. If he did, he paid the highest price, and made Richard pay it, too.

"It went well in the beginning," Bernard murmurs, "but in the end it did not. In the end they had three men for every one of ours. Many were killed and many wounded, near the same on both sides."

And one was Richard. "Where is he now?" I ask, and Bernard assures me that he is brought back to St. Louis and somehow Bernard will get word to his parents and I need not worry myself about any of that.

So his father who so angered Richard will tend to him now.

Those parents, I am sure, know nothing of me, know nothing of Richard's true life. I suppose he will go to New York to be buried in that ground, in a place he did not love and that I will never see.

From upstairs I hear a rap on a door, then a door opening and female voices. Then laughter. I would be angry at that laughter if I could feel a thing at all. I feel as if I were like the gas lamp on the table beside me, empty and cold to the touch.

I squeeze Bernard's hands. "You are very kind, Bernard, to come and tell me. You are kind as your father." I might never have known Richard if not for Bernard's father. Now it is his son come to tell me this. The circle is full drawn.

"I will never know another like Richard," Bernard says, but I can no longer listen, and wonder how I will make myself do so in the endless days and nights that loom before me.

IT IS NOT Richard our city mourns, but Lyon. For Lyon, flags are lowered to half-mast; for Lyon, crepe of black is strewn across public buildings and homes and shops. Not across all, of course, because for many Lyon's slaughter is a victory they fête on the sly with toasts and quiet cheers.

In my parlor, where I sit of an evening pretending I am same as I ever was, I am told that Frémont takes no responsibility for the Union defeat on that hill, never mind he ignored Lyon's pleas for troops and provisions. I think to myself that Frémont makes very clear the kind of man he is. Why cannot all see it? Why cannot Lincoln, even Richard's Lincoln, see it?

Daniel tries to comfort me, and Charity, too, and maybe if my heart were not turned to stone they could help me. As it is, I watch them try and thank them for it then move away from their pitying eyes. If I could feel better for them, I would do it.

It is a week or so later, on a sun-filled forenoon that taunts me with its brightness, that I am walking empty through the streets—a vessel of a woman; I am sure all can see right through me—and I realize Richard must be gone from this city. So many days have passed: surely his coffin has been taken to New York? And though it matters not where he falls to dust—who could care if it is here or there?—I am stabbed by the agony of it and must turn my face into a wall of red brick to hide the tears that would not come before and now will not stop.

I am thinking I have nothing of him—not a button, not a shoe, not a shirt; well, I suppose I do have his battered gig, and, yes, the toy carriage he gave me near the time we met—when I remember I do have one important thing. I run back to Poplar Street. There it is, in my armoire, tucked behind gowns I will never again wear for him: the portrait he wished painted of me.

On the day Richard told me he wanted such a silly thing we frolicked in the snow. What did he say while he held himself above me, both toppled in the drifts? *So I may forever remember how beautiful you are in this moment.*

I gaze at the portrait. I am solemn in it, for that is the way of portraits, and there is sadness in my eyes, for I suppose there was, even then; but how much the painter would have to lie now to put any light in them.

Richard made such a fuss bringing this oil from his boarding-house. I must hang it somewhere. It is part of him, somehow, is it not? His eyes looked upon it every day. From now on, yes, mine will do the same. I do not know what is the proper place for it, but as I tote it to a different wall I see there is something tucked in the frame behind.

An envelope made of fine thick paper. With one word written on the front.

I can guess what that word must be. Have I not seen it every time I put my X to a deed? *Eliza*—her mark—*Haycraft*. Eliza.

Charity is where I wish her to be: in her bedchamber. I hand her the envelope and she raises astonished eyes to mine. "Is it from—?"

"Is that my name on the front?"

She nods.

"It must be from him," I say. "It was crammed in the frame of the portrait." I remember then the night I woke to find Richard crouched beside my bed and the doors of my armoire ajar. All is fine, he told me. "Please read it to me," I tell Charity, and she pulls a single sheet from the envelope, unfolds it, and reads.

My dearest Eliza,

There is a word we do not speak, you and I, a word you may mock and may not even believe in, but I have come to believe in it because of you.

You made me a happy man, Eliza, and I tell myself I have given you some of that same gift. Every day with you was a joy, every day away a torment.

I will think of you in my last moments, my beautiful Eliza, and wish you happiness for the rest of your days. I am not a man who can say he believes he will see you again, but oh! if I do, I will shout for the wonder of it.

My heart you stole the very day I met you. Please keep it safe and hold it fast, for it is forever yours. My heart, my love, Eliza.

Richard

Chapter Thirty-Five

"Mr. Lincoln's highest aim was to save his deeply-wronged country, and upon the altar of his country he was ready to risk all, and for his untiring patriotism he lost his life...

"Mr. Lincoln now sleeps the sleep that knows no awaking, but though his body lays cold in death, and his soul with its Giver, his noble deeds of patriotism, of virtue, of generosity, and of humanity will live in the hearts of the American people for ages to come."

— *The Weekly Perryville Union*

— April 28, 1865

"YOUR DAY WOULD BE SHORTER," I tell Noah as he brings the gig to a halt, "if you did not waste your time bringing me here. You well know I can drive on my own."

He cocks his chin at the gates of the cemetery. "Do you want to walk the rest of the way or will you let me ride you in?"

"This time is the same as every other, Noah," which means I would be alone. "Do not worry about me," I tell him as I step down from the gig.

He says nothing, and away I walk knowing he will worry, and however long it takes me to return I will find him waiting.

I have lost so many dear to me, but I have not lost Noah, not after all these years, not with us both gray of hair, our faces lined, and so fitting in with most all the rest, for who did not age during this war? It is finally over, people say, though I dare not believe it. Are not the rebels trying to make Negroes fight for them now, desperate to find men to thrust into battle?

I could get up a head of steam about it if I could about anything. Instead I will walk through the gates of Bellefontaine Cemetery and listen to my boots crunch on the pebbled walkways and enjoy the canopy of trees above my head and allow spring's green stillness, broken time to time with birdsong, to calm me.

I have come here so often that even if it were full dark I could find the spot where Dr. Farrar is buried. If I were in New York I would go where Richard lies, but alas I visit this place where first I saw Richard and he me. I have tried to recall the location on the road where we spoke, but there is no hope for that and I have too much pride to ask Charity to aid that pitiful quest.

I begin as I always do, by paying respects to the excellent doctor. This time I will be glad to tell him that his namesake son fares extremely well. Bernard served the Union so ably they made of him a brigadier general. I hear that another of that rank, Sterling Price, has removed to Mexico, trying to settle a Confederate colony there. That is fine with me, for if ever I saw his face again I would spit at it. The same I would do to Frémont, too late removed from his post by Lincoln.

I walk to the tree that shaded me that July day I met Richard. Sixteen years later, how tall and leafy it is… I sit, lean against its timeless heft, and shut my eyes. I call Richard to mind.

There are those amber eyes. There is that slow smile. I hear his laugh. I feel his touch. I hear him speak my name. *Eliza.*

Richard. What have I to tell you this time? Ah, yes. There is much news. Finally they found Lincoln's assassin and killed him. You will be glad of that. But on the Mississippi a hideous accident happened. A steamboat called Sultana *exploded. It was carrying north freed Union prisoners. They say over a thousand perished. The pilot had far too many aboard and steamed ahead despite a leaking boiler.*

That man in charge made grievous errors, just as Lyon did, though time and again Mr. Stewart tells me it is not so clear in Lyon's case. Perhaps one day I will believe him. I have come to understand that after the battle at Wilson's Creek, Price's side was too battered to pursue the Union men in retreat. His rebels lacked the strength to take the whole of the state. Missouri stayed with the Union and people say that kept Kentucky, too. I know what Mr. Stewart is telling me, though he must grow weary making the point: that Lyon did not die in vain; that Richard did not die in vain. Will I let myself believe it? Soon I may. I am getting old and long for that comfort.

There is another sorrow, too: my father is dead. It was not war that took him but a sudden ailment. Never did I see him again, for he would not have it. Him, too, I conjure in my mind, but too often when I do he is unsmiling.

Oh, these pains no longer wrack me as they once did, but still the colors of my life are faded, like fabric too long in the sun.

I sit a while in the shade of the tree, my old friend, before I force myself to rise. I must return to Noah and then to Poplar Street. Tonight is like every other and I have work to do.

———

HOW MUCH LESS WOULD I know of the world if I did not sit in this parlor and listen to gentlemen speak? Oh, the stories I have heard! —from men who move freely about merchant houses and court-houses and state houses. Now I hear murmurings among a trio that intrigue me very much. If I am not mistaken, I hear whispered the name *Chouteau. Charles Pierre Chouteau.*

I shush Daniel, sitting beside me, and perk my ears.

"They say," one man mutters, "old Cadet will not last the year." That is the nickname for the father of the Chouteau I despise. "Six long years he is gone blind," the man adds. "That would be the only thing to keep him from counting his money."

"So Charles Pierre will soon get the pile of it," another man murmurs. "I hear he is nearly done with selling the family fur trade."

"That is not all," the third whispers. "The mansion, too, he intends to put on the block." The others arch their brows in surprise. "Yes," he confirms, "the property on St. Charles Street."

I turn to Daniel. There are times I wish I were blond like he is, for then my gray might be hidden. "Why," I ask quietly, "would Chouteau sell his mansion?"

He eyes me with interest, long enough that I remember his watchfulness those years ago in Planters House when he was the one to tell me Chouteau was betrothed. "Perhaps he desires a still larger place. Do you ask because you yourself would care to purchase the mansion?"

"Oh, I'm sure not," though even as I speak the words I know they are false.

In a day or two I visit Daniel in his office, taking joy in the bustle of the city that has nothing to do with the business of war. It is simply, as Obadiah would say, commerce. "Do you know if it is indeed the case?" I ask Daniel when I am settled before his desk. "Is Chouteau selling his mansion?"

"Well, well, well." Daniel smiles. "I begin to think I might soon earn an enviable commission."

So the rumor *is* to be believed. "Do you know the price Chouteau seeks?"

"I do not but expect it will be upward of twenty thousand."

I am near breathless hearing that. Have I ever paid so much? "I doubt there will be many bidders at that price."

"And none"—again Daniel smiles—"quite like you. Tell me: what is it about the place you admire?"

I look down at my lap and run my hands over my skirts, though there are no creases to be seen. "Well, it is very attractive, is it not? Quite large, built of brick"—that is hardly a recommendation in this city; near everything is built of brick—"and nicely situated, too, don't you think?"

"It is many blocks north of Poplar Street. Perhaps you have a hankering to return to that side of the city?" He asks as if he does not believe that possible. "Or perhaps this should remind me of your first purchase of property? When part of the allure was the boldness of the scheme?"

I raise my head to meet Daniel's gaze. "I do like that one such as me can afford to buy the property from one such as him." Oh, the shock in this metropolis that would follow such a purchase! For once it would be a bawd triumphant.

"You know," Daniel says, "Chouteau does have his good points."

"If so, they are few in number."

He chuckles. "Well, he did help found our Academy of Science. And people say he is quite the steamboat pilot."

To my mind come words Obadiah once spoke. *I don't know Chouteau to be a liar, but if you're rich as he is, few would say it if he were.* I like to think it might be the same with his piloting: praiseworthy because he is Chouteau.

"Given your low opinion of him," Daniel is saying, "you will enjoy this story I heard. I'm told he was aboard the steamboat *Yellowstone*—perhaps he was piloting—at the time news came that Lincoln was assassinated. It seems Union forces in the area got wind that jubilating broke out on board the steamer."

"Well, Chouteau might have made a show of doing a thing or two for the Union side, but who would believe his heart lay there?"

"Not one particular colonel, who apparently fixed his eye on the Creole and threatened to toss him on the riverbank and shoot him like a dog. I'm told Chouteau was petrified."

I should have liked to see that. "Why do you think Chouteau would sell in quick order the fur trade and this property?"

"The fur trade he should have sold years ago, for it has long been in decline. And though it would please me to say he needs the money, I cannot. It is said his father soon will depart this life and you know what that will mean."

"That the younger Chouteau will grow richer still, for he is the only son to survive. You know he has lost two of his own sons," I add, "and a daughter, too."

"That is a great deal to bear." Daniel says it with solemnity and I must agree. "Still," he goes on, "is that all there is to the matter? It is only that Eliza Haycraft wishes to show she is as formidable a citizen as any other in this city?"

"That is all I have to *say* on the matter, Daniel." I rise and give him a smile. "Perhaps I will say more when you secure for me the property."

CHARITY KNOWS me well as Daniel—probably better—so it should not surprise me she says what she does when we finish our business at that excellent tailor on Olive Street, G. W. Alexander.

She gives me a sideways glance as she returns to her slim hands her short white kid gloves, ornamented with tasseled silk cords. "There is a secret reason," she says, "that you wish both of us to purchase new gowns, for I do not believe it is merely to celebrate that the war is done."

"That is not reason enough?"

"There is another."

She will be stubborn about it. And, really, I only borrow trouble if I delay telling Charity important things. "You are right. There is a particular reason why I wished us to come to this shop. Reasons," I add, "and they are outside."

She smiles, for now I have put a mystery before her and few things entrance Charity more. One would be a wealthy, attractive, unwed William, but after all these years, after so many men, such a one still eludes her.

We step outside to stand on Olive Street and I urge her to join me in turning about to survey the storefront. "What do you think of the pair of lions?" I ask her. For two made of cast iron, posed as if crouching, guard the shop's entry.

"They are exceedingly large."

"Life size, or so Mr. Alexander tells me. And he will allow me to purchase them"—her eyes grow wide—"so that I may set them beside the entry stairs of what I hope will be my new property on St. Charles Street."

"You wish to make another purchase? Where on St. Charles?"

"Between Fifth and Sixth. Number five hundred twelve," though really there is no need for a number as the property claims the whole of the block.

I watch her mind work. Then: "But Eliza, is that not where Chouteau lives?"

"It is the very place."

"Do you mean to make it a cathouse?" There is shock in her tone.

"I mean to live there, and no, not as a bawdy house." Imagine that: Eliza Haycraft living in a house that is a residence only. And not a house: a mansion. "And should you desire to live there with me, Charity, I would like that very, very much."

She is shaking her head: maybe that prospect does not please her. "But will Chouteau sell to you? He might think it an insult to him, and to his family, to have one such as you, such as me, take over his home."

"Daniel and I have discussed the very thing." I take Charity's arm to leave the lions behind us and continue downhill toward the river. "Daniel proposes that he not say until the last moment that I am the party of the second part, so called. And that I not go to the deeds office to set down my mark."

"It would still be full legal?"

"He says it would be, so long as the language on the deed is correct, Chouteau receives and acknowledges the money agreed upon, and he signs the deed."

She is silent for some time, as this is a great deal to ponder. Then her mind moves where I would expect. "And what of Poplar Street?"

"It will go on as it ever has." I am not one to sell a property unless I must. And where would I put the money from one property but into another? I do not full trust banks. I have heard reports that the men of banking got into mischief during the war giving money to the secesh side—our scoundrel Governor Jackson might even have planned the scheme—so I have not changed my view.

I realize Charity has not said she wishes to accompany me to St. Charles Street. "Should you desire to stay on Poplar," I tell her, "of course you may have my bedchamber. If you would like it."

Perhaps this will cheer her as she nears her fortieth year? And indeed her eyes do light, before they darken again. "But if I don't go with you, you will be lonely by yourself in that great mansion."

Oh, I will not tell her I am ever lonely, for I do not wish to sadden her. And really, that is not the full truth of it. Always, always some part of me has stood apart, even from those dearest to me. Well, I do wonder if I sheltered any part of me from Richard. If I did not, I do not wish to think on it, for that will mean even more that I have lost.

I squeeze Charity's arm. "I will be fine. After all, I am purchasing this grand house that I desire."

She stops beside me. "Do not try to persuade me that such a thing could make you happy. I know better."

"I will not go that far. But this is something that would please me. All the same, I wish to know what *you* think of living there."

"Well, I do prefer more people about. More noise and bustle. Are you sure you do not wish the same?"

"I wish for a change. But you stay on Poplar Street." I step forward and she does the same. "As it is, I will be there much of the time, same as always."

———

"You are sure the family is full gone from the house?" I ask Daniel. It is one thing to push open the gate, stride up the walkway, and mount the entry stairs to 512 St. Charles Street. It is Boldness herself to thrust this key Daniel has handed me into the front-door lock and turn it.

He chuckles. "From what I witnessed this morning, Eliza, I believe it safe to say the Chouteaus have put this house behind them."

So I do it, and after only the merest hesitation push open the door of my newest property, my greatest property, for which today I paid twenty-two thousand dollars in cash.

It stands empty, as the Chouteaus have had their furnishings removed, and so it sounds hollow as an abandoned ship as Daniel and I walk about, examining this and that, the gilt-edged moldings, the coved ceilings, the ornamented fireplaces, the double parlor.

"I should have guessed it would have a double parlor," I tell Daniel, and think: *Here is where I will hang my portrait.* "Truly, were you worried Chouteau would run from the deeds office when he learned I am the second party?"

"I have never seen the olive-toned skin of a Creole turn so white so fast." Daniel smirks. "He might have run if his wife were not sitting beside him. How could he explain to her the reason he would do such a thing? Even I," he adds pointedly, "do not fully understand the business between you two."

"The thing you need to know is that I do not like him."

"Years ago I would have guessed you liked him overmuch."

"Oh, but many years have passed, Daniel, and many things have changed."

The smile quits Daniel's face. He steps forward to take my hands. "I know you feel the pain of those changes very deeply, Eliza, and for that I am so sorry."

There are days Richard seems near enough it is almost as if he haunts me, and this momentous day is one of those, and somehow Daniel knows it. I am trying to think of words to jolly us out of this mood when I hear footsteps in the foyer and turn to see standing there the tall figure of Chouteau himself.

I see Chouteau about, so he is no mystery to me, but I am reminded anew that the years have been kind to him. He is still a striking man with a look of strength about him, his dark hair only threaded with gray, his air confident as a king.

Daniel drops my hands and strides toward him. "You are not simply to enter, Chouteau. This is no longer your property."

"The front door was left wide open, Godfrey."

"There must be a reason you have come here," I say to Chouteau. "What is it?" And this time when he turns his eyes to me, they settle.

A woman with forty-five years is not the same as one with twenty-four and it is a rare man who will let her forget it. Chouteau is not one such; I will never see kindness from him; I can tell from the coldness of his gaze that he would dismiss me if he could. "I would speak with you," he says instead, "alone."

He wants something from me and already I am bound and determined not to give it. "Of course. Daniel, do you care to look about the second story?"

"I will do it," he says, and then I am alone with Chouteau for the first time in twenty years, since he tried to bed me in my chamber at the house of Madam Lantos. Enough of a flush rises on his cheeks that I believe he remembers the very thing.

"In light of our long history," Chouteau says, and now I hear him struggle to put warmth in his voice, "I wish for you to sell back to me this house."

"It is only hours ago that I purchased it!"

"Long enough for my wife and children, and myself, too, if I am honest, to realize it is too dear to part with."

"That is not the reason you wish me to give it up," I hear myself say. "It is because it humiliates you to have sold to me this house where you yourself lived."

His jaw clenches. "You did a great deal to mask your identity, I will say."

"Because you are easy to predict as a coming storm. I have as much right to this property as anyone who has the money to buy it."

"Money you procured"—he eyes me with malice—"by the vilest means."

"Not too vile for *you* on a certain occasion you will prefer to forget. And do not try to tell me the Chouteaus are pure as new snow. There are many who call your family business corrupt, in how you deal with the Indians, your rivals, and the government, too. Your father is famous for such dealings."

I have been hearing Daniel's footfalls on the floor above. Now they cease. He must wish to hear what Chouteau will say to that same as I do.

Chouteau steps nearer, fire in his dark eyes. "Do not speak of my father!" he bellows. "He is a saint next to you."

Again I hear Daniel, now racing down the stairs. I am sure he worries about leaving Chouteau alone with me. I hold up a hand to keep Daniel on the staircase and speak to Chouteau. "This is how you hope to persuade me? You have lost the charm I once saw in you, if it was ever there."

He lowers his head and tries, I can see, to compose himself. Then: "I am prepared to offer you twenty-four thousand dollars for the property. Two thousand dollars more than you paid just hours ago, for no effort on your part."

"I understand the mathematics. What *you* need understand is that the number of dollars is not at issue here."

I believe I hear Daniel, still on the staircase, wince.

Chouteau swallows. I will say it gives me pleasure to see him struggle. Finally he speaks again. "I am sorry that I insulted you all those years ago."

"But here is the thing: you insult me again *now*. Because the reason you want this house back has nothing to do with how dear it is to you. Well, Chouteau, I have something to tell you. You wish for me to be ashamed of what I am, but I am not."

He stares at me as if he would throttle me to the death if Daniel were not here watching. "It was an error to come here," he spits, "an error to expect one such as you to understand love."

I have one thing only to say to that. "Get out of my house," and I follow every step of his with one of my own until I reach the foyer, where I halt.

There is Chouteau, on the walkway looking back toward the place that is now mine. I watch him standing there until Daniel shuts the door to leave him outside.

Chapter Thirty-Six

"In the name of God, Amen!

"I, Eliza Haycraft, being of sound and disposing mind and memory, calling to mind the frailty and uncertainty of human life, and being desirous of settling my worldly affairs and directing how the estates which it had pleased God to bless me, shall be disposed of after my decease, while I have strength and capacity to do so, do make and publish this my last will and testament... "

— Last Will & Testament of Eliza Haycraft

— August 30, 1867

THE MONTH OF AUGUST IS NOT ONE OF WHICH I AM FOND and so I wonder why it must have thirty-one days? Why can it not mimic February and in so doing allow me a measure of comfort?

I sit in my double parlor of a sunny Friday forenoon and already am fatigued by the young day. Oh, that is common now. But it does give me an excuse to enjoy quietly what I have about me, least until my relations return from their promenade: the Brussels carpet underfoot, the secretary with mirrored doors, two mantelpieces with a pair of vases on each, the three-tier mahogany whatnot laden with small pretty things, and of course my portrait, on which my eyes linger. How long since Richard's eyes did the same? Six long years...

"Aunt Eliza!"

I hear it dimly. Is that a prod on my knee?

"Aunt Eliza!"

I open my eyes to see shocking near my own face that of my niece Martha, Asa's second daughter, with eleven years now, bright-eyed with dark hair straight as Charity's and a sweet way about her.

"You are awake," she tells me, "and we are back from our walk."

She is correct on both points. Behind her my nephew Alfred appears. Fifteen years he has now, the smallish light-haired fellow who is Visa Ann's fourth boy—and after him are three more boys and two girls and I suppose we could see still more.

"Amanda and I have a wager," Alfred tells me, "that you won't let me drive your carriage. I bet you will." Beside him stands Amanda, Asa's oldest at thirteen. Sadly for her, she shares her father's dark and forbidding looks. With her eyes she sends me a plea.

"You will win the wager, Alfred," I tell him, "so long as you have Noah beside you, for I believe you are old enough, even in this busy city," and I watch Amanda's face droop until I offer "a visit to my favorite dress shop for you and your sister," at which both girls jump and scream.

"You spoil them," Visa Ann tells me, settling on a stuffed chair and removing her bonnet, but I do not believe she minds—she smiles as she says it—and from what she tells me I am sure her husband Benjamin, left in the countryside for this visit, would not, either. How is it possible this sister could bear nine babes and still possess her fair-skinned beauty? But she has done it.

"Did you enjoy your walk?" I ask her. I am less for walking now, as my feet and ankles too often swell.

"I would have enjoyed it more," Asa frowns, "if the city did not roast under red brick."

I am not surprised he complains about something and on this I must agree. "People say it is like Nebuchadnezzar's furnace."

"A Babylonian warrior was he!" Alfred shouts, and thrusts an imaginary sword at Martha.

She shrieks before she pulls from an imaginary scabbard her own sword. As the jousting begins, I listen to Amanda heave a deep sigh. "Will you read to me again?" I ask her, and she brightens. "The newspaper is there, on that side table," and I point to draw her gaze.

Always I have a newspaper about for Charity or Daniel to read to me and indeed I am pleased that my nieces are able, even if Asa keeps repeating it is only so they can train their own children to do the same in due time.

Amanda comes to sit beside me on the sofa and clears her throat while scanning the newsprint. Then her young voice pipes out with importance. " 'A Negro Empire in the South.' "

"What manner of trash is this?" Asa scowls.

"The *Missouri Republican*," Amanda tells her father.

"You allow such tripe in this house?" he asks me.

"Come now," Visa Ann chides, and rolls her eyes in my direction knowing our brother cannot see. "The war is done and all that is behind us."

Her husband Benjamin enlisted in '62 with the volunteer infantry, the very year our brother Asa was arrested for aiding the enemy. When pushed, he swore allegiance to the Union. He did not ask me to post his bond, though I would have.

Diana Dempsey

"Go on," Visa Ann tells Amanda, and again the girl clears her throat.

"No, I do not care to hear more," Asa raises his voice to say, and perhaps it is the perfect time for Cicily James to interrupt us, that good woman introduced to me by Noah. She came from Poplar Street to be housekeeper here, as she is of an age she wishes for a quieter life than can be had at a bawdy house. Oh, she is kindness itself!—despite all the troubles she has suffered.

"Madam Eliza," she says now, "the ladies from the orphan asylum are outside by the gate."

"Oh yes." I hoist myself to my feet, a struggle as I have been sitting overlong. "I put together an envelope for them."

Martha ceases her jousting. "They should come inside for it."

"They won't do that," I tell her, "even though this is a respectable house," and it must be for how else could my church-going relations reside in it for their visit? I suspect they were curious to see this new residence, for I am told word of Madam Haycraft's immense profits from the war flew even far as Cote Sans Dessein. Well, my houses earned well from the many men in our city, but did they not do the same long before the battling started?

"I will walk you outside," Martha offers, and I wonder if she does so because she has never before seen anyone from such a frightful place as an *orphan asylum*.

The pair is earnest and simply dressed and, though they would prefer to look anywhere but into the eyes of a trollop— even one long ago judged of little use in the bedchamber—they cannot stop thanking me for my generosity.

"How much did you give them?" Martha whispers when we are walking back to the front door.

"Two hundred dollars."

Her eyes grow wide as plums. "That is a great sum!"

"Do you think it too great?"

She seems astonished I could care what she thinks. "I suppose not. Not if they are truly in need."

"Oh, they are, Martha. The war made for so many widows and orphan children. I can help them and so I do." How I pity those poor souls who lost those dearest to them and their way of surviving, too. How could I not help, when I have so much? I am thinking all this as my niece and I halt at the bottom of the stairs for me to catch my breath.

Her expression grows pensive. "I suppose I understand what you say."

To my memory rises the astonished face of Obadiah aboard the steamboat that first carried me to this city. *Nobody ever give you a hand up?* "A few people have helped me," I tell Martha. "I have been given a hand up. And it made a great difference to me. So I try to do the same."

I will not tell her the other thing: that in this life of mine, many times I have had to stop myself from feeling anything at all. Yet when I give to those in need, I see from them no criticism. No, I see gratitude and relief. Then how I bask in joy!

Martha climbs a stair or two before she thinks to step down to take my arm. "Uncle Benjamin says it is not just orphans you give to but fallen women."

"Well, your Uncle Benjamin might not realize how easy it is for a woman to become fallen, so called. But it is true."

She lowers her voice to a whisper. "And to Negroes, too, he says."

Apparently Uncle Benjamin speaks a fair amount on the topic. "He is right. I give money also to convents and churches and relief funds of all kinds."

I watch Martha's dark eyes go wide. She must know enough about my business to be surprised that such institutions take money from one such as me. Oh, but they have for years. "And you must still have a great deal left after all that," she says, "for you live in a very grand house and own many more besides."

She blushes after she says it, but I can only chuckle. For that I must stop and rest again. "Does your Uncle Benjamin say that, too?"

She will pass that question by. Instead: "I know what my father says," and I steel myself but need not. "He says you have a very generous heart and God knows it and will reward you for it when the time comes."

Well. My brother does sometimes surprise me. I can hope God will, too.

"YOU'LL BE WANTING some sweet tea," Cicily tells me, "cold sweet tea."

We are in my bedchamber and she is loosening my corset, for I have worn it long enough for a steaming day. Already my throbbing feet are loosed from their boots: a mercy. "It is quiet," I tell Cicily, knowing she will understand I don't mean outside the open windows, where the din of city life streams in like the scent of the garden lilies: the squeaks and squeals of unseen machinery, carriages, horses, shouting, and far away a drawn-out locomotive horn.

"You'll be missing your family." Cicily chuckles. "I do enjoy the scampering of young feet."

"And the shouting. And roughhousing."

"Oh, yes. Less to pick up from now, but I miss them."

"I will miss Visa Ann most. And Martha." Perhaps I should not speak them aloud, the names of my favorites. But I do.

"That one is still young enough to speak her mind," Cicily says.

"Women should do that same as girls."

Cicily shakes her head. "Maybe someday. But not long as I am in this world."

I stop myself from saying more, for there is a thing bothering me that it would be improper to discuss with Cicily. Even a hussy like myself cares about propriety from time to time. "I've changed my mind, Cicily. I would go to Poplar Street," and so my corset is re-laced and my feet once again shod.

Is it different to walk into my house there—yes, I still have the compound entire—when I am no longer an inmate? It is, but I can bear it, for now St. Charles Street feels like home. I ask Charity if we may speak in her bedchamber, that beautiful room that used to be mine, for I desire privacy.

It is no longer a splendor of jade tones but now a riot of pink. Charity has kept the gold stenciling upon the cream-colored ceiling—from the first that was her idea—and like me has placed two armchairs before the hearth, though hers have cabriole legs and tufted upholstery in an amaranth hue.

We settle in those. "I wish to discuss a thing," I tell her, "that I worry will upset you, though truly there is no reason for disquiet. I am fit as a fiddle," for what are my aches and pains but the complaints of an aging trollop?

"Are you ill?" Her voice is a screech.

"No. But I come to think it past time to have my will written." I watch Charity's features contort in distress and lay a hand upon her knee. "For what if I were to be felled by a dray tomorrow? The men of business would find a way to take for themselves everything I own. Why, Chouteau might lay claim to the house on St. Charles Street as if it had been his all along."

"Yes," Charity allows. "I can imagine it."

"And what would happen to you in the case?"

"You are not to worry about me, Eliza."

"Of course I am." I must stop then, for tears sting my eyes and I can see they do Charity's as well. "You are my dearest friend and have been by my side all these years and I wish for you to be protected. Whether," I add quickly, "William appears later or sooner." Already it is later, but for now let us pass that topic by.

"Have you come to think about this because your family was here?"

"Yes, but not because they press me, though a few might if they had the chance." I am thinking of Benjamin.

"Those few will wish for you to leave everything to them, not set aside a bit for a strumpet like me."

It will be more than a bit, for I intend to leave Charity a house entire. Why should I not? Am I to forget those dearest to me when I leave this life? "And that is why all must be written out by the clerk," I tell Charity, "and my X set down upon the line. That is the only way to assure things."

"What does Daniel say on the topic?"

"I have not yet discussed it with him," and I can see by the light in Charity's eyes that it pleases her to hear this first. "And there is something I wish to put in my will that I fear is not full legal: that my sisters control what I bequeath them."

She frowns in concentration. "You mean... not their husbands?"

"Men believe it is theirs to mind such matters, that only they can understand them, but that is foolishness. Of course we women cannot understand what no one explains to us, but that can easily be remedied."

Charity snorts. "It will sooner happen that the Mississippi River flow from the south to the north."

"I will ask Daniel if I can do it."

"There is a good reason for it," Charity tells me. "For in the sad circumstance that one of your sisters dies, her husband might give what she inherited from you to his new wife and the children he begets with her. All of them strangers to you."

Yes. Charity knows too well that a father's new bride may turn her back on the wife and children who preceded her.

"Will you leave the same to Sarah that you leave to your other sisters?" Charity wants to know.

I had not thought on the matter but can decide it quickly. "I will not. She does not deserve it. Also, you remember Mr. Stewart decreed she cannot come back to this state. So how could she lay her hands on it, if she still breathes?"

Then there is my brother. Oh, there are times his heart is hard to me. But it is not always so, as I know from what Martha said and from what I myself have seen. And what of Martha, and Asa's other children, if I forget my brother when I die?

"It is much easier to be rich than poor," Charity observes, and we both laugh at that statement plain as the sun in the August sky. "Your family will be astounded at your riches, Eliza," she adds, and I believe her correct on the point.

IT IS the thirtieth day of August in the year eighteen hundred sixty-seven when my final will and testament is written, with Daniel at my side.

It is written into a large leather-covered book with lined pages, the same sort of volume I have many times inscribed with an X in the case of a deed of property. Here, though, a portentous phrase or two makes my heart thud. *First I commend my immortal being to Him...*

"Yes," I assure Daniel, "I do wish to include such a sentence about Sarah," and I am told the clerk writes: *I bequeath unto my sister Sarah the sum of One hundred dollars, as her portion of my estate and no more.* To Asa and Lucinda and Nancy and Minerva and Visa Ann, and to their heirs, I bequeath all I own. Oh, and here is the phrase I am so pleased to hear: *free from any interference or control of their said husbands.* More than once the clerk raises questioning eyes to Daniel, but Daniel urges him forward and so it is done.

"Your hand will suffer the rest of the day," Daniel tells the clerk with a laugh, and he laughs, too, and says he is amazed how many properties he must describe. Eighteen: and this clerk does not know about the others to be deeded separately to Charity and Daniel.

Three men witness me setting down my mark: Mr. Meeke, Mr. Cunningham, and Mr. Moorehead. Over coffee that morning Daniel explained why he desired such a thing. "So they can testify, Eliza, when the time comes, that you were the one to mark your X and were of sound mind when you did it."

"This will make the will more sure?" and he said that it would.

Oh, there is another thing I wish would be sure: that my brother and sisters will manage wisely all that I bequeath to them. I believe I can say this is a fortune I amassed, over long years. Yet when I die I fear it will become the same as me: dust, to be blown away if not carefully tended.

Chapter Thirty-Seven

"Old and young, we are all on our last cruise."

— Robert Louis Stevenson

— "Crabbed Age and Youth," *Virginibus Puerisque,*
1881

"HOW MANY TIMES, ELIZA," Mr. Stewart says, "have we sat together of an evening before a hearth fire?"

Tonight we sit thus in my parlor on St. Charles Street. And though it is only September and the nights are not yet cold, for the likes of us with greater than fifty years, we desire the fire lit. "It may be as many as a thousand nights," I tell him.

He lays his hand upon my knee. "And, dear friend"—I am warmed to hear him call me such a thing—"tonight shall be the last."

"You cannot mean that." I speak those words, but all the same

I see how frail he is become, this man with only five years more than me. He is a barebones when once he was a giant.

"I do mean it, for I shall not quit St. Joseph again." That is his favorite place, where he began his law practice decades ago. "Not in this life or the next, for I have purchased a burial plot in a most beautiful cemetery called Mount Mora. I do not wish you to be sad about it," he adds when I make a noise to protest, "for I am ready to say goodbye to this tortured world of ours." I gaze at him and think I might see a tear in his eye, a rare thing for a man who once wielded as much power as he.

"I know," I murmur, "you feel greatly the loss of your mother." It was last winter she passed, in New York, and many years since the two saw one another.

It takes him some time to speak. "Eighty-three years she lived. A much stronger constitution than mine."

I will dispute that. "I saw with what strength and wisdom you steered our state before the war."

"Only to leave it in the hands of a traitor."

"It is Jackson's fault he was treacherous. Not yours." I sip my whiskey, glad that scoundrel is long dead. "And unlike him, you would have carried a musket into battle if allowed to."

"To be judged unfit was a great frustration to me. But now, Eliza"—he pats his chest—"there are times my heart pounds with such a frightful anxiety I fear it will leap through my very ribs to lie thumping on the floor in front of me."

I shudder, for in these last months I can too easily imagine my own heart doing the same. I have heard what the doctor says: that my heart suffers a weakness he can do nothing about. Did I survive a great fever as a child? For that could be the cause of the trouble. Whether it is or not, he has told me I do not have long for this life. Oh, somehow I must find the courage Mr. Stewart shows.

"You know"—he says now, casting me a sidelong glance—"some speculate that *you* gave particular assistance to the Union side."

I make a scoffing sound. That is a secret I will carry to my grave, same, I am sure, as Lyon—and Old Peter—carried it to theirs. And Noah carries his secrets, too, though with time I came to understand the bravery he showed for his people.

Again Mr. Stewart speaks, his gaze still upon me. "Specifically, it is said that you took some action to benefit Nathaniel Lyon."

I force a laugh. "Well, it pleases me to be a woman of mystery. And I am flattered that any would judge a bawdy house madam so capable."

"Well, if it is true, I envy you that satisfaction. I envy you something else, too, even more fiercely." Now I am sure I do not mistake it: there is a tear in his eye. "You have been loved. And you loved as well. Do not try to deny it, Eliza, for I saw how you and Dr. Bonner looked at one another."

Even now, *love* is a word over which I stumble. "I will tell you" —now I am the one who can scarce speak—"I miss Richard every day of my life."

"I am sure. But you have that love to remember. That is a joy I never knew."

We sit in silence after that, needing no more words to understand one another, a man with his secrets and a woman with hers.

———

"ARE YOU QUITE SURE, ELIZA"—IT is a wry tone Daniel uses—"that you wish to pass eternity here at Bellefontaine? Near the likes of Sterling Price?"

It is mere moments since we entered the cemetery and began to roll along its meandering roads. Even wrapped in my thickest cloak with a blanket over my knees, I shiver in the chilly brightness of a late October day. "So Price is here?" I heard tell it was cholera that took him. From time to time that thief of lives is still among us. "But how could he afford to lie in such a place as Bellefontaine? Did he not die a poor man? I hope it is not just that I wish it so."

"I have heard the same and believe it true. But Price has many who admire him. Perhaps they opened their pockets to help."

"He is fortunate to have generous friends, then."

Daniel chuckles. He knows my low opinion of Price. "You do not think Price generous for sparing your sister's life?"

I will not tell Daniel I am far from sure it was generosity that moved him. "I will say I am forever grateful to him for that one thing."

As I prepare to leave this world, I must wonder if Sarah still walks among the living. My far better sister Nancy does not, and more tragically still, Sallie and Alfred do not. They are two of Visa Ann's own, both lost last year, her daughter just sixteen and Alfred eighteen, the very youth who stood in my parlor brandishing an imaginary sword. How can I curse my fate when I think of them?

"We are awaited," Daniel tells me as the gig curves along another road, "in the Keepers Lodge."

"Well, I do not relish this prospect, Daniel, but once I do it, it will be settled and done." It did not take dear Mr. Stewart, laid to rest weeks ago, for me to know it is past time to make my own arrangements. "And," I add, "I feel at peace here." I keep to myself that this is the place I feel closest to Richard: I am embarrassed to sound sentimental as that. "In the end, this will make matters easier for you."

"Yes, I will have only to execute your estate." He pats my knee. "That may prove challenge enough."

For I am a harlot and none will let me forget it. Of that I am reminded anew soon as we arrive at the lodge, a forbidding stone structure with a turret. I wonder: what are those high-set windows for but to keep watch for specters wandering the grounds? Inside is a parlor where I am surprised to see two gentlemen of vaunted station awaiting us. Were we not to meet with a clerk who could handle such a simple transaction as the purchase of a plot? Yet before us stand Mr. Conard and Mr. Primm, affluent merchants both.

I must hold back a smile as they usher Daniel and me to a tufted sofa. Oh, I know both these muck-a-mucks!—and very well, too. But this afternoon I will skirt the topic of how in our younger days we frolicked and tumbled.

I must sit quietly for a moment, for even after such a short walk my swollen feet ache and my heart must settle into a calmer rhythm. Finally: "I am such an admirer," I say, "of the dignity and tranquility of these grounds. Both of you are to be congratulated on their beauty."

Mr. Conard, thin and with a disapproving air, inclines his head. "I will speak for Mr. Primm in saying that we are honored to serve on the Board of Trustees of such a remarkable place as Bellefontaine Cemetery."

The portly, red-faced Mr. Primm hastens to agree, though he cannot quite meet my gaze as he does so. "And on that Board, we certainly consider ourselves guardians of the heritage of our great city."

"For where else but here"—Mr. Conard will stare at me full in the face, and with meaning—"would the most eminent person-ages of our metropolis, indeed of our entire state, enjoy their eternal repose in peace and honor, away from the taint of the mortal world?"

Ah. I believe I am sent a message. And I can tell from how Daniel shifts beside me that he hears the same. It is as I feared: these two scheme to stand between the bawd Haycraft and the plot of ground she seeks. That is why *they* sit before me and not a simple clerk. Well, never before have I desired a property that I did not in the end possess.

And this is the last one I must have.

"It is gratifying to hear," I say, "that on the Board sit such careful stewards. That adds one more to the many reasons I wish to purchase a plot here." I gesture toward Daniel. "Mr. Godfrey, my executor, tells me he had a fruitful discussion on the topic just the other day with the gentleman who handles such matters."

"Mr. Bryant, yes," Daniel says. "He surprised me with how

much he knew of Madam Haycraft's extraordinary generosity over the years, both to the people of St. Louis and to her institutions."

Mr. Conard and Mr. Primm glance at one another, then the latter speaks. "Laudable as your charity may be, Madam Haycraft, we on the Board are of the mind that a different place of rest might be more suitable. Perhaps Wesleyan Cemetery?"

Just up the road from Lindell Grove, where I would pass eternity reliving my nerve-wracking tour of Camp Jackson beside Nathaniel Lyon. "Bellefontaine is where I desire to be," I say with firmness. "Perhaps you gentlemen would be more comfortable if we end this discussion and I set a time to raise the matter with your wives? I am sure both are understanding and forgiving souls."

Mr. Conard's eyes widen to the size of walnuts while Mr. Primm grows red as an autumn apple. They rise as one to confer in a corner and Daniel and I exchange a glance. Oh, I see light dance in his blue eyes!

When they return, Daniel speaks. "Perhaps now is a good time to discuss the many plots at Bellefontaine that remain unspoken for, according to Mr. Bryant. In the family lots," he adds and turns to me. "Those are more desirable than the so-called public lots."

"Then it goes without saying"—I smile—"that I desire a family lot."

Mr. Conard finds his voice. "Now you mention it, there is one plot that comes to mind, in a land mass that is vacant at present and well situated beside Cypress Lake."

"One plot in particular has a coping around it," Mr. Primm adds, "which lends a special dignity to the setting."

"Also," Mr. Conard says, "the plot we speak of is circular, the only of its kind. And it is quite sizable."

"How sizable?" Daniel wants to know.

Mr. Primm hastens to the mahogany secretary to consult a document. "Thirty-two feet in diameter, or eight hundred four superficial feet."

So I would be alone in that great space, forevermore: among but still apart from others, as I have ever been. "May I see its placement on a map?" I ask.

The plot in question is far from the main gate as can be. That also means it is far from Sterling Price. I know full well Bellefontaine might wish to hide such a one as Madam Haycraft if they cannot banish her entirely, but that I can abide.

Mr. Primm clears his throat. "I must make mention of another point." He forces himself to meet my gaze. "The Board is unlikely to approve a headstone for you, Madam Haycraft."

"I see." Daniel begins to object, but I raise a quieting hand. "I would like to ride out to view the spot," and I push myself to my feet.

In the end, I do not care about a headstone. I stand on the grassy earth and amid drifts of fallen leaves I feel a calm in my soul I have not oft enjoyed. Is it the nearness to Richard I always sense here? Or the grass beneath my boots and blue sky overhead, the very scene to take me back to those girlhood days when I would lie on the ground and dream? I daresay it is both.

Daniel and I are returned to the gig and have left Bellefontaine behind us when I am startled to feel his body shake and to hear a sob escape his lips. He halts the horses on the roadside. His cheeks are wet with tears.

I turn toward him and take his hand. "Oh, Daniel."

He is sputtering like a small boy. "I do not know how I will bear it, Eliza."

"You will bear it because you must. And you have Alice to help you do it."

"When we had business to conduct in that lodge, I would not give in to such feelings. But now—"

"Now"—I recall the words Mr. Stewart spoke to me—"you must not be sad, for I am not. I can feel my hold loosening on this world of ours, but it does not frighten me." That grows truer with every week. Perhaps it is that I am full tired and ready to rest. "I have had a full measure of life, Daniel. Not the way I dreamt about when I was a girl, no, but it is enough all the same. The way I have lived, it has cost me. But it has given me freedom, too, more than most women."

"I will miss you horribly, Eliza. But if you are to be so strong" —he wipes his face with a handkerchief—"I suppose I must be as well."

"I don't know that I am strong. I only know there is nothing to be done."

We are silent for a time, then: "Would you allow Alice to pay her respects to you?" Daniel asks. "She wishes to thank you for all you are giving to us."

It is something for a woman like Alice to enter the home of a woman like me, perhaps an even greater accommodation than her husband conducting my business and remaining my stalwart companion. "Alice is kindness itself," I tell him. "But let us leave that topic for another day. For I wish to be home to rest."

Hearing that, Daniel picks up the reins and drives like the wind, so fast that I must laugh from the rollicking joy of it. He does the same. Oh, that is what we have ever done and what I will ever remember.

In the end I do not see Alice, for I do not wish her to witness the condition to which I am reduced. Are there days entire when I am clothed in nothing but a wrapper? Oh, I will admit it. There are days entire when I do not leave my bed, for if I try my heart flails in my chest like a river trout seeking to escape a net.

"Shall I ask Dr. Benkendorf to visit again?" Charity wishes to know, for she is with me on St. Charles Street so often now.

"Bring him," I pant, my breath hard to find, for in these dark days of late November I am desperate for relief, though there is little the physician can provide.

Dr. Benkendorf is German, for what man born and trained in this country would tend to such a one as me? Dr. Bernard Gaines

Farrar would have, that good man, and of course Richard, too, but no more like them live and breathe.

After the bloodletting is done and the gruesome bowl removed, Dr. Benkendorf stands at my bedside with Charity beside him and Cicily at the foot. He is a somber, bespectacled man who dispenses advice in an accent thick as a slice of German bread. "You must avoid excitement, Madam Haycraft."

As if there is any of that in this bedchamber.

"Do not attempt violent exercise," he orders me, and I could laugh at such a warning if I did not worry it might threaten the tincture of digitalis I so desire he give me.

Finally Cicily ushers him out and I am left alone with Charity. "Will you do a thing for me?" I ask her. "Will you bring my portrait from the parlor so I can see it?"

"I will prop it on a chair across from the bed." She drags just such a chair to just that position. "I will ask Noah to carry it up."

She does so, and after Noah sets the portrait in place he stands at the bedside to grasp my hand. We neither of us speak a word. The squeeze of his strong hand, the warmth in his brown eyes— oh, they are enough. What a true friend he has been. And I hope I have been to him.

After he leaves, I pat the bed so Charity will sit beside me. "I wish to ask something more of you, dear Charity. Something for me and something for you."

"What?" She croaks the word. Can I believe that her hair begins to gray?

"Will you write to—"

"I have already done it. Visa Ann and Asa will arrive in a day or two, with a few of your nieces and nephews. I don't know which."

A day or two: I will stay for that, though the weight on my chest is so very heavy now. "And when it is done"—I must speak slowly to find breath—"all done, I wish you to place the letter in my casket with me."

She knows which letter. "The one Richard put in the back of the portrait."

"I wish it to go with me," I tell her. "I wish that very much. You will find your William," I say, but she is shaking her head. "You will find him because you have the softest heart of all and it will draw him to you as it drew me."

"There can be no dearer friend than you," Charity tells me, and really it does not matter that I have no more breath to speak, for what is there to do but grasp her hand and squeeze it, sending her some of the strength I still possess?

MY RELATIONS, they come in and out of my bedchamber, and we speak quietly of this and that, days of old mostly, leaving off topics that chafe. I am with them and yet I am not, for I will go on a frightful journey soon and they will not come with me. Will I see them when they make that journey, too? Soon I will know.

It is December, a Tuesday, and excessively cold. Ice chunks float in the river—so Charity reads in the newspaper—hence we must all agree it is good my family is already arrived in St. Louis for they would not get here now. " 'Navigation is ended to and from this port,' " Charity reads. "Also, it snowed in Chicago."

"What does my sister care about Chicago?" Asa grumbles, staring out the window, but Charity will smile at me and wink.

At midday my soup is so dull I wonder if it has no taste at all, making it exactly the sort of thing Dr. Benkendorf desires that I eat. Instead I abandon the spoon, allowing it to clatter onto the tray.

"That is not what a proper lady would do," Chantal says.

"Chantal?" My head jerks up. I look about my bedchamber. I am alone—I do not care to be gazed at while I eat—though Cicily will return soon to collect the tray. Chantal cannot be here, yet I heard her voice clearly. "Chantal?" I call again, but as I hear no response—did I really expect to?—I settle back against my pillows.

Oh, there is my portrait across from me. Chantal would think it shows vanity to possess such a thing, yet of course I am not the one who commissioned it. Richard did and why he did so, Chantal would understand. And Obadiah? He would applaud me for climbing so high that I would have an oil portrait of myself, regardless how I came by it. Oh, what must my family think that I insist on passing my last days gazing at my own likeness? It does not raise their opinion. No matter. They are not the important judges now.

I must doze off, for there comes a moment when I startle awake. The tray is gone and I am alone. The draperies are full open, for I like to see what sun these December days can produce, but now a ray cuts me sharp across the eyes and I do not like it.

I struggle to sit up then push away the blankets and move my legs to the edge of the bed so they hang over the side. I will walk, very slowly, to that window and pull closed the drapery. Carefully I stand—that makes me dizzy; it is some time since I have done this—and so I halt.

Oh, it is as if an ox has mounted the stairs and come to sit upon my chest. What weight! I try to find breath, I gasp for it, but it eludes me. The feeble strength in my legs gives way. I tumble to the carpet, that fat carpet with a floral pattern, for I have admired those since the days of Madam Lantos. I try again for breath. Oh, dear angels, let me find it! But I cannot, no matter how I struggle.

At the carpet threads I stare, navy and crimson. Then a musty smell fills my nostrils, as if I have poked my head deep inside my armoire where my oldest garments lie. Where are my favorite gowns, the bluebell and the jade? I wonder for a time then forget those, and perk my ears. Is that the horn of a steamboat I hear?

Now I hear a man's voice. *Eliza.* Dare I believe it? I stare at the carpet. Navy, crimson, gold…

No. Not gold.

Amber.

Chapter Thirty-Eight

"There was perhaps no resident of this city, male or female, saint or sinner, who could point to such a record of charitable deeds as this woman. Those who knew her declare that no deserving call for pecuniary help was ever passed by unnoticed...

"Her treatment of the girls who lived with her need no further illustration or explanation than a glance at the numbers of these unfortunate creatures who flocked to her house last night with unfeigned expressions of sorrow.

"The expression of such facts as these regarding the character of the woman will not be construed as a defense of her life. The very fact of such qualities being united with her life-long ways of crime only made her the more dangerous to society."

— "A Noted Character Gone"

— *St. Louis Times*, December 6, 1871

MARTHA SAW IT WOULD BE ONE SHOCK AFTER ANOTHER now her aunt was dead.

The first was the shriek from Madam Charity, who found her aunt gone. Anyone who heard that wail would know Madam Charity's heart had broken from lamentation. Martha's father and Aunt Visa Ann raced upstairs faster than Martha had ever seen. They'd cried, too, even her father, but not the way Madam Charity did. Even the Negro housekeeper Cicily sobbed, and the man about the house, Noah.

Then came raised voices, even though they were standing beside her aunt's body. But Martha's father didn't like Madam Charity taking charge, as if she had a right to. "No, I will summon the undertaker," he told her. "It is right and proper that a family member handle such business, not—"

"Hush, Asa," Aunt Visa Ann said.

"Fine. You do it." Madam Charity's face crumpled again, but she kept speaking. "The undertaker is Mr. John Smithers, on—"

"I will take Mr. Harper there," Noah said, "and when we return, we will have Mr. Smithers and the casket with us."

"That has already been purchased?" Aunt Visa Ann asked, and Martha could tell she was surprised.

"It has," Madam Charity said. "Noah, please remember to bring back the black crepe, too, the English crepe," and then she couldn't say anything more.

"English crepe," Aunt Visa Ann murmured. "What will our sister have paid for her casket?"

"A fair sum," her father guessed, and he was right, for word followed that it cost three hundred fifty dollars, what with it being rosewood and lined with cream-colored satin and ornamented with a great deal of silver.

"It is an exceedingly comfortable-looking couch," her aunt said when it was brought into the house and carried upstairs, Mr. Smithers stepping up behind.

That is not where the coffin stayed, though, not once Aunt

Eliza was washed and dressed and laid inside. For all eternity she would wear a rich figured silk robe with leaves and flowers, as if she wished always to think of springtime.

The night after her aunt died, Martha watched Madam Charity and Cicily make the double parlor ready for the casket. They pulled down the blinds, drew the lace curtains, and shut the jets that made the chandelier sparkle, lighting a few candles instead. When finally the coffin came down, it was set upon two benches beneath Aunt Eliza's portrait, where Madam Charity said it must be. As a family they gathered in the shadows, Martha's cousin Nancy, too, Aunt Visa Ann's only daughter still living.

"She looks shrunken," Nancy whispered. "And it's strange how her hands are crossed over her chest."

Martha shushed her cousin, worried what the eleven-year-old might say next. On this night the four years between them felt like a great gulf.

But this time her father said the right thing. "It is a comfort, Nancy, that your aunt bears such a placid look, placid and serene, as if she has been blessed by her Maker," and then he made the sign of the cross and all of them did the same.

Martha tried to sleep that night, but it was impossible not to think about her aunt in the parlor. Someone from the undertaker was sitting with her—Aunt Eliza had paid for that, they were told —and Martha was glad of it.

The next morning, when it was still black as night and the whole mansion quiet, she tiptoed downstairs in her nightdress. In the parlor only a single candle burned, down almost to the nub. The old man the undertaker had left was sitting beside her aunt, dozing and so poor company. Black crepe covered the mirrors and Martha knew more was draped over the knob of the front door and other places, too. She expected everything to be the same as before, but here came another shock. For tucked inside the coffin, where her aunt's hand could reach, was an envelope with *Eliza* written upon it.

Martha was filled with great curiosity. She thought, not for the first time, that there was a great deal she did not understand about her aunt, who could not even read and yet here was a note precious enough to go with her to the hereafter. Martha was sure she could sneak a peak: she would be extremely quiet and the snoring old man would sleep through. She went so far as to reach out her hand but in the end pulled back.

No. It would be unkind. And her Aunt Eliza was always kind.

It was Noah who insisted on keeping watch over Aunt Eliza that day, when people would pass through to pay their respects. One of the first was Mr. Godfrey, who came to the house every day. Martha heard Aunt Visa Ann whisper to her father that Mr. Godfrey was the executor and would know what was in the will. When would that be read? They must remain in St. Louis to hear it; that is what Uncle Benjamin said. Most of the others who came were young women and Martha knew who they were: the reason none of her male cousins had been allowed to journey to St. Louis. To a one the women were crying, which made Martha think they must also have found her aunt to be kind.

Soon it was nighttime again, late enough that the visitors had left and Noah had gone to the kitchen for stew. Martha remained with her aunt—she did not want her to be alone—when a woman walked through the front door and into the parlor bold as could be. She was not young like the others, but she was still pretty: tiny, with green cat eyes and hair white as a rabbit's. She spent a long time staring down at Aunt Eliza but did not shed a tear. Martha was worried she might take the envelope into her hand, for she bent down to peer at it closely. In that case, Martha worried, she might have to reach over and slap away the woman's hand.

Then: "Who are you?" the woman asked, and Martha thought she might fall asleep if she heard too much of that voice, soft as brook water.

"I'm Aunt Eliza's niece," Martha said.

The woman eyed her. "She always told me she didn't have family."

Martha did not believe that. This woman wanted to insult her. "Who are you?" she asked, and the woman laughed.

"You have some of your aunt's spirit. Do you know I taught her everything she knew?"

Martha was not convinced. Judging from her garments, this woman was not as rich as her Aunt Eliza. Martha knew about such things, a little, from the shops her aunt had taken her.

"Do you know why I came here?" the woman asked. "It was to make sure your aunt is really dead."

That declaration came as a shock, too. "I think it's time you go," Martha said, and was about to say it again when Noah returned to the parlor. In moments he herded the woman back out into the wintry night.

"You'd best get some rest," Noah told Martha. "You'll need it for tomorrow," and she knew she would, for in the morning was the funeral, here in the mansion, for she heard people whisper that no minister would allow it in church.

MARTHA LOVED Aunt Eliza's grandfather clock, whose moon dial boasted a scene of a castle behind a golden field. When the clock tolled ten times, Martha looked out the parlor window and saw Negro women on the sidewalk murmuring to one another and nodding at the mansion. Then men of every age began to appear, to stop and stare. Other women came, too, some with children by the hand. Boys perched on the fence surrounding the front garden. Everywhere were people—white and black, young and old—until the street was filled. The hearse and eight carriages Aunt Eliza hired had to roll very slowly so as not to hit anyone. Some women weren't paying any mind, as they were crying too hard.

The clock tolled eleven times.

"Madam Charity and I agreed," Martha heard her father say to

Aunt Visa Ann. "We sent Mr. Godfrey to request policemen to keep the mob in order."

"Why are there so many people?" Nancy wanted to know. She turned from the front window, where she was staring out same as Martha.

"Your aunt had many people who loved her," Aunt Visa Ann said.

"Nobody has that many," Nancy said.

"People who were grateful to her," Martha said, and shushed her cousin before escaping to her bedchamber upstairs.

The funeral could not begin until Mr. Godfrey returned. With time suddenly on her hands, Martha felt a need for solitude. Though her aunt had died two days before, the finality of it was striking her hard now, like a woodpecker drumming a tree. Oh, the questions she wished she had asked! At fifteen Martha understood how her aunt had made her fortune. None of it was pretty, and her father wouldn't want her to know a single thing about it, but Martha wished she'd probed why her Aunt Eliza had lived the life she did.

Martha walked to the window and received another shock. People were not simply blocking St. Charles Street: they were blocking all the streets around the mansion. She had never seen so many. And she knew they were out in their numbers because of her Aunt Eliza.

She was watching them, astonished, when she saw Mr. Godfrey thread his way through the crowd to the mansion's front gate. She raced downstairs to open the door and he gave her a smile. "Your aunt was very fond of you, Martha." Then he spoke even quieter. "She called you a favorite."

"I'm only realizing now how much I'll miss her," Martha said. "And that I'll never know another like her."

"You and I have that in common," Mr. Godfrey murmured before Martha's father came near to ask if policemen had arrived.

Mr. Godfrey nodded. "You should know, Asa, the crowd is in the thousands."

Martha watched her father grow near as white as Aunt Eliza. "So many?"

"I'm told they line the route to Bellefontaine." Mr. Godfrey put his hand on the other man's shoulder. "It is because your sister gave before she even had much *to* give. To think there was a time I tried to talk her out of it."

"You wouldn't have been able to," Martha's father said.

"She once told me," Martha heard herself say, "that someone gave her a hand up. And she wished to do the same for others."

Both men turned toward her, her father with a frown and Mr. Godfrey with a face full of interest.

"It must be an odd thing," she went on, "that a woman in that business had such a kind heart for those in need."

Her father's frown deepened. "You spoke with her about her business?"

"I wish I had," and Martha watched her father's face twist in shock. Yet that was another thing she had seen of her Aunt Eliza: she was a woman, but she said what she thought.

From behind them in the parlor came a commotion. The Reverend Dr. Linn had risen from his seat beside the casket and cleared his throat. "Lord," he intoned in a loud voice, as if he were trying to be heard all the way in heaven, "Thou hast been our dwelling place through all generations."

All were quiet but for their crying. Madam Charity could not stop, or Aunt Visa Ann, or Cicily, especially when the lid of the coffin was closed and locked. It was the most final sound Martha had ever heard.

She pictured her aunt in that silent blackness, alone forever. But at least she had that envelope with her, to reach if she wanted, tucked safe.

Characters

Real and Imagined

ELIZA HAYCRAFT

Needless to say, Eliza is real. I will write more about her in the author's note that follows but will relay here a wonderful post-script to her life. When Eliza was buried in Bellefontaine Cemetery, her gravesite was as far as could be from the main gate on Broadway Avenue. A century later, the main gate was changed to the entry on West Florissant Avenue. That put Eliza's grave right in front.

That said, she remains, as I wrote in Chapter Thirty-Seven: "alone in the large space, forevermore: among but still apart from others, as I have ever been." And as of this writing, no headstone marks her grave.

SARAH HAYCRAFT

Real. Three years after Sarah was pardoned and banished from Missouri, an item in the *Weekly California News* placed her in San Francisco. The article reported that a man stabbed her above the knee as they fought over a coin, producing "a bad wound." I don't know if Sarah survived the stabbing, which took place in her house on Jackson Street.

Jackson Street is the only street in San Francisco on which I have ever lived, at two different addresses over eight years. That kismet has only strengthened my feeling that I was destined to write Eliza Haycraft's story.

JOHN NEVILLE HAYCRAFT

Real. It appears that the scoundrel had a wife and two children in Kentucky at the time of his 1843 "marriage" to Eliza. At some point after Eliza's departure from Cote Sans Dessein, Haycraft moved to Indiana, married three more times, and fathered several more children.

OBADIAH DARBY

Imagined, but Eliza reportedly traveled to New Orleans with "a male companion" soon after her initial arrival in St. Louis, remaining for a few months in the Crescent City before she returned to live permanently in St. Louis.

CHANTAL ROSSIGNOL

Imagined

CHARLES PIERRE CHOUTEAU

Real. Chouteau died in 1901 as he was born: a member of arguably the most illustrious family in St. Louis.

He was survived by four of his eight children with Julia Augusta Gratiot Chouteau, who predeceased him by six years, and left a library of more than a thousand volumes, in both French and

English, a testament to his lifelong interest in literature, history, science, and Americana.

MADAM EVALINE LANTOS

Imagined

CHARITY / ELIZA STUBBLEFIELD

Real, though renamed, as I judged that a second important character with the name Eliza would only confuse readers. An item in the *St. Louis Post Dispatch* of February 1874 indicates that after Eliza Haycraft's death, Eliza Stubblefield—sometimes known as Little Eliza—continued her quest for love, including at a masquerade ball: "(she) appeared in a blue domino with white stars, and from the manner in which she made love to her spectacled escort it was very evident that she had entirely lost sight of the sweetheart who was destroyed in the *Oceanus* disaster." That unfortunate steamship blew a boiler and exploded in April 1872.

DANIEL GODFREY

Imagined

BERNARD GAINES FARRAR, SR.

Real. Three years before Eliza was born, the good doctor served Thomas Hart Benton in his two duels against Charles Lucas, though it was Lucas who needed the medical help, as he died in the second supposed affair of honor. The two lawyers clashed in court and, unwisely, Lucas demanded they settle their dispute on a spit of land in the Mississippi River that came to be known as Bloody Island.

FREDERICK NORCOM

Real. It appears that Norcom died in 1865, the father of eight children with his wife and an untold number of children with women he enslaved.

HESTER WILLIAMS

Real. In the book *Redemption Songs: Suing for Freedom Before Dred Scott*, author Lea Vandervelde writes that there is "circumstantial evidence" that Hester Williams moved to New York City after she won her freedom suit against Frederick Norcom.

I am fascinated by the slaves in antebellum Missouri who, like Dred Scott, sued for their freedom. I had no idea how many succeeded. Given that Frederick Norcom purchased Eliza's first Green Street house, I thought it likely that she intersected with him, and possible that she met Hester Williams as well.

NOAH MOBERRY

Imagined

CAPTAIN THOMAS TARGEE

Real, as was his wife Sarah. I found Targee's bravery on the night of the 1849 Great Fire astonishing. When he perished, he left behind not only Sarah but six children ranging in age from four to seventeen.

RICHARD BONNER

Imagined

REVEREND JORDAN WINSTON EARLY

Real. The Reverend died in 1903 and is known as a pioneer of African Methodism and ardent advocate of Black Nationalism.

LOUISA CLARK

Real. The 1860 census lists a 30-year-old Missouri-born prostitute of this name living alongside Eliza Haycraft.

ROBERT MARCELLUS STEWART

Real. The land speculator turned lawyer turned politician is a character I intended to play a small role. But as always happens in the writing of a novel, some characters step forward toward the footlights and others retreat into the shadows.

STERLING PRICE

Real. In this novel in which Eliza is no fan of Sterling Price, she would have been irritated that in the 1870s Price's friends paid to erect a 30-foot white granite obelisk at his Bellefontaine gravesite. It features the Southern Cross of Honor and this inscription: "His purity of character was equaled by his exalted patriotism."

VISA ANN BABB

Real. Visa Ann died in 1875 at age forty-four, survived by her husband Benjamin (who lived until 1907) and seven of their nine children.

There is a postscript to Visa Ann that does not reflect well on her. Eliza did not include three of her properties in her will but deeded them separately to friends. A year after Eliza died, three of her siblings—Visa Ann, Lucinda, and Asa, along with Visa Ann and Lucinda's husbands—filed suit arguing that they as family members were entitled to those properties. Attorneys took the suit on spec, agreeing to accept twenty-five percent of whatever proceeds were achieved, if any. However, a settlement was reached behind the attorneys' backs and Eliza's relations reneged on the agreement to pay their lawyers.

ASA HARPER

Real. Asa died in 1884, survived by his wife Sarah Chambers Harper and at least four of his eight children, one of whom was his daughter Martha, through whose eyes we witness Eliza's funeral. (See below for more on Martha.)

BERNARD GAINES FARRAR, JR.

Real. Farrar died in 1916, two months after burying his wife of sixty-four years, Isabella Jerdone Mitchell. The father of four, Farrar served the Union Army throughout the Civil War, at one point forming an all-Black regiment that would become the 6th U.S. Colored Heavy Artillery. Later a successful businessman, he served as Missouri's Assistant U.S. Treasurer, an appointment made by President Benjamin Harrison. Farrar and his wife are interred at Bellefontaine Cemetery in the Underground Farrar Tomb.

NATHANIEL LYON

Real, and a difficult character to write about, as many of his military exploits, particularly against Native Americans, are horrifying. But there is no question that Lyon was an early hero for the Union side owing to his bold maneuvers in Missouri.

CLAIBORNE FOX JACKSON

Real. In October 1861, after Lyon died in battle, Jackson tried one last time to put Missouri in the Confederate column. In his

Pulitzer Prize-winning *Battle Cry of Freedom*, author James McPherson writes:

"Claiborne Jackson called the pro-southern legislature into session at Neosho near the Arkansas border. Less than a quorum showed up, but on November 3, 1861, this body enacted an ordinance of secession. The Congress in Richmond admitted Missouri as the twelfth Confederate state on November 28. Although Missouri sent senators and representatives to Richmond, its Confederate state government was driven out of Missouri shortly after seceding and existed as a government in exile for the rest of the war."

FRANCIS PRESTON BLAIR, JR.

Real. Blair died in 1875, three years after being stricken with a paralysis from which he never recovered. He served as colonel for the Union Army, U.S. senator from Missouri, and, after switching to the Democratic Party, as vice presidential running mate to Horatio Seymour. He is buried at Bellefontaine Cemetery alongside...

APPOLINE ALEXANDER BLAIR

... his widow, who died in 1908. The mother of eight children, two of whom were lost to infectious diseases, she organized a group of women to raise money to found a hospital for needy children. (At the time, hospitals for the poor excluded children.) She was the first president of the St. Louis Children's Hospital Board of Managers and served on the Board until her death.

MIRAH MADISON ALEXANDER

Real. Appoline Alexander Blair's mother, whose daily carriage rides entertained the residents of St. Louis, was born to politics:

she was the daughter of Kentucky Governor George Madison, who died in office in 1816. She herself died in 1886 and is buried in Bellefontaine Cemetery.

OLD PETER

Real. In his book *Rebellion in Missouri: 1861 - Nathaniel Lyon and his Army of the West*, author Hans Christian Adamson describes Old Peter coming to collect Lyon in his old-lady disguise: "A black barouche, whose body gleamed like ancient onyx, wheeled lightly through the portal, drawn by a span of coal-black geldings. On the box perched Old Peter, regal as a king."

JOHN CHARLES FREMONT

Real. Frémont died in 1890, survived by his wife Jessie Benton Frémont and three of their five children. In 1864, he briefly ran for president under the banner of the Radical Democracy Party and later served as Governor of the Arizona territory until widespread annoyance at his prolonged absences from Arizona forced him to resign.

MARTHA JANE HARPER GRAGG

Real. This second daughter of Eliza's brother Asa died in 1930, nine months after losing her husband of forty-eight years, R. M. Gragg. A lifelong resident of Missouri and mother of five, her obituary states that: "She loved her home and children, and enjoyed the many occasions during the last few years of her life when her children and grandchildren would gather for a Sunday dinner and visit."

CICILY JAMES

Real. In the lengthy December 8, 1871, piece in the *Missouri Democrat* entitled "Funeral of Eliza Haycraft," Cicily James is listed by name as a "servant of the house," all of them "colored women." She "waited upon Mrs. Haycraft for the last seven or eight years and nursed her in her last illness," exhibiting "more heart felt grief than any one else."

DR. EDWARD BENKENDORF

Real. Benkendorf tended to Eliza twenty-three times in the last month of her life, earning five dollars for each visit to the mansion on St. Charles Street.

Note from the Author

I first heard the name Eliza Haycraft in November 2014. My husband and I were visiting dear friends in St. Louis for Thanksgiving week, as we often do, and went to see a Missouri History Museum exhibit commemorating the city's founding two hundred fifty years before. Fifty St. Louisans were profiled. Eliza was one.

Her display included no image, for none was known to exist, and the write-up was brief. It included the phrase: "a rags-to-riches story unparalleled in St. Louis history." I had published eight novels by that time, none historical, yet the bare bones of Eliza's extraordinary tale captured my writer's mind. I took a photo of the exhibit, though I needn't have, for I was not going to forget Eliza Haycraft.

I doubt I will ever again come upon such an exceptional true story not yet fully told. And though I delved deeply into her life and era, Eliza will always remain an enigma, for she never learned to read or write and so left no letters or papers. We can never know how she expressed herself or what she believed. We can judge her only by her actions, as revealed by public records and newspaper accounts.

I approached this novel with a guiding principle: I would not contradict anything about Eliza that I knew or believed to be true. Given how little about her can truly be known, I was left with wonderful room for invention.

Here is what Eliza's legend holds to be true. She was born on February 14, 1820, in Cote Sans Dessein, a township on the Missouri River a hundred miles west of St. Louis. The area— comprised of small farms but at one point boasting both a fort and a steamboat landing—was settled initially by the French then mostly by people from Kentucky and Virginia. In her twenties, Eliza made an abrupt departure, by canoe, alone, floating down-river toward St. Louis, a booming frontier outpost. After a brief sojourn in New Orleans in the company of an unknown man, she returned to St. Louis never to depart again.

Here is what public records indicate to be true. While still in Cote Sans Dessein in June 1843, Eliza married a John N. Haycraft. (Her maiden name was Harper.) In 1846 she purchased her first prop-erty, in St. Louis, with cash. Her 1867 will reveals she owned eigh-teen properties at that writing; separately she gave away three more. One of that trio was her crown jewel, in my estimation: Charles Pierre Chouteau's family home on St. Charles Street in St. Louis.

(As an aside, I found the deeds of property for Eliza's transactions to be fascinating and full of valuable information. For example, in her very first purchase and sale she intersected with Dr. Bernard Gaines Farrar and Frederick Norcom, both of whom became gate-ways to key storylines.)

As part of my research, I was thrilled to visit the Civil Courts Building in St. Louis to see and touch the enormous leather-bound volume into which Eliza's will was written. There, in clear script, were the stipulations I describe in the novel. And there was her X, her "mark."

Newspaper accounts are an important source of information that is not, alas, entirely reliable. These describe Eliza's philanthropy and the reaction to her death on December 5, 1871. I believe her generosity, more than her notoriety, is why thousands of mourners, Black and White, young and old, filled the streets to watch her funeral cortège make its way to Bellefontaine Cemetery. To this day, historians differ as to how much she had to battle to gain entry there.

(Also as an aside: the *Missouri Democrat* describes an oil portrait of Eliza hanging in the St. Charles Street mansion where she died. In my telling, I chose the portraitist Sarah Miriam Peele, who lived in St. Louis in that era, as the artist. Of course I yearn to find that painting, for I would love to see Eliza's likeness.)

On one fine day of background research, I was reading *Redemption Songs: Suing for Freedom Before Dred Scott*, by Lea Vandervelde, and came upon the story of Hester Williams, an enslaved woman who sued for freedom from Frederick Norcom.

The man's name was familiar, but it took time to realize why: I had read it on the deed for Eliza's first sale of property, at a loss, months after the purchase. And this same Norcom was the very man who tore up the freedom paper he himself had written for Hester Williams. Eventually Williams was vindicated in the courts, as were dozens of other enslaved people, an important piece of pre-Dred Scott history. It is primarily through the fictional character of Noah Moberry that Eliza comes to understand a bit about the lives of her Black neighbors both free and enslaved.

I am eternally grateful to Michael Hingerty, excellent attorney and genealogist both, for without him I would not understand nearly so much about Eliza's family tree. On one branch is her sister Sarah, who appropriated Haycraft as a surname for her own labors as a prostitute. In early 1856, Sarah was convicted of murder and sentenced to hang. Newspapers around the country covered the scandalous trial and noted Eliza's "immense" wealth. Clearly, years before the Civil War, Eliza benefited from St. Louis's explosive growth to build a fortune. And though we will never know why two governors, Sterling Price and Robert Marcellus Stewart, showed mercy toward Eliza's murderess of a sister, I had a fine time concocting plausible explanations. Also, I altered the timing of Stewart's pardon to better suit the flow of the story.

In *Friend and Foe Alike: A Tour Guide to Missouri's Civil War*, Gregory Wolk writes that: "Missouri suffered more battles or engagements during the Civil War than all of the states except Virginia and Tennessee." I limited my storytelling of that period to the fraught months between January and August 1861, when St. Louis was most in play. As Eliza might have known Dr. Bernard G. Farrar, so, too, might she have known his namesake son, who served as aide-de-camp to Nathaniel Lyon.

Historians debate whether, as legend has it, Lyon disguised himself in widow's weeds to tour Camp Jackson in Congressman Frank Blair's barouche, with Old Peter driving up top, but many judge it possible. In this work of historical fiction, I exercise my discretion as a storyteller to place Eliza at the center of the action.

I exercise that same right in inventing Dr. Richard Bonner, for I am of the mind that a woman of Eliza's special character deserves an exceptional love story. Though I introduce the two at Dr. Farrar's burial at Bellefontaine in 1849, the good doctor was buried else-where initially but reinterred at Bellefontaine in the 1860s, according to the famed cemetery's Dan Fuller. Given Bellefontaine's eternal importance to Eliza, I used that setting for her crucial first meeting with Richard.

And then there is Eliza's purchase of Chouteau's mansion. In the novel I made use of the fact that while both Charles Pierre and his wife Julia were present when the deed was executed, Eliza was absent. I could not resist crafting a backstory to explain Eliza's acquisition of that particular property. For what should we think of a formerly penniless prostitute buying the home of one of the city's premier aristocrats and founding families? To me she was making quite a statement. Surely there must be a story behind it? Now we have one.

It appears that Eliza chose not to clarify her marital history, as her contemporaries seem befuddled on the point. Note this in a *St. Louis Times* obituary: "There is a rumor that she was first married to a ship carpenter, who lost his life in the Mississippi, but this seems to be without foundation."

Again I must thank Michael Hingerty, this time for diligently searching for John N. Haycrafts. He found only one of an appropriate age, named John Neville Haycraft, originally of Kentucky but with an uncle in Missouri living about a hundred miles north of Cote Sans Dessein. Haycraft was married to a still-living Kentucky woman in 1843, at the time of the "marriage" to Eliza. He got around: he went on to marry three more women in Indiana before returning to Kentucky in the early '70s to die there in 1872. Given Eliza's notoriety, I feel sure he would have heard tell of the fabulously wealthy St. Louis madam who hailed from Cote Sans Dessein.

To me, Eliza's "marriage" creates a fundamental mystery: why would a legitimate husband not appear in St. Louis at some point to lay claim to her fortune? The laws of the time would have allowed him to do so.

Well, John N. Haycraft the Bigamist would have had no legal leg to stand on.

This also helps explain the confusion over whether Eliza had been married. Perhaps she wanted to keep mum about this embarrassing chapter of her life. Or she thought the ongoing mystery would add to her allure. Or she didn't want to encourage a husband, legitimate or not, to make a claim on her wealth.

Lastly: why, some time after her marriage, did Eliza suddenly flee her hometown, alone, by canoe?

Well, perhaps she found out that her husband was a bigamist, which gave her ample justification to grab her things and go.

For Eliza Haycraft was, by every account, unstoppable.

Acknowledgments

So many generous people helped me with the research and writing of this novel. I am indebted to every one of them. First and foremost, I thank Michael Everman, historian and archivist. Both when he was heading the Missouri State Archives office in St. Louis and since his retirement, Mike has been my number one go-to guide for all things Missouri and all things Eliza Haycraft. He has also become a dear friend. His wife Diane Everman, also a historian, has been very helpful to me as well, as has Pat Barge of the St. Louis archives office.

As I wrote in the author's note, Michael Hingerty has truly been a standout, donning his genealogist hat numerous times on behalf of this project.

Dan Fuller, historian and Events and Volunteer Coordinator at Bellefontaine Cemetery, not only provided juicy historical information, but along with Joe Shields gave my husband and me (and Mike Everman) a personal tour of the grounds.

Katie Bowen, in the Archive Department of the St. Louis City Recorder of Deeds, scrounged among dusty records to help me out. And Michael Meyer, archaeologist and Senior Historic Preservation Specialist for Missouri's Department of Transportation, was very giving with his time and information.

I am also grateful to: Amanda Claunch, Archivist of Photographs and Prints at the Missouri History Museum Library and Research

Center; Sheila Guthrie of the Kingdom of Callaway Historical Society; Andrew Hahn, Executive Director of the Campbell House Museum; Matthew Hathaway, Communications Manager for the St. Louis Art Museum; historian Lynn Morrow; Jeannie Rabbitt, formerly Probate Clerk of the 22nd Judicial Circuit, State of Missouri; Madeline Reichmuth, Public Information Officer for the Missouri Historical Society; Lauren Sallwasser, Associate Archivist Photos and Prints for the Missouri Historical Society; Sandra Vandelicht, Deputy Director of the Recorder of Deeds Office for Callaway County; Clare Vasquez, Public Services Librarian at the St. Louis Art Museum; and Andrew Wanko, Public Historian of the Missouri Historical Society.

For more than twenty years I have been privileged to be part of a writing group whose advice on both writing and publishing I could not do without. We lost one of our members, Lynn Hanna, during my writing of this novel. The only thing that consoles us is that Lynn was en route to her beloved Scotland at the time of her death. Much gratitude to the rest of the band: Carol Culver, Barbara Freethy, Candice Hern, Barbara McMahon, and Kate Moore.

I also owe an immense debt to other writer friends who have been readers, advisers, and cheerleaders all these years. My very deep thanks to Will Fuller, Tracie Donnell, Karen Parrish, Sarah Ladipo Manyika, and Ciji Ware. (And Sarah, an extra dose of thanks for really sticking your neck out for Eliza and me.)

Other friends who are not themselves writers have generously given of their time and insight, from encouragement to reading the manuscript to helping with promotion. I am very grateful to Raya Albin, Chantal Combes—*merci beaucoup, Chantal!*—Juliana Jensen, Miranda Jilka, Allison Pharis, and Cheryl Popp.

Speaking of promotion, there is the matter of the Jade Gown. Yes, such an item is being designed and sewn as I type. I am thankful to Kate Hertelendy for turning me on to Professor Catherine Amoroso Leslie of the Kent State University School of Fashion Design and Merchandising, who in turn introduced me to Trista Grieder, Senior Lecturer. Trista, your design and workmanship are spectacular. Thank you for your enthusiasm, keen attention, and great skill.

St. Louis-raised Amanda Martinez Robiolio will indulge me by wearing the jade gown and in so doing will endear herself to me even more deeply, if that's possible. I can never thank Amanda and her family enough for all they have done for me on this project. It was their idea to see the exhibit where I first learned of Eliza. Then they hosted me while I conducted research. Amanda and her mother Aixa Martinez went so far as to spin through microfiche beside me at the St. Louis Central Library. (Aixa went further by reading the manuscript and offering valuable notes.) And Paul Robiolio took time out from saving lives to drive Aixa and me to Cote Sans Dessein, where they waited patiently while I snapped photos of grassy riverbanks and stands of cottonwood and willow trees. If memory serves, we did end the excursion with lunch in Hermann, complete with a tasty libation.

And to you, Jed, boundless thanks for all kinds of things, from encouraging this book from the very early days (when I had my doubts), to cheerful brainstorming, to the painstaking reading of bumpy first drafts (and seconds, and thirds). You have been the most steadfast champion of not only this book but of me, which is a wondrous gift to receive.

About the Author

Diana Dempsey traded in an Emmy Award-winning career in TV news to write fiction. The first of her ten contemporary novels, *Falling Star*, was a finalist for a Romance Writers of America RITA award for Best First Book. *The Unstoppable Eliza Haycraft* is her first historical novel.

A graduate of Harvard University, Diana was born in Buffalo, New York, enjoyed stints in Belgium, the U.K., and Japan, and now resides in California with her husband and a West Highland White Terrier, not necessarily in that order.

Diana loves to hear from readers. Email her at DianaDempsey.com or contact her via social media.

Discussion Questions

1/ Do you think Eliza was justified in leaving John and taking his canoe to do it? Did your opinion about that change over the course of the book?

2/ Do you think Obadiah treated Eliza well or poorly? Did your opinion about that change over the course of the book?

3/ In Chapter 4, Eliza thinks: *I know where we're headed—I think I've known ever since I was in Obadiah's stateroom and told him I'd take his help. I don't know how to think about it except I do need help and far as I can figure I've got only one thing to give in return and that's as clear to Obadiah as it is to me.* Do you understand why she would think that way? Do you agree with her?

4/ When you realized that Eliza would take Chouteau's proposition and leave New Orleans, did you think she was making the right decision? Do you think you would have decided the same if you were in her position?

5/ Why do you think Eliza did not believe Chantal and Obadiah's warnings about Chouteau, in particular that he would never marry her?

6/ What do you think of Eliza's decision to become a prostitute?

7/ As Eliza embarks on her life as a prostitute, she thinks this: *Perhaps I can find a way to close some part of myself off, as if it is some other woman doing what I must and I myself, the true part of me, is watching only. I don't want to be coldhearted and unfeeling—then it is my mother I become—but I must pick and choose my times to feel. I must remember my aim: to have my own money, to have the money to be free.* Do you think it is possible for a woman to do that?

8/ What do you think about Eliza's "burning desire" to pile up money?

9/ In Chapter 13, after Eliza interacts with a woman reformer, she thinks: *Does she think the souls of the men who come to me are destroyed? I don't think so. She says that women should be treated the same as men, but even she thinks us weaker. Perhaps my great whorish sin is thinking as a man would: that sex is sex and that is the end of it.* Is a woman thinking "sex is sex and that is the end of it" taboo even today?

10/ In Chapter 14, when Charity balks at leaving Madam Lantos's to join Eliza's new bawdy house, Eliza thinks: *It is the same old thing. It is myself I must rely on. I believe I will go to my grave with this feeling. It is very sad, though, because it makes even those dearest to me seem apart from me.* Why do you think relying only on herself makes Eliza feel apart from other people, even those she loves?

11/ In Chapter 19, when a man from whom she buys a property calls Eliza a whore, she thinks: *That is the thing with some men. It is to bed us women that they want us—for some men it is all they want us for—yet never are we to profit from it? Ever in this life would a man agree to such a thing? That question is so easy even a bawd could answer.* Do you agree with Eliza?

12/ Do you think Eliza should have done more to help her sister Sarah? For example, should Eliza have given Sarah a job? Do you think that would have kept Sarah from stabbing Sam Hudson?

13/ What do you think of Eliza asking Governor Price to pardon her sister? Do you think she was obliged to try to save her sister's life, especially given her connection to Price?

14/ Do you think Eliza takes enough, too little, or too much responsibility for her sister Sarah's behavior?

15/ Do you think Eliza is wrong to encourage Charity to leave Martin Terris and return to the bawdy house? Does Eliza have Charity's best interests at heart?

16/ When Charity sees the portrait of Eliza, she remarks: "And to think, Eliza. You are the one who doesn't believe in love." Do you think Charity is correct, that Eliza doesn't believe in love?

17/ Eliza and Richard met in 1849 and he died in 1861. Do you believe a love that lasts a finite time is lesser than a love that lasts a lifetime? Do you think their relationship is diminished by never having spoken to one another the word "love"?

18/ Do you think Eliza was wrong to leave some properties to her friends rather than leaving all of them to her relations?

19/ Do you think Eliza was making a statement by buying Chouteau's mansion?

20/ Why do you think Eliza was so generous to the downtrodden?

21/ Returning with Daniel after purchasing the plot at Bellefontaine, Eliza says: "I have had a full measure of life, Daniel. Not the way I dreamt about when I was a girl, no, but it is enough all the same. The way I have lived, it has cost me. But it has given me freedom, too, more than most women." Do you agree with her assessment, as portrayed?

22/ Are you surprised that thousands of people filled the streets to pay their respects to Eliza after her death, given that she was a prostitute and madam?

Further Reading

Contraception and Abortion in 19th-Century America by Janet Farrell Brodie

Daughters of Joy, Sisters of Misery: Prostitutes in the American West 1865-90 by Anne M. Butler

The Gateway Arch by Tracy Campbell

History of Early Steamboat Navigation on the Missouri River: Life and Adventures of Joseph La Barge, Volumes I and II, by Hiram Martin Chittenden

In Her Place: A Guide to St. Louis Women's History by Katharine T. Corbett

The Gilded Table: Recipes and Table History from the Campbell House by Suzanne Corbett

Old and New St. Louis: A Concise History of the Metropolis of the South and Southwest, With a Review of Its Present Greatness and Immediate Prospects by James Cox

Personal Recollections of St. Louis by John F. Darby

The Homefront in Civil War Missouri by James W. Erwin

Inside War: The Guerrilla Conflict in Missouri During the American Civil War by Michael Fellman

Civil War St. Louis by Louis S. Gerteis

Wild River, Wooden Boats: True Stories of Steamboating and the Missouri River by Michael Gillespie

Fire, Pestilence, and Death: St. Louis 1849 by Christopher Alan Gordon

A Most Unsettled State: First-Person Accounts of St. Louis During the Civil War by NiNi Harris

The Chouteaus: First Family of the Fur Trade by Stan Hoig

The Broken Heart of America: St. Louis and the Violent History of the United States by Walter Johnson

Civil War Day by Day by Philip Katcher

Stamped from the Beginning: The Definitive History of Racist Ideas in America by Ibram X. Kendi

Nell Kimball: Her Life as an American Madam by Herself and edited by Stephen Longstreet

Bitter Brew: The Rise and Fall of Anheuser-Busch and America's King of Beer by William Knoedelseder

Absinthe - The Cocaine of the Nineteenth Century: A History of the Hallucinogenic Drug and Its Effect on Artists and Writers in Europe and the United States by Doris Lanier

Battle Cry of Freedom by James McPherson

Damned Yankee: The Life of Nathaniel Lyon by Christopher Phillips

St. Louis: Its History and Ideals by Philip Skrainka

Southern Queen: New Orleans in the Nineteenth Century by Thomas Ruys Smith

A Battlefield Atlas of the Civil War by Craig L. Symonds

Redemption Songs: Suing for Freedom before Dred Scott by Lea Vandervelde

Food in the Civil War Era: the South by Helen Zoe Veit, editor

Food in the United States, 1820s – 1890 by Susan Williams

Friend and Foe Alike: A Tour Guide to Missouri's Civil War by Gregory Wolk

Also by Diana Dempsey

Falling Star

To Catch the Moon

Too Close to the Sun

Chasing Venus

A Diva Wears the Ring (novella)

Ring of Truth (anthology in which novella appears)

Ms America and the Offing on Oahu

Ms America and the Villainy in Vegas

Ms America and the Mayhem in Miami

Ms America and the Whoopsie in Winona

Ms America and the Brouhaha on Broadway

Ms America and the Naughtiness in New Orleans

CPSIA information can be obtained
at www.ICGtesting.com
Printed in the USA
LVHW041451100723
752008LV00001B/131